I0546192

Schaffer Press
PO Box 50971
Eugene, OR 97405

All characters, events, and locations depicted in this book are
fictitious. Similarities to anything real are merely coincidental and
unintentional.

First Edition: February 2014
Printed in the United States of America
ISBN: 978-1-941976-00-5

# TABLE OF CONTENTS

Advice is like prophecy without the virgins.

"Down!"

My warning came as a startled squawk, as much as a yell. Follow your own advice, right? The dive forward clipped my chin on the pavers and carried me under the path of the spear that scored a hole down the middle of the passage.

That's the problem with unguarded secret entrances. Eventually someone notices that an exit is an entrance and decides to discourage visitors.

One moment it's a wetly glossy blackened bronze door. The next the surface is melting like a sideways pool of water after the rock hits and before you can adjust to the change, green pseudopods covered with chitinous spikes are leading a beak, the size of a child's head, out of the pool of black water - door.

All your holes try to close at the same time while your head tries to outrun the feet that haven't gotten any messages. When I caught up with myself I tried to turn and to run without any interval between the two and promptly over balanced. Then I fell on my face, arms windmilling. Who knows, maybe they thought since the legs weren't doing the job they could put a hand in and help out.

I bounced up off the turf, spat loam out, and darted towards Sylvie and Dugal like a schooner catching full sail. Sylvie's eyes had gone wide, but she already had her sword half out and the other hand was completing a precise follow-through. She'd underhanded that dagger of hers while I was faceplanting.

My brain started clicking and I immediately tucked my sprint into a roll.

It was not a good time to be an obstacle between missiles and the Deepspawn.

Thad A. Wind

# Ebb

# Tide

Tides of the World
Book One

www.schafferpress.com

Eleven

Twelve

Thirteen

Fourteen

Fifteen

Sixteen

Seventeen

Eighteen

Nineteen

Twenty

Twenty-one

Twenty-two

Twenty-three

Twenty-four

# ACKNOWLEDGMENTS

Writing a book is easy; finishing a book is hard. Publishing one is Herculean, if not Sisyphean…and that is enough literary references for one work that would never be in your hands without the efforts of a pair of people.

Thank you, Sadie, for encouraging me even when the names were changing. As well as cover illustration and design.

Thank you, Brandon, for reading first, second, and even the seventh time. And that editing thing – this work would never be more than something I wrote without that.

# DEDICATION

For Porter. You can show your friends now.

# ONE

Jak thought big and acted small. His pants sagged where his belt hadn't found the loops and the coat looked handed down from a brother twice his size. He liked to think of himself as a stylish man about town. The current fashion on the hillside favored a degenerate sort of equestrian mode replete with riding boots and two inch heels. Never mind that nobody but the merchant lords could afford a horse in Myrport, it was more likely to see one as a menu item than transportation. Jak had the boots anyways. Maybe pulled them from the former owner's corpse himself.

He ran a little Sevens game outside a place called the Net and Hook. Not for big stakes, small enough that I could use my own dice. That little fact made sure I'd been bleeding him and his friends slowly but regularly for the last couple months. The game's played with dice shaped like pyramids, usually made from carved shell. Hard as a six pin lock with a pearlescent luster. The set I used were made from fired clay and then lacquered to give it the same burnt cream shine; virtually indistinguishable from the real thing. The artist who'd made them was inspired. Dice that always came up threes and fours would get you killed, but dice that were just a little more likely than not? Those dice could make you rich.

Jak's usual spot was along the north wall where the boardwalk fit nice and tight. Bets and dice didn't fall through to the mire. Plus, the wine and ale from inside was cheap. A few lighter for a jug of unwatered wine, I joined the game. By second bell or so it was just me, Jak, and his friends: Ferg and Gev.

My plan was to keep things small for a while longer, no sense rocking the boat, and I'd been keeping the wine going as well. It wasn't great wine, possibly not even worth the cost to ship it in. The vinegar smell was better than fish and urine; it was still wine.

Then I got greedy.

"Your toss, Renn. Time to give me money." Ferg was the sort of gambler everybody loves. He drank too much and thought the gods of luck were fair. Mostly it made up for his breath.

The gods of luck aren't the objects of worship around the inner sea. They aren't even named. They are mad as a harpooned whale and drawing their attention is considered the same as drawing their ire. Even warding them off is considered risky since they might take offense. There's a legend about them taking offense at the sun traversing the sky in the same direction every day so it's not impossible.

"I know. Just a moment, need to make room for your coin. How about three?" I said. Even with my dice that wasn't a great call. Sevens is played on a chalked out circle, bets go in or out of the circle - depending on if you think the thrower is going to make their call or not, inside if he is short, outside if he's over. The man with the dice names a number of sevens he'll roll and, if he does, he gets everything. He gets to keep rolling until he makes or he gets ones on all the dice he rolled. Pretty simple. I scooped up the dice, gave them a couple shakes and tossed them into the circle.

"Three and a four, Reroll the rest." Jak liked to narrate.

"Bets? Excellent Gev, I need more of your money"

"A one, that's out. Reroll."

"More bets? Four dice left, take my money." Winning at that point would mean not losing another die. Not looking good for father's little Renn, may he rot in the deep. The sound of coins stacking up against me was music though. The dice flicked out revealing another seven and the last two still in play.

"Last two, Renn. How much you got to lose?" Jak could smell blood in the water better than a shark.

"Enough to cover, thanks for asking." Trying not to smile when you're about to double your money is hard. Normally he'd be right, either die coming up a one and I was out everything they had bet. It wasn't impossible but it wasn't odds I'd have taken on anyone else's dice.

"That's good, we aren't the loan types." Gev actually popped his knuckles at that. Gev came to Myrport on a slave barge. Nobody had any idea where from but they grew them big there. He had to turn sideways and duck to get through doorways and the only reason he wasn't still a slave doing heavy labor meant for three men had to do with him never leaving the docks. No slave catcher with an interest in walking dared set foot in lower Myrport.

The dice floated out of my hand, bounced around the circle, and came up threes.

"Drown me! Threes." Ferg was keyed up tight. He expected to win and it was all he could do not to scoop up my match while the dice were still in motion. I favored him with my best lazy smile and slowly scooped up the dice for another toss. Small of me, but the wine and knowing brought out the smug.

"Clear the circle, Ferg, you're crowding fate."

"Shut up and roll, Renn."

I took my time, making a show of blowing on them and rubbing the dice for luck. When he had suffered enough, I let them bounce gently into the circle. Three and a four, the craftsman who made them would have been proud. A fish talks more than the three of them did while I scooped the winnings over and started to transfer them to my pockets.

"Hold up a second," Jak interrupted my work, "It's my turn to toss."

"Ok, it's your money...well, mine now. What's your call?"

"Three. Everyone bets." Ferg and Gev scowled at him. They'd lost on top of losing already.

"Everyone bets." Jak found the lead dog inside himself and used it to stare the other two down. Each threw a few dirhams inside the circle.

There was no way Jak was going to let me walk. Ten dirhams was enough to satisfy him. When I reached out to gather my dice so he could roll, quick as a silverling he grabbed my wrist. "I'd like to use yours; mine have attracted some attention from The Three lately. You don't mind do you?"

My sigh probably went unnoticed, it wasn't nearly what I'd taken off them, but who likes to kiss good dirhams goodbye? Besides, with Gev and Ferg there it wasn't likely arguing was going to be healthy.

"No, that's just fine, feel free." I finished my wine and refilled it from the bottle.

Jak pulled his gloves off; set them on the bucket he'd been using for a seat and then picked up the dice. He cupped all seven in his hands. Rising up off his haunches, he performed a full circle twirl as he shook the dice. Goddess of midday tides strike me down if he didn't throw a couple squat kicks in. We all took a step back as he pranced. One especially ambitious flying kick hit my wine cup, catapulting it at Ferg.

"Dammit Jak, just toss the damn dice and be done." Ferg grumbled, wiping the dregs off his vest. Jak ignored him and continued his good luck caper. For a moment I thought about sticking a foot into the middle just to see him flat on his face. Gev and Ferg were tight with him though and they were already sore from losing to me all night. My father taught me my letters, lock picking, pocket diving, and a whole lot else. One of his best lessons, delivered with the stick as usual, was never start a fight the other guy's friends can join.

The stick was a polished length of beamwood, capped on the narrow end with bronze and then thickening at the other to a rounded knob carved into the shape of a leering goblin. That was the stick. Minor corrections called for the narrow end, major ones with the heavier end which left patterned bruises.

Also, the man with the stick gets to do the talking.

Jak finished his ritual, bouncing to a stop. Legs spread wide, he let the dice fly. Straight at the wall next to the chalk circle. The dice shot out of his hands and bounced clean off and past the four of us hitting the wall behind before rattling to rest in the middle of the alley in eight pieces.

Sevens dice aren't made from just any shell. They're made from something called a sawclaw. Sawclaw shell attached to a sawclaw is one of the many reasons not to go down below lower Myrport into the mire. A sawclaw is just a large crab really, a crab the size of a small dog with a shell that takes an axe to split. There are a lot of things that might happen, rolling a third seven with one die out for instance, but shattering a dice made from sawclaw shell against the wall isn't one.

We looked at the shattered seventh die for a moment. Lantern light glinted off metal core and spilled wine while we stared. A slightly sick feeling washed through me. The feeling you get right before a fight. That combination of stomach clenching and heart racing that brings out the sweat on your palms. I stopped looking before they did; a moving target is a live target. - more useful lessons from my father.

A couple slow steps backwards bought me some space. Dicing with Jak and his friends had just come to an end. It was nice winning more than I lost, but I was under no misconceptions about the nature of our friendship. The money they'd lost was piling up in their heads right then and as soon as all the ropes got tied off they were going to want an explanation. "Gee, I've been cheating you guys blind for the last couple months," didn't seem like a good starter. Ferg stopped looking first. He locked eyes on mine and swatted Gev on the shoulder. He nearly had to tiptoe to reach up to do it.

"Well guys, it's getting early, I'll see you around sometime."

My feet were moving with my mouth; any second they'd decide to come collect.

Jak was staring at the remaining fake dice. They'd come up six singles, a bad omen if there ever was one. If the wine and the hour kept the three of them sleepy slow, it might not be for me.

"Now don't worry about me, you lost some money, but that just makes us even, right?" I turned and sprinted toward the building at the far end. A stray bucket connected with my foot and rebounded off the alley wall tumbling me into a sprawl. I ignored splinters in my palms and lunged back up.

Jak and Ferg both started talking at once, each giving the others different directions. Gev ignored both of them and charged after me. For a half second the hope that he might bust through the planking and fall straight through to the mire flitted through my brain. Rotten slapdash planking was the only part of lower Myrport more predictable than the tides, but I ditched the thought just like my winnings back at the circle. The Mad Three, gods of luck and more commonly misfortune, had turned their eyes my way; suitable punishment for loaded dice if you ask me, but they weren't asking. No chance they'd give up their fun so easily.

Lower Myrport is built on the piers and abandoned barges of last year's shipping trade…and the year before that and so on. As the harbor recedes, new piers are built to accommodate shipping and the old formerly floating piers become the cheapest building space around. The entire low town floats or squats just above the mire. Every so often a pier will sink or rot and any survivors usually just board over it and rebuild. Streets are a goulash of shipping piers and walkways built to connect them. Any given one is just as likely to end in a newly built shack as it is a cross street. Building codes are the hobby of upper Myrport and inspectors have better places to be than the docks. This works out pretty well for people in my trade. Guards and watchmen wear armor and are habitually bad climbers. Likewise, spears and crossbows are usually all the impetus someone like me needs to take the high road….or two gamblers and their mutant giant friend.

Gev slammed along behind, sounding like a galley drum. Looking back gets a runner caught. Two more strides - and a well-timed leap - got me to the far wall. With one leg, I kicked up onto the wall before kicking off. Back the way I'd come. Hands extended, arms windmilling to catch the overhanging eave of the Net and Hook. Momentum carried my feet, still pumping, to power myself up and over to the roof.

No time to congratulate myself on an escape until it was an escape though. The watch would have called it a night as soon as I was a floor up. Even a golden dinar a day doesn't buy climbing in armor. Jak wouldn't want any his regulars finding out I'd been scamming them. Everybody cheats on the docks, but getting fleeced is sloppy. Sloppy people end up in the mire.

A low hunched scuttle saw me up and over the roof peak where I made myself part of a second story window casement. The sound of Ferg laying it to Jak wafted up from below.

"Drunks've got more brains. If he starts talking..."

"He's not going to talk, Ferg. Gev, give me a lift." There was a grunt and a rattle followed by the shattering of tile.

"Tides! You lubber! That nearly hit me." Ferg said.

"Blame Gev! A lift, I said. Winds take you! You just about threw me into the bay."

There was a grunt from Gev and then silence from all three as Jak tried to see where I'd gone.

"Don't see him. Ferg, check around front."

"Check yourself! Not leaving so you and Gev can scupper off with the bets."

"Ferg, I get down, you and I are gonna have a talk." Jak started making his way up the peak of the roof. He wasn't used to being up top and the continual stream of curses and raining tiles gave me an excellent fix on his progress.

"Kraken take you Jak! Who you trying to kill, us or him?"

"Shut up Ferg, I'm not rope dancing 'cause you're a loudmouth." Ferg snorted, most days nobody even bothered to pull a fresh body out of the mire, far less investigate its provenance.

The window and I got even more intimate while I thought about my options. Slinking off might work, Jak wasn't going to make it very far in a chase. Those boots he had on would kill him. That footwear was probably why he was raining roof tiles on his companions. My clothes tended more to the functional; soft leather soles coated with a layer of tar and finally dipped in sand.

The tar and sand mixture made a little more noise but the traction was well worth it.

Problem was, even if I did shake loose, I'd have to spend the next few weeks looking out for all three of my fellow gamblers until they decided the damage had been done and the effort to kill me wasn't worth the return. And there was the small matter of the dirhams. Well the coin and a pair of earrings inset with what looked like sapphires and were probably glass. Dirhams could buy a tumble but jewelry bought effort.

The winnings scattered across the boardwalk could buy a weeks' worth of gin. The feel of the burn as it coated my throat sounded really good right about then.

Carefully - sudden movements draw snakes and eyes - I located Jak, straddling the roof peak, peering and just a bit wobbly from my wine. The light wasn't good, pole lamps, like they have in upper Myrport, wouldn't last the time it took to find a ladder Dockside. That left whatever moonlight forced its way through the rain, or fog when the weather was nice.

Waiting comes in flavors, like stew. There's the wait while someone else takes their turn, the wait until the girl you like comes to the window, the agony of waiting for the crack and searing lash because you didn't pop the lock quite fast enough, but the wait while a guard pokes the bushes until he can't decide if it was a cat or the wind takes the longest. That flavor calls for slow shallow breaths through the nose, eyes fixed in some other direction. Some'll tell you a man or woman can feel you watching them, I've never seen proof, but why make things harder?

Jak had just about finished another complete turn when he was interrupted from below.

"Find him?" Ferg stage whispered from where he and Gev waited.

"No." Jak muttered. Awareness was creeping up on him. He edged close, some distant animal sense guiding him toward my hiding spot until I could smell him; wine, sweat, and just a hint of fear. He had a blade out - some sort of chopping knife about the length of his forearm - at some point he'd filed down the back of the blade into a hook. I shook my head, no idea what he'd thought that would be good for. It seemed unlikely Jak had ever been outside of lower Myrport; much less somewhere he'd need a gut hook on a knife that size. What was he going to skin, a whale?

When he turned back toward the others I came up in a rush, knife in one hand, the other reaching up and around until I had his face, fingers anchored by an eye socket and his nose. A swift hard jerk back to overbalance, entirely too successful, I nearly stabbed him as he fell back into me. For a second I thought we were both going off the roof. The point of my weapon on his throat cut short any attempt to alert Ferg and the giant.

Motivated by the point of the knife boring a hole into his side, we crab walked back up to the top. Anyone sleeping below probably figured the weather had gone from worse to hail.

"Lose the knife" A little extra pressure for incentive helped him see my logic.

He dropped it, hands held wide and open. The hilt bounced, and then slid with all the speed of an anchored barge, scraping down along the tiles. It caught for a second, as Jak and I stared, and then fell, right where Ferg and Gev had been standing. There was a moment of silence - and then a loud thunk as it hit the planks.

"Tides! What the hell?" Gev never said much of anything so it must have been Ferg. "Jak? That you, you got him?" Ferg was never the sharpest tool.

With a little extra pressure, I minuetted Jak down the roof until I had him perched on the edge with my blade poking at his kidney. The lantern we'd been gaming by made it so I could see him and Gev staring up at us. Heads tilted to the sky, mouths open. Ferg was armed with Jak's knife, lucky break it hadn't hit him. Gev just had plate sized hands and reach the length of a full grown man.

"Jak can't answer right now, but he's authorized me to speak for him"

"Jak you ok?" You can lead a horse to water but you can't make it swim, or something.

"Ferg! Ferg, take a moment. This is why you lose so much at dice, you know. Well that - and loaded dice."

"Renn?"

"How many people did you think were up here, Ferg?"

"Tides take you Renn, when we get up there..." He motioned Gev over to give him a boost. Ferg was not keeping up. A sharp poke in the small of his back prompted Jak.

"Wait, don't, Ferg, he's got a knife!"

"Yeah Ferg, I've got a knife. Right, how about you both back off so we can work this out?"

"Not much to work out, Gev's going to twist your head off as soon as you let go of Jak"

"That's not really an incentive Ferg; I'm beginning to see why Jak does the thinking."

"What? I'll kill you myself, that better?"

"Not really, did you get dropped as a babe?" This may not have been the wisest thing I've ever said. Ferg was keyed up for a fight, and half drunk. His face scrunched up and flushed bright red. Without another word he wound up and hurled Jak's knife, like he was trying to throw a stone.

Throwing a knife is about practice and measured distances. Throwing one in a fight is a clever way to disarm yourself, as often as not. If it hits at all, it either hits hilt first, flips to the flat of the blade, or - even if the point goes first - it lacks the weight to do real damage. That knife was exactly the sort of knife you don't throw. The thing fluttered and spun flashing lamplight like a herring before burying itself to the hilt in Jak's throat.

Jak spasmed and twisted out of my grasp - choking and spraying blood everywhere. Without me holding him balanced on the edge, he pitched forward straight at Ferg who was in the process of following the thrown knife up onto the roof, spewing curses and spit in apoplectic fury. He stared, momentarily frozen as Jak's body wind-milled out of the darkness and plowed him off the crate he'd leapt onto. The two bodies flipped backwards slamming into the planks at the giants feet, with rib crushing force. Ferg hit without even a chance to break his fall, crushing whatever he'd been about to say in a strangled gargle. The wood gave way beneath the combined weight of the three sending Ferg and Jak twenty feet down into the mire in a shower of rotted wood, blood, and my coins.

Well damn.

Gev managed to catch himself on the splintered edges of the walkway. The other two hit the mire, sending a gout of mud and green slime up from below. Gev's grunts combined with periodic yelps as he stabbed himself on splintered wood, trying to pull himself up. The entire section was bottom-of-a-trawlers-hold rotten though, splintering and crumbling away as he struggled. With a twist, I caught the overhanging roof and let myself down, making a detour for the wine bottle. It had fallen over in the commotion but hadn't rolled into the gap and there was still some left that hadn't spilled. I took a long pull and squatted down out of arm's reach as Gev pulled himself up onto his elbows. He was trying to fit a leg the size of a ship's mast , up onto the splintered wood. Waving my knife at his face got his attention.

He grunted and kept trying to swing a leg up, until I placed the tip just under his left eye. He was breathing heavy - that's the problem with being really big or strong, after a while people get used to it and they stop making you work for things. Everyone had gotten used to Gev being too big and strong to fight and so he'd gotten a bit soft around the middle. We looked at each other for a moment. If I left him, he'd probably get himself out of the hole. Whether he came looking for me was another question.

"Yer dead, y'know that, right?"

Question answered.

Gev didn't talk much. When he wasn't dangling from a collection of busted wood scraps over low tide in the mire, he stuck to glares and the occasional slap to get his needs across. Since his hands were also useful as oars, that worked most of the time. Right then, his voice was pitched pretty high and more than a little hoarse from the exertions of the evening. One hand had a splinter the size of my finger embedded in it and blood was welling up from a series of gouges where the broken wood had got him.

"I don't know Gev, seems like things are pretty well resolved. You wouldn't happen to have any money on you?"

He shot me a disgusted look. It was probably asking too much, but hey, if you never ask, how will you know?

"Clar's gonna kill you."

"Clar? What does Clar want with me?" I had already gotten where Gev was headed. If Jak was working for Clar, I was in more trouble than the night was worth. Gev wasn't really a thinker though so he just grinned and spat phlegm to clear his throat.

"Clar finds out you killed Jak, he'll kill you."

"I didn't kill Jak. That was Ferg. You saw him."

"Don't matter, you cheated, Clar'll blame you soon as he finds out."

"You could not-tell him." That just earned me a snort and renewed effort to get up.

Jak's death had been sort of my doing. Not intentionally so. I knew Clar would see it the same as Gev said and, if Jak had been part of Clar's gang, then things were going steadily south. As soon as news got to him my life wasn't going to be worth a mug of bad ale. One man dead, Ferg would probably live if a sawclaw didn't get him and he hadn't landed face down, and the third wounded. It wouldn't matter that I hadn't really done any of it. Clar couldn't take it as anything but a challenge. Backing down from that would be as fatal for him as taking a knife to the throat was for Jak.

Ferg started screaming from below; clearly he hadn't landed face down. Gev took his moment and made a grab for me. Not a fast grab, he was tired, it was late, and he may have been distracted by the ruin of his arm. Pain will do that to a man. I slipped under the swing. Without thinking, I stabbed his other hand. He bellowed as his face contorted in pain, lost his purchase on the pier, and crashed down into the mire - right where Ferg had landed. Ferg's screams choked off as Gev hit, sending another massive fountain of mire water up to splatter against the alley walls. It was too dark to see them, but I could hear the splashing and cursing well enough. Lower Myrport's underside isn't something I'd ever wanted to see up close, nobody sane would. Upper Myrport has sewers and they drain under Lower Myrport. Lower just has holes cut into whatever castoff barge, decrepit boat, or floating wreckage the residents had built onto.

"Hey Gev, if you get out, see a priestess, that's probably going to fester."

A second later a glob of mud and sea grass whipped past my head reminding me that just because I couldn't see down didn't mean they couldn't see up. I ducked back before they remembered to throw anything sharp. After scooping up what I could find of the last bet, I went to find somewhere in Lower Myrport that Clar wouldn't look.

# TWO

I was riding high on paranoia by the time I made it to Whistlers. As a tavern it is quite possibly the worst. On a good day, the ale consists of water. On a bad day Corliss is too lazy to make the trek to land and dilutes with any liquid he can scrounge. Nobody with a choice drinks there and those that do range from suicidal to suicidally insane. It had a couple strong points from my view though. It wasn't near the boats and it wasn't near land. At some point in the distant past Whistlers had been built on top of a sunken barge to serve the needs of arriving sailors but the constant ebb and flow of lower Myrport had left it adrift as its foundation slowly decayed. It sat at the bottom of the worst part of the docks, The Runs.

Generations of owners had shored up the structure long enough to pass it on to the next owner, but never enough to make it a sound investment or a desirable location. The outside had been rebuilt and patched so often it looked like a collision that hadn't finished. The inside was pretty much what you would expect: dark, smelly, and full of the sort of people that if you ran them over with a horse you'd do them a favor by going back for another pass.

At night it got worse. I went there because it was the one place in the docks Clar wasn't willing to be hip deep in. Corliss would have sold out in a second, but he'd yet to find anyone dumb enough to buy. Clar was definitely not stupid.

As soon as I made it past the door I kept to the darker corners. Habit really. The clientele were probably too far gone on whatever combination of disease, powders, and vomit-inducing ale they favored to make much note of their own mothers in the gloom.

The nice thing about paranoia is the lack of consequences if you turn out to be wrong. It might turn out that Jak wasn't working for Clar - a lie to scare me. Maybe all three of them would get eaten by whatever inhabits the mud below the docks. Or maybe something with three eyes and teeth the size of my head would crawl out of the nether and drag them naked and screaming back to its eternal lair. Ok maybe not that last part, but it's not like  The Mad Three got crazier if you asked big. If Jak was working for Clar then I had just made the most sadistic would-be crime boss in Myrport angry.

Every so often someone or other got ambition and decided to organize things. Mostly these efforts ended with the body disappearing below docks or by attracting the attention of upper Myrport and a subsequent hanging. In a town where bodies mostly were fed to the mud below, Clar avoided these fates, by making a point of leaving bodies where they would be found. The last one had been fed his own intestines and I had plans on keeping mine in their natural order.

The tables in Whistler's were mostly old doors or the tops of casks, propped on crates or busted barrels and secured with the odd nail. An empty seat, away from the entrance, made me think my luck might be changing. The bottle I bought had no label, either because he'd bought it straight off the back of the barge or because whoever made it didn't want people to know of his crimes. The seal looked intact though.

Its possible Corliss had resealed it but that sort of effort wasn't his style. He was an accumulation of bones and pale sagging flesh topped off by bulbous eyes like some sort of landed puffer fish just prior to panic and full inflation. Nobody had seen him outdoors since he acquired the place. Whistler's changed hands frequently enough, but rarely by purchase - rumor was Corliss had won it in a card game. That seemed unlikely; he didn't seem crazy or dumb enough to take it on a marker. It left him with a steady source of marginal income and he spent most of that sampling what he served. This said a lot about his lack of judgment and probably explained how he ended up with the place, after all.

Buying the bottle bought me residence rights for the foreseeable future. So I carved off the wax, took one look at the cup Corliss had provided and drank straight from the bottle. The faint sting of alcohol - well I hoped it was alcohol - was a welcome friend. I slumped back against the wall, grateful to have made it skin and head intact. The chair-crate creaked a bit as I shifted, but held.

Getting drunk probably wasn't the best thing I could have been doing. Stowing away on the nearest boat going anywhere but Myrport was probably the best, but it had been an eventful night. Truth was, I had never left Myrport and the thought of doing so didn't hold much appeal. Myrport was a loathsome wallowing pit, a boil on the backside of the world, but it was home. It had rules, predictable and mostly safe even when I wound up on the wrong side of them. A fresh start in some other part of the world might sound good to some, but I had a fair idea that every other city was pretty much like the one I had. Sailors might not be the best example of their native lands, but they all talked about the same press gangs, petty nobility, taxes, and tithes.

Philosophical drinking is the best kind. The bottle turned up empty and I bought another. Things were starting to look better. Sure, a man was dead, but I hadn't killed him. Besides, the world wasn't going to be worse off for missing Jak. He had been a thug, a loan shark, and a welcher. His bad qualities didn't even bear mentioning. Congratulating me on my narrow escape required a third bottle. After all, I deserved a reward.

At some point past slightly drunk I started thinking about buying something to eat. If Corliss even had food available, I was very sure that eating anything he had touched would be suicide. My legs tried to stand and then gave up as the walls wobbled and shifted.

I eyed Corliss. He had one bulbous eye squinted at me and was rubbing down the busted door he used as a bar. The door looked like it might have been on upscale house once until something had ripped it off its setting, hinges and all. One of them still clung to the door, a warped chunk of dark metal shaped to meld with the salt scrubbed inlay carvings that were significant to its former owner. A bottle and a half had passed since I'd been sober but there's no amount of alcohol that could hide the oddity of Corliss attempting to clean anything. The dirty rag he was using was just working grime into the grooves and sworls of the carved surface.

Suspicion forced its way up past the layers of drunk and stupid. Corliss' mouth split into I wide, toothless grin as he stared at me and I knew. Whistler's was most definitely the sort of place you could expect people to ignore the tavern hands going through a man's belongings before shoving the unconscious body out the door if he was lucky - or down below if he'd really offended them and it was possible he'd just drugged me to roll me. The odds were good I had money if I was drinking this close to dawn - the results of a hard night's labor. Unlikely though. It was just a bit too much coincidence that he'd try to roll me the same night I'd managed to inconvenience the latest would-be king of the docks.

The room swung wildly to the right and then back again. I staggered upright as whatever he'd laced the last bottle with slammed into my head. My last conscious thought, as I fell forward and the table gave way, was at least the toothless freak would have to get a new barrel. Cheap bastard would hate that.

# THREE

I heard a smacking noise first and thought I might be on a boat - the motion of a boat, back and forth in time to a sound like someone slapping a side of pork. The rocking and the sound went on and on while something weighted my eyelids - a sinker weight trying to keep me asleep. I tried to go back to sleep but the noise and motion kept pushing, poking me conscious.

I opened my eyes, in time to see a plate sized hand hit the side of my face with enough force to rock my head to the side. The pain shot through the remaining fog, clearing away the remnants of the alcohol and drug that had put me under. I tried to duck the next slap but was tied, kneeling, with my back to some sort of square post. It felt like they'd used wet leather straps to tie my hands and feet. It's a good trick, the leather shrinks as it dries, making the normal methods for getting out of ropes largely useless. The blow slammed my head against the post, sending sparkles around my vision as I croaked out in pain and spat blood from a split lip I had acquired.

"I'm awake!" Blood and saliva drooled down damaged lips, my tongue felt like I'd chewed it for breakfast.

The next backhand pulled up short as I peered around the room. Part of it was obscured by the bulk of Gev. He'd been hitting me for some time judging by the blood and loose teeth in my mouth. He had one arm swathed in bandages and bound tight to his chest and the other - also bandaged - raised to administer another slap. Behind him a man in worn brown leather breeches and an equally worn leather coat straddled a chair. He was resting his chin on his arms which were crossed over the back of the chair and was sucking on something deposited in between his gum and cheek. His skin showed the lined and creased look of someone who'd spent years confronting the weather, with narrow inset eyes that gave him a sunken unhealthy look.

As I watched he turned his head and spat a glob of viscous

black saliva onto the wooden floor. I didn't want to be whoever had to mop that up after they were done with me. Of course, that unlucky soul wouldn't have spent the evening getting drunk, drugged, and then beaten awake, so perhaps trading places would be worth the scrubbing.

Crates and barrels were stacked around the part of the room I could see. Two lanterns were placed on stacked crates to provide ambient lighting. No windows or doors, there was a stair up making me think it might be underground.

"Hey Gev, how's the arm?" I said.

He scowled and slammed by head back against the post with another swipe of his good arm. My left cheek was starting to swell; he'd clearly been putting some effort into waking me up. I wasn't really surprised to be where I was. Waking up tied with a beating seemed pretty much the prayer to go with the sermon after all, but I needed to find a way to keep this service from turning into a memorial. Gev looked like he'd be happy to keep right on rearranging my jawline, but the man in brown cleared his throat and Gev dropped his hand and stepped back like he'd been caught sneaking a loaf in the market.

I tried to shake off the last of whatever I'd been drugged with away - along with bad wine and a slight concussion.

I cocked an eyebrow at the man in brown. Hiring refuse like Jak didn't say much for his judgment, but then I was the one tied to a post so maybe I shouldn't be chumming the water with my foot.

I settled down to wait. That part was easy, the tips of my fingers were numb from the tie job and the room refused to stay still. It kept lurching to one side and then the other. Vomiting might feel better. The man holding Gev's leash was just a little too far to hit though. Instead I composed my face in what I thought was a bored expression.

My father spent a lot of time impressing upon me what he thought of as life lessons. One of his favorites had to do with negotiations. "He who speaks first pays most!" he'd bark as I was frantically scaling a wall or sweating over a disassembled lock. Some things he taught me haven't really been all that useful - I've never really needed to poison a horse. I'm not even sure there are any horses in Myrport - but I will swear by the power of a long steady stare. Silence makes people uncomfortable and they generally start talking.

The room was quiet for a moment while we each looked at each other, I could hear feet on the floor above and the periodic mumble of a voice but nothing else intruded. Finally, the man I had presumed to be Clar squinted for a second and gave me a tight lipped smile.

"You'n made a bad decision last night." He said at last.

I shrugged. Since I was still alive to be tied to a post, it wasn't as bad as it could be. It wasn't great, but over the last few months it'd been worth more than the dice had cost but pointing that out in my position seemed like a fine way to get hit again.

"Jax was'n very bright, but he worked for me. Usually I'd have you'n fed to the sawclaws for that."

Sawclaws feed off carrion and whatever they can scavenge. Anything too big to fit into their mouths they shred with their claws. It was commonly accepted that anything thrown below docks was consumed by scavengers like the sawclaws. They didn't get all that big though and my confusion must have shown.

He snorted and made a handwave at Gev like he was conducting a string ensemble. Gev smiled at me - grinned really - a big happy grin as he moved past me and out of my line of sight behind the post. A moment later I heard him dragging something in fits and starts. Scrape, pause, scrape. After a few pulls, I heard panting, big wheezing breaths. He really needed some regular exercise. Gev reappeared on my left side, one giant arm straining as he slid a crate big enough for him and I to fit inside. It barely fit between me and the wall. Over the top was strapped a sheet of oiled canvas tarp. Grommets around the edge had been strung with rope to keep the tarp in place. A few more seconds of heaving and grunting and he had the thing slightly more than arm's length from both the other man and myself. He stopped, looked at his boss, who made a 'go on' gesture.

Gev fumbled for a bit with the ropes and straps and then fumbled some more. Finally he had them all loose. He spent a second longer turning the crate slightly toward me and then, with a look toward the man in the chair, whipped the tarp up and off in one smooth pull that was ruined at the last second when it caught on the top edge rocking the crate and then slamming it down on the wood floor.

The lone occupant of the cage had already been in motion towards the mesh front that now faced me. A sawclaw the size of a skiff, with two giant serrated pincers, raised to slam against the wire. The rocking and subsequent impact with the floor sent it into a pale-brown, chitinous, crab frenzy. Clearly bent on vengeance for the dice made from generations of its brethren, it emitted an ear rending whistling screech and began pounding the cage front and the side walls with its claws. One of its other legs slammed through the wire as it tried to climb up the side of the crate.

That was all I needed to motivate me. I tried very diligently to increase the distance between it and me, slapping my head up against the post and sending another wave of nausea through my throat. The man in brown stood up, chair raised as a shield but otherwise calm. He snapped his fingers at Gev who scrambled to re-cover the crate with the tarp. He fumbled at it with one arm, as the crab rocketed from side to side, all the while screaming in that high pitched shrieking tone driving a spike into my head. I was really beginning to think about giving up drinking and gambling. Either one…maybe both.

Finally Gev got the tarp over the front of the cage. The monstrosity inside crashed about for a few more seconds, inching the crate forward and back, until it subsided and the screeching stopped. We all stared at the cage for a few moments until the man carefully placed his chair back on the floor and sat, legs crossed, in front of me once more.

"That is a convincing argument." I offered. At that point I was far more interested in not seeing the inside of that cage than winning any negotiating points. There are no good deaths, but that thing seemed worse than most.

"She is."

"She?"

"The males are smaller."

"That must be awkward"

He shrugged, "You have a problem."

"Several actually." I nodded towards my arms.

He flashed another tight lipped smile at me. "Clar has a business deal with…with someone. Before you killed him, Jak was going to act on Clar's behalf."

"You are not, in fact, Clar?"

"You don't want to meet Clar." He said. Gev chuckled.

"Alright. I don't want to meet Clar. What do I call you?"

"Not important," He aimed another black glob at the floor between us.

"Alright." Sir? No, too formal. "I assume you have a plan for how I can make up for my bad decision. Does it involve this business deal?"

This got me another tight-lipped smile. I was starting to wonder if he had teeth. A beggar I knew pulled all of his - he just wiggled them one by one until they got loose enough to pop right out. He could chew steak with his gums and part a man from his dirhams with a toothless grin faster than I could with a knife.

"Clar thinks that you should take Jak's place."

"I don't think I need to know what will happen if I refuse. Is there any chance you could untie me while I still have fingers?"

My new, unwanted, employer eyed me for a couple more seconds and then gave Gev another graceful wave of a hand. The giant scowled like a child without a treat. Something permanent happening to him in the mire was definitely a missed opportunity. My fault for getting fancy. Something my father had never managed to correct. Enemies are a part of any endeavor, but live ones are optional. Gev's attitude left no doubt in my mind, I would have to deal with him eventually, and now there was a good chance I wouldn't be able to pick the moment. He never blinked as he fumbled for the knife hanging from his belt. Eyes locked on mine as he walked around behind the post. I tried not to show the concern I was feeling. It probably wouldn't go well if he stabbed me while cutting the straps, but people do stupid things when they're upset.

He sawed at the straps for a moment, tugging at numb fingers, and I raised my arms a bit to provide better access and to keep my wrists clear. Using a knife one handed probably wasn't going to improve his outlook. After a moment he cut through. Rubbing a little life back into my fingers sent tingles and spikes up into my wrists. I studied my new employer while I did so.

Mostly I worked for myself, solo, but I'd worked with and without other members of my profession before. Not something I cared for. There were enough mistakes of my own making without covering for others and the discussions about shares and splits could turn fatal in the time it took to take your eyes off the loot.

"So, not-Clar, what precisely am I expected to do for Clar?" I motioned with my chin at Gev who had walked back around to stand next to the chair, "I'm not really the muscle type."

"You're going to pay a debt. If that goes well, Clar may consider your debt with him good." Gev snorted and the man in brown glanced at him and then back at me. "You might be favored by The Mad Three. You might survive, but probably not."

I had a sudden urge to go see a priest, having the favor of the gods of luck wasn't something to wish on anyone. People blessed by them usually ended up dead, disfigured, and insane. Hopefully, in that order. The gods are not friendly to mankind. They are capricious at best, dangerous in the middle, and horrifyingly terrible at worst.

"Ah. I don't suppose there's some way for us to work this out without an unspecified length of potentially lethal indentured servitude? No? I thought not." I sighed. So far this wasn't turning into the sort of day I'd treasure in my memories. "So, what now?"

"You go to the Sailor's Rest. There you meet a man named Dugal. Do what he tells you to do. If we see you in Myrport without Dugal...Well, Clar isn't going to be making this offer twice." He and Gev smiled at that last part. I wasn't really all that gratified at their amusement since it involved mortal peril for me.

"How do I know who Dugal is?"

"He knows you."

"That seems unlikely." It wasn't impossible, I wasn't famous - that was the sort of condition that led to branding and eventual hanging - but I'd done enough dockside business that I could have dealt with someone from Clar's organization without knowing it - especially if he'd used a different name. Names are one of the many things I learned to take with a certain amount of tolerance over the years. In a city where the location of buildings can change with an especially high tide, changing your name to avoid official notice is easier than breathing.

"Oh he knows you. He helped carry you here."

"Ah."

The man stood up, brushed at his leather pants, and flicked his coat into place.

"Wait a bit and cut his legs free." He eyed Gev squarely, "Don't damage him." With that he stepped past me. Gev and I watched him mount the stairs without another word, leaving the two of us alone.

With my feet still tied Gev had the advantage, even with one arm, if he decided to get in a little pre-failure exercise. My options didn't look great. Do whatever nonsense Clar was on the hook for, which would probably kill me. Or don't, and either leave Myrport, or try and lay low until something unfortunate and permanent happened to Gev and Clar.

That last part was as sure as the tides. Sooner or later someone would smell blood in the water and decide that being in charge was better than paying Clar his cut. That might not be for years though and until then Clar wouldn't be keen on letting someone like me being the sign of weakness that started the process.

As the footsteps on the stair faded, Gev crouched in front of me. As he leaned in his head grew alarmingly large. He breathed on me for a moment. Sour cabbages, fish - naturally, and beer nearly made my eyes water. For a man his size I was still impressed at the size of his face.

"You and I will meet." he ladled an extra dollop of menace on the last word.

"Why wait Gev?" I waved at my feet, "Not enough going for you? Or are you afraid of that guy?" I jerked a thumb at the stairs.

He just snorted and glared into my eyes. All of his size and muscle hadn't left Gev with much experience when someone didn't back down. I didn't really have a plan in provoking him, but I was pretty sure he'd follow orders and any information I could get would help.

"Were you and Jak close? Ferg not man enough for you by himself?" I hit a nerve with that one. His scowl got deep and dark. Faster than I would have given him credit for, one hand slammed into my jaw. I rolled my head with it a little but still tasted blood from where my teeth cut into the inside of my cheek.

"Ferg's going to gut you while I hold you down." He promised.

"I think you're supposed to leave me undamaged." I really was a little too fond of my own voice sometimes. It would be a good idea to find the giant with a weapon in my hand well before his arm healed. Especially if he found out I wasn't doing Clar's bidding.

"Yeah. Stupid idea, but yeah." He stood up and went behind the post. He stood there a moment while the waiting crawled up my spine and sat in between my shoulder blades. The same feeling that lets a wary man know someone is following him, brought on by knowing that someone who wants to kill you has a knife and a view of your back. We sat there in the basement for a long moment, until he buried the knife into the post behind me with a loud meaty thunk, startling the sawclaw into another fit of rage. I ducked at the sound and then again as the crab rattled the wood of its crate.

Gev laughed. "Cut yourself loose. Don't forget about Dugal. I hope you live. I really do."

"I'm touched. Say 'Hi' to Ferg for me."

He snorted and started for the stairs. The knife was buried to the hilt in the beam. It might have been a part of the wood for my attempts to pull it out. I sighed again and began working it back and forth. Provoking him was turning into another in a chain of great ideas.

# FOUR

I thought about my decision making while crouched along the eaves of what had once been a major shipping warehouse. The building had been several things since then: a dance hall, a processing building for cod, and now a low rent flophouse. It stank of fish guts; that could be said of just about anywhere on the docks, but it was smack in the middle of the ebb and flow of lower Myrport. Buildings in the docks tended to conform to the needs of their owners. As the city expanded outward, structures rotated through functionality to match. It did have an excellent view of the entrance to the Sailor's Rest; a not-irrelevant feature in its current incarnation as a flophouse.

From my perch I was able to observe and consider. Perhaps I should have been doing more of that, prior to winding up on the bad side of men like Clar and Gev.

They'd left my belongings at the top of the stairs. Minus any dirhams, but being armed again was comforting. I'd also lost a silver neck chain bought from the proceeds from my first uptown job. Under normal circumstances I would have been checking with the various places known to buy up easily transportable goods for resale, of course if one of Clar's people saw me wandering about the docks I'd likely end up killing someone. I wasn't sure if there was a daily limit to the number of bodies that could be disposed of, it seemed unlikely in Myrport, but a wise man never tempts the tides as they say.

It was probably time to get off the roof and out of the rain. While I wasn't excited about doing Clar's bidding, it wouldn't hurt to know what he wanted me to do, while I figured a way out from under his thumb.

The side of the flophouse looked like an impromptu dump for people too lazy to cart things to a gap and toss them into the mire. It was dark, smelled worse than usual, and was an easy drop from the roof away from the entrance to the Sailor's Rest. It's always best not to advertise.

Sailor's Rest had no door; just a few blankets nailed up to keep the heat in and the weather out; duck through one side or the other and be quick about it, or make enemies of those nearby.

A wall of moist hot air and sound brought me up short. Thanks to the rain, the tavern was a busy place to get out of the wet and do business and drink, or game away the day. Several tables had been converted to temporary dice games using the point of a knife or chalk to draw out the circles for bets and squares for held throws. The owner probably wasn't thrilled at the damage to his tables but the sale in drinks would ease his hurt. Nobody made a show of noticing my entrance. There were probably twenty tables worth of patrons and almost all of them the normal mix of day laborers and less socially acceptable jobs, like me, who made it their business to transfer wealth.

The sole exception was a table to one side of the lone fireplace. Wood costs dirhams and nobody burns money if they can avoid it. A noticeable gap ringed the table's occupants. If a fight broke out, the inevitable brawl would have still left that iron-walled space free. There were enough weapons visible on one of them, a narrowly gaunt man, to outfit a squadron of the watch. No idea what he thought he'd need a great sword in a bar for. Even money said the crossbow propped against the wall, but still within arm's reach, was his as well. Of course most everything looked to be within arm's reach for him. He was tearing off bite-sized chunks from a loaf of dark bread while listening to the person to his left. His legs were too long to sit square to the table so he slouched and held his head tilted.

The talker had a round face incompletely covered with tufts of dark hair; like a badger that's lost a few fights. He wore a grey robe with the sleeves were rolled back, showing blackened steel underneath. Between the two of them, they had enough plate to drown a village-worth of soldiers. Since the watch didn't wander lower Myrport, it wasn't usual to see armor of any sort and I was certain I'd never actually seen anyone wearing armor made of lacquered ebony plates.

On the other side of the table, another fellow in a robe was following the same conversation. He had dark hair managed with too much oil. The fabric of his robe could briefly be seen under the pinned or stitched surface of rustling paper scraps and strips of parchment; all covered in fine lettering and splotches of ink.

Next to him, the remaining two, a man and a woman, were in their own conversation and it was clear the woman was not impressed.

She wore a leather coat covered in polished rivets and fastened from neck to waist with matching buckled straps. Her hair was braided behind her, held in place by a worked comb, revealing smoothly pale skin and a well-defined jaw. The firelight danced off the metal in glints of silver and gold; like a crystal throwing off light in all directions.

She was scowling at the other and, as I watched, she began shaking her head. He was selling something and she wasn't buying. All I could see of the other was his back, but he appeared to be trying to make a point, which the woman was having none of. As I watched, she cut him off with one gloved hand.

I decided to live the rest of my life in a manner more pleasing to the gods of luck. Clearly, I had done something that The Mad Three found incredibly offensive. In the last forty-eight hours I'd been caught, drugged, rolled, and beaten. Throw in the death of a man - not my fault - and pressganged for sauce. Whatever madness the sideshow at that table was overdressed for, I wanted no part of it.

The man with his back to me had to be Dugal and now I understood perfectly why Clar would have employed a failed gambler like Jak. It didn't take a palm reader to tell me why he would be happy to have someone outside of his organization take Jak's place.

Whatever else can be said against making a living by the redistribution of wealth, it is a fairly safe version of crime. Sure, if you get caught they might hang you but you might also catch the death cough or have a piece of the stars fall out of the sky and crush you. Bad thieves get caught and my father made sure that whatever I am, I'm not a bad thief. If I ever had any doubts, he made quick use of the stick to correct my thinking.

It never came up but I could conjure a perfect image of him in my mind, stick in hand, lecturing as I hung upside down from the lock post. It wasn't really a post as much as a large wood frame that had locks of every size and shape fastened to it. Everything from padlocks to key holes to manacles, placed so that access to anyone of them required me to climb the frame and then prop, hang, or suspend while I practiced. My father felt that this helped to instill the proper amount of difficulty into the training. Touching the ground or dropping anything was rewarded with the stick. I had no doubt that, were he still alive, he would have had quite a few things to say about getting trapped into consorting with the sort of people who went on 'adventures.' A sick twisting feeling churning up my intestines argued that was exactly the sort of hobby the group beside the fire was interested in.

My better instincts had just convinced me to duck back out into the rain when the woman finished poking at the man I presumed to be Dugal. He turned away from her, saw me standing at the entryway, and immediately stood up and made his way through the crowded tables to where I was pondering flight.

He was a narrow faced man with a long nose that ended in a downward tilting point. The effect reminded me of a wax candle as it melts. His hair was pulled straight back and fastened in a braid which he kept draped across the front of his jacket, probably to show off the gold wire woven into the braid. He was dressed in a silk blouse with a shorted jacket similar to the style farther up the hill in Myrport proper. Gold stitching worked patterns of leaves and various fauna, most of which I doubted were real, into the fabric. His outfit included knee boots, tights, and some sort of short pant I couldn't even identify. Spurs, fixed to the heels with tiny chains, tinkled as he walked. All topped off with a light bladed sword suspended on a worked silver chain.

How he managed to make it this far into the docks without either winding up naked in the mud below or killing an aspiring mugger every few feet might be one of the Goddesses miracles. It's not every day someone dressed for court gets lost on the docks.

As he reached me, he turned his lips in a smile and nodded slightly. "You are later than I expected." He snipped each word off like a merchant clipping coins, each word started slow and ended in a rush. "Sober. That is good, but you stink."

I stared at him. Silence is a general purpose tool.

"I will introduce you. Do what you are told and feel free to not share your motivations for joining this venture. Clar wouldn't appreciate that." He said the last with a smile intended to impart the difference between what Clar might appreciate and what he might have me killed for.

"I live to serve" I said. That got me another, identical, smile.

"I am sure you do. Of course, you have already shown your willingness to put that at risk. We had to be quite firm with Gev. I think he actually intends to twist your head off. I doubt that it is possible to de-stem a human being but I may get to see that I am wrong."

"Maybe I'll get lucky and his arm will turn septic."

"Decidedly unlikely, Clar paid for a priestess."

Things were just getting worse and worse. A full priestess of the Goddess could heal even mortal wounds. They rarely did so though, and required a great deal of convincing - usually in the form of donations - large donations. Rumor was they coated the effigies in the temple with gold from those donations. In a fit of secular optimism, I'd visited the temple once. The statues had silk drapes over them, only true believers were allowed to gaze upon the visage of the goddess, but I was suitably awed by the surrounding fresco and engraved tributes. The guards appeared to be overfed monks armed with oversized tridents. Full of sharp edges and shiny phalanges, but I doubted their utility in a fight. An intruder was more likely to be injured by having one fall on him than any intended thrust from an easily startled monk.

Two things had occurred to me. It was generally bad business to offend deities. And nobody sane in town would buy a single thing I stole. There isn't much use in thievery if all you're doing is decorating your home. In the end I decided to opt for caution.

Dugal looked equally useless, but you drink what's in front of you. "So, what am I supposed to do for these...Ah...people?"

"Just what you do; nothing beyond your natural assets."

"Ok, but why? Not that I'm ungrateful at this startlingly fantastic opportunity to make amends..." I trailed off hopefully.

He just smiled again and turned to lead the way back to the table. I fought down the impulse to head the opposite direction and followed after. He moved with care and was surprisingly adept at weaving through the crowded tables without smacking his sword into everything he passed. That didn't tell me if he knew how to use it for poking holes in things, but it did seem to indicate that he wasn't just "dressing" like a hilltop dandy, he might be the actual thing. We got to the table and Dugal made introductions starting with the woman he'd been talking to.

"Sylvie, this is Renn, the expert we promised." He gestured towards the man sitting next to her, "Isaac Fontein."

Isaac looked at me quickly and then back at the two in armor opposite. Compared to those two, he looked small and thin. If nothing else armor makes you look imposing.

Dugal continued around the table pointing first at the shorter one, "Brother Hospur and Lye of Goldpoint."

Hospur eyed me for a moment and then resumed stuffing the loaf of bread into his mouth chunk by chunk. Lye gave me a smile and a nod before returning to whatever he'd been discussing with Hospur. I hooked a free chair and set it between the table and the fire.

Sylvie sizing me up, felt like fingers on my skin. Her problem was that, while it may be possible to tell if someone can fight by their appearance, a thief should spend as much effort as it takes to make sure he doesn't look like a thief. It sort of ruins the surprise. People start investing in better locks and booby-trapping their doors. Her face was expressionless, but I watched her watching me. Her eyes were large and dark and her nose had just a hint of an upward tilt.

After a few moments, she scowled at Dugal. "If he isn't an 'Expert' as you say, I won't very well be able to ask for a refund, will I?"

"My employer has every reason to hope for your safe return."

"Which will do me exactly no benefit at all if I don't."

She had a smooth alto - smooth and listenable. It was pleasantly conversational, even as she was clearly both irritated with Dugal, and suspicious of me. It sounded like they had been over this already, probably more than once.

"You asked for someone of specific talents. If you did not trust us to provide the appropriate candidate, why did you ask?"

"Well, he looks like he'd be great at carpentry or maybe bricklaying. Maybe we'll be lucky and whatever awaits us will be brought low by a well-constructed wall."

That hurt a little, but I wasn't going to help Dugal, unless it involved handing him ballast when he was sinking.

The fop snorted, "I doubt our expert would be much use at either if it comes to that."

As it happens, I had spent more than a few afternoons working a site with line and pins. The pay wasn't very good, but timing guards looks a little suspicious without something to occupy your hands. Pointing that out didn't seem useful so I leaned my chair closer to the fire and tried to think dry, warm thoughts.

"How much have you told him?"

"He is as clear as he needs to be." He stared at me as he said it.

I rolled my eyes at him. Sticking a dagger in whatever scam he and Clar were running on this woman and her overdressed friends would be stupid. The setup smelled like tripe - especially if they'd been pawning off Jax. Nothing about the dead gambler's reputation said he'd had any skills worth noting, much less being an expert of any sort. It made me think he hadn't been expected to return. If they'd been willing to discard a member of their outfit like that, the odds of me surviving whatever they had in mind, didn't seem very good.

"This wasn't our deal." Sylvie announced. Her voice clear and loud, cutting through the room.

The tables next to us paused and then consciously resumed their activities. Not much deters the average man from the pursuit of his distractions in a tavern like the Sailor's Rest. Start noticing and pretty soon you're in the middle of a fight or waiting for a knife between the ribs because you've overheard the wrong people doing business. Nobody wants that. So you keep your head down, drink your ale, roll your dice, and try to put off the next day's work as long as you can.

Lye and Hospur turned and waited. Dugal pinched the bridge of his nose with one hand and waved her on with the other. It was that moment when two people approach each other down a narrow walkway and each continues forward, yet one or the other will have to stop or step aside. The first is not quite sure what to do, does he stop? But if he stops will he appear weak, or less of a man? Meanwhile the other guy is thinking about how his sore tooth is going to fester soon if he doesn't get it pulled.

Since I had seated myself to take advantage of the fire, Sylvie was forced to have her back to me while she addressed the others.

"We've spent too much time; we've all worked too hard, to put this to chance." She really did have a captivating voice.

"It's not like we can put out for applicants, Syl." Hospur said.

"We've gotten this far, send the two of them back, we can do without that sort of help, I should think." Isaac rustled as he spoke; each little shift whispering.

"You've done the reading; you were the one who suggested we find someone. Besides, there are things that Hospur can't fix and Lye can't kill." Sylvie said.

Lye shrugged. The loaf was gone, devoured, and he'd

picked the crumbs off the table. He started in on a second, rolling the bread into balls before popping them into his mouth.

Isaac fluttered a bit more, "True enough. But, I don't like him."

As far as that went, I didn't care for me either. So there.

"That wasn't part of the deal." If Dugal was offended, he didn't let on, "Breaking the deal isn't going to go well with my employer."

A verbal contract could be binding in Myrport. There were all sorts of laws the council didn't spend a lot of effort enforcing: murder, theft, extortion, to name a few. But violating a contract or being known as a welcher could ruin a man faster than the gibbet.

"He is rude, smells of wet dog, and we hardly need a hired hand to carry our bags." Isaac reminded me of a prodded seal, grumping as it waddles off. "We do not owe this employer of yours…"

"If your employer has provided what he agreed to, there's no problem." Sylvie cut Isaac off, leaving him grinding down molars. "If not, he'd better hope the crypt kills him instead of the Vevoda"

That brought me up short. I hadn't ever seen the Vevoda. She ran one of the newer merchant houses and her money had bought her a seat on the council along with the sort of dubious title currently in vogue. Since money was the only blood that mattered in Myrport, the market stall mentality of the rich and worthy meant they had bargain-shopped for titles to impress at parties.

Rumor, always a loose and willing tart, had it that the current Vevoda of House Mara was also known for taking special delight in dealing with her opponents. This was supposed to involve extreme pain and suffering and, depending on the ambition of the storyteller, may include demonic rituals performed under light provided by flickering souls consumed in hellfire.

I found those rumors to be doubtful. My experience in the homes of the rich and mighty led me to suspect that the normal motivations a man might have, amplified by wealth and power, were sufficient without invoking demons. The rumors I did believe were more than enough to make me want to avoid any hint of this scheme.

Fortunately, I had a plan.

"You know sweetpea… If it helps, I would be happy to stay out of whatever little tea party you and your friends here are up to" I ladled all the condescension I could into a nice slow arrogant drawl. "Nice outfits though, Honey." I threw in for good measure.

Sylvie froze and her neck and ears flushed scarlet. Lye stared at me, half chewed mouthful visible. Hospur got caught with a mouthful of ale, choked for a second, swallowed, and then leaned back from the table glancing between Sylvie and I.

"You will speak when…" Isaac stopped as she held out a hand. He ruffled like a disturbed owl, one offense away from smoothing his paper feathers.

Time to go all in. "Oh. Sorry. I thought she was in charge."

Getting fired, or short of that, a nice bar fight would provide a plausible way out of both the turtle-brained plan and any usefulness I might have to Dugal and his master. Clar might still decide to do something permanent, but getting out and abroad in the world was starting to look like the better part of valor. It looked like I had caught Dugal unprepared as well so I used the momentary lull to lean back and adopt an appropriately disrespectful expression, something halfway between a smirk and a sneer.

Sylvie turned with all the deliberateness of a barge. Her eyes were slits and her lips formed a tightly compressed line in between high boned cheeks that had flooded the same iridescent red as her ears. Even so, she kept her composure. She stared at me for a long moment as I tried to hold my smirk.

"Can you do anything that Master Dugal has suggested you might?" Each word was handled with care and delivered as if it were glasswork from the northern factory cities.

Dugal was giving me the same narrow gaze. Scams aren't my usual fare. I much prefer leaving without being seen. You never know who you're going to run into, and starting the day off running from a former victim isn't my idea of fun. Still, I'd spent enough time talking my way into trouble to know that abandoning a con early was the mark of an amateur.

"What's that, honey? I just got done with my shift. Got near to all the north wall up, with a view of the Orchid the whole time." A wink and a leer for emphasis. She was formless in the reinforced leather she was wearing, but I doubted she recognized that.

That coat cost more than I would make in a decade in my supposed role as a day laborer. Before sanity caught up with me I'd learned all about the craftsmanship and materials costs. The specimen she had on was even nicer than anything I'd looked at. The coat was fastened along each side by a series of three buckles worked into likenesses of human faces with the strap coming out as the tongue. Each was as big around as a mug. I suspected that they'd be pretty good at blocking a blow to the side as well as being decorative. My money was on running like I was about to get stabbed, over getting stabbed.

For a moment it looked like I was about to get a chance to try my skills in outrunning. She held my gaze while one hand drifted behind her back. She was a lefty and had some sort of weapon that wasn't visible. That wasn't really a surprise. Only a fool shows all his toys.

Before I could find out what sort of toy she had hidden, she stopped - hand still behind her back. As we looked at each other she returned my leer with a slow smile of her own. Her teeth were immaculately white, even and disconcertingly. It matched the look in her eyes.

"On second thought, Dugal, maybe that was hasty. He'll do fine."

"Syl!"

"It's fine, Isaac. He may not be able to do what we need in the traditional sense, but if not, I think I would enjoy seeing whatever happens to him." She favored me with a decidedly feral grin and turned back to the group, leaving me with nothing to do but scowl at her back as she finished off whatever was in her mug.

"Excellent. Then if that is settled," Dugal glanced at me, he was definitely planning on revisiting the conversation later, and then focused back on the others, "when do we start?"

My half apologetic shrug didn't seem to placate him.

"Better yet, what are we starting?" I asked. "Or even, what am I supposed to do?"

Isaac cleared his throat, started to talk then stopped. He didn't like me; no real surprise.

"Tell him, Isaac." Sylvie said.

"We are attempting to recover an object thought lost to the world, it has been hidden and protected, you are going to help us with those protections by, ah, you know..." He waved one hand at me like I was a small, excessively irritating, child he wanted to get out of his way.

"So what is it?" I asked

"What is what?" Issac looked at me blankly.

"The object."

He set his jaw and adjusted his seat with a mutter of dry leaves. So I tried again,

"What is so important that people like you," I waved at the four seated at the table who had so obviously not made their place in the world by scrabbling among the docks, "that you would make deals with Clar and his friends?"

"Is that a problem?" He peered at me.

Dugal cleared his throat and favored me with what he probably hoped was meaningful glance, which I ignored.

"Clar. You know...extortion, prostitution, smuggling, and probably slavery? Not the sort of people I hang out with, but I'm sure whatever you are doing must justify whatever you promised him." Hospur had stopped talking to Lye and was looking at Sylvie, brow furrowed. The other looked at him then at Sylvie, shrugged, and went back to his bread. She locked eyes with Hospur for a moment and then turned back.

"I really am going to enjoy watching you." She said. "I'm starting to think I would prefer it if you aren't at all what we were promised. As Isaac mentioned, we are recovering an object. Regaining it will be difficult. It might even be fatal. In your case, I'm beginning to think not fatal enough."

"It's always nice to have a fan." I said with a smile.

"I assure you, he will be exactly what you require." Dugal attempted another quelling glare.

Not all partnerships end by splitting the take. If this was going to be one of those, I wanted to know. That meant getting as much detail as I could.

"So what's it for, then, if you don't mind telling the help?"

There was a long moment of silence as Sylvie and the others looked at one another. Hospur sat back with a smile and gestured, palm up, for her to go ahead. Her eyes narrowed as she gazed back at him. While she thought, she tapped the nail of her forefinger on the table.

"Call it…Call it a key." The statement sat between us, squatting, like a beggar on the wrong street corner waiting for someone to speak up and roust out the interloper.

"A key to what? And why?"

Asking questions probably explained my career as an independent. Nobody likes being used, but I took it personally. That's why I'd never taken up with one of the various dockside factions. They styled themselves unions and guilds and so on, but mostly they were just gangs of thugs. The big ones on the top, feeding off those on the bottom, who in turn, fed on each other and the infrequent lower Myrport resident who looked like they might have something.

Not that anyone on the docks had much. Upper was where the money was, along with dry land and houses that don't collapse into the muck during a storm.

"Why what? Why do we want it?" Isaac said.

"Sure."

"Because…" Hospur tended to start talking before his lips, muddying either end of his words. "…if we don't, robbing the Temple of the Goddess will be pointless."

"Oh. That's insane."

My understanding is that normally, when dealing with someone whose ships have slipped their moorings, it is best to avoid directly pointing out that you think they are detached from care and reason.

Devout, wealthy, patrons of the priestesses were buried in the crypts underneath the temple grounds dedicated to the Lady of Tides. Unsurprisingly the crypts were rumored to hold the wealth of generations of the rich and entitled, usually literally. Normally such a target would have been inundated by waves of the sort of moral reprobates that make a living off acquiring other people's wealth. People like me. Of course, that would make further burials and donations unlikely. Sensibly, the priestesses took measures to prevent that sort of recreation. Obviously, the potential thief would be committing blasphemy of awe-inspiring magnitude as well as facing the usual run of traps and wardings. But that wasn't the really bad part. The bad part was the Tugali.

Rumors about the Tugali were a favorite pastime late at night when money had run dry, but the cups hadn't. People would claim to know that they were cannibals, devotees of animal cults, sacrificed babies, and then they'd start getting inventive. Of course nobody really knew, since they never left the temple grounds and spoke only Tugali. They were nearly identical. Short, albino pale, and festooned with blades chipped from a blue translucent stone. These blades were used liberally on any intruders, who were found flayed and pinned – insect-like - to posts. Since I had no desire to end up with the meat of my legs carved into paper-thin slices, the thought of going anywhere near the place wasn't comforting.

"No really. That's crazy." My brain was stuck. The gibbering in the back of my head had overcome my mouth.

Sylvie smiled again, a lazy, slow smile that was all immaculate whiteness. She was tapping the table again with her fingernail. It was my new goal to get as far away from these people as possible. Maybe join the army, except Myrport doesn't have an army.

"So, I get you this thing and you go commit suicide? Fine

then. Where is it and when do we start?"

# FIVE

The answers to those two questions were fairly straightforward. The thing was buried with the body of one of the Vevoda's grandchildren. An uninheritable second son who contracted the falling sickness while on an expedition to the Citadel Ring - a series of semi-mythical frozen castles that line the roof of the world.

Traipsing up north to the vacant, deadly, halls of long abandoned fortresses was something of a hobby of the un-inheritable scions of the rich and powerful:

Scholars claimed not to know what the forts had been for. The only thing that lay past them was vast sheets of ice and storms of snow that turned the world past your nose white. A man could reach out his arm in one of those storms and not see his fingers and likely as not, pull back a frozen stump.

Whatever people had built the fortresses had been wealthy enough to build a line of stone castles that outlived both them and whatever threat they were meant to ward off.

Getting to one of these castles was more dangerous than profitable. There were plenty of easier ways to get dead and rich, as the dead auxiliary-son learned. Something he found sickened him. He died on the return voyage, losing whatever spoils he had gathered on the outbound journey. He was buried with the one item he had managed to salvage from the wreckage of his ambitions.

Sylvie and her fellow suicides planned to break into said crypt that very night and retrieve it, along with whatever other valuables were interred with the dead man. Those would go to Clar. At which point, I was free of my obligation. I very much doubted that would play out in even close proximity to the plan, which was how I found myself standing outside the walls of the Vevoda's estate about half way up the hill.

Standing on the street in the middle of the night was the sort of behavior that the watch was designed to both detect, they used patrols of armed men for this, and, post detection, stop.

Since it is fairly easy to tell the difference between legitimate nighttime business and mine - honest people didn't walk about in the middle of the night - being spotted by the watch, standing about like moonstruck halfwits was a sure bet.

The walls were just the thing, tall, smooth, and no doubt topped with shards of glass or pottery, anything sharp really. Taking a running leap to grab the top and heave yourself over would shred your hands. If the owners were especially viciously minded, the shards and spikes would be coated with something poisonous.

If I'd been living a more virtuous life, I would have gotten a good look as I made the jump - with a nice tuck and roll from a convenient adjacent roof onto what looked like lush and lovingly tended crocuses. Instead I was crouched in front of the side gate with my hands up to the wrists inside of a worked iron monstrosity that passed for a lock. Since no sinner ever stands for judgment by herself, Dugal was leaned against the wall next to me. Ostensibly, to provide a lookout I didn't need. Instead he was mostly blocking what little useful light there was while delivering a lecture on the proper comportment of someone doing Clar's bidding. Apparently my mouth wasn't a useful addition to my skills. Who knew?

Any moment, one of the packs of half drunk, tabard-makes-us-gods wearing fools would round the corner and what would I say? Working late, I'm a lock polisher? Then I could just tell them the roll of leather with individual, hand sewn, pockets - each caressing a highly polished and shaped length of steel for getting at the secret soul of even the most reclusive lock - I could tell them it had fallen from the sky. A gift from a benevolent sky god, no doubt. Quite a gift it would have been too, those tools had taken me a year of every contract and freelance job I could scrape together to pay for. Nothing to eat but bottom fish that year, I still couldn't stand the taste. I snorted to myself in the wet darkness and got back to work.

The others were waiting, under the eaves of what looked like a dressmaker's; enormous concoctions of lace, silk, and bustles obscured any view of the shop interior. Heat ripples of impatience wafting off of them, like steam on cobblestones when the sun decides to follow the rain. Dugal could probably pass for a citizen of uptown, but three of the others were festooned in armor and sharp objects and Isaac was so odd that just the sight of him would probably give me the head start I needed to escape.

Every minute or two, one or another would bark a scabbard against a wall or scrape rivets along the stone; sending worms up my neck to burrow in my ears. For a second I thought I heard wooden boot heels against cobblestone, my heart lurched like the first time I'd been pawing through a dresser when the lady of the house rolled over in her sleep.

"Sorry" Hospur whispered followed by more clanking as someone else elbowed him.

The uselessly loud whispered conversations grated worse than the metal on stone. That's the thing about whispers, they aren't quieter. A man whispering is just announcing to everyone within earshot that he's about to say something worth listening too. That, amongst a bevy of other heavy and impractical but intimidating reasons was why we weren't doing the smart thing and going up and over the wall and the wear and use on my nerves was making, what should have been a quick pop and release, into an extended affair.

There were more ways to commit murder than hands to apply them. Hospur had spent a good part of the walk uptown extolling the virtues of his mace over a sword. Since I'd become a devout worshipper of the church of shut-up in that same distance I hadn't given this dissertation the attention he thought it had deserved and suffice to say, my suggestion that we avoid the gate in favor of a more survivable method of entry had been met with a fairly dismissive wave of one mailed hand.

My fingers finally worked their magic; the click of the hasp release was like a sunny day after a month of rain. "Finally." Sylvie wasn't a fan.

"If you'd like to do it..." I offered.

She snorted, "Oh no, Sir Expert, I'm still holding out for some sort of grisly demise, preferably with screaming." Her smile didn't contain any humor.

"I doubt you'll get any luck there, most of these people rely on dogs and paid thugs."

Where did she get teeth like that anyways? There were tribes the sailors talked about that filed theirs down; the better for eating other tribesmen they said. Somehow Sylvie didn't seem like she was eating people on the sly.

Dugal cleared his throat and pointed towards the now unlocked entrance. I'd worked the dock a few times, casing arriving shipments and so on - warehouse robbery goes better when you have an idea where to look. Dugal was beginning to remind me of some of the dock bosses, they could spend entirely too much time riding their crews and make a day drag worse than the harbor dredges. It had still been worth the sweat.

A friend of mine had spent an entire evening searching an especially large warehouse. The place had been cobbled together out of several adjacent buildings and one three story ex-floating barge. He'd fed the dogs drugged salmon by punching a hole in the roof and dropping it onto the barking, half-starved mongrels below. We all agreed it had been a good plan up until he spent so long searching the multi-floored storage that the hemlock he'd laced the fish with - not only didn't kill them but wore off. The dogs hadn't been at all grateful for their meal either. He'd been covered by bandages where they'd expressed their feelings on finding him wandering about their home. He died of lockjaw not long after.

The gate slid smoothly inward. Well, smoothly after I applied a dab of whale fat to each of the hinges. As my father used to say, "Preparation is the path to old age." Not that he would know.

Beyond the gate lay a cobbled path, wide enough for delivery carts and lined on each side by closely trimmed shrub roses planted to keep outsiders from straying into view and disturbing the sensibilities of the wealthy. Deliveries would continue around a hedged corner, presumably to the kitchen and storerooms that lay at the foundation of wealth and power in upper Myrport. We were looking for the family crypt that most of the top shelf families who didn't follow the Lady of Tides, had. Followers were buried under the temple if they could afford it, at sea if they couldn't or under the docks if they couldn't manage even that. Unless someone didn't want the body to be found - under the docks was a good place for that too.

Halfway to where the path took the corner, stood worked-stone archways creating a protected break in the thorny barrier and covered with climbing flowers that had been meticulously managed up and over the top of each. The thick smell of honey coated the back of my tongue. In the darkness the vines shrouded most of the granite, glistening and dripping from the constant drizzle that kept most nights company.

The rain dampened noise, a useful feature once you got used to being cold. Even dogs grew incurious unless roused by something really strange. If they had dogs, the weather was enough to cover the noise, as we blundered through their gardens. We sorted into a line. Me leading the way, followed far too closely by Dugal who'd decided I needed supervision. Hospur and Lye bracketed Sylvie and Isaac behind him. Thank the Goddess they were far enough to keep their noise from distracting me.

The path to the left seemed as likely as any.

It opened up into a precisely trimmed expanse of spongy turf interspersed with small fruit trees leading toward a squat stone building nestled against the outer wall. It wasn't a great leap to guess that this was the crypt, so I waited for the others to notice it and then went that way.

My feet sunk slightly into the ground. A small puddle of dark beneath each tree covered me as I moved closer.

The gardener was going to die of apoplexy when he saw the holes left by hobnailed boots on his lovingly tended grass. The crypt's entrance was lit by the oil-fed lantern; replete with storm glass to keep the flame from drowning during the local weather –

rain, mixed with water falling from the sky, often sideways, thanks for asking.

Waiting under one of the plum trees gave me a chance to examine the entrance. Something wasn't right. If I somehow became as rich as a prince, replete with foreboding family tomb, I'd probably seal the entrance with a solid bronze door. The crypt up ahead had that, artistically engraved with many-armed tentacles representing Deepspawn. The walls were made of a dark, glassy stone, in blocks the size of my head. I could just barely make out the lines where one block joined with the next. There was no sign of hinges or a lock, but nobody pays for craftsmanship like that and doesn't lock it., unless it was guarded.

That's what was sending tendrils of worry, cold and seaweed clammy, up my spine. No guards, no patrols, and no dogs. This estate was a pie left cooling on a windowsill. A lifetime of larceny hadn't ever presented me with such a wide-open target. All my instincts were queuing up.

Normally, if a storefront is unlocked, a guard is right around the corner. Thrift or bad information leads people to think a guard will work better than a good lock, preferably coated in contact poison. It might even be true if the same thrift didn't lead people to take the lowest bidder's services. That's where sleep, bribery, or a touch of battery comes in. "After a concussion all men are reasonable," as the wise man said…or something like that.

I took advantage of my location and grabbed a plum while reviewing my options. This is why working alone is always a better option. The time to consider the consequences far outweighs any benefit to be had from an extra pair of hands. Thinking things through is a solo activity and generally adding participants just means someone gets impatient.

"Problem?" Dugal was up to being someone.

"No. Yes." I said around a mouthful of plum. Something squirming around in my gut pulled me back to the door. Eight feet of cast bronze with row upon row of Deepspawn depicted down the face. Deepspawn are the stuff of evangelical doomsaying and the stick to any good priestess' carrot of eternal paradise.

The story goes that the Goddess of Tides had four sons. She gave each son dominion over the winds that steered the boats of man over her body. Three of them mirrored the temper of the winds. By turns fickle, dangerous, and helpful. The Three were content.

But the fourth, who took as his the howling implacability of the north wind, was as proud and dangerous as the wind he controlled. Not satisfied with power of storm and ice, he sought to use his brothers in a bid to gain power over the whole world. Sly as the scuttering clouds that turn into a wall of iron-tinged death, for boats large and small; he convinced his younger siblings to play a game with their mother.

Full of the impetuousness of youth and blind to their brother's intent, The Three tricked their mother into a drinking contest against her envious son, the lord of the North wind. The Goddess, in her aspect of the devouring bottomless ocean, sought to win by turning the drinks into water as the contest went on, but even she had trouble keeping up with the pace and volume the other divines were consuming, seemingly without effect.

The line between insanity and inebriation is thin indeed. The more she drank, the more they drank, matching her one for four of their own. The priestesses say the ale they consumed by the barrel would kill a mortal man with a drop. Finally she succumbed.

Her son took this moment of weakness for his chance and lay with the goddess, thinking to gain power over her. Of course, as any gambler will tell you, bargaining with The Three is a fool's option. Even then, the madness they would eventually be known for was upon them. They used their power to make sure there would be evidence of the blasphemous union.

As many a drunk has, upon waking the following morning, The Goddess cursed the excesses of the night before. As a god, those excesses were far more numerous than any wine soaked human dalliance. She banished her new offspring to the bottomless chasms of the glacier covered northern seas, where they became known as Deepspawn, along with their father.

Every so often some cabalist, with even less sense than normal, will strike the sort of bargain that shrivels the tongue of a sane man and summons one up to do his bidding. What comes forth reeks of decaying fish and can supposedly crush a man in armor with their squid like tentacles. Other, more lurid, tales claim that they carry off virgins, small children, the unfaithful, and so forth. What they don't do, or at least I'd never heard of it, is provide comfort and protection to the dead.

"Well, Expert, time for you to earn your keep." Sylvie could hold a thought.

"I'm not being paid." I said.

"What's the hold up?"

"Nothing. Just checking." I couldn't very well admit that a door with creepy faces on it scared me, after all.

Sylvie looked at me for a second, then at the door and then a slow, happy, smile revealed; precisely spaced, uncomfortably sharp, teeth.

"It's just a door." She said.

"I know that!" Right then I knew that she knew what was bothering me. Knew and was perfectly willing to enjoy my discomfort, of course. She was standing so close I could smell something that tingled my nose mixed with roses. That was the time to do something; say something clever. Instead, I turned back and strolled up to the half circle of marble that led up to the door. It was a solid slab of grey stone sanded and polished to a smooth finish.

It wasn't going to be a fun evening if the crypt was full of mourners, but it didn't look like that was the case.

Rites and observances for the dead in Myrport varied widely with wealth and religion. Some folks disposed of their deceased and then never another thought, some spent part of every day with their ancestors. Most Lowtown folk practiced burial at sea, or mire, as the opportunity and need struck them. They spent more time on the next meal than for those that don't eat any more.

No way to know how much traffic the crypt got, but there wasn't any sign of rubbing where the door swung open and the rain washed stone kept any footprints from lingering.

Unfortunately that was the end of reasons to delay that I could come up with. Now that I was close enough to work out the details on the door I could feel the hairs on the back of my neck stiffening. Doors did a lot of things, but eating people wasn't one. Past time for me to get to work.

Running my hand lightly over the stone, barely contacting, just brushing at the moisture created a slick, nearly imperceptible layer between the stone and my hand. The idea is to keep your touch light enough that you can feel the imperfections left by triggers and false fronts without setting off whatever gifts were left by the owner. The surface was smooth, with the perfection of shaved skin.

My face pinched and I could hear the shades of older and wiser thieves telling me to walk away. Just stand up, turn, and run. Nobody in armor would catch me. Lye and the crossbow bothered me a little bit, but he'd only get one shot, and that through the trees with a wet string. Besides, even if he hit me, I might not die. Those older, presumably wiser, thieves knew that the way that a young thief gets to be an old thief is avoiding things that look too good to be true. No guards, no dogs, and no traps. Sure, the gods could be making amends; they and I agreed that the last couple days had been a bit much, even for them. This could be an elaborate divine apology, after which we would all kiss, make up, and sing hymns together in some sort of ale inspired fever dream.

Sure, and right after I could start buying boats sight unseen. A smart man examines a boat for leaks and makes an effort to keep people like me from taking what he's earned. That's the way the game is played. Keeps things interesting for both of us. If nothing else, it keeps me honest. Well, more honest. Which meant that what lay past that door was either worthless, which people don't generally house in elaborate imported stone crypts, or defended in some other way. Probably horrible and every bit as lethal as Sylvie had insinuated.

"Expert?"

Right on cue. There was laughter burbling in her stage whisper. I turned my head and tried a quelling glare. It failed.

"Is there a problem?" She was all innocence.

Next to her Dugal had his arms crossed and jerked his chin at the door. The image of him dangling over the edge of a building helped me smile back.

"Do you want to do this? Don't rush me, Sweetpea."

That earned me a scowl she failed to hide as I turned back to business. Nothing happened when I tapped it with my left toe, weight balanced back on my right to propel myself away from whatever might be waiting. I shifted my weight towards center as I reached out to touch the bronze.

"Perfectly saf…ghhhhhh" I said. Well gurgled really.

Everything was fine, no traps, just a creepy bronze door to a scary tomb until I touched the metal. That's the thing about magic, isn't it? Everyone thinks they'd cope…they'll adapt and move on if they ever face it. It doesn't work like that though.

One moment it's a wetly glossy blackened bronze door. The next the surface is melting like a sideways pool of water after the rock hits. Before you can adjust to the change, green pseudopods covered with chitinous spikes are leading a beak the size of a child's head out of the pool-of-black-water door.

All your holes try to close at the same time while your head tries to outrun the feet that haven't gotten any messages. When I caught up with myself I tried to turn and to run without any interval between the two and promptly over-balanced and fell on my face, arms windmilling. Who knows, maybe they thought since the legs weren't doing the job they could put a hand in and help out.

I bounced up off the turf, spat loam out, and darted towards Sylvie and Dugal like a schooner catching full sail. Sylvie's eyes had gone wide, but she already had her sword half out and the other hand was completing a precise follow-through. She'd underhanded that dagger of hers while I was faceplanting.

Dugal was doing a fair interpretation of me, both feet planted, jaw open, with the sort of look on his face a mule gets right before it turns into a wild ball of hooves and teeth. My brain started clicking and I immediately tucked my sprint into a roll. It was not a good time to be an obstacle between missiles and the Deepspawn.

Lye's crossbow made a broken fiddle string twang followed by a squelching slap as the bolt hit home. Hospur shoved Dugal aside with his shield as he yanked the mace from his belt.

Dugal promptly slammed into the tree trunk, pelting ripe plums from its branches. It was like someone pulled out the bottom of a stack of crates, he collapsed in a pile of expensive clothes and panic.

Once out of tentacle range, I unfolded back on my feet. Mostly it was time to find a good place to run or hide. Both would suit fine. Beyond identifying it, my knowledge of Deepspawn didn't cover if the thing could see or smell, or if it was just flailing out to drag anything it hit towards that beak; running seemed like the correct call. Instead I was caught by whatever makes people stand and watch a falling ladder only to end up covered in whitewash.

Lye had dropped his crossbow in favor of the sword. He lopped a tentacle clean off in a spray of translucent ichor and then somehow had it levered back around to slap aside another. The Deepspawn yanked the stump back towards its mouth while crashing a succession of blows into Hospur's raised shield, driving him back onto Dugal.

Dugal howled and scrambled back around to put the tree between him and the 'spawn. All the while Sylvie left inch-deep slashes on any part of the creature she could reach with her sword. At the same time flicking a steady stream of knives toward the thing's body; a squat barrel shape covered in thick hairless hide. Finger length tentacles poked out from small folds of skin and waved eagerly in our direction, seemingly eager to join with the larger robust arms sprouting from the top. A beaked mouth the size of my torso nestled in the center of the larger pseudopods, snapping and clacking in anticipation of whatever the arms could bring.

During a festival, I'd seen a thrower working the crowd. He used flat, hiltless, knives - several to a sheath. He'd flick them in rapid succession, splitting half-inch sticks and nailing moving targets. Sylvie had that talent. Blade after blade sprouted out of the 'spawn's hide anywhere she thought might be vulnerable. It seemed impervious to anything she inflicted.

One arm reached out and grabbed the crosspiece to Lye's sword, plucking it out of his hands as easily as I might take a child's toy. Another swept towards Hospur's feet, forcing him back. For someone who looked like a steel-banded barrel he moved like girl at her Sixteen. The tentacle stretched, elongating and thickening as it grew to reach. It flicked out again, flowing around the tree as Hospur ducked. The tendril pulsed, searching for a target, and found Dugal, slithering up his leg as it drew the screaming fop towards its mass of tentacles and beak.

I had no illusions about how a snap of that beak would treat him. A not insignificant part of me was looking forward to it.

"Isaac, now would be good" Sylvie said. She may as well have been at the market from her voice. Perfect calm, all while fending off a mythical abomination from a priestess's fever dream.

"Working on it, Sylvie."

Isaac was standing a couple strides back from the fight. As I watched, he wadded up a palm-sized scroll, probably took a monk a month to copy, and shoved the whole thing into his mouth. He took a moment to chew a couple times, swallow forcefully, and then began to chant while tracing words out on another, larger, scroll. It was really beginning to be past time for me to find somewhere else to be. Even if whatever Isaac was about to do - did work, there was exactly no chance that every single watch patrol in the city wasn't able to hear the steady crash of poorly aimed tentacles or Dugal's increasingly high pitched screams.

The suckered arm that had Lye's sword wrapped itself up onto the blade, slicing knobbed skin open, before flinging it away. The blade arced in a flashing spray of steel and ichor toward Hospur who was smashing down tentacles and blocking those he didn't get on his shield. His attention never seemed to waver. At the last second he flicked the shield up, sending the sword up and over his head to land behind Isaac, buried feet deep in the soft grass.

"Hey Lye, you dropped your sword." Hospur said.

Lye shrugged. He had a pair of hand axes out and was industriously severing tentacles that reached past Hospur. His arms were so long he could reach past his friend's shield and take some of the pressure off. The spawn was inching closer but losing tentacles as it did. Hospur was now moving forward to meet it, trying for a blow at the body mass instead of just whittling at the arms.

Lye paused, counting his moment. One axe flickered out, cutting off Dugal's sobbing, as the grasping tentacle went limp in a spray of ichor. .

Sylvie began to work around the thing's side, darting lunges that left little oozing gouges in the body mass. It didn't respond. It just continued forward, propelled by the few tentacles left uncut. I couldn't tell if it didn't feel the blows or couldn't express pain through that snapping beak. The garden had acquired the semi-hush of high-stakes gamblers; a focused intensity interrupted by grunts and the rending scrapes of bone on shield or steel.

I was flatfooted in the middle of the lane of trees from the house to the crypt, mouth half open as I watched them work. My plan to make for safety was being overtaken by just a little bit of awe, I did ok when push came to stabbing, but knowing how to lift a purse doesn't make you less impressed to see a master fleece a mark. Knowing how it's done means appreciating the real mastery. That was it. The part of my head that keeps me from getting hung made a special note not to start a fight with any four people who worked that well together.

Isaac's chanting rose out of the background, growing in

volume as his voice gained confidence. Steam began to rise off the severed appendages and the creature. Hospur drove his shield full into the face of the thing with a shout as both Lye and Sylvie buried their weapons deep into its body. It tottered, smoking, for a moment.

Isaac strode forward, shoved between the two men and vomited blue fire, full onto the weakened 'spawn. Within a matter of seconds its tentacles had withered and melted, scorched by the flame that poured out of Isaac's mouth, pinning and searing away the creature. In a few moments more, there was nothing left but the arm that had been wrapped around Dugal, a viscous black puddle of sludge where it's body had been, and the odor of burnt fish. Finally, Isaac closed his mouth with a snap - cutting off the gouting fire - swallowed forcefully once more, and then coughed out smoke and a few scraps of scroll.

Sylvie wrinkled her nose at the smell and poked at the sludge with the tip of her sword, "Remind me not to kiss you."

"Oh I don't know, Sylvie, from the looks of it, he'd warm you right up." Hospur adopted the look of a rat that just got all the cheese.

"Ugh, really? Fire puns Hospur?" She said.

"They're just burning to be used!"

"Don't you have prayers or something?"

"Nothing that can't wait, my child…unless you've decided to convert? I'd be happy to perform the rite…"

The conversation had the rote feel of well-traveled ground. Both of them were checking their gear for damage caused by the brief struggle.

"I don't think I could take vows with a religion based on low puns and bad taste in companions" She said.

That earned her twin glares from Isaac and Lye who were performing the same assessments. Dugal stared at them from where he sat, mouth open, eyes a little wide. Sylvie finished her check and took out a flask and handed it to Isaac.

"Come now Sylvie, It's not so bad, it's not as if we sacrifice virgins. " Hospur drawled, watching Isaac take a swig from the flask, rinse and spit, and then take another long pull. "Not that you'd need to worry there."

Isaac's eyes went wide and he tried to exhale and drink at the same time.

"Now, Sylvie, that's no sort of gesture for polite company." Hospur slapped Isaac on the back, rocking him forward with each blow "See there, you've turned him all red. You need to get out more, son."

"Not like I have to worry about polite company with you around, do I?" She looked at me and Dugal, reached down and pulled the man to his feet. "With stalwart companions like these, I'm beginning to wonder that the thieves in this town don't starve."

"What was that? And will there be more?" I asked. Not my best question, for some reason I was having trouble focusing.

"A Deepspawn…probably not. The ritual to bind them is…expensive. Come now, Expert, this is where you show us your worth!"

She was enjoying this far more than was good for my health. Corrupted mythological spawn of incestuous deities are supposed to put a damper on things, right? Not provide fodder for jokes. Her enjoyment was entirely too sharp for my comfort. A knife fight would have been less threatening.

"Alright, keep your skirt on, Sweetpea." I forced a smile, checked my boot for my dagger, the odds on needing it were going up faster than a flood tide. Time to double check the door. Anyone willing to pay for that sort of guardian wasn't likely to assume the monster would stop everyone.

# SIX

Traps are one of the hazards of my line of work. A single trap can be a marvelous deterrent to the would-be distribution, well re-distribution, of portable wealth. Oftentimes the best traps are the ones that an intruder finds. Once you find the first one, the question of others can take up the rest of the night.

Fear is more effective than a crossbow. Guards can be counted, timed, and distracted. The sprung trap can't. So you spend more time searching, checking, and rechecking.

One of my peers, Lucky Todd, got so spooked by a missed trigger plate that he spent entire evenings poring over doorways and windowsills. Todd was the master of hidden switches, tripwires - he even discovered a guillotine designed to be triggered if some poor fool's body blocked the flow of air from one side of the hall to the other. The mechanism was probably worth more than the valuables it kept safe.

Overachieving like that isn't common though. Most of the time it's locks coated in poison, spring loaded needles, and the inevitable tripwire connected to a crossbow.

Wear gloves and don't slide your feet and you're fine. Failing that, most traps are pretty worthless once they are triggered - cut the line with a knife or pop the pressure plate with something long and that's that.

Otherwise you end up like Lucky Todd. He spent an entire night running down hair triggers and so on until dawn broke and the homeowner woke up to find him rifling through the jewelry box. Paranoia can be too much of a good thing.

I reminded myself of this as I fought the urge to duck as the door to the mausoleum swung open and, probably two hundred pounds of bronze, pushed fresh air into the darkness beyond. Since I wasn't instantly pinned by a bolt or split by a blade, I poked my head inside.

The door opened into a landing decorated entirely in

metallic burnt orange. Square tiles of bronze led to a spiral stair at the back. Sheets of more bronze, etched and sculpted, covered the walls. Sea creatures turned into Deepspawn monstrosities carried sailors off ships, ravaged towns and maidens, and undulated before the priests that led them. Others depicted spawn pouring out of towns and buildings down into the depths of stylized oceans leading towards the same staircase. The ceiling was layered in the same tiles, this time with carved gods and angels being gutted, strangled, or torn limb from limb, by yet more Deepspawn. No two of which were identical representing the infinite mutations of depravity.

"Well. That's not creepy" Sylvie said into my ear.

I hadn't even heard her approach as I absorbed the details on the walls. My stomach lurched toward the sky. I jerked forward and then fought back a curse. At the same time all I could think about was the tangible, vibrating, sense of her mere inches away.

"Hmm," I cleared my throat and felt her giggle.

"Steady now, Expert, If Isaac is right - and he isn't known for error - we're just getting started."

"I'm fine, thankyouverymuch."

Not true, but it seemed the thing to say. My ear tingled from her breath. The inch between us became a solid layer that transmitted every shift and exhalation. I could have turned my head and put my lips to her cheek and for a mad second I felt I couldn't not do so. Like standing on the edge of a roof and having that mad impulse to jump just to see what it would be like to fall.

"Ah, a little room here?" I said instead.

Her smile shouted across the space. I gave myself a mental shake and moved one step at a time into the room. By the time I got to the spiral stairs there was a layer of sweat under my clothes.

Focusing was impossible; I was in more danger of death by snapped nerve than any trick left by the builders. Performing for an audience was turning a standard evening into a confidence-shattering ordeal. Step, shift weight, ears strained for the nearly sub-audible click that would result in humiliating death or humiliating narrow escape. Of course there was always the looming possibility that there wouldn't be any warning, just the twisted results of whatever insane conjuration resulted from the work of someone like Isaac.

There was plenty of fodder for imagining what that might look like, sculpted into the walls around me. Having my head ripped from my body by a clawed tentacle was beginning to look like the most appealing of my many, many choices. Do tentacles even have claws, is that possible? I decided not to check.

The stairs down were polished white marble, smooth to the touch and unsupported by any metal or wood frame. Each step sprouted out of the central column as if it was a branch on a tree. The walls leading down were equally smooth and seamless white. giving the entire structure a softly glowing luminescence in the unlit crypt. Not that it was like any crypt or tomb I'd been in. Your average crypt is used to store bodies. Unless this particular family believed in cremation it would be awfully difficult to get a body down that staircase.

The image of the grieving family, trying to fold and maneuver some freshly dead sainted elder down and around slickened marble without some sort of accident leading to recriminations and a lack of eye contact for years to come, popped into my head.

"The room is safe and the stairs look fine. I don't suppose you all want to come clean about what's really at the bottom of those stairs?" I locked gazes with Sylvie for a moment before deciding that Isaac's eyes were safer. Eye contact with her made me feel like I had something to confess instead of the other way around.

He fidgeted and shot a glance at her before answering, "Not that you should bother, but it is just a family crypt built some forty years ago in secret. Everything is written somewhere, though. Not that you will have read it."

"Isaac." Sylvie said.

"Fine. It is the final resting place of one of the grandchildren; an insignificant child who thought to better his lot and instead is buried with something worth more than the grounds it is under. Poor sense or ignorance is hard to tell on observation." The look he gave me was meant to impart that last part was about me, not the son.

"As you say, fine. What about the key? Or was all that clam fodder?"

Isaac got that lecturing look and began popping his knuckles as he explained.

My father had taught me to read, sometimes books and letters were more valuable than the wife's jewel box, but mine was an active vocation for the most part. Hours spent watching guards or mapping floor plans came with the job, but I didn't have much use for being told something I could just go see or do. It's not that I'm not curious. Just like knowing how to read, I'd seen people walk right by a fortune while looking for gold. It just seems that a little time with my hands wrapped around something was worth hours of someone else's explanations.

"No, you misunderstand, it isn't a literal key. It looks a bit like a carved statuette, as it happens. The literature varies; some describe it as a representation of The Goddess, others as one of her handmaids. One particularly…vivid account dwells on its state of dress more than I would think is appropriate."

He kept popping joints as he talked. I had a moment's sympathy for his students. Finally I caught Sylvie's eye as he kept going. Her face warped as she fought down a smile, "It acts as a conduit or a valve control or something, right Isaac?"

"The Keystone can be applied in a number of ways, concurrent effort by perhaps five or ten, with appropriate training. That would be fairly obvious though. The chanting would be loud and that many people would be hard to explain to any observers. It's a bit like using an anvil to kill a cat of course, not that I would, kill a cat I mean. Or use an anvil really. I presume I could learn to use one though." Somehow he could pop a knuckle and then re-pop it a second later. Between the rustling of paper and the sound of tendons shifting he was like a possessed glockenspiel.

"It, the Keystone that is, can be used directly, of course. If the practitioner was highly trained and very careful it would, in all probability, not result in death or madness. Probably." All the while pop, pop, pop. It was like he was tapping along in time with his own song. My eyes started to film over as I got lost in the rhythm. Sylvie had stopped trying to hide her mirth and I could feel the desperation take over my face.

"On second thought Isaac, this is probably more than I need to know. In fact I should go make sure the stairs haven't been rigged. Or, you know, shove my face into a spike." That last earned me a glare from Sylvie as Isaac nodded to me and kept talking his way through the various options for using this keystone thing. How does anyone even do that to their fingers? My own ached in sympathy and I fled down the stairs to escape.

That's the thing about advice, of course. Advice is like prophecy, without the virgins.

Tales of prophecy recognized too late is the bread and butter of playwrights. Luckless hero realizes that he's gone and released the kraken unwittingly and all is doomed. Advice is just like that. It lacks the theater, no sacrificial goats, droning priests, or tithes of gold and nubile maidens. It's just a good suggestion to chew on right up until the realization that you've hit too late and your arm is in it up to the shoulder.

Don't tip a bar wench in advance, for instance. You tip her early and she loses her wiggle and before you know it the bottom of your mug is parched and you're sober as a rookie watchman. Of course that sobriety is what allows you to reflect on the gem of wisdom that would have kept your mug and eyes, full of ale and cleavage.

My father used to pepper his lessons with chunks of lore, some useful, some not. It took me a long time to realize that it probably didn't matter which direction I was facing to snap a lock, but as it happens dogs do prefer lamb or beef to fish. That probably had more to do with how much fish they got in a port town, but still.

Along with suggestions on telling when a fence has sold you out (they overpay), he especially liked to remind me about focus.

Before you take the silverware, remember what you went in to get. Something to sell usually, whatever someone was willing to pay enough for sometimes, but whatever it was came first and last. Forget that and trouble was more than likely all you were likely to get for your night's effort.

Nothing is more humiliating than sneaking past the guards, evading the dogs, busting the locks, and then walking out with silverware when you were supposed to get the wire wrapped bracelet inset with garnets that your employer gave to his mistress in a moment of ill-timed passion and it turns out his wife really did miss it. People who give their wives' jewelry to their mistress, the wives, and the mistresses don't tend to be the forgiving sort.

The sound of the snapping joints drove me down and around the turn in the stairs. It was all I could do not to cover my ears and babble nonsense phrases to avoid hearing it. About a step before I decided to stop, I felt the grinding shift as the marble sank under my heel.

My body was tucked into a ball and rolling forward before my brain even registered the implications of the sound of stone rubbing on stone. That was followed a heartbeat later by the clatter and pinging of something rattled off the steps behind me. I kept rolling, ignoring the slamming edges of each stair leaving its mark. Whatever part of me hit and bounced off each step, would just have to heal.

Somewhere in the middle there was the screech of metal on stone, like a sword being sharpened -if the sword and stone were the size of a man - followed by a cracking and a shower of stone dust. I caromed off an especially insistent stair, unfolded long enough to push off the rounded stairway wall and arced into a dive as if the landing below was water. The floor rushed to meet my outstretched arms and face, driving the wind out of me as I skidded to a crumpled stop.

"Ow." I informed the sudden silence.

There was a brief pause. From far off and above Sylvie's voice, "Expert? Are you alive?"

"Fine, thanks for asking."

"That's too bad." Her voice sounded vague and distant, or that might have been the dizziness.

"Your concern has been noted."

None of my parts appeared to be broken or punctured. Always good when that happens; especially when you've just been a complete idiot. Once in sitting position, I took a second inventory, nope, no holes. I'd just performed a career, and normally life, ending descent down a fully trapped stairwell and nobody had witnessed it. That was more luck than The Three normally allowed.

The room stank of burnt lamp oil and stale anise. Several benches of blackened and polished hardwood occupied the middle, leading to a raised area at the far end. Evenly spaced lamps hung from brackets in the stone walls each just far enough that a grown man couldn't reach from one to the next, leaving the room in pools of darkness and dimly reflected light.

I'd come a hair away from testing the first row of benches with my head so I used them to pull myself up just to see if I could still stand.

Other than mildly shaky hands, I appeared to be in one piece. For once, things were improving. The unmistakable ratchet clack of a crossbow changed my mind. My hands were up and away from my body faster than my re-revision of my luck.

"Safe to come down?" Sylvie's voice floated down the stairs.

My mouth was sealed tighter than any door. Don't provoke people who can put holes in you; redundant advice but valid. Whoever it was had me cold. By the sound, they were close - somewhere behind me and towards the stairs.

Life would be better, and longer, if I could get one of the very solid benches between my puncturables and whoever had my future in their trigger hand. I worked for a butcher once; being junior, that meant I had to reach into the grinder when something jammed it; every time I fought down the feeling that someone would heave on the handle with my fingers as tomorrow's sausage. Eying the mahogany bench and steeling myself to jump, was that same feeling. My fingers went cold and my heartbeat drowned out the sound up the stairs and even my own breath.

Then he shot me.

One second I was trying to think of a way to not get shot, the next I was looking up at the benches on either side of me with something hard in my stomach pushing against my guts thinking, "Well. I got over the bench. That's good." From off in the corner towards the stairs, I heard the ratchet clack again. That was bad.

All I really wanted was to stop whatever was twisting in my stomach. The stairwell was visible under the bench and to one side I could see a pair of muddy boots. There wasn't any mud upstairs though. That was odd. I decided to call out. After all, being shot wasn't so much of an issue anymore. Then I decided to sleep.

Pain is one of those things - like food really - that's most noticeable when it's missing. Sure there's the moment of impact sort of pain, getting hit in the face during a fight for instance, but usually pain is an ongoing sort of event. Like the food at Whistler's, it stays with you for hours, or days, or one time when I tried the fried flatfish, for weeks. If it goes on long enough you stop paying attention; a fellow might get a little meaner, but a month on, they probably couldn't even tell why.

That might be how aging works. Life adds little pains up. First the back - from years of unloading bales at a few dirhams a day. Then the hands - they start aching when the weather changes - in Myrport, that's every day - or a knee twinges from an especially vicious kick some gutter slurper got in.

Each one piles on the last, each making a man a little more snappish, a little more willing to throw an elbow on the way to the bar. After a couple decades, the hairline is heading back, wrinkles have taken over, and all that's left is burning bile when he swallows and mean with nothing but surprise for how he got that way.

But take away the pain, even for a little bit, and all sorts of things get better. Sleep is great for this. Maybe that's why old people sleep so much, and why it's so hard to get them out of bed. Before he died the surest way to feel the stick was to wake my father up when he was sleeping. He'd rap my knuckles for bending a pick or a shin if I jostled him while practicing dipping. But by the time I was ten, I'd learned the difference between little corrections and when he was really angry. Waking him up from one of his drunken spit-pooling slumbers meant bruises.

"Is he dead?"

"Yeah, that's a fair way of putting it."

"Damn. He probably could have told us what was below."

"Sure Sylvie, he tried to murder Dugal's pet but for us he would have talked, no problem."

"It would have been worth a try. Will you put that down?"

"What? I thought you wanted to talk?"

"Funny Hospur. He'd need a jaw. Aren't there rules about dead bodies in your religion?"

"Blame Lye for that. If he'd aimed lower the jaw would be...well, findable. And no, not really. There's a long bit about making dead bodies. Mostly, it boils down to 'only sinners.'"

"Isn't everyone a sinner?"

"So?"

"Never mind. Can you do anything about that? We still need him."

I went from sleep to waking as suddenly as I'd made the reverse trip. I kept my eyes closed until I was fully awake though. People were less cautious around someone they thought was asleep. Most of the time that wasn't an issue, but since I'd made something of a trend lately of waking up in strange places, it was paying off.

"Probably. If it hit anything important he'd be reacting differently. That's just shock." Hospur said.

"Differently?" She was far more academic about a crossbow bolt through my stomach than I would be.

That's when the pain hit me and a moan escaped before I could stifle it. My stomach felt like someone had set fire to it.

There's a bar game popular in some of the more dangerous dockside taverns. Pretty simple really, each contestant holds their hand over a candle flame while downing mugs of ale or beer -

whatever is cheap and can be served in quantity. It's a combination of stamina and speed really. Very sophisticated. The faster you can drink or the more pain you can withstand the better you do. Of course it gets tough to swallow when your palm is scorching black and you can smell yourself cooking. Minus the smell, it felt like I'd used my intestines to try and win the game.

"Screaming, puking blood, more screaming. Different like that." Hospur said.

"Oh." I opened my eyes and caught a momentary look of concern on Sylvie until she saw me watching. "He's awake."

"Bad luck for him. Going to have to get the bolt out and he's not going to like that part."

"I'm…I'm right here, you know." Mostly, anyway, the stick through my insides was highly distracting.

"That's great. Now don't scream. I have to see if the head went through."

Hospur was on his knees next to me. He'd taken off his gloves and his hands were wetly red in the lamplight. The distant me, that likes to say sensible things right before he gets ignored, pointed out that was probably my blood on his hands. That's why he gets ignored, never anything helpful. Hospur reached one hand under me and pressed down on the center of my chest with the other to keep me still. Even so the shifting from his probing hand turned everything white for a moment and then dissolved into sparkles and dots. At the last second, I clamped my teeth down, turning my scream into more of a keening whine like a kicked dog.

Hospur scowled at me and kept up his search and then smiled as he found the tip of the bolt.

"Excellent! All the way through. This won't be so bad after all. You're a lucky man. Not many people get shot without either slicing open their guts or having to have the point shoved through after the fact."

"Seems you're good at something after all, expert." Sylvie flashed me a smile. My return smile was weak. The best it could be called was a grimace.

"Alright, this next part is easy, I'll just break off the fletching and pull it through, remember, no screaming."

It didn't really seem like he needed a response, so I just kept my teeth clamped and shut my eyes. A moment later there was a loud snap that I felt down in my toes and then a combination tugging sliding as he heaved me up onto one side and simultaneously pulled at the head of the bolt. Accompanied by a keening moan that I realized must be coming from me. Each time he tugged I could feel it pulling at my insides, stretching them. My body had a guest that it didn't want to give up because then who would my spleen have to talk to? Each tug filled my vision with little sparkly motes of light. I'd had enough and tried to push him away with the arm that wasn't trapped under. He ducked his head to avoid my pawing hand.

"Sylvie, a hand wouldn't go wanting."

She snaked a hand past him faster than I could follow and caught my wrist before I could make a repeat try and knelt smoothly in front of me. She rested her other hand on my forehead and gathered my eyes as easily as she'd got my arms.

"Better," He said.

Hospur grunted and gave the bolt a yank followed by a long hiss of breath as he drew the shaft out through my back. I felt like I'd just run the length of the docks without resting, all heaving breaths and sweat. The spots had taken up permanent residence and my mouth was dirt dry.

"Any religious preferences?" Hospur was rooting through a satchel.

"What? Can I have some water?" Something to keep the skin in my throat from chaffing on itself was all I could think of.

"Spiritual leanings, pacts, devotions? Not judging, but this next part is harder if I don't know." Hospur said.

The question didn't make sense. All I wanted was a drink and to lay still. Sylvie frowned and flicked a look at him.

"Enh. Well, hold still. This part doesn't usually hurt but..." He shrugged complacently as he draped a length of orange silk across his shoulders. The entire length had been embroidered in blue threaded patterns of geometric shapes. Each one was formed by rows of a symbol repeated over and over to make lines that then made a larger copy of the same symbol and so on until they formed a line or arc of the shape.

Hospur arranged himself so that he was kneeling next to me with Sylvie facing him and then started to draw in the air with one hand and the other lay lightly on the entry wound from the bolt. After a few passes it was easy to recognize the pattern as the same as the one on the stole draped down his chest. After a minute or so of this he began muttering something low and droning, vocalizing it in the far back of his throat without using his lips to form the words.

Sylvie's hand stopped me from turning my head for a better look until he started to apply pressure to the wound. As soon as he pressed down, I clamped my teeth to hold back the scream I knew was coming but didn't since the pain never came. It was no different than as if he'd rested his hand on my shoulder as a friend.

I liked Hospur. He was a good man, someone I could trust. I could depend on him, he'd be there for me. He and Sylvie would stand with me against whatever came. I could tell him anything. Here was someone I could unburden myself too who wouldn't judge, wouldn't try and use it against me.

Goddess of tides, I wanted to share, to talk. In case I haven't been clear, my upbringing wasn't the sort of childhood that led to long reflective discussions into the night. In case I haven't been clear, my upbringing wasn't the sort of childhood that led to long reflective discussions into the night. I wasn't big so I learned to be quick with my feet, my hands, and my mouth, more often than not.

Turns out my father didn't appreciate that any more than you'd expect. If I got a little too wordy, my father was prone to editing with his stick. There were two types of tasks in his world view, ones you finished and excuses. With that sort of incentive, and the example of some of my friends who ended up at the end of their rope - hanging isn't too good for anyone really, I didn't spend too much time sharing my inner secrets.

But here I was, sure I could unburden myself, confess any crime, reveal the litany of small and large sins that made one day run into another.

"I'm sorry. I didn't mean to..." Sylvie stopped me with a hand on my mouth.

"Damn, can't you do this without that?" She said at Hospur.

He shrugged, but kept up the chanting drone. His free hand continued to trace in the air over me and I was starting to see the pattern left in the air. Like staring at the sun and then looking away but still seeing the round spot when you blink. The hair on the back of my neck was straight as an oar.

Somewhere in the back of my head there were thoughts and opinions about what was happening, but they were swamped by the conviction I felt. I had to share...needed to share. I was trying to talk through the hand on mouth, but Sylvie tapped me, hard enough to notice but not enough to hurt, on the forehead and then broke my view of the symbol with her head. I had no choice but to stare at her eyes. Mostly green, with a faint brown ring around the outside. That close I could see the faint traces of liner and shadow she'd applied to appear as if she wasn't wearing any.

My stomach squirmed, somewhere in between the lurching panic as a watchman starts to turn your way and the day after a hangover when food seems like poison.

"It's the spell, it isn't real." Her breath tickled my lips when she spoke.

As she said it the need, the trust, was gone. I made myself relax, stop fighting her but right then I wanted...needed to get as far as possible from Hospur.

Her hands were cool and dry, smooth. My mind seemed to have taken a rest day. How did anyone have hands like that? Staring at her eyes was nearly painful, but shifting my gaze just made it worse and what was she thinking as I stared first at her nose, then her lips, back to the eyes (the left one had a fleck of gold), then away again. For a moment a nod of the head was all that separated kiss from awkward magnetism. So close that the need to keep people away is trampled by the urge to jump.

The droning chant from Hospur had stopped and I didn't know for how long.

Sylvie stood, wiped her hands and walked to stand over the corpse without a word.

Hospur removed the stole and was wiping blood from his hand with a rag. The need to trust in him...to confide, returned, smaller now - the thirst after the initial burn for a drink. It made my hair prickle again, nothing good came from magic.

You're a priest then?" I said.

"What gave me away?"

"Aren't you going to start converting me or whatever?"

"No. How's the stomach? No pain?" He sat back and stretched out his legs, rotating his ankles to restore circulation.

A few prods, gingerly to start, told me there wasn't. Sitting up to take a look, the muscles felt a bit like I'd been doing sit-ups, slightly shaky. My skin was as smooth as ever, no scar to show off later; just a pair of matching holes in my shirt at the center of larger wet spots. Stained beyond. Wearing by my own blood.

"No pain. Thanks I guess. What sort of priest are you?"

"Doesn't matter. Next time I'm getting a stool, my foot's asleep."

"Sorry." I realized I meant it.

He gave a short laugh, "Don't worry, it wears off. By tomorrow you'll be back to normal. That's how it works. Sympathetic magic. Convincing the wound to become like the...unwound. Like attracts like. What you're feeling is a side effect of that. Eye contact makes it, well, worse I guess. It works differently for some than others but by tomorrow you'll be fine."

"Expert? Ready to continue? There's plenty of opportunity to get mutilated in ways Hospur can't fix." Sylvie called from the far end of the chamber.

There was a plain wooden door to the left of the dais. Easy to miss in the darkness; dirt brown and sturdy in the light of a lantern. Polished wood flickered back orange light as she swept it in an arc, beckoning me onward.

"You are the soul of comfort, you know that? Hospur was just converting me to his pagan worship."

Sylvie and he snorted in unison, "No he wasn't."

What sort of priest doesn't try and convert? That's like a bartender who doesn't serve ale. I was almost offended. Not that I had any intention of joining his heretical cult, but he should have tried.

Shaking my head, I joined her by the door. The others joined us as I examined the latch and jam for more surprises. We were probably past the traps, but I wasn't ready to be wrong.

# SEVEN

A friend of mine once told me not to trust him. It was just after I got away from my father and getting to the point where I could eat regularly.

There's something you don't think about on those long nights, sleeping on your stomach because every time you roll over the bruises wake you up. Grand statements as you slam the door? Sure. Semi-magical combat skills that let you turn the tables on the thug-parent that outweighs you by fifty pounds and a lifetime of terror? That you think about. Often. Stealthy midnight escapes only to fall into the waiting arms of a merchant princess who inexplicably cannot live without your wit and masculine good looks? Less frequent, until your voice changes, then all the time.

Where you're going to sleep and how you'll eat - not so much. The wet and cold after midnight is the worst part of the day, the hopeless hours. It takes an equally cold resolve to make it through those hours. Men who'll take kicks and abuse all day long for a handful of shaved coins will gut you without a second thought for taking their spot, in the hours before dawn. Some part of the Goddess was watching out for me. I found my way beneath the wood planks and pillared platforms to the subfloor of a sail maker's workshop. Whatever the building started as had long since been floored over, when the current owner built his shop - leaving a three foot space comprised of mostly rotting planks.

The parts that were still solid were dry and enclosed on three sides providing me with a mostly safe place to sleep and store the few belongings I had. Stuff grabbed when I tipped from planning to action; driven by a conviction that I might not survive the next drunken disciplinary session.

I fed myself in much the way you might expect, given my upbringing. Stealing anything not fastened to something too heavy to lift.

Fairly quickly, I'd taken up with others pursuing the same

lifestyle. Most of them were orphans, runaways, the by blows of whores, or just abandoned by whatever dockside vagrant spawned them before deciding feeding an extra mouth wasn't an option. Some of those found others who were, or pretended to be, willing to make a stand for them; they started or joined gangs.

The ones who were entrepreneurial usual ended up part of the sludge under the docks. Sometimes they were just a little better than the existing competition, like my new employer Clar, and they did well for themselves until the next combination of ambition, rage, and amorality came along. On instinct, I avoided those. No part of me was in a rush to replace one lopsided abusive relationship, with another. So the friends I had were either too crazy or not good enough for the gangs. But they were lucky, fast, or stubborn enough, not to die either.

My friend was all of those; his name was Johan but he went by Joh. Joh was a little big for his age; all bones and tendons with the combined slouch of the insecurity of youth and the paranoia every thief struggles to cultivate and ignore. He was as clean as anyone who bathes when it rains can be and he was vain enough to spend the extra dirhams he could on getting his hair trimmed instead of chopped with a knife if it got in the way. He seemed older than me, so fairly early into our partnership he took the lead.

Neither of us had gotten to the point of braving the watch and guards of the hill, so we were parasites on our own as much as thieves. Opportunists mostly. We'd stumbled on one another one evening when we'd both tried to roll the same drunk. We practically fell over each other as we were both creeping up. At first we each had a hand on whatever weapon we'd stolen or fashioned. On that thin three way line between fighting, flight, or cooperation. Turns out the drunk had been less drunk than he ought to have, but ready enough for a fight. By the time we'd worked it all out, Joh was standing on the poor sot's head while I searched for any change that hadn't been spent on wine. We split it two ways and worked as a team from then on. He'd decide where and do the parts that required muscle; locks and so on were my job. Before long we had enough money to buy food and shortly thereafter ale and wine.

Drinking is one of those moments, much like splitting up the proceeds of a night's work, when you can find whole other people hidden inside the people you thought you knew. Hiding inside is a singer, a gambler, and so on. There's no pattern, the shopkeeper who keeps a meticulous business, trustworthy and staid, turns into a punch-throwing puking mess just as readily as the soldier sings the anthem of every country she's ever been to after a couple rounds of ale.

Joh turned maudlin. Make-a-jester-slit-his-own-wrists-and-then-hang-himself maudlin. Since I just got mellower and more content the more I drank, it didn't bother me. It was a little rough trying to make way with a girl when he got like that, though. Turns out there aren't many lines that work when the object of your attentions is crying.

If that was something I was after, I learned quickly to start him drinking and then wander off. One night he trapped me into staying with him while he got progressively blind drunk.

We'd split a particularly good take earlier that day. He'd convinced me to spend the first part at a place, within shouting distance of uptown, called The Pike. It was more expensive than the places we usually drank at, but we were flush and it seemed like a good way to celebrate. The sign over the door featured a fish being impaled on what was supposed to be somebody's idea of a pike. It had long since weathered into just a long pole. The inside was shy of high class. Patrons provided their own knives, but the glasses were eponymous and the brass on the lanterns was polished.

We claimed a table easily enough and, after a few minutes, the owner shuffled over, giving up on glaring us out. We hadn't started upgrading our clothing so we looked and smelled as disreputable as we were. His face said he was wishing he'd hired a bouncer. Business was light, so instead he sold us ale without water by the pitcher and tried to avoid being seen at our table.

Joh started off two fisting; he picked up the pace from there.

At first I tried to keep up, but I'd already learned all I wanted about staring down a latrine hole praying for an angry god to finish you off. When it became clear my friend was trying to bury something under shipping tonnage of alcohol I backed off. One of use needed to be able to find the way back to my subfloor hideout at the end of the night.

An hour or so on, he was full into the wind and alternating between long dead silences and half formed muttering. Then he put down his glass and glared over where I was lounging, one foot on the table and two legs of my chair off the floor. The glares I was getting from the owner made me happy inside.

"Stelk made...made an offer" Joh said.

"Yeah? When did you see him?"

Joh waved the question off with his mug hand, sloshing onto the floor and table as he did. That earned us another scowl from the owner. Joh just topped off his glass and took a long pull before continuing.

"Wants us. You an' me. Wants us to join I mean." He said

"I knew what you meant. I don't like him."

"Told him that...doesn't care."

"I care. We're doing good. Why change it? Besides, we start working for Stelk or whoever, we have to give him a cut."

We'd had this conversation before. There was a certain amount of safety in the gangs. Word was some of them could even protect you from the watch. From where I could see they just fed off of their members. Every so often they got a few people killed. Right about when someone decided they could do better as leader.

Joh refilled his glass again, "Be nice to have a safe spot to sleep. A bed even. Hell, standing 'd be nice."

He kept getting taller and, now that we were both eating regularly, he was filling out too. Me, I was starting to think I'd never grow.

"Sure, right up until he wants a little more, or wants us to avoid someone's place, or winds up face-down below the docks and the new guy has a different split. No thanks." I said.

Joh's reply was a grunt and he went back to staring into his cup.

The groups that traded control of the docks around, like a bottle of cheap wine, didn't have much use for most of the independents like Joh and I. They'd squish or tolerate us as the mood or business interest dictated. But success creates demand. As we'd started establishing ourselves, recruitment offers started to come in along with the odd job.

It wasn't a regular thing, but when we got something worth selling we started to learn who would buy and who wouldn't. Eventually those buyers started hinting that silver spoons were easy to sell, or Verlosian Red sure would be nice this winter. After we turned up a crate of the Red from the assistant dockmaster's office it turned out the guard had a similar desire for the stuff.

It hadn't taken me very long to decide that the gangs were just many to one versions of my father and I wanted nothing to do with them. Joh liked the attention.

"You can't trust people, Renn, you know that right?" Joh spoke up, surprising me.

Usually he sulked for longer after that particular conversation.

"What?" I'd heard him but that wave had hit from the back of the boat.

"Nothing. Forget it."

"Whatever Joh. You alright?"

He was making me uneasy but I was younger, I wanted it to be ok between us.

"Fuh, fine. I'm fine."

He was scowling at his cup now. It was empty again and so was the pitcher. He'd pass out soon. It was time to get him home before I had to spend the night in an alley. He was too big for me to drag or carry. I'd threatened to leave him a couple times, but couldn't bring myself to do it.

"Come on. Time to go before we get kicked out." I dropped a couple coins on the table and got up to leave.

"Not done drinking." He waved at the owner.

"Yes you are. You can hardly walk now, you have anymore and you won't make it."

"Piss off. Not done." He got the owner's attention finally and signaled for another pitcher.

"Dammit Joh. Cut it out, I don't want to spend the night fending off alley trash."

"Don't. Not done."

"You'd wake up naked and dead if I didn't" I said.

"Piss off. Not done."

The owner showed up with the new pitcher and scooped up the money with a cursory wave of his rag at the table. He didn't like us but he liked getting paid. Waiting until he walked off, I tried again.

"Tides Joh, we've had a good day, don't muck it up by getting puke drunk and rolled."

"Great. Got a new mommy. Piss off."

The flush burn of acid hit my stomach. Joh and I knew each other pretty well, Goddess he was as close to a friend as I understood how to have. That didn't mean he wasn't a mule-headed ass sometimes.

"Fine. You know what? You can drown for all I care. I'm going to get some sleep. Maybe one of the serving girls will keep them from going through your pockets and tides know what else." With that I turned and made for the door. My eyelids felt raw at the edges.

"Renn?"

I stopped, usually that was where he said something funny or pitiable and I would relent and stay. The room rocked a bit, I wasn't nearly as sober as I felt. "What?"

"Sorry."

Somewhere, awash in ale and the impulse driven anger, the little part of my brain that keeps me from crazy women and leaky boats was desperately signaling for attention.

"I'm not staying Joh. Sleep it off. See you tomorrow."

A moment later saw me out of the Pike and into the evening mist. The full breaths of wet air stung the face and did a decent impression of sobriety.

Later it would get cold, seeping into your clothes and making you feel damp inside and out as everything touched would slip or splatter droplets. Until then it was refreshing though and the lamps glittered and shined off the dock-ways and the walls.

The taste of the air cleared my thinking and I thought about going back inside, but realized I'd rather just wait Joh out under an eve where I could enjoy the fog without a barkeep's judgment to keep me company. I stood outside for a long moment, staring up at the sign showing the pike on a pike, watching droplets fall and letting my head clear. A couple breaths later a thin man wearing a knit hat and a waxed canvas coat rounded the corner and stopped a couple paces away, head cocked as he examined me.

The agreeable fuzziness created by a night's drinking prompted me. I stepped to the side to let him enter. He stood and eyeballed me.

"Something I can help you with?" I stepped back as I said it, trying to give myself an extra second to run. It's the size thing. Big people win fights; small people run away.

The knife I carried had been a momentary flirtation with being tough after meeting Joh. He was a big proponent of being armed and so he'd insisted I start carrying a real knife as soon as we'd gotten one. It was a meat knife that we'd ground a point into. It had a four inch blade and no guard. Not exactly the sort of weapon destined to give me trumped-up ideas about facing down someone with a foot of reach and unknown motivations.

The man didn't say a word and didn't close the distance. Risking a look behind told me I was in big trouble. The shadows of a grocer facing the Pike disgorged a pair of burly thick-necked thug types. The lead one swung a short club from a lanyard on his wrist and split off to the side after a few steps to bracket either side of the way down the walkway with his friend. On cue the other one rolled thick shoulders, stretching his shirt to splitting, and then began popping his knuckles one by one. It's a cheap trick, the intimidation equivalent of the street magician who pulls a copper out of your ear, but plenty effective for all that. My fingers ached in response.

It could have been the ale, or maybe I liked Joh more than I realized, but I still hadn't put all the pegs in the holes. A quick half-step by the man in the waxed coat cut me off as I tried to edge back toward the Pike.

The dark kept his face obscured, but I knew he was smiling as he slowly shook his head back and forth. Moving slowly, I fished the pouch holding the coins I carried out. No sense in provoking rashness after all. Dangling it from one hand, I offered it to them.

"It's all I got, no need for convincing."

One of the ones behind me chuckled. A laugh that was low, slow, and full of more menace than humor. Probably practiced it with small children, honed it until it carried the message he wanted.

The other one spoke up, "We don't get paid that way, son." His voice was higher than I expected; a smooth, almost alto, pitch.

"It's more than a ship'll give you for me. Maybe we can make a deal?"

Pressganging isn't a big concern in Myrport. More than enough people are desperate enough to leave the docks. I was at ends for why they wanted me though. Mostly people wanted big, grown types for that sort of work.

The two behind me were close enough to feel; a looming presence that sent chills up my spine. They hadn't grabbed yet, but I knew it was coming. If they meant to kill me, there wasn't a lot I could do about it until they tried. If they didn't, it was in my best and most fervent interests to avoid pushing them into a mistake.

It was always possible they would be satisfied with a few kicks and whatever message they had been sent to deliver. If not, well, things can get a bit confusing in a fight. It wouldn't have been the first time I'd rolled with a punch and vacated the premises. Call me a coward, but somehow it never really occurred to me that taking a beating was better than a good sprint. It was best to take a deep breath and wait. So that's what I did, forcing myself to keep my gaze roughly where the leader's eyes would be.

"How old are you, anyways?" I still couldn't see his face, but he spoke slowly, his voice rough and deliberate.

I shrugged. An honest answer, I didn't know really, didn't seem like making up a number would help.

The faint murmur of food and drink trickled out of the Pike and somewhere even fainter the low complaining from an animal pen. Their plight and mine felt pretty similar right then. Sooner than they would like, they'd be slaughtered or sold up the hill at the whim of someone unknown. It looked like the three of them were set on adding me to the menu.

"Not feeling chatty? Maybe beg a little? Promise you won't do it again? Yer taking the fun out of this."

The high pitched thug behind me giggled, not all the fun, I guessed. I gave them a small shrug.

"Names Jargo, Jargo Three Finger," He held up his gloved left hand. The thumb and last two fingers were normal, the index and middle finger of the glove flopped about as he waggled the glove. "Want to guess why? No? You know how I lost those? I turned down a job offer."

"Job offer? Is there an interview?" My voice didn't even crack.

It did that sometimes, Joh liked to point it out when it happened.

"Heh. Funny. That ship's sailed son. You shouldn't be so picky about yer employment." Jargo said.

"That's Ok, I don't really see myself as the joining sort. Say, I was just leaving so don't let me slow you down..."

Both the men behind me latched onto an arm as I tried to step past Jargo again. There wasn't much use in fighting; their hands were iron hasps latched to me.

"That mouth is only going to make things worse for you son. You were better off before."

Casually, he reached out with one balled hand, no speed, no

windup, but it felt like someone had dropped a barrel on my stomach. The air in my lungs exploded out, choking me, and turned my knees to jelly. Leaving me hanging there, supported by Jargo's unnamed hired help, coughing and trying to inhale but accomplishing little except a pathetic squeaking.

He waited until I finally got breath back in my burning lungs, "You remind me of me."

"No need to be hurtful." I said. Choked really.

There was a long slow moment and then Jargo slowly reached out and hit me with his open hand, snapping my head back and sending sparkles dancing in the dark. My mouth flooded hot with blood and saliva. The taste made me nauseated and I spent a moment with that and finally settled for spitting at Jargo's boots. Turns out there's a skill to that, one I hadn't practiced, so I ended up dribbling long strands off my lips instead.

"Listen you. Yer a mirerat small time thief. You have a choice about how this ends. Piss on me and it's face down in the mire after I let these two relieve their frustrations for a few hours. Suck it up, and get some sense, you might live. It's too late to get a better deal like your friend Joh, so make the smart choice son."

I wiped my chin on my shoulder and tried to shake the spots from my vision.

"If I was smart, we wouldn't be having this talk, would we? What'd you do to Joh?"

"Heh, he made a better choice, son. Yer right, you aren't smart."

He stepped back and nodded in the dark to the two who had my arms vice-d, "Take yer time, I'm going to have a drink with our newest member."

He turned, strolled over to the Pike's door, and entered without a look back. The one with the high voice was giggling nonstop by the time the door swung shut. The other one waited until the door closed and then slammed his fist into my kidney. Agony and nausea raced up my back and I might have screamed. They threw me down hard enough to bounce off the wooden walkway. The one who sucker punched me walked past, stopping to stomp on my hand, twisting the wooden heel into the small bones. I could hear the cracking as they gave, in my inner ear, reverberating through the bones of my arm and neck. As soon as the weight came off I rolled onto my back, cradling the useless hand to my stomach, determined to protect it from more damage. The high pitched thug stood over me, straddling my legs as he giggled, and worked at the knot holding his pants up.

"Wait. Wait." I managed to grit out through the pain.

This earned me a chuckle from the other one, "Now's a little late for the begging, Jargo's gone inside."

He had stepped back, out of reach and was standing, arms folded, waiting for his partner.

"I have money, dirhams."

It hurt to move, to talk. I didn't have money really, but it seemed like the thing to offer. With my good hand I palmed my knife. Using it was going to get me killed but it looked like there were things a lot worse than death.

"Told you son, that's not how we get paid." His high voice was breathy now and he had his pants undone.

For a brief second I was grateful for the dark. Some things can't be unseen. He reached down toward me and I lunged fast and with all the force I could muster from bruised muscles and no leverage. I hit something, I didn't know, didn't want to know, what. There was a spray of blood that nearly blinded me. His voice turned into a scream that rose to an ear splitting pitch.

My knife hand was slick with blood in an instant. One giant paw tried to grab at me and clamped onto my head, fingers digging toward my eye socket; he couldn't get purchase but his nails left grooves in my skin as he clawed. With an awkward half torque, I lunged again, striking flesh and bone with the point of the knife and I dropped it as my hand slipped on the grip, flaying my fingers. We screamed together as he let go to clutch at his wounds.

I threw my abused body forward into a roll between the wounded would be rapist's legs, rolling through the spraying blood and away from his friend before he could come to the others aid. If they caught me after what I'd done I suspect death would have been a longed-for mercy. I tried to come up into run behind the bleeding thug, but my roll turned into a sprawl as the muscles in my back spasmed from the punishment I'd taken. Instead, I scrabbled forward on all fours trying to put distance between us.

"Where is he? Get him, kill him!" His voice went even higher and shrill from pain, as he staggered off to one side to clear the way for his friend.

Surprise is the great equalizer, but once it's gone size and strength win most fights. There was no way I'd get an even shot at either one of them without a weapon. Even wounded the first one could knead me like bread; his friend wouldn't break a sweat doing the same.

That's when I resolved to do whatever it took to make sure the next time I got in a fight I had a better shot than relying on a hidden knife and stupid luck, no offense to The Mad Three.

My feet finally found themselves and I shoved myself into a hunched sprint to the corner of the grocer, hurtling off the wall of the warehouse opposite and down a slim passage between the two. Twenty feet later the passage stopped dead against a connecting wall but terror and the sound of the unwounded thug coming around the corner propelled me up the wall and onto the roof of the grocer.

There was no point in sticking around to see if he could climb. Big people have a reasonable fear of heights. But as my father had been fond of telling me, "Winning is good, gloating is fatal." I went to find a place to hide that Joh didn't know about. If he was willing to sell me out once to join a gang, there was no reason he wouldn't sell me out twice.

That's how I learned not to trust my peers.

# EIGHT

The door next to the altar led in and down. Underneath the estate of the Vevoda and her family, was a series of hallways and stairs - apparently created by moles with bad directional sense. Every doorway had to be checked. Closets and alcoves, designed for sitting and perhaps pondering the dearly departed - mostly. Some I couldn't begin to guess their use. Tables with drainage holes, racks of storage for casks - I wasn't brave enough to test, and serrated-edged marriages of knife and saw.

Part of my father's attempt to educate me included reading works of literature and philosophy. He used to say that more wealth had been overlooked by thieves than had ever been stolen, merely because the worthy entrepreneur couldn't understand what he was tossing aside to get at gold and silver. Things of true value aren't generally made of gold. One book, bound in a blond wood unstained or lacquered but polished by unknown hands as they held it, talked of principles of logic and thought. I didn't understand most of it. That earned me a good couple of bruises from the stick, but one long passage concerned the difficulty in proof that a thing wasn't.

It is easy to prove that a box is a box, merely show the sides and put something smaller inside. It is a box. But try and prove that a thing is not, that was said to be impossible. Finding traps is like that. No matter how diligently you search, how much time you spend, how soft and light your fingers might be, there's always that little bit of doubt.

Since I'm a big fan of the continuous nature of my skin, after a couple hours of this I was getting a little tense. Also I was wondering how and who could possibly have dug out and built the warren of stone lined passages.

Sylvie finally called a halt while she and her three companions discussed our progress, leaving Dugal and I standing off to the side. The hired help didn't get a vote, apparently. I leaned against the wall and admired the fit of Sylvie's leather pants. It was a fine consolation; I didn't care much for voting anyways.

"Renn," Dugal interrupted my appraisal.

"Mm?"

"Walk with me." He nodded up the passage the way we had come.

I sighed. Something like this was inevitable, like the burn of fire when a child sees it. Some people's minds are just twisty. They can't help themselves. Dugal fit the type and I was pretty sure whatever he had to say wasn't going to make my night. Morning? I couldn't tell anymore.

"Yeah, sure."

We edged back out of the reflected lamplight. As soon as the dark covered us Dugal stopped. He fidgeted restlessly in the dark until I got close enough to feel the warmth roiling off of him. That close I could smell the stress coming off of him in waves and I wondered if whatever he had to say was his idea or Clar's.

"So?" I said when he didn't say anything.

"Shhh," He whispered, "I've been thinking."

So, his idea then. Great, another whisperer! Maybe he should hold up a flag and hire a crier while he's at it. Definitely time to make an offering to the Goddess, whatever I'd done, The Mad Three weren't done with me yet.

"Do tell."

"Clar didn't know what they were after when he made his deal. I think we can do better."

"Dugal..."

"Shh, they'll hear you."

I gave him my best 'you're an idiot' look in the dark, "Dugal. Did you see what they did to that thing at the door? Or what they did to the guy who shot me?" My voice was as mellow and reasonable as I could keep it. The sort of tone you use on a friend when you find him standing on a chair with a rope around his neck and the tail end up over the rafters.

"Hear me out. If we play this out right, Clar will…Well, whatever they are after has to be worth a fortune. You and I could sell it, ourselves"

"How about, I pretend I never heard that, and you pretend I don't know you, before they finish their little chat and notice we aren't waiting?"

I turned back toward the others but Dugal grabbed my arm before I could go find some way to look both casual and ignorant.

"Look, someone went through an extraordinary amount of effort to hide whatever it is down here. And those," he waved a hand toward the group huddled next to the oil lamp, Isaac had a large bound book out and was pointing at something while loose pages kept falling out interrupting his speech, "idiots are going to get themselves killed by the Tugali or the Priestesses, or worse. Better that I…we should profit. No? Besides, you owe Clar, and that debt is only paid when I tell Clar that it is. I don't have to share. Surely you don't feel any obligation to them? Or, is it the girl? You can't seriously be thinking you and her?"

"No, but I like the me that doesn't have to put out flames while dodging Lye's sword."

"It's all about picking the right moment. Be ready to move when I say and there won't even be a fight. It'll go down just like a mugging." He said.

Dugal let my arm loose and gave me a small push back toward the others. Clearly, he'd never tried to take a drunk's bender coins. Sooner or later someone always decides to fight.

It's not that I had a particular problem with the idea, I didn't owe the others anything. I was only there because Clar had decided I was worthy enough to screw over, in whatever scheme he had running. Anyone who made a deal with Clar was either rotten to the core or really desperate. This group could be either…or both. My problem is more of an independence thing. Taking orders made me itchy. Otherwise I'd have joined a gang when I left my father, or when Joh had brought it up, or sometime, anytime, after that. Besides, Dugal was a twisty, slimy, sort of lowlife. As opposed to the fine upstanding sort of lowlife I preferred to spend time with.

Putting on a blank face, I strolled over and tried to look like I hadn't just been discussing betrayal and naked greed. They finished discussing our progress and Sylvie waved me forward. Isaac stood next to her trying to get his book back in order. It was bound with sheets of embossed metal but I couldn't quite see what the art depicted. Scraps and sheets of paper were stuffed in between the vellum pages and he was trying to get several of them back into their appropriate spots. Every page seemed to be written in a different hand, as if someone had an entire monastery write a book by having each monk write one page.

"Isaac remains convinced that we are in the right crypt" Sylvie said.

"You weren't sure? Wait, there's more than one of these is Myrport?" I said.

"Most of the important houses have a family crypt." Isaac said. In that voice adults use on children when there's something obvious for them to notice.

"Family crypt – sure - labyrinthine tunnels that go nowhere? Not so much. Not that I would know."

She twitched her lips into a half smile with no amusement and waved me down the hall in the direction we had been heading with a smooth flourish.

The corridor opened up into a natural cavern. The builders had leveled off the rock formations on the ceiling and floor but hadn't stopped the water from oozing out and dripping to the floor below, leaving standing pools of chalky slick water throughout the cave. Every so often the drops would fall either singly or in waves reverberating and echoing with pings and plops. At the far end of the cavern, torches lit up a raised tomb.

Flames flickered gently in the slow current of air that distributed the spores growing between the pools and up the walls. Someone had kept the torches lit  and, from the look of it, scraped the mold from the raised dais and the tomb constructed on top.

It sent wiggly chills up and down my spine. More so,

because I could vaguely see under a layer of green and blue, that the walls were covered in row upon row of palm-sized carvings. Bulbous, stiff-armed, humanoids going about their business reaching from the floor to the roof some twenty feet up or more.

There was no sign of whoever was responsible for the torches but, given the air current, maybe that there was some other way out of the cave, if they weren't waiting hidden, in the room itself.

Giving myself a good metaphorical shaking, I crept back down the hall where I'd made the others wait when we saw the light up ahead. Sylvie and Isaac were nearly beside themselves when I got back.

"Well?" She hissed at me.

"It's something, maybe your tomb."

"Is anyone in there?" Sylvie said.

"None that I could see, but who knows if they heard us."

Isaac waved that off, "We have to be close, if this isn't it. Nobody is to touch the tomb. There's no telling what protections they left."

"Will you be able to figure that out, or is that my job?" I said.

"This will be beyond your...abilities." Isaac said.

"Aww, that's too bad, I'll just have to cope somehow."

Sylvie's smile showed her teeth, "I'm disappointed too. I'd hoped for at least a spike pit, preferably covered in poison."

Her smile showed those teeth again. I was caught between wondering how they were just a touch too long and deciding that her smile was better than her lips. What would it be like to have those teeth nibbling...down boy. There were easier ways to get hurt. Just because a girl doesn't like you is no reason to fall in love. Maybe not love; probably more like lust. With a mental slap, I dragged myself back to large caverns of unknown provenance and led the group forward.

"Could be worse. I did get shot." I said.

"In the stomach, hardly counts."

"Disappointment is our lot I guess."

At the entrance again, I tested the slime-covered floor, "Maybe I'll slip and break something."

"Consolation prize at best." She favored me with another smile and leaned against the wall, arms folded, to watch me navigate the distance to the tomb.

The floor was as slick as I'd feared. Keeping low and weaving in between the puddles and pools, I was determined to avoid falling and giving them all the show she was waiting for.

Traversing the cavern took me a good five minutes of stealthy movement and long pauses to listen for lurking mobs of deranged cultists eager to offer my heart up to their Deepspawn patrons. By the time I'd gone about half way I could start making out the raised carvings on what was clearly a sarcophagus or similar resting place. The lid was a separate piece that had something sculpted onto the top. The sides I could see were covered in similar rows as the walls.

The floor was as slick as I'd feared. Keeping low and weaving in between the puddles and pools, I was determined to avoid falling and giving them a show.

The lid of the sarcophagus had something sculpted onto the top. The sides were covered in carvings mirroring the walls. The closer I got the better I could see them and I quickly started preferring the concealing mold slime of the wall. Without the overgrowth, I could see rows of executioners eviscerating captives. The victims were depicted as kneeling and chained and I assumed them to be humans. Someone had really put extra effort into the scenes. Right down to spurts of blood and gore - with hideous expressions of pain and misery on decapitated heads held aloft to spatter on the waiting prisoners. It was like watching a public execution - you don't really want to but you can't look away either as each twitch and spasm revolts and fascinates.

I was reaching out to trace the carvings on the lid, to follow the lines of misery and horror, when a voice boomed out, crashing into and swirling echoes around me. The sound reverberated in my stomach. It was felt more than heard and I instantly stopped. Arching my back to avoid touching it at the last second, I threw myself back and landed flat on my back, staring at it in shock. The echoes continued to bounce and fragment across the cavern, finally dying away into a mumbled muttering followed up by Hospur's voice.

"Well, no need to sneak about anymore."

Isaac coughed, "If he hadn't ignored..." He spit out a scrap of half chewed paper.

"No, no. Another second and he might have touched it. No telling what would have happened then." Hospur said.

"Nothing good," Sylvie said. "Watch your step, if there's anyone else down here, they're on their way. Best we not be in the middle when they get here."

She moved carefully out into the cavern followed by the Isaac who took three steps and went down like a sack of flour. A second later he pulled Sylvie down with him as she tried to help him up sending a spray of slime and water over the others.

Hospur spat and scraped at his tongue with the edge of his gauntlet, "Tastes like salad. If it gives us the runs, I'm not healing either of those two."

Dugal shot him a narrow glare and edged around the side to join me on the dry edge next to the tomb. I tried not to make eye contact. It would be a decidedly bad move on his part to make his move right then, which convinced me that was exactly what was on his mind, since he'd spent the entire night hanging back. Whatever was in the tomb, I didn't want to be the one to try and retrieve it after what had just happened. The wall carvings gave me an excuse to move away from him and I gave my attention to things other than the sarcophagus.

The end of the cavern was dry and finished stonework lit by a series of torches. They burned well, giving off a flickering orange light that displayed the wall carvings to good effect. It made the larger figures dance and move. It looked like it was a dead end now that I could see the other side behind the raised dais.

If there were guards or priests, I decided we'd be at an advantage unless they tried to smoke us out...or wait us out, come to that. If we had attracted any attention they had us well and truly trapped. They could just wait until we got hungry unless we fancied licking slime for food and water. Tides.

"Sylvie, I don't mean to be difficult, but can we pry whatever it is out of the hands of whomever is interred there and get out of here before someone shows up to check on the noise?" I said.

"We'll just have to deal with it Expert, rushing at this point will only make things worse."

Worse, how?" I hated to ask but the words flew out of my mouth before I could stop them.

She shrugged, "We don't know what protections these," She waved at the carvings on the walls, "will supply. Hopefully not much beyond what we've already seen. If not, well Hospur and Isaac will probably take care of it. Meanwhile we watch the entrance and make sure they aren't interrupted."

"I'll just throw myself at the breach, shall I?"

"Lye and I will take care of it. You and Dugal can catch any stragglers. Sound fair?" She smiled easily but her voice had the firm expectation of a sea captain coming into port and the expectation of obedience from her troops.

Lye was ratcheting a bolt into his crossbow. He ignored the winching system and just hauled back with both arms on the string; the stirrup hooked into one foot. Maybe whoever came to investigate would line up in the doorway, he could probably punch that bolt through the lot of them.

My dagger didn't give me the comfort it might have for a bar fight or a back-alley cut and run. After the encounter with the Deepspawn and being shot, I'd have preferred something a little longer. Dugal hadn't even drawn a weapon. He'd positioned himself behind Sylvie and Lye. As soon as I looked at him, he motioned back toward where Isaac and Hospur were deep in discussion over Isaac's journal.

Instead, I faked not noticing and faced front, just out of reach if Lye decided to swing instead of thrust with his sword. He glanced over and raised an eyebrow at me, so I shrugged. It wasn't like I could explain. My reasons weren't entirely clear; certainly I couldn't explain them.

Dugal was an ass. That part I was definite on. But, that hardly made him unique. Most of the people I knew could fit that description. It was hardly a qualification to get myself in the middle of a stand-up fight. Doing whatever Dugal had in mind and getting out, before someone tried to kill me had to involve a better plan. But the thought of doing his dirty work was bitter, like stale wine. Besides, nobody had shown up yet, maybe nobody would. Stranger things had happened.

Steady dripping from the cavern roof was accompanied by low conversation around the altar. The sound, as each drop hit was tossed about, magnified, and then reverberated into a larger choral refrain that mixed with the next. The three of us stood in silence. Dugal tried a couple times to get my attention but ignoring him amused me. There were worse ways to pass the time.

My stomach kept twisting about, fighting with my intestines. Mostly the scrapes I'd been in were the inconclusive sort of dance meant to establish the relative masculinity of the participants without risking any serious injury. A few punches, the infrequent stabbing - without malice, and afterwards everyone has a drink. Disease, cold, starvation, and the gibbet were much more likely to shorten your allotted time. It took really bad planning or some greater offense against the gods to change that.

# NINE

The job was a commission bit by my favorite fence, Josie. He was my favorite since he paid in dirhams and didn't try to run tabs or markers, when you had something to sell. He wasn't the sort of guy you'd have drinks with; besides being cheap, he disliked bathing, and was excessively fond of cod oil.

He claimed it was for his dry skin and it was good for the hair. It didn't seem to do much for his rashes - his skin was usually some version of splotchy red - but it did keep his hair combed back and the smell was a quick way to tell if he was open for business...from half a block away.

Josie was finishing counting out my cut while I practiced holding my breath and then he stopped before letting the last silver dirham drop into my hand.

"Thirty-nine. You laying low for a bit Renn?"

This was unusual and unusual raises the hair on the back of my neck. There was only the one door out and the bars between me and Josie looked solid and well seated. Josie was a moneychanger by day, his place of business was one of the few over the mire that sported solid structural features. A quick glance back eased my paranoia a fraction. A non-committal grunt encouraged him to continue.

"Got word about something that might be in your wheelhouse. You interested?"

Giving me the last of my coin was what really interested me, but if Josie wanted to take our relationship somewhere new, I was game.

"How about a few details so we can discuss?" I said.

"Well it happens that one of the merchant houses lost all of their gold knives a couple months back..."

We both smiled at that. Josie loved anything he could melt down and I loved anything that Josie loved; the cutlery in question was a masterwork of goldsmithing. Each handle crafted to represent one of the pieces on a chess set, the carving knife was the king, bishops for steak, and down to pawns for butter and marmalade. By now they had all been turned into dinars with the council stamp on them. A dinar was worth about twelve dirhams. Josie took the captains share of the profits, leaving me with two dirhams for each gold coin his basement stamped out.

Good pay for the work.

"It turns out they've ordered some replacements, those are currently waiting excise inspection since the Dockmaster Mara house is in competition for trade rights. The new set seems to have been misplaced and I know where it is being kept pending the conclusions of those rights."

"Is that so?" I said.

It wasn't that I wasn't interested, but contract work meant you owed someone and I liked to keep things simple.

"That is so. You get me that metal and I'll pay weight." He said.

Josie actually smiled, probably thinking being friendly would help convince me. Forgetting that he only had three teeth, Josie smiling made the skin on my neck tighten and I had to resist the urge to check the door again.

Paying weight meant the same price as the first set, to be melted down. Usually when someone contracts a job they want something for their part, knowing where the valuables are makes stealing them easier after all. Of course if they ask too much they risk the thief just selling it somewhere else. Not really an option with this particular job, but still, the people I associate with aren't known for charity.

"What's the catch, Josie?"

His smile fled faster than a jailbreak.

"No catch Renn. Straight deal." He saw the look on my face and shrugged, "Look, I need the metal for a deal. You do this, you get paid and so do I."

If this wasn't a set up, it was a fine deal. And if he really was trying to broker an exchange that required gold, it probably was for him too. He didn't break eye contact, as I thought about it and that convinced me.

"Alright. Where is it and when do you need it?"

"Forty!" He dropped the last coin in my hand with another smile.

"Next week. It's in the dockmasters apartment, on Lordsway. He's keeping it there so the Poulsen family can't get at it. Get at least a pound of it and we'll both be celebrating their misfortune."

He rapped the iron bars to ward off the bad luck he was invoking.

Once I was outside and enjoying a few breaths of air that only smelled of swamp and fish I headed over to Lordsway to have a look.

Myrport was founded by a consortium of merchants when they decided taxes weren't an expense they wished to pay. Being merchants, they looked around for the cheapest land that had a harbor to do business out of. Swamps are cheap, in this case free; since the swamp was shoved up against a mountain range the locals call the South Wall. It's actually due east; the name makes about as much sense as building a city on a bog.

Initially, the city was built on the foot of the mountain, with boardwalks out through the mire to the harbor. Warehouses faced the harbor followed by the fleas that spring up around any enterprise - sail makers, fitters, and so on. Ramping up the side of the mountain, the newly minted merchant lords built houses for themselves and their families with a nice wide road leading up the hill. Whatever name it was meant to have got lost in the continual shuffle for power and place. Before long it was simply known as "the lord's way" and soon enough Lordsway. The sail makers were soon replaced with shops and houses for the more respectable professions serving the lords and it still serves as the primary path up to the merchant houses that can afford to build up away from the swamp.

It wasn't very difficult to find the home away from home that the dockmaster maintained; he had certain habits involving young men and women that were fairly well known to dockside residents. His needs were well served by proximity to the massage parlor doubling as a brothel calling itself The Orchid. Or the other way around; both businesses seem lucrative.

Methodical planning results in a long career. My father stressed the importance of details and any deviation was rewarded with the ever-present stick.

It is possible to do that preparation, lurking in alleyways and hiding behind sheds, but the city watch tends to frown on loitering and they express their displeasure with truncheons and boots. Bribery works, but that starts to eat into the whole point of this chosen career and like any good merchant, keeping my costs down is essential. Besides, the only drinking problem I like to fund is my own.

In the end, the lure of a quick payout worked its magic. That night I made my way back to the apartment, broke the hinges on the second floor shutters, and wormed my way into what turned out to be a chamber room. In the dark I nearly made a shoe out of the pot.

Collecting taxes and fees was clearly good business. The entire top floor was dedicated to the man's private getaway. The walls were papered over to match paintings of veiled men and women posed next to sun draped landscapes amidst fruit trees and ochre buildings. His decorator had posed silk replicas of trees in corners and out of the way nooks that added to the impression.

I nearly stepped on the cat. Instead tumbling into a fake plant as the creature hissed and tried to run up the wall. It slammed into another wall and finally fled the hall with a yowling screech.

My pulse pounded in my ears and I froze becoming one with the silk tree. A pair of cherries bumped against one eye while I tried to forget how to breathe.

"Scrumptious? Is that you?"

Scrumptious? No wonder the cat was nervous. He, it, wasn't sure if it was a pet or a meal. Neither the cat nor I answered.

Light streamed out from below a door, midway down the hall. That was normally the time when a good burglar makes a speedy exit.

There were three reasons why that wasn't an option. The window I'd come in through was on the other side of that door. If I even breathed, the plant would make enough noise to alert guards out in the harbor, and if I left empty handed it was unlikely Josie would work with me in the future. So instead I pretended to be a tree and sent the Goddess a quick request for whoever had that light to be struck dead. It doesn't hurt to ask.

The door swung open, bathing the hall in flickering candlelight. It was a moment when all the dreams of standing on a table in a crowded room, naked, while everyone stares at you come flashing into reality. Don't judge, some people have dreams of falling or of forgetting something important, I have public speaking anxiety dreams. No, I've never needed to speak in public. Thanks for asking. It didn't help that the slightly potbellied man holding a sword seemed to prefer sleeping unencumbered. He was probably a little past forty and well-endowed with hair everywhere except his head. Nature can be cruel.

The plant and I both tried to think plant thoughts. Scrumptious, the poorly named cat, was nowhere to be seen. I tried to avoid looking directly at the naked man in hopes that he would decide to check down the hall first.

He raised the lamp and called for the cat again, "Scrumpy, here kitty, scrumpy wumpy..."

That poor cat. Then the cat's troubles took second place to my own. He slowly pivoted toward me scanning the walls and crannies as the light swept over my tree and me. For the briefest pause I thought he hadn't seen and then the sword came up and he froze.

Very slowly, I disentangled myself from the tree, both hand held palms forward; naked or not he had the sword.

He examined me, not saying anything while I evaluated my options. Not great. To my right was a carved wooden door, probably to an office, featuring palm trees and primitive dancers in some sort of feast. To my left, another door - plain - with a large lever handle. Either way, I'd have to turn away from naked sword-man to try for an escape. If whichever one I chose was locked, things would only get worse.

"How about I just leave?" I said.

"You're not going anywhere. Do you know who I am?"

"No, not specifically, and given the circumstances I'd like to keep it that way."

"What are you doing here? Who sent you?" He said.

"You wouldn't know them. Just go back in there, put on something. When you come out, I'll be a memory."

"It's the Poulsens, those mire-sucking backstabbers, sending a knife in the dark to do their dirty work."

His face distorted weirdly in the flickering shadow, like a ghost in a stage play telling out doom - aside from the nakedness Actors usually have sheets or something.

"Hold on, it isn't..." He charged before I could finish. Sword raised, belly leading. Frankly it was more disturbing than I expected. Right then I resolved that all fighting should be done clothed.

There was no time to work out options. I slammed into the plain door to the left, madly fumbling for the handle. It was stuck firmer than a support pylon. I bounced off the door and reeled into angry naked homeowner. He decapitated the tree as he tried to pull his swing as I fell back onto the floor looking up and wishing I hadn't.

Definitely clothed.

He kicked at me and hauled back for another try with his sword. Bare foot connected with my shin as I was scrabbling back to put some distance between us. He howled as his toes bent back on themselves and began swinging wildly, while hopping on one foot.

"Hold it! Look...tides take you!"

The sword point skittered down the carved door, spraying chips and splinters. The gouge it left was going to cost a fortune to fix. My shoulder brushed the inside of one hairy, naked leg as I dove forward and through. Once past, I just kept rolling and was followed by profanities that devolved into rage-choked gibbering and the regular chunking of sword as he took swings at me. Finally, there was a crashing smack as he tripped on something and collapsed; the sword shot past me and bounced off the door into the chamber room.

At the end of a final roll, I hopped to my feet and risked a look back. He was prying himself up off the floor, blood streaming from his nose. Some of it was dripping into his mouth, lending a burbling noise to the resumed torrent of death threats and profanities.

It was well beyond when I should leave. A neat sidestep around the sword got me through the door and a moment later I had the latch fastened. Trapped. The window was still open, but if he decided to get through the door I'd end up with a sword up the backside. For once, I actually wished for someone to go fetch the watch. A moment later, the door shuddered with a resounding splat as large meaty and naked man tried to force it. The hinges bulged but held. None of this was working as planned.

Ever since the night I'd parted company with Joh, I'd carried a dagger. This one was designed for a fight, with a cross guard and grip to keep it firmly in hand. Time spent with people who measured age in scars, most of whom had fewer fingers than they started with, taught me how to use it. Most of the lessons may have been bought with beer and ale, but it isn't what you pay, it's where you shop. Outside of practice I hadn't ever had a reason to use it on anything more threatening than an apple, but this seemed like the time.

The door reverberated again, this time as he attempted to chop through. I crouched back into the corner away from the entrance and waited. A few loud kicks and grunts of rage covered pain later and the latch finally gave way. There was a second of silence as he stood, sword tip dragging, out of breath, mouth gasping for air, chest heaving.

So I kicked the chamber pot at him like it was a game of kickball and dinner had just been called. He never even moved. My foot hit the pot toe first and it launched end over end through the six feet between us spraying its contents in a huge looping arc splashing the ceiling and him with a stripe of fouled night waste. The pot bounced off the floor and then his shin. He didn't move.

We looked at each other. Him dripping slightly...naked... sword in hand. Truth be told, I felt a little bit bad.

The finger loop on my dagger chaffed as I worried at it with my pinkie. The blade was angled toward him at a steady forty-five degrees diagonally; hilt toward hip, tip to shoulder.

The sailor who had taught me defense, hadn't had much to say about fighting someone with a sword other than, "Run. If that don't work, give up." Since being hung wasn't how I wanted to end the night, and running wasn't an option, I decided on the defense that gave me the best reach.

Since he didn't attack right away I tried reasoning, "Walking away is still an option. It's been a bad night for both of us, no need to make it worse."

Nothing. No response at all. He just stood there. Dripping. That's the problem with weapons. As soon as you've got one in your hands, that seems like the tool to use no matter what the lock is like. Any movement on my part seemed like it could break him out of whatever spell getting hit by a chamber pot put him under.

"So. I'll just be going, shall I? You go back to bed and we both never saw anything..." I said.

"Do you know who I am? Do you? I am going to have you hung, impaled and then hung, no something worse, impaled, your jewels fed to ship rats, and then hung. Roasted over a fire, impaled, hung while ship rats gnaw at you..."

Frankly it wasn't hard to see where he was going with the negotiations.

I cut him off, "Look, that sounds really nice, but I have to go now."

"I will kill you!"

With that he bull rushed forward, sword raised. There was no way I was going to be able to block an overhand blow like that. It was like watching a ladder tip over with a man at the top. At first it's slow and you think he might stop or grab something. Then it gathers speed and it's just a matter of where he lands and how hard.

His foot hit the pot then stumbled as his other foot slicked out from under him on the wet polished floor. He went from charging to falling as he crashed into me, slamming us both back into the wall then collapsing into a tangled pile under the window.

The force of him caroming me into the wall knocked my air out, leaving me pinned under his bulk, gasping and choking in panic. My dagger was gone and as soon as he recovered all he had to do was cut off whatever pieces he liked, he was bigger, armed with a sword, and I was prone. It took me a long moment to start breathing again and somewhere in there I realized he wasn't moving. At first I thought he must have knocked himself out crashing into the wall somehow. Maybe hit his head while crushing me. Then I found my dagger.

Once my lungs started my brain did as well. I was covered in sweat, urine, and blood. He'd had the phenomenal bad grace to impale himself on my outstretched dagger during his aborted charge. The blade, which I kept razor sharp since tool maintenance had been ingrained in me along with the rest of my lessons, had slipped neatly between his ribs. It was hard to even take credit; if I'd tried I couldn't have planned a strike like that.

From the amount of blood he'd probably been dead by the time he and I had hit the floor. His night had not gone at all according to whatever his plans were and it was pretty much my doing. Well, all my doing. That isn't a comfortable thought. That was the first time I'd even been in a fight that wasn't forced on me, and I'd never done more than wound the other guy. My line of work doesn't lead to a lot of moralizing and ethical debate, but killing someone for a set of knives didn't set well.

Old habits being what they are, the knife came out as clean as it went in. Aside from the black wetness of blood, the only sign anything was amiss was a small line just higher than his heart and an incredibly foul stench. Chamber pots are best kept covered, not spread all over ceilings, walls, dead naked bodies, and your clothes. I sat, arms on my knees, and cleaned the knife as best as I could while my mind settled with itself.

After that was done, I levered myself up and dried off my boots, bloody footprints are unprofessional, and went to find the cursed cutlery.

Five minutes later I crawled back out the window, the knife set had been in the man's office. He'd thought to hide them behind a concealed panel, but the scuff on the floor it left when opened, made my job easy.

There was no telling what Josie was going to say when I showed up. The deal would probably still be on since he'd been planning on melting down the metal anyway, but a dead body off the docks was not a standard contract clause. My clothes were ripe with blood and every shadow on the streets looked like the watch coming around the corner. The path I took toward lower Myrport was as nerve wracking a thing as I've ever done. Every corner I turned was an ambush; every doorway held a squad of the watch stacked two high. It took three tries to get the knocking code right at Josie's.

"Here." I said.

The knives clattered out onto the counter. The delivery method wasn't unusual - the mahogany was pitted and dented from years of cavalier delivery.

"That was a tad faster than expected. Did you slip in something on the way? You smell."

He began inspecting the spoons, checking each for weight and scratching a groove in the soft metal with a tiny horn handled dirk he kept on a chain about a hand span long. A patina of gold or an alloy would be an expensive mistake; for anyone witless enough to try silliness like that.

A grunt was the best eloquence I could muster, "Enh."

Shock and fatigue had long since taken over.

"Perfect, perfect. I don't suppose the Poulsen family is going to be too pleased but their loss is our gain. It really is a pleasure doing business with you, Renn. You are a credit to your breed."

The smile on my face was a bit on the sickly side. The body wouldn't be discovered until daylight in all probability but he wasn't going to be quite so impressed when he found out. Of course by the time he did payment was already rendered.

"As promised, weight." He said and then counted out the coin.

It was a few months before I went back there, the murder got pinned on the feud between the dead dockmaster and the Poulsen family, but I didn't want to give Josie a reason to add facts to the investigation. It left me with a desire to avoid the sort of circumstances that could lead to repeating the event.

Which made me wonder what exactly I was doing. If and when someone showed up to check on their creepy cave, why was I not making extra certain to be somewhere else? Making points against Dugal was a poor reason and I knew it.

# TEN

Semi-rhetorical question here. How can you tell the difference between an irate home owner bent on exacting punishment for disturbing his ancestor's graves and a maddened cultist of forbidden gods? Since one of them was chasing me around the cavern with what looked like a barrel attached to a broom handle adorned with phalanges and spikes, I couldn't really answer that. The plan had worked out well enough at the start.

Beginning at the back of the ears, down in the neck almost, a low droning chant wove in and out of the dripping noise and periodic bursts of muttering from Isaac and Hospur. It was nearly unnoticeable, just a tickle really. When I finally heard the chant for what it was, my first thought was that the pair working on the crypt had finally got started.

There's something about defying the laws of nature and performing acts of unexplainable sorcery that denies witness. The last thing I wanted to do was observe. I had to almost forcibly turn my head to check on their progress. When I did, they were busy, silently, with their books and scribblings.

"What is that?" I said.

Asking never hurt, right? Lye shot me an eyebrow and a shrug.

"What's what?" Sylvie said

"The…I don't know…chanting or whatever."

"What chanting? Getting nervous, Expert?"

Since the answer had long passed 'yes', there was no dignified response I could offer. The chanting got louder as we looked at each other and the smirk slipped off her face.

"That." I said.

"Well, it was probably too much to expect they wouldn't check up on their sanctum. Now we work for a living." She rolled her shoulders and set her feet as she said it.

"About that..."

"Mmm?"

My response, carefully prepared, turned into a strangled gurgle as a seven foot tall bipedal...thing, stepped out of the gloom into the entrance to the cave. This one only had two arms, each ending in a sawclaw pincer that dripped mucous. Each leg ended in a mismatched boot, one a knee high cavalier's the other a hobnailed affair with laces that crisscrossed up to mid-calf. It had no neck to speak of, just a mound in between the shoulders with a pair of beady eyestalks on top of a multi-segmented mouth. The mouth was surrounded by what looked like moss that was alternately sucked in and blown out as it breathed and gasped. It was unclothed except for the boots, but the entire torso was rigid and shined greenish brown in the glow.

Behind the 'spawn, several men pumped swords and axes in time with the chant. They wore deep green robes with the hoods up, concealing their faces. As their arms moved, their robes parted revealing a glint of mail that had me rethinking the usefulness of my dagger. In the back, an especially burly man hefted keg-sized maul on a stick that he'd taken the time to deck out with spikes and blades. His robe was embroidered in glowing purple lines that cast flowing unnatural shadows up on his face. He added a deep bellowing bass to the chanting that seemed to spur the spawn into action; sending it charging across the mossy slime.

Footing didn't look to be the advantage we were hoping for.

Lye waited as it charged, crossbow leveled. Each boot made an alternating thump as it landed, propelling him faster and faster. The back part of my brain - the front was carefully involved in finding the lever for 'wet myself in terror' - made note that the cultists chant went faster in time with the thumping hurtling 'spawn.

The robed men were moving more cautiously, eyes on the floor, as they made their way out unto the slick intervening space.

Twenty feet out, Lye loosed the crossbow, aiming dead center for the mass of the charging 'spawn. The bolt screeched out, propelled by a resonating hum, just fast enough to follow with the eye as it blasted dead on target...and bounced to the floor with a wet plop, like another of so many drips of water falling from the ceiling.

The force of the bolt stopped the creature; its boots sliding an inch or two as the ground through the muck from weight and inertia.

We were dead, extra dead. A sword wasn't going to do anything to a carapace that could shrug off a point blank shot from an arbalest. Those things are designed to punch through siege hoardings, the wooden fortifications on top of castle walls built to protect defenders as they rain down arrows, oil, or whatever. They'd blow right through an unarmored man and leave a plate-sized hole on the back end.

Lye didn't even look concerned. He could have been sipping ale at the pub, face smooth and unworried. Lazily he reached back and flipped his sword up out of its sheath. It flipped end over end once, twice, and then he caught it already set in guard position. He never took his eyes off the spawn. Not the sort of thing a sane man would practice.

The spawn recovered and stepped forward, both giant claws darting forward to impale with impossible reach. Lye rotated on his back leg avoiding the one punching for his stomach and caught the other with the sword. The moment he had full contact with the sword he rotated from the hip throwing the upper claw to the side and then flicked out the tip dead center onto the exact spot he'd hit with the bolt. Sure enough, the sword impacted with the sound of stone hitting stone but failed to even leave a mark on the chitin. Lye snapped back into guard and the spawn cracked its claws, mouthparts clicking furiously.

At that point, someone tried to murder me with an axe. He came in fast, sliding on the wet slicked stone with an axe in a broad horizontal sweep at my neck. It was a really good plan. The crowd of slightly drunk pirates I practiced with would have cheered and placed bets. It was all I could do not to congratulate him for using the terrain to his advantage, as I leaned back to avoid premature decapitation.

The next part got messy. His feet hit the dry stone and stopped but the rest of him didn't. He made a bad decision about the axe, trying to recover for another swing - all of which meant that most of him whipped forward, while his feet remained nailed to the dry stone.

Years of practice took over. Left foot forward, torso shifting in line to follow, a slight wrist flick whipped the dagger around the finger loop into a hammer grip - blade trailing from the fist along the forearm - and then a quick flashing drive into the ribs as he fell past. His motion cleared the blade with a slight jerk as the body slammed face first into the granite...probably dead before it bounced. The complicit axe clattered and rolled to a stop next to the altar.

The thought that I was going to have to deal with what my hands had just done was pushed aside.

"...more pressing matters" I told myself. There wasn't even any blood on my blade...not really. Aside from the body fouling my movement options I might not have just killed someone.

The rest of the robed men piled up behind the spawn in a confused mob. They still outnumbered us. Of course with the spawn they always would, no matter how many of the others we killed. Lye was being pushed back as it made stone-cracking stomps forward. Each ponderous step accompanied by both claws driving in to pierce and sever. Somehow Lye had his sword wherever the claw was or his body wherever one wasn't. But eventually that would come to a flesh-rending, spine-severing end. His periodic strikes back at the creature sounded like someone chopping at a ships mast. Thick hollow gongs that would have collapsed a steel breastplate were having no effect at all on the crab spawn.

"Forward! Drag their screaming tongues down to the dark for the glory of the Son!"

Giant-hammer guy spit encouragement to his underlings and they rushed past the spawn to get at Sylvie and I. She grinned at the oncoming flunkies, white teeth bared; it was easy to admire the effortless precision she seemed to possess.

Every line of her stance was relaxed and practiced. Her right hand held her sword, three feet of razor sharp steel no more than an inch wide and tapered to a needle point. Wrist slightly bent - out and to the right; point inclined in to the left so that the blade would naturally deflect thrusts aimed at her torso. Her left hand was casually tucked behind her back where it might look like she was keeping it out of the way. In reality she held a fan of those flat throwing knives I coveted. I couldn't watch - but at least one had already learned about the reach a flexible and trained combatant can get with a sword like that. His body lay, staring up at the ceiling, where its fellows would have to step over it. Another was dragging a leg, pinned in the thigh by one of her throws.

The chief thug was headed my way, following a couple more conventionally cutlass-armed lackeys, so I couldn't watch - but at least one had already learned about the reach a flexible and trained combatant can get with a sword like that. His body lay, staring up at the ceiling, where its fellows would have to step over it.

The two men approaching me fanned out to either side and then edged in together. If he lived, it was beginning to look like Hospur was going to have to reattach my head - if that was even possible. Three days ago I would have sworn that someone with a crossbow bolt to the stomach would be dead by nightfall, so I guessed I might not be an expert in that field. The one with the maul stayed back, content to let his minions carve me up.

"You two don't want to take turns?" I offered.

Couldn't hurt, maybe they were insane. Well, obviously they were at best half-baked. Cavorting with powers that held the leash on Deepspawn, lay somewhere between wrist slitting drooling self-mutilation and capering feces-smearing insanity.

The one to my left shook his head and smiled a big gummy grin. The one to my right looked like he was about to explain the error in my thinking when he took a step too close to Lye who promptly flicked out a paw, snagged the poor man by the cowl, and then launched him into the path of another claw pass by the spawn. He didn't even get to scream. One enormous claw clamped down on his shoulder and sent a spray of blood and sinew as it cleaved through bone with a wet crack. The other claw hit the back of his head, punching through to create an obscene protrusion where his face had been. Brain, blood, and teeth splattered wetly, as it wrenched the body back and then slammed it to the floor with a piercing whistle of rage.

"He should have taken turns." I said.

The remaining attacker scowled darkly, but still had the cutlass that I suspected he'd used on a few merchant decks. As long as he didn't get careless, like his former partner, he had the advantage and we both knew it. A quick dodge to the left was rewarded with a casual sweep of the sword. He was careful not to overextend and equally careful to keep his shelled ally where he could see him.

A practiced and fit combatant can lunge more or less the length of their body. That extension is what had killed the man facing Sylvie. Unfortunately my new friend seemed to be aware of the danger and was keeping his strokes small and in front of his body. Any lunge on my part would cost me a hand…if I was lucky. The trick would be to get in close, inside arms reach, where the maneuverability of the dagger would be superior to the sword, especially a slashing chopping implement like a cutlass.

The shock of impact nearly drove my dagger into my stomach. Using the hilt as a trap I wrenched it wide and attempted to close. He did a fancy shuffle step and widened the gap again. He knew the trick and was having none of it. He grinned at me and took another small swipe at my face.

There's something wrong with someone who smiles as they try and kill you. His teeth were green. Either he wasn't big on hygiene or he chewed way more Garpa leaf than was healthy.

A quick wrist flick and I held my dagger by the blade. His eyes widened a little and he took another step back, sword up in front of his face to fend off the throw.

In upper Myrport I'd watched a man with a dog once. He'd throw the ball and the dog would fetch it. Every so often he'd pretend to throw the ball and the dog would go tearing off after the ball that was still in the man's hand. Eventually the owner would call the dog back from its search and the game would go on. Not a terribly smart dog. Turns out it wasn't a very good guard dog either.

The way I saw it, the thrown dagger is bluff really, but a good bluff. The best bluffs force the other gamblers to react even when they suspect you're dipping from a dry well. If someone throws a dagger at your face, well you've got to duck, just in case.

When I didn't throw right away, the pirate turned cultist made another chop at my head. As soon as the blade was in motion I sidestepped and whipped my arm down and behind me as if I'd thrown. The smile turned into a grimace and he yanked himself back and to the side to avoid getting a face-full of knife.

Of course there was no knife, as soon as he flinched away I sprinted the few feet between us, shoulder first, while I flipped the hilt back into my hand. We went down into the mud and moss in a jumble of robes and foul smelling cultist - definitely Garpa. As soon as I hit he was flailing at my back with the sword but, without some room to swing, it was only as good as the edge he'd put on it.

My dagger was razor sharp and meant for close in distances. He screamed the first time and by the third he had stopped moving; the cutlass ringing dully off blood and water slick stone.

My stomach heaved and then cramped. Two men were dead because of me. I killed them. Sure, they had tried to kill me at the same time, sort of a mutual sin maybe. It wasn't much of a rational though. A good thief takes things; assassins take lives. A good thief was all I aspired to be. Somehow there was a difference and the line was exactly at the point of killing someone.

Things were moving too fast for me to spend any of it being maudlin. The crab-headed spawn had driven Lye back, maybe trying to pin him against the tomb where its size and armor would be unavoidable. Lye turned it though. So now it was pushing him back toward the slime where Sylvie was holding off a pair of men.

One had a short spear in one hand - not even a spear really, more of a knife with a handle as long as my arm – and a pot lid-sized shield in the other. His partner must have showed up to the mustering last and all the useful weapons were gone. He was waving a club around with great enthusiasm though.

Sylvie danced in among a trio of bodies on the floor using them to forestall attempts to close into range.

Hospur and Isaac were still holding court on the lee side of the coffin. The two of them were now chanting interspersed with one or the other throwing colored powder at the stonework. The skin on my neck tightened when I saw that the powders had created a streaked layer in the air above the surface leaving a good six-inch gap. This was the sort of event that in a normal day would have been worth a good round of beer for years to come but after two Deepspawn, scholars spitting flame, and near death, it was reason to drink rather than talk.

The lead cultist got brave and hefted his hammer as he slid carefully towards me. He mouthed words in a continual stream without vocalizing and kept checking on the progress of the spawn with quick shifts.

He could have been controlling it or he could have just been extra crazy. Being in charge of underground temple crypts seemed like the sort of job you might have to have applied nuttery for.

The maul came whistling down in a looping overhead swing.

A quick roll to the left soaked me like I'd just jumped into the bay and covered me in a glowing duckweed-type plant, but did put some distance between us. Anything that put distance between me and getting my skull popped like a grape was an improvement.

It hit, crashing into the stone floor with a splatter of water and a deep resonating crack that ricocheted around the cave and the inside of me head until it faded away.

Once he got the rhythm of it, the swings came faster and faster until the echoes were overlapping, merging with the grunts and periodic shriek from the Deepspawn and the chanting from the far side of the tomb.

Again and again the cultists attacked. It was all I could do to throw myself back and roll to my feet. There was no way to use the recovery time for anything but putting space between me and the arcing spike-covered head of that weapon. It wasn't as if I could deflect or parry.

That's the beauty of using pole weapons. The fool that tries to take one on a shield or parry is going to get pasted as the weight of the killing end crushes through and permanently embeds a broken shield into their corpse.

The leader spat a long stream of yellow-green juice to splutter down on the slick covered stone. He had the knack of spitting, so it doesn't leave tendrils of drool hanging from your chin. Nothing really ruins the effect like ropey strands of saliva; another indication of the application process for ravening cultist.

Another overhanded looping arc followed up by ear stabbing cracking echo. Sparks flew up from stone where the maul hit a dry patch. The head had been rimmed in iron. Some foresighted blacksmith had really planned out that sledge.

Somewhere I'd lost track of Sylvie and just had to hope she was holding up her end. If any got past her they were going to make quick messy work of me, since all I could do was duck, roll, and run. My muscles were loose and quick after the first few swings but one misstep, one raised bit of stone, or a wet patch where I was expecting dry, meant the entire routine would come to a smashing halt.

One winter my father and I spent the daylight hours learning and practicing games of chance. Of course there wasn't money involved but as usual, the cane was all the incentive he needed. We wagered strokes. What I won he subtracted and what he won he added. The first rule I learned was: don't play the game your opponent is playing. That's gambling and gambling is dumb. If I expected to live, it was past time for me to stop playing the same game; the house was eventually going to win.

It took several near misses and one spectacularly

improvised backflip that would have had Left-handed Horace in tears, "Never get flashy boy, it's a gutting session not court!" It bought me the time I needed to fish the bag of crow's feet out.

The things are fiendishly expensive; there's no legitimate use for fifty or so sharpened four bladed spikes. The smith who made them normally worked silver and gold and didn't change his prices for copper and iron. Josie had introduced us and that had cost me too. They were about twice the size of a thimble, but with nearly the exact opposite intent. Stepping on one with your full weight would puncture a half-inch of shoe leather and some of the foot past that. They were barbed at the points like a fishhook and nearly as difficult to remove.

The bag was made of parchment. A quick duck under a horizontal swipe - the maul left a hollow buzzing noise lingering in the air overhead - and I tore open the sack spraying a gush of the little traps towards his feet. They made a noise like coins as they hit and bounced. That particular noise was normally my sort of music, but was only barely audible over the general cacophony holding forth in the cavern.

The cult leader never even paused. Looping swings, hand-over-hand, to slam the weapon down in a spray of rock dust and motes of fire. His hands flickered smoothly up and down the handle and each swing started with an evenly placed step. Each stomp followed by a hollow whirr as the massive head sought some part of me. My job was to circle and weave to keep him in the area.

We traded anticipation, each waiting in turn. Swing...step...swing...step.

His luck ran out before mine.

He pulled another horizontal swing seeking to break the pattern by flipping the handle around behind his back and continuing the same momentum through again. Mid-swing he sidestepped; weight fully placed to counter the force of the head as it threatened to yank him off to the side like a badly managed fish.

The shock blossomed as his neck muscles corded out in pain

and he struggled to control his balance only using one foot; instinctively pulling his mass off the punctured one. As soon as his mouth got the message he let out a shriek worthy of the Spawn he'd followed in. One foot in the air, sledge transitioned instantly from friend to foe as he hopped on the other foot.

It was like watching a skiff capsize. The crew rushing to the up side to recover and for a moment it looks like it will, and then it shifts inch by inch as ballast and crew lose grip and fall into the ocean; followed by the long stately collapse of the mast until it splashes down in a mess of rope and sailcloth.

Waiting on the ground for him were more crow's feet.

He toppled over and hit another, rolled to escape that one and found more. Each one clung to him, perversely accumulating instead of falling away. All I could do was cringe as his attempts to escape the stings led him directly into the path of more.

None would kill him but that stopped being a blessing as he twitched and jerked on the stone. Some of the points failed to puncture his armor but his limbs weren't covered by anything sturdier than his robes - which quickly became tacked to him as he flailed - trying to find bare ground with some part of hand arm or leg that wasn't sporting a finely crafted sharpened parasite.

It had taken hours to sharpen those, each one had four points adding up to over two hundred fish hooks to be filed and polished. That was a lot of effort to put into hurting someone; I felt the bile rising in my throat.

The hollow gong of sword on carapace broke that train of thought. Lye was still fending off the claws, but sweat was dripping down his face and he'd flushed a deep bloody red. His blocks were starting to give under the relentless pounding. The spawn didn't seem affected. There was some scoring it's shell but each claw crunched in with the same force. Blasphemous summoned monstrosities didn't appear to need as much management as I'd thought.

A knife wasn't going to do anything to that. Sylvie was approaching it from the side but she wasn't going to fare any better. Every couple blows it would pause for a second to squeal and hiss. The crow's feet might have punctured the boots but they were as likely to cripple me if I went to gather them up. Assuming the howling rolling mess of blood and robes didn't forget about his problems and try to kill me if I got close. The screeching was really getting on my nerves though.

The maul lay where it had been dropped and it was almost too heavy to swing. The head made a series of scraping noises that I could feel down below my ears and in my teeth as I dragged it into position and waved Sylvie off. I tried to motion to Lye to try and hold it still, but taking his focus off avoiding and maneuvering claws would get him killed; spitted on the end of a claw or snipped as easily as a thread at a seamstress.

The back of the spawn was covered in the same slightly glossy chitin as the front. Instead of sunbaked chum, the stink of urine and wet leaves punched the back of my throat forcing me to swallow hard several times.

Counting showed me a pattern:
step…claw…step…claw…hiss. That was why the thing needed a controller. If it wasn't as hard as an anvil and the size of three men, it would already be shucked and boiled for dinner. Even untrained men would find some way to crush it, trip it, or simply run away. Bad luck for it that its controller was currently plucking sharpened barbs of iron out of his skin like a dog with more enthusiasm than sense when it finds a sea urchin at low tide.

It never even noticed me behind it. Absolutely focused on its task, it may have never even had the ability.

What sort of existence would that be? Plucked out of - what? - some deep, dank, rotten hole? Judging from the wafting waves of reek coming off of it - plucked out and unable to act or think on its own. There at the whim of whatever had made the sacrifices and performed the unspeakable to get the services of one of the tools of the North Wind.

Hoisting the maul felt like levering a shovelful of wet sand. As soon as I had the head up over my shoulder, I took a couple steps forward and brought it down and forward with everything I had. It was the same motion used to throw bags of grain out of a hold and unto the decks…with about the same amount of finesse. The blades made a whistling noise as gravity took over at the top of the arc. My aim was off. Boulders, kegs, and enormous sledgehammers aren't really precision weapons. Joints popped as I hauled back trying to correct.

The creature hissed at Lye, raised a claw and then the maul hit it squarely in the middle of what served as its head. It sounded like a cross between squished tomatoes and the solid meaty 'thunk' of a thrown knife hitting the target.

The Spawn stopped cold…both claws falling to its side the rest of it immobile. Leaving it looking exactly like someone had decided it wasn't monstrous enough and added a small keg and an assortment of kitchen knives as a head. Things should fall over when they die. Assuming it was dead of course.

"You ok?" I said.

Lye just stood there panting, sweat and grime sheened his face. We both turned at a strangled squawk came from where I'd left the cultist in a field of crow's feet. Sylvie had made her way to him. She wiped the last of the cult leader's blood off her sword.

"Sloppy, Expert. Always finish what you start." She said.

"He was busy and I had other business."

"That was well done." Her tone was approving.

"…part of the service."

People didn't compliment me much. It made my stomach twist a little. She smiled at me and then went to check on Lye. Somehow my nose decided I could smell her after she walked past. After being coated in muck, fighting a handful of men to a standstill, the outbuilding smell of the Spawn and the tang of blood in the air my brain knew better. Still, I could sniff spice and something like pine.

# ELEVEN

Gobineau was a large man stuffed into too small clothes. Parts of him bulged out past his mail shirt, his forehead protruded from beneath the iron banding on his leather cap, and his grasping need for gold had long since extended past his income.

He'd been the favored son of a small merchant and sometime smuggler, who made a bad bet on the price of desert wolf fur. Followed by an equally bad bet on how well the harbormaster's patrols could see in the dark.

Before they hung him, the father had spent the last of his gold setting his son up in the watch. The theory being it would give him the means to look after his mother and sisters. Size and the strength to go with it - Gobineau was big but not fat - had served the son well enough. But rank requires money, and he wanted both.

When his mother passed the next winter of grief, and possibly a pillow, the son had seen a chance to find gainful employment for his sisters. They could still be found at the Orchid or places like it, these days.

The space between upper and lower Myrport grew people like Gobineau in the same way that wet caves grow mushrooms and open wounds grow putrid. By the time he was done selling off his sisters, he'd been made sergeant of the watch. He had his hands in all the little vices that the docks supplied, men like him facilitated, and people up the hill wanted.

Gobineau was especially fond of slavery and prostitution; related forms of income that he'd already shown natural talent for. But he wasn't shy about blackmail, extortion, and of course the family business - smuggling.

Early on he'd used some of his money, and a handful of broken fingers, to purchase a low-roofed counting house. He'd knocked out most of the walls himself and created a sort of warehouse. He used it to store goods, as he facilitated their way up or down the hill, without troublesome paperwork and associated fees. Every beggar, drunken sailor, and fence was talking about it before the mortar was dry.

After a week or so, two things happened. Several attempts were made to inventory and redistribute the contents of that warehouse, and shortly thereafter boots - feet inside - started showing up in pairs on the edge where, what counts for dry land in Myrport, met the wooden docks. As quickly as the news of a warehouse full of easily portable wealth had spread, the disappearance of a few of my peers ended that speculation. Like a bucket of water on a bar fight.

The way I saw it, the problem was timing. The most troublesome guard isn't the old, experienced ones. It was the fresh young recruit; eager to prove his worth shoving a spear point in every bush, and a lantern in every shadow. Whatever means Gobineau was using to protect his stash would grow fatter, lazier, and spendier over time. After a few months, he'd be cutting back on hours and reducing the watch when all the excitement of fresh meat died down. That was the time for an enterprising soul to take a little inventory; practice a touch of unsolicited redistribution.

The sudden reduction in the talent pool made things busy for the next month. While the problem of Gobineau's warehouse didn't escape my attention entirely, I was busy with other projects.

As my reputation and the lack of alternatives spread through Lowtown, I wound up with more opportunities than a shark in a duck pond. Meanwhile, Josie did me a couple good turns. It's one thing to recognize the work of Goljin Fernatson and get the canvass off the wall, out of the manor, and lay it out in front of a fence; that's all the easy part. Convincing a man who thinks in candlesticks and silverware that the undamaged Study in Refracted light #23 is more than a hand painted placemat by someone's primary school daughter is where the real work begins. The warehouse came up again in just one of those discussions.

"It's art, Josie"

He grunted and poked at raised masses of thickened pigment. Fingernail met shellacked paint lump with a dull click.

"The Achmedi's paid the cost of a trawler for one of these, last year." I said.

"Sure Renn, I'll just hold a little soiree and auction it off. Besides, it looks like a gutter rat puked on it."

"I'm saddened by the cultural vacuum that stands in place of your soul. It's worth more than this building."

That part was unlikely. Josie was tight as a hull fitting, but his shop would likely outlast the mountains Myrport was built on. He was careful to maintain the outer wall to match the mishmosh of dry-rot, rot-rot, and decay that the surrounding structures featured. But, he'd rebuilt the interior out of forged steel and jungle hard woods. Somehow he'd even had the support piers replaced with the same stuff. An axe would bounce off and not even leave a smudge.

He flashed me his three teeth and I held my breath praying for ventilation.

"We both know you have someone to buy it, Josie. Or you can give it to one of the boys down at the Orchid, I don't care." I said.

Not true, but bargaining isn't about true, it's about maneuver and position.

"The Orchid? Hah! I'm not one of your victims, fat and happy on the hill with nothing better to do than get my tool rotted off."

"Funny, I could have sworn I saw you there a couple nights back, must have been someone else being carried home."

He slicked back his hair with one hand. It made a sound like chewing gristle and he prodded the crusted paint again. Point to me.

"It's a hassle, I don't like hassles. Why can't you stick to metal? Everybody wins with metal."

"Don't pout, this was worth more. Besides, metal's heavy and I tire easily."

Josie was poking the caked layers of paint again, "Was the

artist..."

"...Fernatson..." I said.

"Yeah, whatever. Was he famous for his painting?"

"Funny, Josie. Tell you what. I'll just go see if The Crutch has better artistic taste."

The Crutch was my other contact for dispersing the things I stole. He was a little squeaky man with tanned leather skin, a fondness for other people's money, and dates from his homeland. His fingers were always a little gummy from eating them, which was a good reason not to take anything to him that couldn't be washed after. Naturally, he and Josie loathed each other professionally and personally. Naturally, I took advantage of that anytime it seemed profitable.

"I've seen pile of mud more artistic but I'll tell you what, you do something for me and I'll take it off your hands so you don't go make a fool of yourself in front of that sleazy son of a rock cod. Deal?" He said.

"What do you want now Josie? And don't pretend you're doing me any favors, you're going to make triple what you pay me and we both know it."

"Got to pay the bills somehow, Renn. You been to Gobineau's yet?"

"Do I look dead? Of course not, that place is stupid-bait."

"Gobineau and I have... a disagreement. I want to rile him up and I think you're just the fellow to do it. Hell, you irritate people just talking to them."

Probably best to let that slide.

"What sort of disagreement?" I said.

"He thinks I should pay import duties, I disagree. Not important. You break into his warehouse and steal something; he'll look weak. He looks weak and he'll be so busy fending off the competition he won't have time to stick his paws in my business."

"Or he'll kill you, me and then you."

"Unlikely," he gave the bars a whack with his knuckle, pulling a dull echo from it.

He gummed a smile at me as the vibrating died down, "Been tried. Besides word is there's some new fellow making his life difficult already. A little nudge and he'll pull in his shell quicker than a snap turtle."

"Who's the new guy?"

"Nobody…short name. Claw? Word is he took over from Helpin when that stabbing he got festered and turned into an acute case of strangling…or drowning. Not important. Thing is, he's been pushing on Gob and Gob isn't going to add to his trouble when he's busy pushing back."

"Fine, let's pretend he won't turn dockside up on its keel looking for whoever is dumb enough to pilfer his special warehouse. What does he have in there that you are willing to take the chance?"

"You heard they elected a new Council of Merchants up on the hill?" Josie said.

"Yes, of course."

Myrport isn't really ruled as much as small corrections made on a runaway wagon as it hurtles down slope. The people doing the course changes are a council chosen through bribery, extortion, murder, and blackmail amongst the wealthy families that live in upper Myrport. The Council runs things until enough of the standing members die, go missing, or otherwise require new blood to maintain the appearance of order.

While the city and the land it is on wouldn't be worth the torch used to burn it down, every so often one of the countries in the vicinity gets the idea that the wealth of the merchant houses in Myrport would look nice in their tax base. The council's main job is to make sure that doesn't happen since taxes are sinful and bad for business.

"First order of business was a new council seal." Josie's gaze would have shattered rock.

"No. No…no…and just in case; no." My fingers twisted. It's best to ward off evil, or in Josie's case, insanity, the moment you see it, "We are definitely done here."

The council might be ineffective, by design of the city

founders any action required unanimous agreement by a double handful of men and women who made their fortunes by destroying the fortunes of their peers. Some of the families had been feuding since before Myrport laid its first pier. Healthy inaction was the order of the day. Anything they did agree on was stamped with the seal of the council and the Goddess of the Tides couldn't save you if that seal was against you. Better to chum a shark school before swimming in it, than to attract that kind of attention.

There was no point in heading for the door; a smart man would kill me for hearing what I'd heard and Josie might be a filthy, miserly, demented, old creep, but he wasn't stupid. You don't spend a lifetime selling shaved dirhams stamped in your basement, without so much as a visit from the Watch, by being slow and Josie would have to be doubly crazy to let me walk out the door after suggesting such hair-brained lunacy.

"Hold up, Renn, I'm not daft. It's just the gold they're going to use for it."

Josie giggled as I paused, "you should see your face, like a ghost was walking up yer back. Gobineau skimmed a few ounces off the shipment. I like to think the city needs some more coinage."

I took a deep breath and made my hands and feet stay where they were. Sweat trickled down my forehead. Josie and I had been doing business for a couple years by then, but that was no reason for sentimentality and he made sure I knew it. He'd stopped me cold a few weeks after I'd started selling work to him. I'd gotten a little too chatty, asked him about his family or something. He'd cut me off, "Shut it kid, we ain't friends and the moment you cross me or I get a better offer, I sell you." He'd snapped his fingers and pointed to the door and refused to take anything of mine for a month. It was his version of nice; nothing was free with someone like that, not even a lesson.

"Funny, Josie. Any idea where it'll be, pretending I was interested in having my teeth yanked out with a gut hook?" I said.

"A gut hook? You think Gob ain't got pliers? His office,

under a rock, maybe he swallows it at night and rinses it in the morning. I don't know. Am I hiring a professional or an errand boy? Figure it out when you get inside."

"How much?"

"I already said. I'll buy this furnace thing."

"Fernatson."

"Yeah, whatever. You do this; I buy your painting. We're both happy." His smile was very nearly authentic, not counting the three teeth and mass of purple white gums.

"You're buying the Fernatson anyways Josie, and I'm not getting someone like Gobineau riled up for nothing. Did you hear what he did to the Galt twins? Conjoining is supposed to happen before birth."

Josie scowled, nearly the same as no expression at all or constipation. All three expressions he wore regularly, "A tip like this has a cost, boy."

"It's not a tip, if I end up like the others."

"Those were weekenders, you ain't."

"Flattery doesn't buy ale."

"Here's a tip; drinking's bad for you. Alright. How about a third weight?"

My father gave me the back of his hand one time when I beat him at Sevens. Split my lip open and then lectured me on gloating over victories. I didn't even twitch a smile at Josie as I countered, "Half and you pay me now for that."

Josie was looking downright discomforted.

"Fine, half weight. But I'm only buying that if you come through." He stopped me as I reached for the painting. "Leave it, gotta shop it around…be easier if I can show it. Unless you don't trust me?"

His smile wasn't any more sincere than the last one, but it was time to walk away with my victory. He wasn't likely to stiff me on it; that's not how a fence makes money. And letting him have the win on that kept the price he was going to pay for Gobineau's gold from tasting too bitter.

Eighteen hours later, I was hanging by my fingertips from a

crossbeam while a pair of dogs comprised mostly of yellow teeth and ribs snapped at my feet. It was possible I hadn't been as clever as I'd thought.

A quick nap, a roasted duck, and a couple mugs of the Pike's finest to prepare, a few hours counting heads and watching for patterns, and I was in Gobineau's personal, private, warehouse. Not hard at all. If it hadn't been for the handful of my peers who'd wound up missing parts over the last month, I'd have put the reputation down to over excitement and beer.

Stacks of crates mixed with piles of rugs, pallets of sacks filled to leaking with rice or wheat, barrels of all sizes, and wooden racks built to fit anything that didn't fit into a sack, barrel, or box. Everything gave off the smell of itself mixed with salt, damp, and their ports of origin. Creating a heady miasma that stank of money.

The building was heavily reinforced from the inside, brick pillars lined walls of unfinished cedar supporting a false roof sealed with black pitch. From the outside, it still faced the world with salt-washed white gray boards patched with cast off pallets and plaster. The old building sat on the new like a storm overcoat - bricked over side doors the only hint of the redesigned security.

A rook Watchman kept himself company in front of the sliding cargo doors facing the street. From what I could tell, he was mostly concerned with staying out of the rain. He knew as well as I did, he wasn't there for people like me. His job was to keep honest folk honest. Wouldn't want someone testing the handles in the middle of the night, might disturb the real guards.

Bypassing those required some careful work with a pry bar and the gap between the fake roof and the real one. Building the new structure inside the old required Gob's people to leave a foot, or so, of space. Good thing I don't have a problem with confined spaces. From there, I swam crawled to the side, pried loose one of the cedar planks, and shimmied my way to the floor. The pitch had smeared all down my front and then mixed with the dust, caking me in a layer of sticky mud. A lit candle would have incinerated me, the warehouse, and half the docks.

Scraping the stuff off my hands in the dark took me a tense few minutes until I could light the hooded hand-lantern I carried. The trick was to light it without turning myself into a funeral pyre. As it was I had every intention of tossing my pants and the jacket as soon as I got home.

Most warehouses have a room built for paperwork or a sleeping crew boss and that was where they were storing the smaller, gold like, things of value. People are predictable like that. With that in mind, I headed to the corner nearest the doors. There I found a square structure made from reddish brick hiding under baskets of silk and linen bolts. A quarter-circle was kept clear for the door on one side and a row of crates held up the other creating a slope of luxury that poured down over the office.

Judging from the patterns woven into the linen, Gobineau had been tithing a few bolts from any shipment he ran across. Some of the other Inner Sea kingdoms were reputed to have zoos filled with creatures from all over the world. Any one of those would have been outdone by the sheer variety of flora and fauna represented by lengths of rainbow colored cloth stacked, piled, and just plain tossed on top of the haul.

The glow of my hand-lamp lit a winding way through the pilfered luxury goods and soon enough it was just me and the lock. A minute and a half later I was standing in a plain brick room looking at a much repaired chair and an ersatz desk. With enough wealth outside the door to buy a fleet of ships, you would think he could afford decent office furniture. Instead, the chair looked to have been repaired with the legs of a second and third chair. The desk was a repurposed door and didn't have legs at all, each end rested on a stack of wood boxes and parts of boxes. A leather-bound ledger, the size of a serving tray, occupied the desk accompanied by a couple half-full bottles of ink and a lonely storm lantern.

Maybe Gob liked to keep track of other people's things? He certainly had an evident fondness for getting his hands on their stuff. Something didn't sit right though.

There are lots of corrupt watchmen - some days it seems like a requirement for the job - each with their own vices. Never judge another man's deeds, isn't that what the priests say? At heart they were all pretty similar though; they fed off people like me and then went and spent it at the Orchid or drank it away. Left-Leg Jack collected wives, or he did until one of them found out about the others and strangled him with her wedding garter.

Gobineau had his fork in deep with smugglers and runners, enough to retire up the hill, if that warehouse was anywhere near as full as it looked. So I couldn't figure out why he wasn't. And why someone who'd had a warehouse built inside a warehouse out of brick and imported lumber was keeping track of it with a chair that wouldn't hold my weight, much less his, and a door as a desk. And where were the traps? Not to mention the guards, or total absence of them. It was starting to raise the little hairs on the back of my neck.

It took me all of another minute to find the gold. He kept it in a locked hardwood box tucked in the back of the crates holding up the left side. Sometimes simple is best, I torqued it open with the blade of my knife, stuffed the contents into my pockets, and quick walked out of the room. If it was a set-up, better to get in and out before the jaws sprang shut. Navigating my way back to where I'd pried my passage through the inner wall was trickier than it should have been. Landmarks memorized oh-so carefully on the way in, can take on new divergent aspects on the trip out. After a couple bad turns, one involved a dead end into several shipping tons of salted beef in barrels, I was near running. I was starting to feel like the lobster as the water passes comfortable. This was definitely a set up and the only question was if Josie was in on it.

The corners started to look familiar and I broke into a full run, darting around corner after corner now that I was on the right path.

The pair of dogs had made a den of old burlap sacks and what looked to be a collapsed bale of seal furs. No odds given on who was more surprised between us. They were up in an instant. Teeth bared. hackles up. The one on the left started a rumbling growl that resonated up from its stomach. The other joined the duet going up and over, with higher less consistent notes.

Every muscle in my body froze, so I didn't wet myself - that was good.

Dogs are one of the hazards of my profession. They cost nothing to recruit or train. Just grab one or two from the feral packs that roam the docks, lock them inside whatever needs guarding, and lure them into a cage with a little food when you need them out of the way. That is one of the two times they get fed. The pair I tripped over were thin even by those standards. The light of my hand-lamp reflected off of each rib and glowed yellow off far too many sharp teeth. Even half-starved they were the size of full-grown pigs. With large square heads and the battle scars crisscrossing their skin, leaving bare patches in short dark hair.

The other time they get fed is when someone like me makes a mistake. Getting eaten wasn't the only risk associated with dogs. A single bite can be fatal if the victim contracts lockjaw, or canine madness, or if the wound festered - as it often did.

Luckily - a relative state, given that my luck had clearly gone over the mountain - dogs are bad climbers. A running start followed by a healthy jump and I would be able to gain enough height that they would have to wait for dinner. Up the hill the dogs are different, pampered, trained, and used to people. Used to food from people. Drugging them was best since they are trained to sound if they think you don't belong. Ferals mostly don't bark. So if I could get out of reach, I could make my way out and away without dealing with Gob's two-legged dogs.

Careful not to show sudden movement, I shifted my weight to my back leg and then edged out my lantern hand toward the crates that made up one wall of the alley I was in. The one in the back tilted her head, apparently confused about dinner that didn't just run. The other followed the lamp steadily droning his growl all the while. As soon as they shifted their attention I took an infinitely slow step back, keeping my weight on the other foot. It was like walking a rope, only less gravity and more drooling fangs. The one in the back was starting to catch on by the time I made it to the corner I'd come jogging around five minutes before. Her growls turned to a whine as she hunched her shoulders down, afraid to push ahead of the larger male but desperate for the meal that was getting farther away.

My palms were slick with sweat and my legs ached from the strain. I took one deep breath, flashed the lamp back toward the crates, and dove for the opposite side around the corner as both ferals leapt for me at the same moment.

The bigger one went for the distraction of the lamp but the small female was having none of that. The Insane Three be blessed, she had to pull up and leap to get around her slow-witted mate. As it was, the sound of her jaws cracking shut, inches from my head, was loud over the other one slamming into the crate. Skittering claws dug into the wood to make the corner and it was after me.

Leg over leg, I launched up the side of a stack of pallets and then harpooned back to the other side, scrambling to gain height. The top of the stack was barely in arms reach when hungry need drove the small one straight up like shot from a sling. It was a bird's eye view of the cat as it defies gravity to snatch its meal off the wing.

My fingers burned as I grabbed upwards, scrambling to get out of range. The lamp in my hand made clawing for height even harder and I heard myself muttering a steady stream of "tides-tides-tides-tides-tides!"

The crushing shear of the beast's jaws crunched into my heel, whiting out my vision as teeth punctured leather, skin and bone. For a second, I thought my shoulder was going to give as my full weight was hurled back onto one hand and the other foot. She was growling again, this time a loud piercing grating fed by my blood as it filled the heel of my boot and dripped down into her mouth. If there had been any sanity remaining to her, the taste of me washed it clean. The male was making almost human yipping noises as it threw itself up to reach us and then was yanked back to the floor, too big to fly like his mate.

The parasite attached to my foot started to whip its body back and forth, seesawing into my foot in an attempt to tear me back down. The pain convulsed up my leg and I made one of those decisions that, in retrospect, seemed really good, actually.

The hand-lamp was a work of art. Small enough that it could be cupped in the palm of one hand, yet bright enough to signal ships, if that ever seemed like a good plan. It had cost the price of a house and taken the silversmith I'd worked it out with six months to fabricate. Normal oil, rendered from fat didn't burn well enough so we'd worked out a combination of pitch, watered down just a little with rum, and purified oil. It was double walled to keep the heat from burning but still uncomfortable without a glove. For obvious reasons I was a little reluctant to part with it. Of course I was more loath to part with my flesh, so that made the decision somewhat easier, in a land-piranha-is-eating-its-way-up-my-leg sort of way.

With one leg and a hand holding up my weight and the dog convulsively tearing up my foot, I worked my hand out of the braided wire loop that normally kept me from dropping the lamp. The loop seemed like a sensible precaution given the cost; always take care of your tools. Dad was keen to reinforce that with anything he could reach. As soon as I had it free, I leaned over, gritted my teeth hard enough to crack, and slammed my injured foot into the crate below me until the female set of teeth below me finally let go. As she was falling toward her mate I hurled the lamp down after her and shot upward, grabbing the crossbeam overhead. The glass shattered and oil flickered into fire.

The dogs collided in a confused series of growls and yips. They snarled and nipped at each other for a moment, and then they resolutely resumed their assault on gravity to get at where I hung pretending that my foot didn't burn like the flames from the broken lantern. The sound of their jaws clacking and snapping shut as they hit the top of their jumps was nearly musical. It could have been worse, right? I could have been food. It worked better than I could have hoped. Aside from the blinding agony of my foot, I was going to need to get that looked at.

The lamp had missed both the dogs, but I'd been clearing my hand more than trying to hurt them. No real point to that, they were just hungry. The glass shattered when it hit the stacked pallets, spraying fuel soaked shards down to the floor where the wick burned.

The light was just bright enough to see rows of barrels lined up under wax stoppered jars directly behind the growing bonfire.

There are three gods of luck and they all hate me.

The muscles in my arms felt like sacks of mire sludge but panic drove me up and onto the beam. My foot trailed droplets of blood that glistened as it rained down on the two mongrels. They were circling each other, the big one kept up a steady stream of yips, scolding his smaller partner. She had flattened her ears and was replying with an undulating growl. Their problems were about to be a whole lot bigger than a lost dinner.

The open rafter I was on didn't lead to the hole I'd made, but it was way past the point of sneak thievery. I half hopped, half crawled to where it met the wall. As soon as I got there I heard a soft thump and suddenly the warehouse flickered into elongated shadows dancing in the light provided by the ignited fuel from the lamp reservoir.

Normally the last thing you want to do at the end of a long night's burglary is make a racket, attract attention, and start a chase. Not only is it tiring running about in the early hours of the morning with your stolen prize, but there's nothing that brings out the hero in the average man like someone running from the Watch.

Circumstances being what they were, I had two arguments in favor: There was a good chance that Gobineau was going to be a little bit distracted, and if I didn't get out I was going to be burned alive.

Smoke was filling the upper rafters by the time I got a hole big enough to get through. Feet first through the hole as my lungs started to burn, I started to slam at the outer wall with my good foot. It held and I heard the first jars give. Just a small cracking noise, like a teacup hitting the floor, followed by a sucking roar as the contents gave themselves to the fire.

It was midday in the warehouse after that. I shut my eyes. Kicking a hole in the wall didn't require sight and I was going to be light blind enough when I got through. My hands were swimming in sweat. My whole body was. There was a steady series of cracks followed by a rolling chain of small explosions from where I'd left the dogs. By the time the outside wall gave I was coughing in smoke that seared my lungs. No grace at all, I threw myself forward; tried to roll as the boardwalk reached up and smashed into me.

The night air revived me a moment later. My lip was pulp where my face had stopped my fall and there was blood pooling in my mouth.

The warmth of the fire was still on my back. Everything smelled of char and acrid blood. The fire behind me had reached that crowd roar, pummeling bystanders with noise as well as heat. Not that there would be many of those, mostly buildings didn't catch fire on the docks. The rain stopped what the damp didn't. Every so often when something did catch the method for fighting it was typical Myrport; surrounding property owners cut away any connecting wood between themselves and the burning house and if the inhabitants of the doomed structure got out before they did…well that was good too.

It was time to get moving, the fire was starting to burn the skin on my back. It was flogging the dead to get myself up and half stagger; half drag my maimed foot farther away.

The fire was growing and it looked like the neighborhood hadn't caught on quite as quick as the gaping howling fire had. Black stick figures near the door were just standing, staring at the maelstrom I'd unleashed. That feeling in the pit of my stomach was not pride. My mouth was dry and not just from the heat of the fire, there might not be enough wine at The Pike for this one. Assuming the entire dock didn't go up in fire.

Who stores oil in a warehouse made of dry cedar sealed with pitch anyways?

The next few days I hid. There was no way I was going

anywhere near Josie, and as sure as the tide comes twice on a full moon, Gobineau was looking for the source of that fire.

Rumor had it; the priestesses from the temple of the Goddess were called in to stop the blaze before it turned Myrport into a smoking, charcoal covered swamp. As it was, nobody died. Excepting the dogs, but I wasn't eager to point that out to the bar patrons marveling over the lack of corpses.

For a week or so the ruins of the warehouse and a few surrounding buildings left an inky black hole in the middle of the docks. It was large enough to see, in a rare fog-free day, from upper Myrport. Then the docks crept back in like mold on cheese, covering the hole so that a month later it was just some slightly less weathered buildings on the way uphill.

When I ran out of drinking money, I went to get paid. Josie never said a word. He weighed out the gold and then counted out the money.

"Not that one, Josie, looks a little fresh." I said.

Since neck stretching isn't my thing, I made it a habit not to take the fruits of Josie's labors. Getting caught with a handful of fresh-struck coins was a good way to spend time twisted around a rack answering questions. After he was done counting, I eyed the pile of dirhams and gave Josie my best suspicious glare.

"What's the extra for?"

"Call it a bonus, for picking the right side."

"I didn't side with anyone, it was…"

"Don't even say it, boy. You done good, and I'm grateful, leave it at that." He said.

"I work for myself, nobody else."

Whichever gang thought I'd done them a favor, I wanted no part of. Once they thought you belonged to them it was a short passage to owing and "what have you done for us lately?".

"Gobineau is going to be looking for your head for years, you sure of that?"

"Gobineau can please himself with a gaff hook."

"Suit yourself, but that's a reward for services rendered. Someday you'll have to make a choice. Now take it and go waste it on drink like you usually do."

He looked like he'd swilled dregs as I scooped up my pay and made for the door, "Going to have to choose, Renn, remember that."

# TWELVE

Lye tossed the corpses over to one side of the cave. They landed with a mixed crunch and splatter from the muck and blood. It made me a little bit queasy. He'd drag one over to the edge of the dry area, and my stomach would start crawling up my throat in time to him hefting the body as it flopped about while he got under it to heave it out onto the part he'd decided was the perfect spot for bodies. Like some deranged version of darts or something. Plugging my ears was out of the question, so I settled for scrunching my shoulders up as far as they would go and pretending the activity around the tomb was suddenly the most interesting thing since teenage boys discovered teenage girls.

"How much longer, do you think?" I asked Sylvie.

She was watching Dugal get in Hospur's way as he drew a pattern on the lid in chalk, "Well, if your friend there…"

"Not my friend." I said.

"What?"

"He's not my friend. Never met him before … last night? Yesterday? How long have we been down here?"

Sylvie shrugged at that, arms folded.

"So if that idiot," She paused and invited me to object with a raised eyebrow, "keeps distracting them it could be hours. But they can touch it without harm, so we're mostly done."

We stood watching in silence. The drip…drip…drip combined with infrequent muttered words from Hospur or Isaac…sometimes both, in unison. Lye strolled up, his task finished, and stood to Sylvie's other side. I could feel her standing next to me… feel her not quite rubbing my elbow as she rocked slightly from heel to toe. My skin prickled with the closeness, the not-quiteness of it.

"What happens next, then?" I asked.

"Mmm?"

"After you get the thing, from the coffin there? What's the

plan, for after?" I said.

"Well, if our information is right - and Isaac is usually right - we grab the artifact and make our way to the surface. You and Dugal there go back to whatever it is that you do, and we do something...what was the word you used?"

"Insane."

My big mouth wasn't my favorite feature right then.

"That's right. Insane."

She flashed perfect teeth at me. Without a response to that we stood in silence, listening. It was soothing, like when you have a fever and your father is talking to the doctor. You can't really hear the words, but for once everyone is concerned about your well-being and you're warm and hazy so you can't think about how bad you must be for him to trade drink money for a doctor.

We stood in companionable silence like that for an hour, maybe two, and when it ended at first I didn't even really notice. Call it fatigue. No big pronouncement or flashy arcane light show, Hospur just reached down, yanked twice, and pulled his hand back. It was later that I realized he'd shoved his hand through the lid to the tomb. Didn't even leave a mark; I checked. The object was hidden by his fist, but there were greyish bits trailing that turned out to be bits of bone and petrified skin. Hospur had broken the artifact free from the dead hands that clutched it. He grimaced, shook it a couple times to shed the remaining bits of the previous owner, and turned to show it to Sylvie. Isaac slumped to the floor next to him, exhaustion overtaking his relief at being finished. Dugal kept him from hitting his head on the stone.

"Well, girl, that was the easy...unh." Hospur said.

"I'll take that."

It wasn't really a surprise. He'd already told me after all. But still, it's one thing to know someone is a treacherous slime worm, it's another to watch him sink a knife into an unsuspecting man and snatch the prize. Hospur dropped to his knees, hand clamped over the puncture in his side. Dugal either wasn't very good or he hadn't meant to kill the priest.

Sylvie and Lye stood, shocked into statues for a second, and then both started forward at the same instant. I waited, Dugal didn't strike me as especially clever but he had to have more cards hidden if he was working for Clar.

Hospur gasped as Dugal jabbed him in the hand with the knife.

"Hold up there, you two. Unless you don't fancy your friend's skin all that much."

He did have a plan; it was just a bad one. Hostages are troublesome at best and detrimental at worst. They only work at all if they are more scared of you than the alternative and even then they'll turn on you at the slightest hint of hope. Of course that supposes that whoever you're using the hostage on has the same priorities you think she does.

"You lowlife dock dwelling..." Sylvie sliced off the words with a razor.

"Ah! Not another step! Now back over there by the bodies, I'm walking out of here and you're going to let me. Or I'll start removing parts of his face."

"What is that going to get you, he'll bleed out before you get to the surface and the four of us aren't going to just wait for you to get there."

"I think you've miscounted milady, Renn?"

Tides...the look she gave me. I was surprised not to catch fire right there. Her face froze up into the mask she'd worn back at the Sailor's Rest. Lye never took his eyes off Dugal. The easy feeling I'd enjoyed for the last hour or so was gone, gelled into condemnation and distrustful judgment with one sentence.

Part of me accepted that. It's part of the job. No matter the misery of life. Most people, they get to die cold and starving, without so much as a kind word from the people who made sure they eked out their last breath in a joyless hunt for the leavings from the table of plenty. No matter that they are playing a game that is rigged to keep the winners winning and drive the pride and warmth from the losers. No matter, they still don't rise up and take from the silver plates what they should have been shared, instead they get wrapped in the blanket that didn't keep them from the ice and dumped off the end of the docks while the survivors cling to the illusion of pride that at least they aren't people like me.

Another part of me twisted like a well-wrung gooseneck. "Dugal..."

The sawclaws could strip his smirking face for all I cared, especially for getting me into this. People like Dugal are formed from the slurry of algae, barnacle shells, and sewage water that pools around ships being refitted. He'd been hanging out with the wrong sort of people for too long. There wasn't much I liked about the gangs in Lower Myrport. It seemed pretty clear they were set up to feed off the people who did the starving just as much as Upper Myrport fed off Lower. Sure some of them started out with...call it slightly less ignoble intentions. Protect each other and so on. Do that for a week and they start feeling like they're providing a service, regardless of how their friends and neighbors might feel about paying for that service.

"Shut-up, Renn, and get over here."

That wasn't nice. Some people spend so long telling people what to do they forget to make sure people want to do it first. Sylvie's gaze felt like a claw boring and twisting its way into my spine as I made my feet do what the rest of me didn't want. I told myself that one of these days I was really going to have start thinking through these things beforehand.

Once I was where Dugal wanted me, he clutched Hospur to him like a fat ungainly sack of grain and crab-walked the two of them around the tomb past where Isaac was slumped, head lolling to the side. Blood was pooling down the stonework leading to the carved inlay of the tomb like little rivers running down the channels created by the mortar in the interstices. Of course, he'd have taken care of Isaac while we were distracted.

Isaac hadn't liked me much.

Putting my hand on his knife hand, I tried for time, "Dugal."

"I told Clar you were a bad idea. Not another inch milady." Dugal said.

He started working his dagger through the layered leather of Hospur's armor with slow pleasure. Smiling as he did it. Hospur groaned as the blade split skin and scraped along a rib.

"Your friend here only has so much blood to spare. Get in line Renn, Clar doesn't tolerate independent thinking in his men."

I'd sooner join the watch.

The thing about a knife fight, the thing that gets people looking down at their guts, wondering what went wrong, is that the normal rules of combat don't apply. One-eyed Horace used to say if you wanted to kill a man with a knife you had to be his friend, if you wanted to live through the event, you'd better love him.

With a sword or an axe, reach and managing distance is key to survival and victory. That and how many fingers you'll have after the fight. With a dagger you want to get in and get extra personal. And the sooner you do that, the more likely you live. Dugal probably should have spent some time with Horace. On second thought, maybe not. Horace was drunk more than half the time and would have sewed his name on a flunky like Dugal before the end of the night. It wouldn't have been hard; the goddess knows how he wasn't already dead.

I shifted my grip to his elbow and clamped down hard, thumb driving into the inside just above the bone where the muscle from the bicep connects. The pain cut him off but it was far too late, I'd made my choice. Driving my shoulder down and then popping up forced his knife hand up and cleared my way to his torso. With the other hand, I flipped my knife out of its sheath, rotating it through the ring to a reverse grip. Using the joint pinch, I kept his arm up as I stepped in and hammered the tip into his exposed side…once…twice…and a third for surety.

His momentum kept turning him toward me as I rained blows down, mouth gaping, first in anger and then shocked pain. By the time the third punched through the thin muscle and tendon just below the rib he was more or less already dead. It just took another couple seconds for him to realize it as he collapsed on the floor still clutching Hospur. The priest tried to fight it, staggering under the weight of the body and his wounds, until he too slammed down on top of Dugal.

For a moment, I just stood there, surprised at myself, splattered blood dripping from the side of my face where I'd turned my head to avoid being blinded. Just like Horace had taught me. "Don't close yer eyes, son, you'll lose t' bastard's knife an' a lost knife finds a home in yer gut." Some of the blood trickled down my lip and I could taste the man I'd just killed. Then I threw up. Heave after dry heave, dropping to my knees finally as sweat swarmed my face and the realization that I'd murdered a man, killed more, and probably wouldn't live out the day when Clar couldn't find his factor.

There was a hand on my back at some point, an argument with only one person talking, but the choking halting heaves roared the blood in my ears, and I just tried to keep my testicles from coming out with my guts.

After about the third round of little wave… bigger… bigger… choking tidal wave of dry heaving, the panic chased the nausea back into its hole. Sylvie was kneeling next to me, one hand rubbing my back the other holding a flask, which she pushed at my face as soon as it was clear I was back in my head. Pushing it away just earned me a thin-lipped eyebrow and she shoved it in my mouth.

"Don't make me hold your nose, Expert."

I stopped trying; it was like pushing a house frame anyways. Being big was never one of my problems, but a lifetime of scaling, clambering, and making sure I was where the watch wasn't looking had made me strong enough for that lack of bulk. She didn't budge. There were stevedores with less steel in their grip.

Whatever was in the flask it tasted like someone had taken licorice, cinnamon, and some of the hottest peppers to come out of the islands - with just a dash of lamp fuel. My stomach tried for a new round of expelling the invaders, while the flesh in my mouth and throat seared away. It stayed down, but not by any margin a sensible gambler would place bets on.

"That's...that's...vile."

The drinker in me was embarrassed at how long it took me to choke the words out.

"Yes, I don't think you're supposed to drink it." Sylvie eyed the flask while my mouth worked for air. She sniffed at the opening and recoiled, "Smells terrible, I know I wouldn't. Feel like standing up? Unless you want to swim your hands around in that for a bit?"

Standing is harder than it looks when your stomach feels like it's been worked over with a sausage grinder. The cave had its charms but it lacked a washbasin, after a second I used part of Dugal that wasn't covered in blood and vomit. Even dead I didn't really care for him.

Running it over in my head I couldn't think what other option there had really been. Before he'd slipped his riggings and started stabbing people, would Sylvie or Hospur have believed me? Assuming I'd tried to tell them somehow? Seemed unlikely on both counts. Prodding the body with my toe didn't make me feel any different about it...or him. Maybe there was some sort of sacrifice or appeasement to The Mad Three I could do, so any brothers or really close friends never found out I'd done it. Equally unlikely, my best interests hadn't shown to be very high on their lists lately.

"Did you know? ...before, I mean." Sylvie said.

Her voice was blandly neutral as she walked back to where I was prodding.

Just like that the dead guy was the most fascinating thing in the room. We have ticks, little glances, a twist of the lips, things that give us away and I hadn't decided if I was going to lie. No use working up a good story if the mark figures out you're lying before the thing gets under way.

Every joint burned with fatigue, and if it came to it, Lye could probably take me apart with that roofing timber he called a sword; if he didn't just shoot me with his over-sized crossbow. My hand prodded my stomach where the bolt had hit earlier, that night? The day before? For the first time in memory I just wanted to see daylight. My stomach hurt where I poked it but I couldn't tell if that was from getting gut-shot or just soreness from asking too much for too long. I yawned, started to stretch and gave that up as a bad bet. Things just hurt.

"Yes. No. He didn't say anything about..." I pointed back towards where Isaac had fallen, "Is Isaac ok?"

"He's fine. Mostly it was fatigue and the good sense not to give your friend a reason to stab him again. Isaac has his strengths..."

"We weren't friends." I said with a hand wave at Dugal.

"Well, I gather not."

She stepped forward next to me, joined me in staring down at the body.

"Never met him before the Sailors's Rest...before I met you. Isaac's alright then? What about Hospur?"

I felt her smile through the frisson between us. She was close enough to disturb the zone around a person beyond personal space. If you're the ticklish type, that's when you start squirming. Mostly even people who hug everyone skip me, something about body language I suppose. Having someone that close without touching made it harder to think.

Of course, the way I was feeling, if I didn't sleep soon I was going to pass out. My head was a block of wood with pain as a varnish. Even chances I'd get my name wrong right then, if someone asked.

"He'll recover...more irritated at getting jumped than anything else. I've seen him pull an arrow out of his own leg and then sew the hole shut while critiquing his stitch size. He may not be unkillable, but the difference is small."

"He doesn't just, you know...what he did to me?" I said.

"It doesn't work that way I guess. He won't say why and he won't take it from anyone else either. One of the rules or something."

"There are rules?"

Behind us, Isaac laughed, well half laugh, half cough. The humorless laugh of someone who's heard the joke before but didn't think it was funny the first time.

Somehow it seemed like if you could do that, you could just do it, like picking a lock. Once you learned how, that was it, no door was safe with a little patience and very steady fingers. I got the sort of look that a conman learns to hide before their first payout. Sure son. That ship's for sale. Where's the sign? We take it down so it don't get ruined in the rain.

"There are always rules, Expert. From what Isaac says, that's all there is to magic, learn the rules. I can't really say. It wasn't the sort of thing covered in lessons, not the topic for polite company, really."

"The world…" Isaac paused and blew air out his nose to cover the pain of movement "…is a set of rules. Grescal's Third Law is illustrative. Provide impetus and the educated can move an object, add more impetus and it flies. Take away Impetus and it falls, simple and straightforward. Even for you."

"Hunh. What should we do with…" I flicked the back of my fingers at the corpse.

Would it bother me later if we didn't bury him? It seemed a little unlikely, the moral equivalence between the unknown nutjobber who'd attacked us earlier and a treacherous brothel whelp who's name I'd known, would have to wait until I could view it from outside a bottle of wine.

"Leave it. Hospur could offer rites, but you'd have to ask. He tends to take stabbings a little personally."

Lye gave me a nod when we turned back to the others. He had one arm looped under Hospur's shoulders. From the tension in his jaw, supporting most of the shorter man's weight, it looked like Dugal might well have ended up killing the priest after all. Isaac was in better shape, a little pale, but blood loss can do that. Sylvie looked at the priest for a second and then waved me on toward the way we came in.

The walk back to the surface should have been shorter but wasn't. Even without searching for things meant to kill, maim, or just alert, we slugged our way to the top. In part that was my decision, my idea of how the day should end didn't include stumbling on top of a rear guard or the morning shift.

Do worshippers of forbidden horrors work in shifts? I didn't know and, if they did, I wanted to hear them before they saw us. It didn't take long before even that pace wasn't possible. Isaac and Hospur were leaking and going up taxed them beyond what we could do quickly. Before long, I had acquired Hospur's shield and weapon while Lye shifted Hospur into an over-the-shoulder carry. Isaac groaned and winced at every step, but was self-powered, if only barely. An hour later and my hands were slick with sweat; the carry strap had chaffed a groove into my neck that made me look like a strangulation victim.

The rest of the trip was a haze of fatigue. We made more noise than an army on the march and, if there was anyone left alive, none of us were in any condition to fight them off. We'd amused the trickster gods enough for the while though. When we got to the carved and tiled entrance the only thing stopping me from some sort of ill-planned and possibly blasphemous offering to the gods was fatigue bordering on catatonia. I barely managed a croaked "Wait." Before dumping Hospur's gear in a loud heap at the top of the stairs.

The temptation to add myself to the heap twisted with the urge to heave. I imagined that second shift of cultists opening the door "Oi, hey Lucius," - cultists were named things like Lucius in my head. "Someone left their stuff. Dibs on the thief!" My snort at that turned into a gargled choke that earned me a look…I was willing to call it concern…from Sylvie.

"Nothing. Any idea if it's daylight outside?" I said.

My sense of time had been gone for hours, days for all I knew. Lye started to shrug, stopped when Hospur groaned, and settled for a twisted grimace.

"No…probably not. It always seems longer when you can't see outside." Sylvie said.

"Always? How much time do you spend underground?"

That earned me a small smile. For some reason that made things better. Isaac scowled at us both and that made me feel even better.

"Some. More than you'd think, actually. The nice thing about places like this is you can usually tell where things are going to come from. Outside it is more complicated by half. Nothing like having a Tugal fencat landing on your back to make you appreciate a nice simple darkened tunnel."

"Fencat? What's...you know what? Never mind. How do you want to do this? If they're waiting outside, well, that's going to be bad for us." I said.

"Are you always this sunny, Expert? Don't worry so much. The gods are on our side."

"Pretty sure anytime someone says that, everyone dies by act three. Alright, everyone ready-ish?"

Hospur didn't vote, but the other three nodded and I set my shoulder against the door and shoved.

# THIRTEEN

I was drinking. Not drunk. Drinking. Getting drunk required more effort than I'd put to it. Instead there was just a faint buzzing off in the corner just loud enough to make hearing the other people in the tavern difficult and my face warm. Even though I was in the darkest, most suspicious corner of the room, , I was the kind of warm like you get in front of a nice stove. The serving girls knew I was there - had been for most of three days - but the regular patrons filed and sorted me as part of the furniture by the second night. After the third attempt at flirty chatter, the girls stopped working too hard and stuck to taking away bottles as I emptied them and bringing more. Nothing is quite as annoying for a craftsman, as interruptions while he works.

The corner was chosen for a nice view of both the doors. One led out to the fog and periodic rain, the other to what passed for a kitchen. The food might have been nice, but it would have interfered with the task at hand. Eventually Clar would decide that Dugal wasn't coming back and he would start looking for the answers.

With a little extra effort I would slow down the interrogation by being sick. Hopefully all over the newly promoted boots of whoever replaced the not-missed Dugal. Clearly there was more drinking to be done; I could still remember the confused glaze on his face as he spurted and died.

The exit from the tomb was as boring and prosaic as a walk to a funeral. It was still full dark outside, not even the soft glow on the horizon that says you've been up too late and missed your chance to sleep in. The orchard was suitably quiet. The only signs of our passing were a few scorch marks and a pile of smoldered ashes where the Deepspawn had found its inner flame. Someone had stepped in the pile leaving a carefully perfect rendition of hobnailed boot lined in dew. Might have been one of us or one of the dead, down below.

A few tense minutes later we were out on the street. Standing about, like some young watchman's dream collar. Four suspicious characters complete with Hospur's unconscious body - obviously foul play. Skullduggery even.

"Well." That was all the eloquence I could muster. In my defense, an empty safe doesn't really need a goodbye and neither does a bar full of passed out drunks. It was the sort of situation that seemed to call for something. Not that we were old friends, or even friends really, but it was the tail-end of a fairly spectacular night. Sylvie stood looking down the street. The light was edging up, the difference between black and dark more felt than seen.

"Well, the Three be busy, while you do…whatever you're doing, I guess." I said.

For some reason I wanted to keep the moment going, the conversation going.

"I owe you thanks, Expert. You performed admirably today."

She was formal enough for a magistrate's courtroom. Her posture matched her tone. I had a sudden image of her speaking to the council - since I'd never actually seen them, my mental image mostly consisted of really fat men in drapes. Blame the fatigue. I strangled the laugh stillborn, but something between a giggle and a squeak still escaped. Her face froze and her spine could have been used as a ship's mast. Whatever she'd been about to say chopped off quicker than a cod's head on market Wednesday. Pre-morning shadow blanketed her and I found myself wishing I could see better. For once, night wasn't the friend I needed.

"Ah. Thanks, I guess."

For some reason I wanted to apologize, to make whatever I'd done right. It was stupid, she'd let me be pressganged, nearly gotten me killed, twice, maybe three times. She should be apologizing to me, come to that. And nobody clean was friends with Clar, or even business associates. Walking on the same side of the street with him was probably conspiracy.

She smelled nice. Spice and trees wafted back at me as she

led Isaac up the street by one elbow past the dressmakers. The light was bright enough to make them out until they turned the corner. Leaving me standing in the middle of a deserted street like a shill.

So, after they were gone, I turned and watched the sun rise. Well, watched the fog brighten and then drift away as the mist deepened to drizzle and then thicken to rain. It was hard to remember the last time I'd been in uptown during daylight. It is significantly harder to hide other people's stuff in the daylight. When the rain had soaked through my jacket I went looking for a drink.

That took a while. Most respectable drinking establishments don't open at dawn. That leaves disreputable places like Whistler's, I put the odds of Corliss selling me out twice in one week far too high to risk that, or places that haven't closed. Simply find one where the drinkers never stopped buying and there was very likely to be an exhausted, but wealthy, proprietor. After a bit of searching I found the perfect spot. By day two I couldn't remember the name of the place and by the third as best as I could recall it had a galleon carved on the sign...or maybe a trawler... definitely a boat of some kind.

It was past time to step up to drunk, I couldn't get the smell of pine out of my nose and I wanted to be drunk when Clar killed me. The next time one of the girls came by to take away the empties I switched to gin. When she came back I could smell spice again.

"Expert, you're drunk." She said.

"Nope. Not yet. Was about to start, though."

I tilted my chair back till it was propped against the wall with my feet on the table. Her face wasn't visible, just an outline framed against the lamp and firelight. No armor this time, but she was still armed.

"Join me?" I said.

"Thank you."

She sat with far more grace than I could have mustered with a sword in the way. She shoved a cup towards me, and then another for herself. Drinking alone doesn't require cups. While I was eyeing the tableware she snagged a candle from a nearby table. Darkened seclusion destroyed by calm efficiency. Mulling that over carried me through pouring. Steady hands are useful for picking, lifting, and pouring drinks while plastered. She took her mug back and sniffed at it while I emptied mine and waited.

"What is this?"

"Gin, made from berries or something. It grows on the hillsides. Cheap with a nice kick."

It also seared any sense of taste you had left going down. My father claimed it was medicinal. From which I learned that medicine should taste like the bottom side of your boot. Sane folks don't sip gin, but I started on the next mug a bit at a time.

The girl tending bar saw the mostly empty bottle and headed over to collect it and a tip. She was young for the job. Still jutting elbows, pimples, and baby fat. That night she was trying to sway her hips like her older sister. It turned her normal tripping gait into a waddle.

"Something f'yer friend?" The girl scowled at the back of Sylvie's head. She'd been overcharging the wine and scooping tips when they came without talking. Benefits of serving a solo drinker. Now that someone was here to keep me in hand she was watching her income sink like a kid on his first swim.

"No, we're good."

I caromed a few coins at her and she swayed off with her prize.

"New friend?" Sylvie's smile was all lips and no teeth, "You've set yourself up quite nicely here. Is this what you do when you aren't stealing from honest folk?"

"Stealing from dishonest folk can be hazardous to your health."

"So will drinking things like this," She poured her mug out on the reed floor matting, "Goddess help you around open flame."

"Stop that, wasting perfectly poisonous rotgut is sinful. What are you doing down here anyways. Don't you have a suicide to be attending to?"

"Hospur needed a couple days. We decided to wait until he was feeling stronger."

We sat in silence. Normally when a conversation dies, it eats away at you until someone says anything they can to stop it from dissolving your sanity. This was nice. With my thoughts muffled by several blankets of wine and gin, I was left in that warm predawn when nothing needs to be done and nowhere needs to be gone too. Slightly fuzzy thoughts and a half smile on my face…until I sobered up anyways.

Of course there's always something that intrudes. A full bladder being the most likely.

At last she let out a long slow breath, "Are you really going to wait here until Clar finds you?"

"Good chance Clar already knows. Just hasn't made a decision. Maybe waiting until his sawclaw is good and hungry. Do sawclaws get full?"

"Sawclaw? What… never mind. You didn't answer the question."

"Well I was, yes."

"Why?"

"If I'd had a choice, I wouldn't have let Dugal lead me around by the strings."

The space over my head became fascinating, she stared so hard I was tempted to turn and look.

"About that. Look I'm sorry. We're sorry."

Her cheeks were flushed straight back to her ears. My thoughts drifted in a sea of bad wine and thoughts about what else would make her blush like that.

She went on, "It isn't what we do, it isn't right. But sometimes when you have a net, you take the fish you get. We got you. "

The words just flowed around me, it surfaced in my brain that she was going to ask me for something, and I was going to say yes. Anything to make her think well of me.

"Alright. I'll do it."

Her mouth went wide enough to fit a skiff.

"You! You said it was insane!"

She actually looked indignant, like I'd offended her by not letting her ask.

"It is. But then, so is waiting around for Clar. How did you ever hook up with him anyways? You really need to keep better company."

"Like you?" She said.

Her smile was all teeth and flashing white again. The skin on my face was instantly molten and I found religion, praying to any god who would listen for a distraction. A meteor or volcano would do.

"Why, Expert, are you well? You look flushed!"

Lighthouses had less gleam than those eyes. This is why relying on the gods is a bad idea. Prayer, offerings, and the odd soul but they still leave you hanging. I slammed back the mug, hiding behind it, and sucked on the burn it left on my tongue. Sylvie absently scanned the room while she waited for me to regain my footing. As if she had nowhere to be and wasn't in a back dock dive for the first time in her life.

"I do have a question though." May as well ask it now, I told myself.

"Which is?"

"Why? What are you and the others doing?"

She didn't move but I could feel her muscles tense in the empty space between us. She had to know I would ask but whatever it was still bad enough to get ready to fight just at the mention of it. There's bad news and there's whatever she was about to tell me.

# FOURTEEN

They hung my father in the middle of the winter. The watch surrounded the house in the middle of the day, like they knew exactly the sort of person he was. When he didn't come out, they rammed the door open with a rafter beam. The first one in the door was a watch captain from Upper, big blond man with expensive tailoring and the bad sense to lead from the front. The loose board slammed down with his first step, mashing the trigger that sent two feet of steel tipped mahogany punching out the back of his neck. It was meant to hit an average man between the eyes and, like I said, he was a big man. It was fatal enough for him and the two men behind him though. He might have lived, but choking does strange things to people. The blond watch captain panicked when his throat acquired a novel piercing. He gargled and plunged into the room sending a hailstorm of blades, darts, and shafted projectiles at himself and his unfortunate men.

Given who he was, my father and I weren't close; sneaking out under cover of a rum-induced stupor, after another in a long string of observations punctuated with a stick will do that. He probably could have found me after a bit. He knew the right people and they'd talk if he wanted them to. The note, that had told him my reasons, had politely pointed out that my other option had been to stay - after disposing of his body under the docks. It said the things I couldn't. The sort of thing brought about by a lifetime of tears and bruises. He deserved to be hauled off by the watch a thousand times over. Even after Jo sold me out I wasn't tempted to go back. Still, I wanted to know why. Justice - whatever that was - would be served regardless, but I still wanted to know why. The watch lost most of a squad arresting him and left nothing behind but smoldering foundation cobble. Someone was very unhappy with him.

"No such thing as overkill, son. Now set it up like I said less you'd like another!" My Father's voice still rang in my ears. It couldn't have been much past my fifth year; other kids were rolling barrel hoops down the hill outside the open door. It was an unheard of clear day in summer. The heat wreathed houses in steam and forced Myrport to choose between baking or the soup-smell of the mire. The day's task was learning trap triggers. There's almost as many ways to set off a trap as there are to maim and kill when it goes off. My father believed in testing as many of them as he could while deterring unwanted visitors at the same time. He was nothing if not efficiently horrible.

Since most of them were meant for full grown men, the danger was slight and nothing quite beats the sound of razor discs as they fly overhead and bury themselves in a wall for instilling caution. Sort of a shushing noise followed by a trio of tocks stacked up on top of each other instead of spread out from a clock. There were murder devices that some of the houses I've cleaned out would have paid good weight to acquire. The worst featured blades with holes drilled in them so that they'd scream and whistle as they flew through the air. Made me want to wet my pants right up to the day I left.

Noise is generally the real enemy. With a little planning and the right approach, guard dogs and men can be dealt with. Make too much noise and all that goes out with the pot waste. Darkness affects sight, but hearing is always full sail. Make a racket and every dog and would-be hero with a weapon comes to see the show. Even if the screamers didn't hit, a trap like that would end your night and maybe your career.

It was a dive built onto the wall of one of the merchant houses in Upper that catered to the fine fellows who kept the city safe from the docks. The skin on my head prickled and fighting down the urge to run from the place had left my muscles in a permanent state of twitch. My clothes were expensive enough, and clean enough not to draw attention. No reason to be worried. But these were exactly the sort of people it was my business to avoid. Years of training, reminders, and the general loathing common to the lower class for the people who protect and enforce the will of the upper made me twitchy as a cat in a fish market. A watch corporal, rope thin and well past middle age - the sort of man who always makes certain to be in the back - was holding forth. He claimed to have been there, "maintainin' te permeter," and was being bought mugs of beer for his version of the truth.

I knew every trap in that place as if I'd set it myself because I had. Taking apart, oiling, re-stringing, and setting was a weekly routine. Hearing the table of Watch next to me marvel at what had happened to the squad that went in to take my father, I could follow along in my head.

"Yer'all shoulda seen Fitzsimm, twitchin' like an eel, an just as blue. Thet give a poor thirsty man of te watch wit night terrors, tides if it don't!" His newfound friends took the hint and he throated the mug in one go. Grimaces all around but they forked the coin for another, this was more excitement than they could expect all year. A watchman spent twelve hours a day staring at nothing, boredom was a habit.

"Was there a fight?" "How'd they capture him?" "Like as not someone'll hang him 'fore trial, mark my words." And more, questions came faster than the beer, the lucky storyteller parlayed it all into refills.

They hadn't killed my father, goddess knows how that happened. Watchmen weren't shy with the boot or the blade and they got extra dangerous when one of their own died. The corporal's numbers changed depending on how willing his fellows were with the beer, but by any of several counts they'd lost a handful, before the survivors dragged my father out by his heels. They gave up marching him when he couldn't be roused. Of course that might have helped him. Lynching a comatose drunk lacks a certain visceral panache.

Instead, justice waited at the pleasure of whichever councilor had ordered his arrest. Which detail was the reason I dressed up, bought bad ale, and listened to a professional liar and drinker parlay one into the other. Eventually he let loose the name of the councilor and I discovered where my father was. Eventually. The man was a professional...a master of his craft. I wondered if his friends would pass out before hearing the whole story.

Hours later the inside of my left eye was burrowing back through my brain but I had what I came for. The early morning air slapped fitfully against my cheeks as I made my way farther uphill. No time like the present for a little casing and the rain helped sobriety along. My father was the personal guest of one Reinhard Poulson, Greve of Myrport.

The Poulsen family was the Myrport equivalent of old money, meaning they could trace their fortunes back farther than breakfast. Papa Poulsen took a few too many gold trade bars to the head and decided he was entitled to be nobility. Since he had the dinars he was able to get one of the kingdoms lining the sea to grant him a title which he took great pleasure in using. Normally that wouldn't have worked out very well with the rest of the council but the Poulsen family was flush and demonstrated a willingness to practice piracy. After the first couple houses that objected started losing ships by the dock full, they quickly saw the benefits of the odd bow and milord.

What my father had done to incur their displeasure was unclear, but they were exceedingly unhappy. The orders to capture him alive had been so ironclad that even after losing the better part of a double handful of men, the watch merely wrapped him in chains and drug him up the hill to the Poulsen estate, where they'd turned him over to the personal guard of the current Greve.

On the surface, all of the guards were members of the watch on assignment to families with enough wealth and power to demand them. In practice, they were the private armies of the councilors who hired them. At least twice, in recent years, open fighting in the streets had broken out after a contract breach between members of the council. Most of the time, the council kept things from getting that far and the personal guard did little besides executing the justice of the council.

That was apparently the fate planned for my father. The corporal with the hollow keg for a stomach hadn't known the charges, but the punishment was supposed to be dock dredging which meant that someone besides me was very unhappy with my father.

Dock dredging was akin to keelhauling, but without a boat. More room for spectators. The unfortunate soul had a rope fastened to their ankles and wrists and then one of the ropes was threaded through the piers holding up the docks. That end was fastened to a crank, or sometimes a ship if the tide was going out, and the other end was fed out as the condemned was pulled along the underside of the dock, dredging the wood of barnacles, slime, baby sawclaws, and whatever else lives and eats in that space. The crew doing the rope work would make sure the victim didn't drown, but only barely, while the skin flayed off and shredded. A good team would repeat the process for an hour or more. It was the sort of thing reserved for traitors and spies from the kingdoms.

The father I knew was a drunk and a bully. Neither was the sort of sin that got you dredged. Most places on the docks counted those as virtues. Some part of me knew that there had to have been more once; the house wasn't much but it was on dry land which made it more valuable than any part of the docks that wasn't actually tied to a ship. As far as I knew, my father hadn't left the house in the decade or more that he'd been raising me either. He paid a man to bring things he needed to the door when I was younger, and then when I was capable, he sent me to fetch food or drink, mostly drink.

It was akin to the midwinter farces, where the kindly servant pulls off his mask to reveal at last that he's the hero's father helping him all along. Only in this version the father pulls off his mask to reveal that he's something else, but what?

The legal system in Myrport is exceedingly simple. People with money were immune to it and the poor went without. Unless my father had allies or a secret stash of shares and gold, the Poulsen action would stand and he'd be executed within a day or so. No reason to feed someone you were about to execute so best to do it quickly before he starved and made for a poor execution or found friends amongst the other families. All of which meant that if I was going to get any answers this side of the deep, I would have to ask them quickly.

Which is how I found myself hanging upside down from a lintel while the blood pooled behind my left eye doing nothing for my headache. It felt like a spear was being shoved into it.

It was somewhere past midnight and the watchman had marched the forty feet of his route in the exact same time – thirty six slow breaths for the curious - for the last twenty trips. Across the hall - about five paces beyond his normal path - a cherub rested atop a pedestal in a nice quiet alcove. Just as I prepared to make the dash, he decided to have a smoke.

Some smokers can tamp a pipe, light it, and have the whole thing puffing like a smithy in seconds. This man was not one of those. Smoking on watch was probably forbidden, anything that distracts a watchman usually is, and he was bad at it. Normally I'd be grateful. Incompetence is its own reward, but I had somewhere to be. The smoke was making my throat itch and as long as he stood there I couldn't make my move. After a few seconds I was swallowing spit like it was ale and trying to keep from coughing. About the time I was contemplating swinging down and relighting his pipe for him he resumed his route - saving us both a world of awkwardness.

Ten heartbeats later I was across the hall - carpeted, thank you vast wealth - and safely admiring the backside of the prepubescent angel in the targeted alcove while happily enjoying the laziness of security that hasn't had to work for a living.

Sometimes when things have been quiet a while, the hapless individual in charge of the money will decide to be frugal. This usually shows up as a decision to only guard the outer ring of a building. Once some enterprising thief gets past that ring, well that's when the natural redistribution of wealth happens. Or in my case, as long as I didn't set fire to the place or start a horn ensemble, I could go anywhere I liked.

So, downstairs I went, on the theory that prisoner cells would be in the basement. Getting in was no problem, the builders had sensibly built to prevent escapes - not entrances.

Within a quarter of a candle I was standing in a short underground hallway lined with ironbound wood doors. Each door had a bar across it and a small hatch at the floor, sized for a bucket. It was admirable simplicity, no locks to maintain, the only way a prisoner got out would be for the bar to be swung up and the person doing that would be shielded by the door.

It would have been an ideal place to store apples, cool, not too damp.

There were four doors and nobody had thought to put nameplates on the doors. Turnover was too high probably. The doors were a hand-span of solid hardwood, plenty enough to keep anyone in these cells from disturbing the residents. There was nothing for it but to open doors until I found my father while hoping that the process didn't get loud enough to bring the curious.

Sometimes I worry too much, but then that means that each day I get to worry.

All but one of the cells was empty, not even a pad of straw left behind for future inmates. The fourth held my father. I'd taken the time to force a dagger nice and tight between the floor and the wood, they'd probably have to rehang the thing to get it to swing again, but the thought of it clicking shut behind me, made me break out in claustrophobic sweat and was well worth the cost of a new dagger. Tempting the Mad Trio wasn't really a good idea.

He didn't even look up when I swung back the bar and poked my head around the door. He was curled into the corner, back to the door. They didn't add creature comforts with occupancy either; bare stone for your last night on earth.

I stood in the doorway tasting the stew of my emotions. In the flicker from my candle he looked small, a nearly child sized bundle that twitched and stretched with the shadows. This was the man who'd raised me, taught me. That was the problem really. Along with how to break a lock in less time than a swallow's thought, came lessons in fear. Sure I could scale a rain-slick wall better than a sticky footed lizard, but with that came a combination of sick terror and mind squeezing rage that twisted and corrupted. Like a green-grey mold starting out as faint spots on cheese that turns into a furred monstrosity overnight. I wanted to help him and I wanted to kick and beat at him until he felt all the bruises he'd given me.

Instead I cleared my throat and opted for talking, still with the door shielding me from the room.

"Well, you're probably sober. What's that like?"

At first, there was no response. He wasn't asleep, one of the things you learn halfway into an occupied bedroom is the difference between asleep and pretending. A conscious person imposes structure on a room, they can't help themselves.

"You're a damn fool." He finally said, back still turned toward me.

"Maybe. But then the council didn't drag me drunk and stupid out of bed."

"I wasn't drunk."

"Why lie? You're always drunk. You were the day I left and you'd be now if you could."

I choked down worse…the words I'd thought I came there to say, but just then they didn't seem as important. Maybe it was the defeat. He was beaten. Probably physically, it was tough to tell from the doorway and I still couldn't put myself in arms reach of the man. He'd given up inside, whatever they'd done to him. I swung the door open, hiding behind it felt silly.

"Didn't figure you'd last a day, you left, figured you'd come back, hungry, wet, and tired. Guess I beat some sense into you after all. I got that done at least."

"I hate you, you know that, right?" It felt good to say it out loud, without screaming, suddenly I wasn't even angry. It just came out as fact. It's raining; I hate you.

He shrugged and then gasped, "Mhm." It looked like his captors had explained how they felt about their dead.

Would have been a miracle if they hadn't. He deserved worse.

"Had to. Had to be done. Head like yours, sometimes a man's got to break through to be heard. Had to make you ready.

Failed though, you ran off like a fool, years wasted."

"Ready for what? Wasted for what?"

The moment of clarity was gone as quickly as it had come. I wanted to hit him, make him feel what I felt. His back started shaking, him gasping. Like an addict on a high seizure. They do that sometimes, after the drug stops working, snort or smoke so much it kills the brain. He was just a drunk though, did drink do that? What do you do for someone when that happens? I didn't know. Didn't know if I wanted to help.

He gave off a choking rattle and I darted into the cell before I could make up my mind. Turning him over I was not sure what to do, but he was still my father and that couldn't be worth nothing.

He was laughing. Laughing and choking on it, spasms of mirth twisting whatever the watch had broken inside. Choking on the pain and still laughing. Eyes bulging…tears running down the lines of his face making tracks among the bruises, dried blood, and snot.

The first kick surprised us both, I think. It was really more of a stomp as my heel slammed down into his floating ribs, turning his wheezing into a dying rabbit squeal. The sound echoed through the boxed-in cell. He gaped like the landed fish. He'd lost most of his front teeth, raw red craters standing in their place. The second kick was more of a proper kick and was nearly soundless; he had no more air left. He tried to roll away but there was nowhere to go, just stone lined wall and hard packed dirt.

Some folks, they get up in the morning, the afternoon, whatever. They go to work, move boxes, sell trinkets, or gut mackerel. Whatever, they earn their coin and go home and then do it again the next day. They don't get in a fight but once or twice during a particularly rowdy celebration. Too much drink to walk away, not enough to sit back down. Spend enough time in other lines of work though, or every night dropping back tankards, and there's bound to be someone who thinks he can change his outcomes by the application of fists and the odd boot. Most of the time the two of you work out your differences and part ways with a little skin and blood. Then there's the other times. That's when the other guy brings his friends and they decide to impart a message. If you can't buy them all a drink and come to an agreement then you have two choices. Run, my personal favorite, or take it. The secret to taking a beating is actually pretty simple, curl up in a ball and try not to make them mad. Or as the man who taught me this said, "Tides take you boy, your mouth's goin' to get you killed, and no son of mine is going to talk back while I have a say!"

One of the regulars at Whistler's is a man that goes by Bolly. Maybe in his mid twenties, used to run a little dice on the side of one of the dens close to the boats. A couple years ago he got greedy with the crew of a triple deck privateer. In the middle of the discussion that followed, he pulled a knife. Their displeasure at the escalation broke most of the bones in his hands and he had blood pooling out of one ear. Somehow he didn't die, but about all he can do is unload crates and I haven't heard him speak two words together since. Better to take your bruises, fight another day.

Some lessons are harder in practice, I guess. It wasn't until the third or fourth kick that he stopped trying to get away and started covering his ribs. It didn't matter. I could taste blood from biting my tongue to keep from screaming. No words...nothing to say...just a desire to express pain, and the opportunity to do it. For a handful of seconds it was just the sound of booted foot thwacking into flesh. The sound of the butcher as he maneuvers a side of beef - dull smacks with an edge of bone crunching - until my father finally got his elbows down to cover. By then my rhythm was going and it was too late to pull the kick. My foot hit the sharp bony part of his elbow, driving it into cracked ribs one last time to a crunching pop.

Like kicking solid wood or finding the table leg with your bare foot in the dark, the sound echoed in my skull, more than in my ears, followed by a sharp pain piercing the haze of rage. Still without thought, I stepped back - trying to be human again - and instantly collapsed as my foot, followed by my knee, recoiled from the hurt.

From my new perspective on the floor I can't say the cell held more charms. My lungs were burning like I'd just run the length of the city. I was taking huge gulps of the dank cellar air, injured foot held to avoid the ground as my fists pounded at the dirt packed floor. Specks of spittle and blood foamed from my mouth. New pain had catalyzed the old pain into impotent rage that couldn't even express itself in violence.

"Goddess take you, hanging'll be too soon if you don't quiet down, you're like to wake folks up!"

Cold sweat washed away the mindless rage. Whoever owned that voice hadn't reached the door to the cells but I was seconds away from discovery. Right after that I was likely to get a room of my own followed by a double feature in the morning. The throbbing waves shooting up my boot focused my thoughts. In my head it was a scullery maid or a cook, some scrap-stuffed flunky roused out of a dead sleep. The sort of person who thinks yelling at a catfight will make everyone straighten up and slink away in silence so he can shuffle off back to the last hour of rest before he actually wakes. In a moment he'd see the propped open door, the open cell door, the glow of the lantern. By mutual agreement my limbs tensed, waiting for the moment of alarm before the sprint, the mad rush to get out of the collapsing circle. Nothing motivates the bored guard like the prospect of actually catching someone. It wouldn't be difficult.

…a grunt…

…and then the sound of the cook's slippered feet shuffling back to whatever cot and still warm blankets waited as he navigated blindly away. Goddess protect and keep that poor fool. May he have a long and fruitful life.

I've taken less time paying debts than I took crawling on all threes over to the candle stub. One last glance at my father, his eyes agate hard as he watched me, and then I snuffed the light and made my way out of the cells by feel. Whatever I wanted to know when I came here wasn't worth dying for, what was really? I even left the door open. He could escape if he had it in him. The spite in me thought about dropping the bar closed, but I was done, I didn't even owe him the effort to hurt him.

Experimentation taught me how to use my heel to shuffle hop with only a little more noise than I would have made. Retracing my way in, was exhausting and painfully slow in every sense. My good leg ached from the strain. The stairs were the worst. Whatever bloody snot-nosed social climber had designed the interior had decided the stairs were better off without rails. Try it sometime. Hop on one leg up a couple stories, stopping every step to listen for someone with a small bladder or the urge for an afterwards snack. By the time I reached the alcove with the cherub, sweat was dripping off my nose and I was giving full consideration to stabbing the Smoking Guard if he got creative with his patrol.

As it was, the options for getting past him unseen were limited. The reverse of my entry - a short sprint across and out the window - was out. Tucked away in the recesses of my new home in the alcove, I took shallow open-mouthed breaths and looked for inspiration. Some sort of distraction at the far end of his route would be a godsend. The gods don't send gifts like that much, and after the cook I wasn't expecting two in one night.

Ten feet from a clean escape. My foot felt like I had a lit coal instead of a toe. My legs were rubbery and my shirt was sticking to me under my jacket. I wanted to curl up somewhere behind a locked door and a blanket to rock myself to sleep. All in all, it had been the sort of night a man drinks to forget and I was done with it.

On the next pass, I waited for Smoking Guard to turn back the way he'd come. Then I picked up the cherub off its pedestal and over-handed it at the man's head. Some part of the poor fellow's brain heard the anguished grunt as I traded pain for leverage on the swing. He was turning as I brought the angel down with all the force I could muster. I felt a little bad about it afterward. Turns out, the thing was sand filled porcelain.

It exploded off the bridge of his nose, in a spray of shards and sand. Cut off of any instructions from the brain, his legs called it a day and he went down in a multi-limbed pile of guard. Sand rained down for a couple more heartbeats, but it was going to be a good long while before that man was smoking on watch again. Perhaps his wife would think the broken nose was dashing.

After that it was a simple matter to fasten my rope to the, now unemployed, pedestal and lower myself down. Losing the rope didn't make me happy, but given the costs I could have paid, I was prepared to call it even for the night.

A few hours later they hung my father. He was in no shape for dredging; I had no way of knowing if he tried to escape after me, but heard he could barely stand on the scaffold. Public executions are top tier entertainment dockside. Whatever he knew, he took with him to the mire. That night I drank until I passed out and left it to rest.

# FIFTEEN

Sylvie examined the tables around us as she talked, "Are you familiar with the Citadel Ring?"

Not much for her to see…a few patrons drinking away the day's work, freight men by the thick wool tunics and calloused hands. Closer to the fireplace an assortment of local stall owners and small ship officers; what passed for the well-off and wealthy this close to the water.

The Citadel Ring. The castles that line the vast field of ice squatting atop the world are a staple of what passes for bards. Easier to find an unclipped coin than a man or woman ignorant enough that they hadn't heard of the Citadel Ring. Someone, gods or men - maybe both, built them and lived in them for an age. There were a hundred, maybe more. I'd seen paintings, blocks of grey stone rising out of open ocean like support pillars for the sky. Built to defend against something, since they were castles, that wasn't a hard theory to find.  Other gods maybe, or another – stranger - race of men or monster they feared more than the endless slam of wave and howling wind. It was the sort of mystery that the learned spent a lifetime not answering.

A  few were scoured rubble, broken barnacle covered rock barely out of the water. Just the thing to rip out an unwary keel. Some looked as if the owners left for the afternoon. Sages noted the advance of glaciers where the fortresses were mere pilings of stone and claimed the Citadel Ring was a creation of elder forces to hold back the North Wind from covering the land with eternal howling emptiness.

Storytellers made their bread off of tales about doomed love and tragic last stands featuring the vanished peoples of the Ring. *The Lay of Captain Hogart, Farrels Lost Love,* and the decidedly bawdy *Estelle and Pauper Jack* were common favorites worth a dirham or two on long nights of sleet and rain. Pauper Jack was supposed to have found a den of mermaids and silk cushions to lure him away from his patient Estelle. Fish tailed women seemed unlikely, it was Captain Hogart's boat full of gold that motivated most listeners.

Every so often an expedition would sail north to pillage the wealth of those vanished people. Since the north seas could swallow ships and crush masts as the wind ate sails, mostly they came back empty…or not at all. Some came back with delicately carved ivory statues, skins of animals none could name, and dishes made of gold and pearl. Such items would make a man if he were able to settle on price and collect before Myrport stole his fortune away.

Even better tales could be told of the doubly rare objects that somehow held the forgotten magics of the vanished people. Powerful artifacts of unknown intent, invariably cursed. That was the fate of the wretch whose grave we spent so much time in. Until that night I would have put my money on some exotic disease borne of some equally remote tumble in one of the cities between Myrport and The Ring. Tides know there's a full range to be had locally. That was before I'd watched a Deepspawn burned to ash by flame gouting out of a man's mouth. Before I'd played catch-me-if-you can with a giant crab-headed man. Blame the gin, but I was prepared to give previous theories a second consideration.

"I've heard the usual. Songs and so on."

Sylvie made a face, solid bite of lemon, "That tripe? So, nothing useful. Are you familiar with the Tugali?"

"Nobody is familiar with the Tugali except the Tugali. Maybe not even them. They don't exactly wander the city. They guard the Temple of the Goddess. They don't leave the temple except to leave the city. Which they do by boats only they use. From what sailors say, those boats shouldn't be able to make it out of sight of land, but nobody I know is fool enough to claim to have been to the Tugali islands since they have a rather inhospitable tendency to skin and flay people who try."

I finished off my cup and refilled it.

"They reserve that for criminals, actually."

"Well, that's ok then." I said.

"They are very concerned about laws. The Tugali believe all of creation is governed by laws. In fact, life is a process of learning and then following the laws, which is why they guard the Temple Priestesses. Generations ago, before Myrport was founded, the Priestesses and the Tugali bound themselves to each other. The Tugali guard the temples from trespassers and the priestesses prevent any of the kingdoms from acting against their Tugali guardians.

"Nice. No king is going to risk an eternity at the mercy of the deep, and no thief is going to risk the Tugali."

"Exactly. Did you know that Tugali means, roughly, 'People of the Watch?' Most of those who do assume they took the name from their relationship with the Priestesses. In reality, it is far older than even that. The Tugali get their name from the Citadel Ring. They built it. Well, their ancestors did."

"Well that's that, you've had enough. No more drink for you. Shame you can't hold your booze, but there's no shame in it unless you keep drinking past your limits."

The skin of her cheeks flushed slightly, but her gaze was dry land firm.

"Look Sylvie, I don't care, but those men are scary as an executioner's axe, they eat the flesh of those they kill...and they can navigate the seas in what amounts to be an oversized canoe without a sail. What they don't do is make fortresses of stone without a seam and they definitely don't have anything to do with magic artifacts. Tides, they don't even work steel! They won't touch the stuff."

"It would be like you resorting to wearing furs and using torches." Sylvie replied softly.

"Excuse me?"

She looked at me like she was announcing the color of the sky, "Steel. They have no use for it."

"Sure. Look, what is it? Their gods forbid the use of fire? Glass or whatever is sharp, but what are they going to do with a breastplate and a sword?"

What can I say? Old habits break hard and my mouth tends to free roam around her.

"I have seen them shave slivers off a longsword with one of those knives. If armor was any use, do you think the temples would have withstood the likes of Black Alaric and his host?"

A couple generations back, a hardy chap from one of the inland nomadic tribes rounded up a few thousands of likeminded friends, threaded the mountain passes, and pretty much burned anything taller than a house foundation to the ground. Myrport escaped because there are no passes through the wall and the nomads turned out to be exceptionally bad at building boats. Sylvie was right though, not a single Temple of the Goddess was touched. After a few years the faithful called it a miracle, but writings of the time that survive talk of piles of bodies and moats that could be crossed without getting your feet wet…from water anyways.

She continued, "Something happened. They don't remember or aren't saying. The Tugali fled their fortresses and settled as far from them as they could, abandoning whatever charge they built those fortresses for. That is where the priestesses come in. Somehow the Goddess hides them from whatever they served before, whatever they fled from maybe. The People of the Watch live in fear of two things: If that pact ever breaks the Tugali believe that will be the end of their race, and if the ring fails that will be the end of the world. Maybe they are right. The Ring is failing and the glaciers are spreading wherever the fortresses have been destroyed."

She finished off this assessment by pouring herself a slug of gin and downing it while pinching her nose closed.

"Alright. That isn't very helpful. How do you know this? The Tugali don't speak to anyone. That's part of the shtick. Creepy, pale skin, cannibalism…if you're lucky, and stone silence."

"Not true," her voice was a little ragged, gin shots aren't for the uninitiated, "they talk to the priestesses."

Her eyes held mine like a forty-pound clamp. It made my

spine twist between my shoulders and my mind went quiet. For once it had nothing useful to offer. I wanted to stare and I wanted to chew my arm off to get away. Instead I was pinned to my seat by a pair of night-dark eyes that did nothing to explain.

"You are…were…a priestess? Is that even possible? That's not possible. Nobody leaves the service of the Goddess, what the Ocean takes, it keeps."

She answered with a thin-lipped smile and a shrug. Her normal assurance, easy forthrightness I'd admired in the tomb, was gone. The thought of her in the cowled woolen robes of the priestesses just didn't work. But then, maybe that was why they did it, after a while it was easy to stop thinking of them as people, as individuals. Just another unseen servant of the deity - interchangeable and effectively invisible.

For all that, they could take off the robe and who would ever know they were a priestess? Paranoia flashed over me in a damp sick sweat. I had visions of alluring young women luring lust addled roguish types (that's me) to their doom in cryptic sacrificial ceremonies. This was all some strange, excessively elaborate scheme to trap me in the commission of a heinous crime preparatory to a slow, hot coal agonizing torture, ending in ritualistic drowning. My hindbrain started screaming, "Get out!" Get. Out!" Fortunately I was drunk enough that my mouth got moving first. Usually that isn't a good thing for me.

"You're not…still one of them?"

The Tugali were rumored to eat the flesh of those foolish enough to enter the crypts, maybe the priestesses shared in their unholy repasts. There's a chance I was drunker than I thought I was, "I won't be sacrificed to your, or anyone's god, even for you."

She blanked for a second, flat footed as a sleeping watchman. Then a giggle turning into a snort, that she couldn't quite hold back and then dissolved into laughter…howling stomach cramping peals of laughter. People started to glance and then stare as she subsided into giggles. Every time she started to get it under control, she'd glance at my face and start over until tears were streaking her face and breathless wheezing replaced the giggles.

Somewhere in the middle I grasped that I was being exceptionally stupid. My best bar room glare convinced the gawkers to return their attentions back to their drinks and the troubles they were quenching. Then I folded my arms and waited for Sylvie to recover. It's an occupational hazard, I spend a lot of time telling myself to shut up and get back to business. Blame the stress of the moment and the gin. After a few deep breaths she sat back up and crinkled a smile at me. It made her nose even cuter.

"No. No, I'm not, not anymore. Long story, suffice to say we have parted ways and the temple wouldn't be any happier to see me than they would you."

She got my best eyebrow.

"I promise there will be no sacrificing; no secret altars. Not even for me." The sidelong glance I got, told me she was going to remember. Call me Lord Smooth. "I am sorry, it is just so absurd. The Goddess is not well pleased by human sacrifice."

"Well, since you're the expert, I guess I'll have to take your word for it. I don't suppose the part about the Tugali and eating human flesh is wrong too?"

"No, that part is correct."

"That's unfortunate. So…why?

"Why, what?"

"Why leave, why go back after you left? Is this some sort of revenge thing? Revenge is unhealthy, you know."

My mouth was leading again. Time to stop it before I got really offensive. A mouthful of gin helped.

"I was thirteen. There was a boy, blond, green eyes. He was older, fifteen, maybe more. He was apprenticed to one of my father's clerks. All summer I swanned about, trying to…Ah, trying to get him to notice me. Eventually he did…as did my father. He was livid. My mother was horrified. She went to bed, overcome by the stress. I cried myself to sleep for a week. The clerk couldn't be fired, his family and mine had been partners since my father was a clerk in their house. Their fortunes waned as our waxed.

There was no question of allowing the match, but old debts are the hardest to pay. As he usually did, my father charted a path between the rocks and the shoals, between family honor and the rules of society. All that was required was a place to put me where I was no longer a liability to his business affairs."

She paused for a moment, sipped at the gin and made a show of scraping her tongue off with her teeth.

Families often get rid of unhelpful daughters that way, you know. Some find the Goddess and perhaps, happiness

The first few years are spent in seclusion, prayers, study, healing arts, history, and so on. At the end of the fourth year the sisters who find favor meet the Goddess. The ones that do not, serve in whatever ways their talents and the order's needs require. A lifetime of mopping, emptying chamber pots, and other, less palatable, tasks. Many of the girls chose a third option."

"Mopping isn't that bad, I did that for a month once, for, um, this thing."

I was just a market stall gossip. Pretty soon I'd be telling her about losing a fight to Mudface Horace when I was eight and how I'd named my favorite set of picks. That last part may or may not be true…Sarah.

"Perhaps, I will take your word for that. Regardless when it came time, I saw the goddess."

She paused and examined the bottom of her mug.

I'm not sure what I expected, like most in my line of business, the gods are remote sorts who, with three exceptions, don't have much play in your average day. Those three exceptions aren't exactly the sort of influence a sane man seeks out, come to that. Even so, on occasion, I'd met people who were as hands-on with the gods, as I was with their money. When those meetings weren't focused on "Stop! Thief!" they were often quite vociferous in their faith. Sylvie acted as if she'd been caught skipping rope or playing dress up.

"That was good, right? No mopping." I said.

The smile that earned was third rate, at best.

"It should have been. Novitiates who see the Goddess tell

different versions of how it works. The aspect changes, of course, the Goddess of the Tides tends to reflect the ocean she represents, the giver of life, the raging storm, the calm sunny merchant's pathway, and the scouring land eating wave. But more than that, what they experience, how they experience it differs in the telling. For some women it is just an appearance, perhaps a feeling of love. For others she has been known to set a task, or give a warning to the temple through the novitiate. Regardless, that moment, that personal touch with the deity, is what makes a priestess. In different places and times the ceremony or the preparations have changed, but the essential union has been the same for as long as there have been temples of the Goddess.

These days the ritual is quite elaborate, so much so that the actual manifestation almost seems an afterthought. In the weeks before the end of the fourth year the girls undergo a relentless series of fastings, prayer, and purification; all the while stone-faced women with tongues like hammers remind you of duty."

"What was the third option? Why do all that?" I said.

Her nose crinkled in amused disgust, "Life as a Tugali bride hardly seemed an improvement."

"Oh. So. Priestess, mopping, or…" Even half drowned in gin, my mouth wasn't quite bold enough to contemplate what being married to a tribal mercenary would be like for the pampered daughters of the rich and powerful. Sylvie waited patiently while I tried to envision an island paradise of bloody-minded men festooned with translucent blue blades and their merchant princess wives minding the home fires while roasting hapless sailors. I shook my head clear, "That doesn't explain you though. You saw her."

"The folly of men? Or women, I suppose. The Goddess has been worshipped, more or less continuously since before the kingdoms. There are references in some of the oldest writings, on scrolls that can no longer be rolled up for fear of destruction, of a time when the Citadel Ring forts were still occupied. That sort of history leads a bit more to pomp and ceremony than faith or observance."

"I'm guessing the priestesses weren't fond of observations like that either."

There was no indication of where she was going with all this, but I'd read worse, the poetry of Sophont Glissone, also known as 'Gassy Glissone' came to mind.

"They have creative ways to discourage those, yes. Idle minds are best repaired with a scrub brush and acres of flagstones." Her lips twisted at that, told as a joke but felt as pain. It hurt to watch. "Surf and Shoals...I learned to hate those hours. Learned to keep my thoughts to myself as well. What the sisters forgot, in countless generations of ritual, generations of repetition, is that Priestess or Servant are not the only aspects that she chooses for the devoted. In different, more turbulent times, some sisters were chosen as champions; they were her hands, just as Priestesses are her mouth."

My stomach burrowed down as far as it could go. As a general rule, people who went around doing the bidding of gods don't buy a big house overlooking the city and grow old. They were either running cons or died horribly. Depending on whether you were seeing them in person or reading a book. She wasn't running a scam, that I knew. Which meant it was more the book scenario. Brutal, hideous death. Somehow I suspected whatever her fate, they wouldn't give the people with her a pass. It sure explained the suicide run into the crypts though. I was looking like exactly the sort of person I'd tried not to be.

"So, that's you then, champion or whatever they call them? Paladin? I read that in a book once." I said.

It might kill me, but I still wanted to help, to have her think I was helping. Her smile was all teeth. That and a raised eyebrow.

"Tsk, Expert, who is telling the story here?"

"Not my fault you're slow."

Her other eyebrow shot up at that. But rather than respond she continued.

"My turn came, and I was grateful. Truthfully, I was a terrible novice. I'd stopped pining somewhere in my fourteenth year, but I hated it with the special rancor only possible in frustrated love. So I sulked…for months.

It wasn't a bad life, prayers for any excuse at all, lessons, I was good at that and I liked the history - the traditions - but mostly I was a ball of bitterness, prone to leak if the wind shifted."

Her raised eyebrow invited comment, but I waved her on.

"Some days I would forget and it wasn't so bad. Most of the other girls seemed to think it wasn't. Of course many of them were there willingly, or at least resigned to it. Some, like my friend Felity, dreamed their whole lives of joining the temple. She used to talk of the feeling, the sense of purpose she got from it. The thought of spending the rest of my life hiding behind the cowl and working the faithful for tithes…becoming the gray faceless robe until I was as interchangeable as the rest of the sisters? Better to throw myself into the waves. At the time it seemed like something that happened to someone else, I couldn't ever think I would do it.

When the time came, I thought about refusing. I wonder what they would have done? Imagine the look on their faces. Faces I'd never seen. Over the years I'd given them features for how I felt about them. Sister Dellore was a giant, nearly six feet with shoulders broader than a man's and hands to match - I gave her a elder's navel length beard and a single eyebrow. Sister Ellery always carried candies she would share as she taught, for answers both correct and wildly imagined – In my mind she had brown, soulful, eyes and pudgy cheeks. Sister Fann I gave warts. Each time she assigned me chores, to "allow me to reflect," I gave her more. She was pretty much all wart.

Felity convinced me to go through with it. She had been accepted the year before, but still came and talked when she was able…usually as I was scrubbing flagstones or washing turnips. The sisters felt I needed to cultivate more respectful habits, so I did my best not to. She was so convinced…so sure. I didn't expect to see the Goddess – wasn't even sure I believed. Saying things like that to Felity made her cry. So instead of running away to a life of piracy, I resolved to last as long as I could, and then I would march out with my head held…well, not high.

By the time the day came I was half crazed. Mad with the fasting hunger, cold to the bone, throat smoke-raw, and kneecaps turned to mush from days of kneeling. The room was a perfect circle, domed at the ceiling with smoothly plastered walls. A statue of the Mother, big enough to dwarf Sister Dellore (not a very good likeness as it turned out), some small pots for incense, and the door. Barred shut - as tradition prescribed. The only way out was to commune with the Goddess or give up. In my mind I could see the looks of satisfaction on the Priestesses.

By nightfall, I had worked myself into a rhythm and stopped checking the non-existent corners of the room. Truth of it was, I half expected to see some priestess in costume leaping out and playing the role. How that would be managed I hadn't really worked through and I don't remember what I'd envisioned it would be like; a clap of thunder and a beam of light from above, undoubtedly. The sort of thing poets write verse about. Instead, one moment I was alone in the sanctum, knees and voice raw in an endless cycle of chanting and prostration before a representation of Her in her aspect of the life giving tide, and the next she was there. Leaning against the stone version of herself. She was about equal in size but that was the only similarity. Instead of a simple smooth robe, she was wearing a multilayer dress of fabric that scraped and rubbed like a wavelet spending itself on the sand.

I heard the sound and kept chanting for a few more moments as it worked its way through my head. If there had been a scrap of food or water in me I might have lost it. Once I put the spoons with the forks, it didn't take but a moment for me to realize I was in the presence of the Mist Queen, Lady of Tides, Mother of the World. The previous four years spent learning to serve and scrubbing anything that wouldn't dissolve at the touch of a brush was for that moment."

Sylvie paused to take a sip.

While she gathered her thoughts, I got the attention of one of the serving girls and a few moments later a loaf of fire warmed oat bread graced the table. I licked my fingers and tore off a chunk, dipped it in the bowl of oil that came with the bread, and then sprinkled it with salt before stuffing it into my mouth in one go. Sylvie watched and then followed my lead but forgot to lick her fingers. She dropped the loaf, blowing furiously on her fingers.

"Careful, hot," around a mouthful of bread sounds a lot like the rumble of a bull seal. Not really helpful, I shrugged off her half injured, half accusing glare and washed down the bread, "It's hot, they bake them the day before, if we're lucky, and warm them in the fire so it doesn't taste stale. Lick your fingers, like so."

I demonstrated again. Once the taste of the oil hit her tongue she came close to decorating the table with it. Finally she poured the rest of her gin on top of it and swallowed the rest.

"That. Is. Vile."

Fish oil might be an acquired taste, the salt helps, but since most people who acquire it can't afford salt, the best seasoning is poverty.

"Don't be a snob, you just need more salt. Also gin kills the taste."

"Yes, I figured that part out."

"So what was it like?" I said.

"What was what..? Oh. Strange, of course. Stranger because I was adjusting to the idea that she was real, while trying to remember all of the proper forms of address and making a wreck of it and knowing I was making a wreck of it."

I made a noise somewhere between a snort and a cough.

"Truth! Goddess strike me," She held up one hand with her pinky crooked. It took me a second to realize it wasn't some arcane gesture.

"Oh sure, isn't that blasphemy? Heresy? I could never keep them straight."

"Blasphemy. It was terrible, I'm still not sure if she didn't notice or she didn't care. Whichever. I forgot some of her titles. Compacted several more into entirely new ones, and didn't realize I'd forgotten the genuflection until she was gone."

"I gather she didn't send you howling into the depths."

"No. She waited through me calling her the Mist World and Mother of the Lady and then she asked me if I was happy."

"Happy?" I said.

"Daughter, are you happy in my service?' Her exact words. I was terrified. I knew I wasn't, and I knew I couldn't lie. So I said 'no' and waited to be destroyed."

"So, not destroyed?"

She laughed. There was an echo of something, some jubilation left over from the moment in that laugh. That was when I believed her. "I spoke to a god" was on the outer edges of quirks I would normally tolerate. It was time to give myself a good shake and possibly a slap or twenty. But that was what I'd been doing for the last three days, wasn't it? Counting bottles of bad gin as slaps, I'd gone through at least twenty. Other than premature pickling, it hadn't really changed anything. My boat was navigating without lights, way past time to fire the helmsman and correct.

"What happened then?" Is what I said instead. I was in trouble; Sylvie kept making me think things. Definitely bad company to keep.

"We talked. It was like, talking to your mother."

"Pretty sure my mother can't wipe cities away if I don't clear my plate."

"Now who is the blasphemer? Actually, the flooding of cities and sinking of boats is where I come in..."

"I would like to offer my most sincere apologies for anything I may have said or implied."

"Too little, too late, Expert. No, can I borrow the bottle?"

The best squint-eyed gaze I could muster didn't dissuade her so she refilled my cup before handing it over. She corked it and then set it label down on the table.

"Our Lady of Tides has power that makes men tremble and moves mountains."

"Yes, that's the Goddess part."

She ignored the interruption, "The difficulty lies in the exercise of that power. Take your example of washing away the

House of Hebrinda, and consequently the city of Hebroak at the height of their conquest. What the legends and songs don't mention, is the near simultaneous leveling of a series of coastal kingdoms on the far side of the ocean expanse."

She tilted the bottle, the gin shifted to the neck.

"In order to amass the force needed, a price was paid by peoples whose doings and lives were never involved in those wars."

She twisted the bottle sending the gin rushing and splashing against the bottom.

"When Hebrinda pillaged and desecrated the Temples of the Goddess, sending the sisters defiled into slavery, he thought the bargains he had made would protect him from her wrath. He was wrong and suffered for it, but so too did even more innocents."

"She wants me to prevent that, if I can. The temple holds the keystone to the fortress that sustains the Citadel Ring. It was taken and if it isn't returned, Another part of the Citadel Ring will fail. Eventually the whole thing will fall and the North Wind will be free. If that happens, the Deepspawn will no longer be hidden from the surface, no longer be hidden from the servants of their Father. Even the most talentless hack would have access to monstrosities that have lain hidden from all but the mightiest and most corrupt practitioners. Anyone with the desire and willingness to bargain with their Father could have armies of them."

"How hard can it be? There were two there the other night." I said.

"The spawn are kept hidden, the Mother forbids them access to her waters, so they must go…around. It's complicated, more Isaac's area than mine, but with enough power it is possible to bend the world. Twist the boundaries of what is and isn't. The rituals involved are blood rites, murder and worse. The North Wind is only too happy to assist, but even so cracking those barriers holds many dangers, more than enough to twist minds and kill those who try. Just learning the methods left me needing a bath for a week. I don't want to know how those two were obtained. We should hope we don't meet whoever was responsible. It is only with the weakening of the Ring that such things are possible. Without the Ring, the ending of the world might be a kindness."

"What about Isaac and Lye?"

I'd seen Isaac burn a Deepspawn to the ground with fire gouting from his mouth. It's the sort of thing that makes an impression with bystanders.

Sylvie's expression twisted my stomach, "Someone like that could flay the skin from you with a word and deposit your fluids in a cup with another. And that would be a best case outcome."

"That's a hell of a pep talk."

The sort of talk that called for a drink...and another bottle after that.

"Power like that takes a lifetime to gather and a willingness to sacrifice. Usually, everyone around them." She said.

"What does all this have to do with you anyway? If it's at the temple, why not knock on the door and ask for it? That takes some of the fun out, but sometimes the easiest break in is through the front door."

"Ah, well, I'll just have to take your word on that. The temples are founded on millennia of tradition. For a thousand years girls have gone into the chamber of communion and come out as priestesses. Before that, when the tribes that became the Coastal Kingdoms were still carving out their traditions and lineages from the wilderness, through the time of Hebrinda's Conquest, the worship of the Goddess was split into three parts instead of the two now. Some of the sisters were called to bear arms in the Lady of Tides' service."

"They had an army?"

Sylvie grinned, "Spreading the faith was more vigorous, I gather."

"I guess! So what happened?"

"The Kingdoms happened. Eventually the kings and tyrants converted and, with them, their people. Ministering to the devoted was more pressing than the few faiths that remained. Healing and the like. So when I lifted the bar to the sanctum and told the waiting priestess what the Goddess had said, well the reaction was not what I expected."

"No?"

Sylvie paused. Her lips were tight and she was even paler than normal. Just because you've decided to say something doesn't make the saying easy. The desire to lighten the moment burbled up inside but I kicked it down like a too aggressive alley beggar.

"They tried me for heresy."

The silence started and I knew I should say something, something comforting. My mouth was open but I couldn't come up with the words. The beggar offered jokes, but I couldn't; anything like that would cut us both. It was a hugging moment. Or I wanted it to be. My ears got warm and I sat rooted to my chair at the thought of how awkward it would be if she didn't want one. I'm not a hugger anyway.

So, instead: silence. Drawn out and eroding the moment, the longer it sat there.

I started looking for one of the serving girls as her statement hung there between us…twisting, but even that was pointless. It was later than I'd thought. Half sober instead of half drunk, out of gin, and the place was cleared out. It was surprising they hadn't started the shooing out and cleaning up.

"How is it heresy? If she can talk to you, she can talk to them, right?"

A small smile, "Not quite that simple. Talking to the Goddess requires weeks of purification, fasting, and prayer. It was a little bit easier to decide that I was lying; I hadn't exactly made friends. There was a trial. They talked about me while I sat and listened to my peers say things true and untrue about my attitude and my actions. The truth was the hardest part, of course. The ones who made up stories of me sneaking out for this or that assignation were ridiculous. When someone tells you what a bad person you've been and you realize it's true, that's hard."

"It's not so bad. Just hold on to their things and keep running."

"Hah! Point taken. I think I was a little more concerned with their opinion. Though I told myself I wasn't."

"What do they do with heretics?"

"Ritual drowning in Her waters. I was given a choice, recant and spend the rest of my life in atonement, or a lot more water than is good for you."

"What changed their minds?"

"They didn't. I wouldn't recant. The High Priestess pronounced my guilt, sentenced to be carried out at the changing of the tide on the new moon. They stripped me of my novice robes and threw me in a cell. It was a low moment."

"Never liked cells either. Hazard of the profession."

Her cheeks dimpled. "I imagine so. Felity got permission to visit me after a couple days and got me clothes. At first she tried to convince me to recant as well. I told her what the goddess told me and she was the first one I think that actually listened. Eventually she believed me and helped me escape. I got the first passage away from Myrport I could. I only came back when Isaac traced the Keystone back here."

"What happened to Felity?"

Any humor drained like a busted keg. "I don't know. If they caught her, they would have drowned her as well. Otherwise she could still be there."

"So we commit religious sacrilege by breaking into the Temple guarded by an ancient race of bloody-minded fanatical warriors where you are condemned to die, find and steal this Keystone, and then somehow get it back to the ancient fortress on the edge of the ice on the northern tip of the world?"

"Yes, that sounds about right." She could laugh with her eyes.

"Sounds like the sort of thing my father would have disapproved of, with a stick. When do we start?"

"A couple days, a week maybe. Hospur needs to be fit, and we could use a better plan than 'break into the crypt, make our way up into the temple, steal the keystone, run.' Of course the longer we wait, the more likely they'll find out I'm back. If they do, they'll be duty bound to bring me back to face judgment and I like breathing air."

"The bar is closing up soon. I'm renting a place upstairs, so they let me be."

That sounded more like a pickup line than I meant it and I felt the blood swirl in my ears. Humiliating myself was a valid way out, right?

"I mean, if you want to talk about it we'll need to leave." I said.

She quirked an eyebrow at me, "We haven't been here that long, these places aren't famous for early closing times are they?"

If asked, I'm sticking to excessive drink as my excuse for not putting it all in the right slots before that. Of course, sober or drunk it's been noted that I would have correctly identified the near empty common room and total lack of staffing for what it was. Given that the normal method for getting the besotted clientele out the door involves yelling and a stick. Besides, I was dry as sand by then.

"Ever been in a bar fight, Sylvie?" I settled my right hand on my dagger and shifted my left to the neck of the empty bottle.

# SIXTEEN

The man who'd made me the un-refusable offer, at the point of an enraged sawclaw, walked in after a few tense moments.

The doors were a repurposed mismatched couple, like most barroom pairings. The one on the left looked like it had seen better days uphill. It stuck any time it rained, so always. I heard it rattle and looked up in time to see him shift to the other door and duck his way inside.

The books I read suggested that leading from the front was a quality to be prized. On the docks, it was a good way to ingest all manner of pointed objects. He was either a fool or Sylvie and I were in far worse trouble than I'd hoped. From where I sat I could see the entrance to the kitchen and I kept one eye there while I waited for the other shoe to hit the ground.

He was still wearing the worn leather pants and brown jacket. Very casually, he took a second to scan the room while flicking water of his coat.

Not much to see there, a couple passed out drinkers, me, and Sylvie. She was perched so far forward on her chair it was a mere formality to call it sitting instead of a crouch. She hadn't answered my question, but she was ready and I had to give her points for nerve. It's a hard thing to sit with your back to someone you know is about to start a fight. Her face was set in a small smile and her eyes were locked on me, trusting me for the queue she needed. That's a strange thing, looking into the eyes of someone putting that much trust in you; my head felt a little light.

He appeared satisfied with the layout of the room and adopted that same tight lipped smile I remembered before threading slowly towards us. I waited for more muscle to follow him through the door, but he either wasn't going to kill me now or wanted to talk and then kill me...or thought he could handle Sylvie and I, by himself...or Sylvie wasn't what she said - I squelched that line before I could spiral off into any more paranoia. With the same care I'd use putting down a freshly cut pane of glass I folded my hands in front of me. If he wanted to talk, that was space I could use. I got an eyebrow from Sylvie and then she leaned back with the same care.

"Here for a drink? Pull up a chair. My bottle's empty but I'm sure you can get one from," I made a show of looking around the room, "well, nobody I guess."

Little lines appeared around Sylvie's eyes as she fought to keep her expression bland…stewed fish in milk, bland. Clar's hatchet man didn't even look at me. With one foot he hooked a chair and then settled into it without checking its position. He leaned to one side and spat a viscous black stream into the matting. Definitely not making friends with the help with that habit. I could probably rid us of him by arming a few of the staff who had to clean the floors.

"You made a deal, Clar war'n pleased by how things played." He said.

"About that…" I stopped. He wasn't looking at me. Sylvie looked like a child who stole candy and got pig fat instead. Spit it out and endure the laughter or swallow a greasy lump of pork gristle? Whatever deal she'd made was due.

"Is that the case? Maybe Clar didn't hold up his end. We didn't get fifty feet before he was nearly killed." She said.

That earned me a quick glance, "Neither her'n there. Clar wants his cut."

"Tell Clar to ask Dugal for it." I said.

"Yeah'n about that, Dugal'n been seen since he went with you."

"That is neither here nor there, as you so precisely put it. There was no gold to split, so no need to complicate things. You lent us Renn here, and now the job is done."

There was exactly no chance that Clar and his enforcer didn't either know or suspect that Dugal was dead. And if they knew, or suspected strongly enough, why was this conversation happening when he could send in a handful or ten of thugs to have an entirely different conversation? Our previous meeting had shown him to be direct. Frighteningly so.

"Clar does'n think you were completely straight with him." He said.

"And if I wasn't?" She'd begun tapping at the table with her fingernail. Screaming in my head for her to knock it off and not antagonize the sort of man who chops fingers off for coming in a little short on the rent - was having exactly the effect you'd expect. More proof of the uselessness of prayer, as if I needed it.

"I'm think'n you killed Dugal and you think Clar'n do anything cause of your family."

That earned him a quick scowl, "My family isn't a factor, as you know. As it happens, your man attacked us. Is that an extra service or just part of the deal?"

"Niether her'n there. Clar wants his cut."

"No, he doesn't" Sylvie froze, mouth open, and both of them locked on to me. "Fish or cut bait, as they say. Not sure why they say that. You want bait, cut your own." I was stalling while my brain caught up. "Clar already knows about Dugal, tides, probably knows Dugal tried to make a second deal of his own. Which is why you're sitting there instead of letting Gev and whoever else talk to us."

The man's squint, as he factored me back into the equation, told me I was right. That still didn't explain all of it though. He'd been honest, all that was really neither here nor there. Clar would be perfectly content to insist on his cut anyway. And he'd do so in the time honored dockside way, a little muscle, some pointed questions, and a discreet trip to the mud underneath the docks. We hadn't walked out with riches. In fact, the only thing we'd walked out with was the artifact Isaac and Hospur wrested from the skeletal grip of the Vevoda's scion. The key as Sylvie had called it.

And it had been looking like such a lovely evening.

The artifact was the key to the Keystone. Without it, the keystone would be so much useless rock for any fool who made it past the Tugali. Assuming there had been any. A couple times a year the remains of some overly ambitious thief decorated a wall in lower Myrport. Since urban improvement isn't a big thing, it stays there until the scavengers and time remove it. For a season or two there's usually a stain to mark the passing of the unwise.

Sylvie would swallow a whale before she gave the key to Clar. Which was ok with me, Clar would only want it for two reasons: Someone who knew what it was wanted it badly - hard currency badly - or Clar knew, and had a reason to stop us. Either was reason enough.

"It doesn't matter, there's no cut to split. So now you can run along back to your master, don't let the door hit you on the way out. The one on the right." I said.

It was petty, but since he was going to try and kill us as soon as he figured out he couldn't bully it out of us, I was alright with petty.

"You know'n doesn't work like that." He left another oily black glob on the matting, "Make this hard'n I'll make it slow."

"That matters? Does that work on people? Dead is dead, the way I see it, and the way I see it you aren't getting anywhere here."

The muscles in his jaw bunched up and he leaned in with both hands on the table. His gloves were the same worn brown leather, he was far too fond of that color. "Look here'n listen good. You give me what you got'n you maybe get a chance to get on a boat'n don't come back. Otherwise, I call out'n that'll be the end of that."

Sylvie gave me no hints. Her face was stiff, jaw slightly forward, but she seemed content to let me do the talking. The thing was to get him out the door and make our break while he was busy coordinating the rush. The docks are a warren of dead ends, hidden passages, and alleys to nothing in the daylight. At night it becomes outright confusing. Losing them would be like mugging a dead man. Waiting for them to come in would be bad.

"Dugal was the smart one I take it. Small words then. No. Tides carry you off. Travel with the wind in your face. Don't stop running at the pier."

He chewed his jaw a couple times, looked at Sylvie, back at

me, and forced his face into that toothless smile. Smooth as a slime puddle he stood, backed out of range and walked quickly to the doors. He paused, spat, then slipped out the door.

The moment the door closed I was up and headed towards the stair, slowing only to grab Sylvie by the hand. She started to draw her sword with the other but stopped when I motioned. Having sharp objects flailing about is not a safe way to climb out windows. We took the stairs two at a time. The door crashed as we reached the landing. Not good, I'd been hoping for longer.

There was a brief pause as the thugs were confronted by a functionally empty room. From the sound there were a couple handfuls downstairs. The sort of crew that'll pick up a dagger and kill someone in a bar with witnesses aren't exactly thinkers. They were milling about, checking the drunks, and arguing with the new arrivals from the back door.

"Well?" Sylvie half whispered, half hissed.

She'd trusted me this far, I had to hope she wasn't afraid of heights or she wasn't going to like my plan.

Instead of answering I tried the first door. The room I'd been using as an excuse to stay up all night drinking was at the far end and I wanted to hold the top of the stairs if it came to it. The Insane Three had their gaze averted, the door wasn't latched. It swung smoothly in to a low ceilinged bed and table sized room. The occupant was passed out face first in the straw. Boots still on, he was going to hate the morning.

With one hand I nudged Sylvie toward the window while I tested the table with the other. In a moment the committee downstairs was going to come to the correct conclusion.

"Shut it!" A loud bawl cut off the bickering, "They is either up or down, Hepper's crew came in the back, they didn't go that way. We came in the front..."

"What do you know, Danl? Nobody..."

Whoever it was cut off by a loud cracking, probably a chair being used to elect Danl.

"Hepper, you lot check the cellar, We'll go up."

Sylvie came back from the window. Her jaw was set again

and her lips had nearly vanished.

"What? Little busy here." I said.

I was trying to maneuver the table to the top of the stair without barking our location out on the walls and floor.

"You need help."

"No, I need you out that window."

Danl was arguing with his troops. They were dumb but not dumb enough to think leading the charge was going to be healthy.

"I'm not leaving you to die because of me." She said.

"If you stay we both die. Look, even if we held them off eventually they'd just start a fire downstairs. Possibly with their thugs still inside."

She looked shocked, "They wouldn't."

"How did you even meet these people? Go. We can argue about it once we're out that window."

By then I had the table tipped up at the top of the stair, balanced so if I let go it would fall. It was dark hardwood; built to be abused by cheap drinkers. Just the thing for what I had in mind.

Sylvie hopped up on the bed, danced past the comatose occupant, shoved her sword belt through the hole, followed by her torso. That's when the selection process downstairs wrapped up.

"Horace, you get up those stairs or I'll tie your guts around your neck!"

Horace turned out to be a short, thick, man with an overbite and a bad case of baldness he was trying to correct with long hair. He ducked his head around the wall to fast to see anything and, when he didn't draw fire, came back around for a better look.

"Hello Horace." I said.

No reason not to be civil.

He looked confused for a second. Then he placed a boot on the first step.

"I wouldn't do that, Horace."

Horace took another step. Since he wasn't dead yet, his friends started to edge up behind him. The tallest one pushing the others forward I guessed to be Danl. He'd lost an eye and the surgeon hadn't sewn the lids shut leaving an angry red crater. Danl was armed with a boathook that he'd sharpened and mounted on a pole. Holding it sideways to push any stragglers ahead. That sort of ingenuity was likely to either get him knifed in his sleep or promoted. Maybe both.

Horace didn't feel like talking and knives at your back is always a reason to be twitchy. He took the next couple steps quickly and then started to rush the last few. So I let go of the table and launched it forward with a kick.

Horace's reflexes were quick, if misguided. He caught the table in mid-stride. For a brief moment he wrestled with it and then took a step back to balance. If he hadn't been halfway up a flight of stairs he would have been fine. Instead he fell back into the mob racing up after him. It was an avalanche of arms, legs, and sharp objects. Danl managed to duck back, clearing the way for the clump to come to a sprawling, bleeding, stop at the floor.

Sylvie had cleared the window. She was crouched out on the roof watching me through my exit. One glance to make sure the crowd at the bottom wasn't going to catch me with my butt halfway out and I ran up, over the bed, drunk occupant and all, and dove for the opening.

"Ow! What in storm and deep!" So not completely comatose, "Wait! Who? Help Thief! Innkeep!"

I am not a large man. This is an asset in my line of work. In this case it meant that I could shimmy through a window frame that couldn't have been much larger than a foot. Then my hips jammed. As I was trying to squirm through I felt a pair of hands clutch my leg. Sylvie was crouched next to me and I grabbed her arm.

"Pull!" I grunted.

She raised an eyebrow and then set her feet against the lintel and threw her back into it, "Should lay off the drink, Expert. Makes you fat!"

"Not. Fat. Aiugh!"

I don't know why the drunk bit me. Maybe in revenge for

stepping on him, maybe he was still so drunk he thought I was a ham hock.

Sylvie stopped laughing at me and just about dislocated my shoulders throwing herself backwards to get me out. For my part I started flailing both legs to dislodge the newly carnivorous drunk. My free foot finally connected with his temple and he let go with a moan. Sylvie sat back like someone had pulled her chair out and I slid forward in a cresting wave of shingles. They never did get the roof repaired right, it leaked for years after that.

Visions of plummeting over the side, ended in a tangled pile of Sylvie, me, and broken shake.

"Drinking doesn't make you fat. This is punishment for blasphemy. Ow. Is my leg bleeding? That mud crawler bit me!"

"You did break into his room and walk on his head."

"Still doesn't call for biting. Ow. Careful, I'm going to need that hand later."

"If you don't move it, you're not going to have it later." She said.

From inside the sounds of Danl mustering the troops for another ascent reminded me of the maxim: the chase is over when they give up, not before. From the voices it looked like Hepper and his team had rejoined them.

I fished some linen out of a pocket, tied off the bite, and crawled the rest of the way to the roof edge to take a look. If I were going to murder a pair of people inside of a building, I'd post a few less disposable henchmen outside, just in case. It was hard to decide between being gratified at my friend in brown's caution or being slightly horrified that we thought alike.

The side of the building faced on an open, squarish, area comprised of a series of floating docks shoved together and laced up with scraps of rope. Later repairs were accomplished with typical dockside priorities; as cheaply and quickly as possible. The entire thing sagged toward the middle and plunging an ankle through a gap was a common hazard. Normally something like it would be built over faster than you can say, "Who needs a deed?" The locals kept that from happening by running a more or less permanent open market in the space. At night the stalls were cleared of goods and the small merchants took it in turn to patrol the space to prevent entrepreneurial land grabs.

Those worthies had been chased off by my long lost gambling partner, Gev. He was standing smack in the middle of the lowest point of the square holding a ship's lantern and bellowing ignorable orders at the crew inside the tavern. Doubtful they could hear the giant anyways.

Next to Gev was a man so fat it looked like the mail shirt he wore would rupture at any point, showering the surrounding stalls in shards of painfully stressed metal. The last time Gobineau and I had met, I'd burned his warehouse down. Well, we hadn't met, and if he knew it was me who'd torched years of graft, theft, and extortion my life wouldn't have been worth the spit he'd lose ordering me dead.

It was him though, and he was working with the people currently trying to do the job which made for some unpleasant conclusions. Lowtown politics worked on the same theory as a school of barracuda. The moment someone thought you looked like dinner any previous arrangements went down under a swarm of teeth and self-interest.

If Clar and Gobineau were working together, that was an exceedingly fine argument to catch the next thing that floated out of town. The lantern Gev held kept them from seeing us; it was time to finish the escape. I crab walked back away from the eave, tapped Sylvie's arm, and scuttled around the roof away from the window. The sounds of Danl's crew, charging back up the stairs, floated out of the window as we passed.

As soon as I couldn't see the lantern, I moved into a crouch for more speed. The men inside were going room to room shouting as they failed to find us. Moving in a half crouch run, we rounded the corner heading directly away from the market square. I was following a memory from a couple days previous when I'd walked down a narrow side alley toward the tavern. Just as I remembered, the tavern stood close up against a series of low flat-roofed structures. Maybe shops, maybe houses, what mattered was the short gap between the roof we were on and them.

"Get out there!" That was Danl.

Things were about to get crowded up top.

A couple deep breaths and a short sprint later I sailed over the gap. I hit the far roof with a tuck and roll and then turned to help Sylvie. She was standing at the corner. Someone smashed a window on the side facing me and a head popped out a second later.

"Time to go!" I called to Sylvie.

It was too dark to see her face but her head shake was answer enough.

"Oi! They's over here!" Bawled the woman with her head out the window.

I grabbed a pry knife from my boot and overhanded it at her. It bounced off the frame and she ducked back. No sense wasting a good weapon.

"So? Get out there!" That was Danl again, from the sound of it he'd run out the front.

"Suck seal bladder Danl! I ain't getting half out that window to get my throat slit."

So much for a speedy escape across the rooftops. Sylvie had her sword out and was facing off the way we'd come. Someone probably made it through one of the windows. The crack of rope stretching floated up from the square which meant even more trouble was headed my way. It was an unfortunate miracle the ropes had held up under the combined weight of Gev and Gob.

"Really no time for that Sylvie, Come. On!"

She glanced my way and then deflected something that glittered and pinwheeled off into the darkness. The sword might not be practical for climbing through windows and running for your life across rooftops, but it beats a knife every time. The man attacking her never finished his first lunge. The lantern light flickered off the blade as she swatted his arm aside, lunged twice and his thrust turned into a gurgling tumble over the edge. Followed by a wet slap as he hit the walkway.

"Sylvie!"

The woman I'd scared back through the window was ducking in and out of view, testing my willingness to waste more knives on her. Farther away, the scuffling of boots on wood gave away the approach of more men on the docks.

"Fine!"

She dashed to the edge, threw the sword in my direction, and then back to get room to build speed, "If I break my neck you owe me!"

With that she hurled herself over the gap.

I helped her to her feet and urged her on, "You're about to ruin a perfectly good escape!"

"We had the advantage," she scowled and sucked in large gasps of air, "no reason to..."

Something whispered past my cheek scoring a trail from my nose to my ear. It burned like I'd been branded

"Run!"

I pushed her forward and bolted for the next gap. Blood trickled down my cheek. We made the next jump in unison, her landing perfectly planted, me rolling and coming up.

"Showoff!"

She stuck her tongue out at me, "Dancing lessons. Translated well to the sword."

More bolts arced up and fell back to ground out of sight. It made my skin prickle to hear the firing and then a few moments later so many little patters as they landed, like someone tossing gravel out onto the tiles.

Gev's thunderstorm rumble counted out, "One, two, unh!"

Followed by a short squawk and man sized shape vaulted the wall of the building we'd just left and crumpled down on the roof with a painful grunt. The impact sent something, probably a weapon, pin-wheeling away. Stupid. Could just as easily have been six inches into his gut. To be fair, it didn't sound like he'd planned the trip.

I waved Sylvie on to the next jump.

The new arrival fumbled around for his weapon spewing

obscenities and unkeepable promises. It was hard not to sympathize but the periodic twang-hiss of crossbows helped my focus.

"Gibb! Shut your yapp! You see 'em?" The question was barked by someone used to ordering and being followed, likely Gobineau.

Which meant that Private Gibb, over there, was at least somewhat competent, armed or not.

Gibb stopped searching, paused to gesture obscenely at the source of the voice before spotting me waiting for him, "Yessir, he's up here, don't see the girl." The reply was obscured by darkness. "Yessir, right away sir."

Gibb didn't sound eager but he took a step back, pulled a knife from his boot, and charged forward to cross the alley between us with a yell.

Maybe he thought I would move, maybe he figured if I didn't move he'd have the advantage. Without the light from the lantern below, all I could see was a dark mass hurtling towards me with black arms outstretched like some sort of murderous bat. Years spent drinking and trading the tricks of staying alive with sailors of opportunity, pirates, paid off. I dropped back on my hands, kicked up with both feet, and rolled back and up. He flew like a bat at least, clean over the entire building. Halfway over he realized he wasn't going to make the far shop where Sylvie was standing and his battle cry turned into a scream as he plummeted head first into the space between. There was the sound of planks splitting followed by a splash.

No reason to stick around for Gev to start throwing more men at me. I followed through with the roll, turned, and sprinted off after Sylvie.

# SEVENTEEN

Hospur looked terrible.

Isaac rented an apartment that would have looked small on a ship. It huddled, perched at the top of a theater, tacked on by a props man looking to economize. The patrons were the sort of people who could afford to live off the docks but not aspire to farther up the hill. On show nights, any night but Monday, it had the advantage of a constant stream of customers, patrons, and actors in absurd costumes, dressed to go on stage inside and out. Sylvie and I didn't attract so much as a glance as we merged into the flow and continued up the stairs.

The apartment itself had two rooms. The first was taken up by books, loose pages, and rolled up scraps of tanned skins covering any surface, floor included, that didn't have someone sitting on it. Lye occupied the lone chair where he was forced to move his feet when someone wanted to enter or exit the door opposite. That led to the other room, probably intended to be a bedroom, it had been Isaac's study until someone had swept everything off the desk and it had become Hospur's sickbed.

The look we got from Isaac when we arrived wasn't reassuring. Hospur wasn't aware of us and his skin had the look of the streets after a wet fog. Lye's already narrow face was lined with worry. It didn't look like he'd slept or gone outside since we'd parted outside the tomb. I found a spot between a pair of scavenged bookshelves, using a sturdy looking stack as a chair, while Sylvie and Isaac wedged themselves next to Hospur and discussed his condition in half sentences and chopped off words.

Lye looked at me vacantly for a minute. Lack of sleep makes you slow; and stupid, my father would add. His eyes narrowed when he noticed my cheek and he fished into his pack on the floor next to him. A tower of loose bound books, without any lettering on the covers, failed to withstand the siege and slid into a neighboring pile. After pausing to scowl at the debris, he silently thrust a roll of linen at me with one hand pointing at my face with the other.

"Tides, forgot about that. Someone got lucky with a crossbow." I ripped off a small piece and dabbed at my cheek with it, "Ow!"

It had stopped bleeding but the wound was still tacky to the touch and the linen pulled open the furrow the blade had cut spotting fresh blood on it.

Lye held out his hand, demanding the linen back, and shook his head at me. He might not talk but the sigh he produced, full of world weary notes, explained plenty. Once I handed it over, he unrolled the linen revealing a small glass vial stoppered up with wax. He popped that off with a thumbnail, mimed daubing a finger in it and then applying an imaginary paste to his cheek.

Well color me stupid, "Sorry."

The extent of my healing knowledge had been exhausted at the blood clotting. The paste in the vial had the translucency of oil. Mushing it experimentally between my thumb and forefinger produced a stinging sensation. Lye's expression could have withstood thumbscrews. After a long hard look at him, I smeared it across the wound. It was slightly pasty and warmer than I'd expected, but it didn't sting immediately like it had my finger. I tried to nod my thanks and handed back the vial.

Growing up dockside my father sent me out for more gin; running over to one or other of the taverns was a regular chore depending on who he hadn't paid that week or year. Often enough, I'd make the chore last all day. The chance to get away and make him suffer a little while he waited was too good to pass, especially if the weather was good.

On the few days of actual sun you could find packs of kids all the way out where the ships tied up to the piers. There would be a mob with stragglers throwing themselves off like sparks to splash and crater into the water a story or more below. A few times I joined in, merging with the pack and then slinking home to the cane and work. One time the entire mass, without a plan, no leader that anyone would recognize, made the jump at once, a waterfall of kids off the pier. Afterwards we recovered from the near-drowning, laying out on bales and crates that we hadn't been driven away from. I sat next to this kid as the heat from the crate cooked my back and the sun prickled up sweat on my chest. This kid next to me had livid lines running up and down his arms. The same lines tracing his back and legs.

Since we were friends, I asked him where he'd gotten those lines. He described the process as his grandmother would take a coal from the stove and draw. He talked about it like it was a trip to get bread, a loaf because your father had run out, because that's the only way to talk about it. Telling someone how bad it hurts is as impossible as rowing a three master with a wooden spoon. Mostly it just makes the both of you awkward facing pain that can't be described.

My face peeled apart and lava shot up out of the rupture followed by the claws of something vast keening as it tried to claw its way out of my head. Tears streamed from my eyes and I grabbed a large tome that later turned out to be a treatise on ink distillation and pounded it against the shelf next to me. Otherwise I would have been perfectly willing to cut my face off to stop the pain that burrowed and twisted like a worm digging through the skin toward darkness and bloody safety below the surface. Not even being shot hurt like that.

My face peeled apart and lava shot up out of the rupture, followed by the claws of something vast that keened as it tried to claw its way out of my head. Tears streamed from my eyes and I grabbed a large tome that later turned out to be a treatise on ink distillation and pounded it against the shelf next to me. Otherwise I would have been perfectly willing to cut my face off to stop the pain that burrowed into the side of my head. Not even being shot had hurt like that.

"Goddess, can you two be quiet!" Sylvie hissed and then her lips compressed and she stared Lye down. "You're a bad man. Did you even warn him?"

He didn't meet her eyes and tried to fend her off with an innocent shrug.

"I didn't think so. Can you try to play nice?"

Lye put on a wounded look and pointed at my face. The agony had died to a slight stinging. He ripped off some of the linen and pushed it at me. When I tried to place it over the wound his sigh sounded like the wind as it came down off the mountain. He snatched it out of my grasp and proceeded to smudge off the ointment. His fingers were like stone pillars, so I just sat through it, expecting the cut to start bleeding. Instead he rubbed the wound vigorously until my skin was smooth as if I'd never been clipped.

I ran my finger along the line from ear to nose and decided Lye's sense of humor was something to watch out for.

"Hmph. Not even a scar, Expert. Now if you two are done?"

My cheek radiated heat, even if you could afford it, magic seemed to come with side effects, "How is he?"

"Not well. Isaac can't tell if the fever is from the wound turning sour or if that whalefat-idiot poisoned the blade."

"Probably not. It's hard to do on the move like that."

There are times I really should follow my own advice, the look I got from both of them combined suspicion and disgust. Poison is impractical in general but I can't say I understand why people who are fine with lopping off limbs suddenly get preachy about a little aconite.

"Besides, wouldn't Isaac have been poisoned too? Or did he get," I poked at my cheek, "you know..."

Just prior to his sudden retirement from breathing Dugal had stabbed both of them. If there was poison, Isaac would have gotten the captain's share of it.

"Hospur was kind enough to heal me, yes." Isaac joined the conversation, standing in the archway behind Sylvie. "It would probably have taken care of any sort of natural substance and its ilk."

His tone said he held the same opinion about poison layered with a healthy amount of surety that I would stoop that low.

"So, probably not poison. Only an idiot would walk around with a tainted blade and I can't see even Dugal taking that sort of risk with something he didn't understand well."

"Alright, Expert, it isn't poison…"

"I do have a question though."

"Go ahead." Sylvie said.

"Why not just have Lye put some of that on him, I mean besides the mind bending agony, thanks for the warning by the way." I said.

Lye grinned at me.

"It does the trick, as you said, 'not even a scar.'" I realized I was rubbing at the healed wound again and stuck my hand in my pocket.

"We can't," Sylvie's lips pursed like she'd taken a sip of sour wine. "Our friend with the low sense of humor here could explain it better than I," She favored her subject with the sort of smile you give someone you've just caught with a gold candlestick that wasn't in the take pile, "But it has something to do with Hospur's god and oaths he took."

"But.."

"No, just no. Even if you could get it by Lye, they won't work on his stubborn friend."

"I think that's the first god I've ever wanted to learn more about. So what about medicine, or an apothecary? Clar isn't going to take long to find us."

Isaac looked up from his pacing, turning really, in the small space between the archway and the table serving as sickbed. Each turn punctuated by knuckles and joints cracking.

"Clar's not thrilled about what happened to Dugal. And he wants his share from our little grave robbing expedition. He's decided that means the key." I said.

Isaac stopped and looked over Sylvie's shoulder at me. "Well that isn't going to happen, we didn't get anything. Our agreement specifically allotted us the key. That was the whole point of the arrangement, was it not? We didn't have any other treasure to split. His share is precisely what we agreed. Two thirds of nothing is nothing."

How do people like that have clothes after a walk to the store? There is exactly nowhere in Myrport that sort of naif wouldn't be rolled, sold, and cold before dawn. Along with not taking 'no' for an answer, people like Clar don't like answers that came up short. They also have no real problem dictating terms midway through the deal. One of the reasons I do so much business with Josie is his reluctance to pull that sort of bilge.

"Clar isn't in the business of ventures that don't pay."

The scholar tried again, speaking slowly and clipping his words precisely, "In point of fact, part of the cause for the way things devolved was his man, Dugal's, actions. He can't think we wouldn't take that into account. He seemed fine with the agreement we brokered."

Isaac's point was sound but irrelevant. He thought they were even without dirhams and the deal was off. Being stabbed is as good a reason as any I can think of to quit a deal, but his math wasn't Clar's.

"If you had gone to Clar immediately, maybe. But the way he sees it, Dugal is dead and he doesn't have anything to show for it. Busted ventures don't float. Too many of those and people start thinking they might run things better. He can't allow that. Besides, after the conversation we had tonight, I don't think he's interested in money anymore."

Isaac stretched his neck making a sound like stepping on gravel. One of the more common tricks homeowners like to use is to line the two or three feet between the house wall and the grounds with mixed gravel or broken shells. It makes a crunching noise when walked on which makes quietly opening windows and such tricky. That sort of noise gives a good sneak thief hives. Coming from a man's neck it was equally disturbing.

"He can't expect that we'll give him the key, the whole reason we dealt with your ilk, no offense, was to get it. Without it we can't use the keystone. As you recall…"

Sylvie cut him off, "Giving Clar the key is out of the question. We all understand that."

"Somehow I doubt Clar is all that bothered by our resolve. The point is we need to get Hospur up and moving or Clar is going to get around to taking it from us." I said.

Lye frowned and rolled his shoulders causing the leather straps of his armor to complain and squeak. He had his sword propped behind the chair and, once he had our attention, he placed the arbalest on his lap with the bolt centered on the door.

"Fair enough. Lye holds them off at the door until they decide to start using the windows. "

That earned me a furrowed brow from Lye.

"How long do you think we have?" Sylvie asked.

"I'm a little surprised they aren't knocking on the door now. This oath business is going to get us killed. What about a leach?"

Isaac and Sylvie tripped their answers over each other, "A what?" "You can't be serious!"

"A Physik, a Chiurgeon. Does the oath prevent it, Lye? I'm not saying Hospur's method," my stomach lurched a little remembering lying on the floor of the tomb with a bolt pinning me to the floor, "isn't better, but where I live the Priestesses won't even look at you. Any rate, if he is poisoned or the wound is going sour, you need to do something."

Sylvie still looked confused, but Isaac and Lye traded glances and Isaac finally nodded, "No, it wouldn't break anything; perhaps they may even help."

"Stranger things have happened. This week in fact." I got up off the stack of books serving as my chair, "I know the person we want, try not to let Clar in while we're gone."

The smile I got from Lye was slightly feral; I made a note not to have my body in line with the door when I came back, no reason to tempt luck or its gods.

"Good idea, better to not get caught alone until we can start." Sylvie said as she started to the door.

"No, not you. Him." I thrust my chin toward the body on the table, "Can he walk?"

Her look turned hard and her lips thinned. Isaac furrowed distractedly at his friend for a minute. "Perhaps, he wouldn't be conscious, but he could, the sympathetic influence could be…"

"No, absolutely not, you'll kill him! Besides he won't be

able defend himself. What happens if we're being watched? No offense, Expert, but no."

"The leach is going to need to see him, and right now they're after you, if they see you they'll know we're worth hitting. Just me they'll figure we split up and they know I'm not going anywhere. Today, next week, they won't forget but there's no rush."

"I don't like it, bring this 'leach' here."

"Anias Lem probably can't fit through his own door. When he dies they'll have to cremate him in his shop. But we can trust him and right now you need to trust me."

"Then take Lye." Her smile was honed and dangerous. It was all the consent she was going to give.

# EIGHTEEN

After my partner, Joh, sold me out to Jargo Three-Fingers and his thugs broke my hand, I'd found a place to hide. An abandoned warehouse deep in what the docks called the runs.

The Mother's waters backed away from Myrport like a fat merchant faced with a knife, sidling away in vain hope of avoiding contamination and violence. That's what forced the continual expansion and rebuilding of the docks. The runs were built before I was born. The barges and piers that formed its foundation were weathered grey and green from moss, all hint of the warm browns long since leeched from the lumber.

Those strong enough to claim new space, either closer to the mountainside of Upper Myrport, or on the fresher - more profitable - seaward side of town left the unprofitable and decaying heart long ago. That left room for those too weak or too poor to even be valuable as marks. The oldest parts of Lower Myrport were dumping grounds and worse. By the time I was making my own way in the world it had acquired the unofficial title: The Runs.

The Runs was the place to go if you wanted something cheap and free of the heavy handed rules of the gangs that kept order on the docks. It was the seedy underbelly of the underbelly. I went there because I had never been there with Joh and it was the sort of place people didn't ask questions. More because the residents had nothing of value, including information, than any danger. If they'd known something, they would have long since sold it to escape. People didn't ask questions in The Runs because nobody cared for the answers.

The warehouse still had stacks of cloth rotting from wall to wall; the final result of someone's bad bet. While I curled up in a corner of mostly dried patterned bolts I fancied a merchant house had tried to corner the market, everyone in Myrport would wear their goods or go naked. More than likely it was just someone's poor decision. Resulting in a building full of textile that was too expensive to move or sell for a couple seasons that turned into years.

My hand, broken from its time under Jargo's thug's boot, throbbed with my pulse and I seemed to have made it a full time occupation to hit it on obstacle I could find. Within a couple days even moving it brought tears to eyes and it had taken on a bloated fish belly hue.

By then, I was feverish, alternating hot as the swampy midsummer days when the winds died and Lowtown became difficult to breath in or even move, followed by icy chills paired with sweat and chattering teeth.

Prying myself out of the nest I'd hidden in was hard. Climbing was nearly impossible with one hand. I was hungry and thirsty. Drinking runoff from the roof tied my guts into knots and by the second day I'd decided it wasn't work the effort. So I walked, stumbled really, through the nest of dead ends and rotted out walkways that were now just gaping holes to the dried out mud flat below. It was the sort of danger the rest of the docks would have built over or barricaded off. Where I was it was an easy place to throw the refuse that collected at the spiritual sink of Myrport. There the garbage decayed giving ample warning of the danger and adding to the odor that covered the area.

Finally made it to Whistlers. Depending on how desperate you were Corliss' dive was either on the edge of the runs or just one of its more prominent businesses. I drank watered down ale until I was numb and then got directions to Anias Lem.

The silver I'd tried to bribe Jargo off with was enough to keep a homeless sneak in food and drink for a week or two but it wasn't even a door offering at the Temple of the Goddess. Healing from a priestess, even normal sort of poultices or bone setting, was more than I could hope to afford, and with my hand the way it was I had no chance of getting more. Most of the docks was in some version of the same steerage I was. Just visiting the temple was beyond the expectations of a woman who hauled grain off a barge for the weeks rent. Claiming to be healed by a priestess was the mark of a bad liar.

That's where the leach came in. They worked in kind as often as dirhams and provided the remedies that the common folk could afford.

Anias was large. He would have been big under any circumstance, he topped out at well over six feet, but he had a fondness for food and did a brisk trade in the remedies he sold to pay for it. A cautious man would not wager on him being able to make it through his own door. Not that he ever tried. He had a sort of rolling stool behind his counter that he would push around the shop gathering the pieces of the cream or draught he was selling and, if he needed something outside his domain, he kept a series of boys on retainer to run up or down depending on the nature of the item.

When I staggered through the split door that led into his lair, I was in no shape to explain or bargain but that just made me the sort of customer he preferred. He glided over the counter that faced the door, flipped up a hinged table that connected the left and right parts and began his examination without a word. He wheezed as he did his work, sounding like the bellows of a badly maintained organ. The sighs and squeaks of his breath mixed with the sounds of his stock, crickets chirped with the scuttle of roaches and alembics chuckled back behind the counter. The walls and windows had been shelved over and then coated with boxes and bottles that mostly seemed to have the job of supporting layers of dust.

He finished looking me over and finally said "The hand, eh?"

If my vacant stare bothered him he didn't show it. He never showed much emotion beyond a vague curiosity.

"Feverish then. Dirhams or trade?"

My pouch was clutched in my good hand. I held it out and tried to sway with the rhythm of the walls. Anias plucked it out of my hand with one vast paw. He dumped the contents in to the other hand, counted out his shot, and then scooped the rest of them back into the pouch before stuffing it into my shirt.

He kicked off and rolled smoothly to the far wall. Boxes were opened and closed, their contents added to a large glass pot with scorched streaks radiating up the sides. Finally he heated the mixture over a dark thick sided pot that owned a clear area of corner. He ignored both it and me while he busied himself in the opposite corner, all without a word. I entertained myself by counting my pulse by the throbbing in my head and trying not to fall over.

Finally he swam back to the pot, from somewhere he produced a bottle of wine and a glass. He poured some of the syrup he had concocted and swirled in splashes of wine until he had a full glass of reddish brown drink topped with a layer of bubbles. He slid to a stop in the middle gap of the counter, somehow not losing a drop and thrust the glass at me.

"Drink, used wine, that should work for you."

It had an odd texture which probably came from the syrup, but mostly it tasted like an old grainy vintage of red. He sat there, wheezing slowly and watching me. Every so often he'd lick a finger to use the moistened digit to smooth the hairs of one of his eyebrows.

"That it?"

"Nnnh." He shook his head and watched me.

When the light filtering through the shelves and bottles started to glow he nodded and grabbed my broken hand with one meaty paw. The inside of my head screamed and tried to jerk it out of his grasp but instead I just looked at the purplish glow coming off the swelling. There was no pain, just an expanding aura of light that walked a minuet with the streams of dust motes.

The rest was Anias probing and prodding bones back into place while I marveled at light that probably wasn't there. At some point he used a knife and drained out blood until the swelling reduced my hand to a club of gauze and linen that I wasn't to unwrap until the next month. He sent me away with a carved wood ball that I was to practice grasping after the bandages came off. I polished it into a silky shine over the following months.

# NINETEEN

Isaac plowed through papers - stacks were reduced to floor covering in a matter of seconds. The three of us watched him from the center of the room as he threw books aside like a watch squad clearing the road. By the time he found the one he wanted, there wasn't a space to step on that wasn't a book or paper.

He made some additional notes in the margins, ripped the page out of the book, and tossed the remainder aside to collide and topple another stack. After a few breaths his face slacked and he began reciting from the page he now held in both hands over Hospur's face. As he read he tore strips off the top, leaving just the unread portion. Crumpling the recited passage strip in one hand, he popped the wad into his mouth. Each successive part filled more and more of his mouth forcing him to rearrange the balls of paper until his cheeks bulged like a rat in a grain bag. When he forced the last scrap into his mouth, spittle was sliding down his chin. He jabbed Hospur in the extremities, swallowed convulsively, and forced the priests eyelids shut with his thumbs before turning back to us. His gaze shifted erratically and it took a moment for him to say anything.

"That should be sufficient. Don't leave him alone, his body won't make very good decisions without his mind." Isaac's legs gave way from under him and he stared at the wall.

We left the arbalest with Sylvie. She wouldn't be able to reload it but a baby could fire it. The bolt would tear a schooner-sized hole through anything in the way. She settled herself in Lye's chair and set to watching the door with the same intensity the over-tall fighter had. Doorways weren't safe with these people around.

Hospur shambled after us, eyes closed. The stairs were slow going, he would pause and then step, always leading with the left foot. His feet would come down like he was trying to punch his boot heel through the stairway, pause, and then the right foot would come down in the same way. I threw Lye a shrug and he waved me on while he stayed with Hospur. His sword was slung over his shoulder and he kept one hand on his friend

The night's show played on the other side of the wall as I worked my way down to the street. The wall would rumble with laughter under my hand each time a line hit home. The street was quiet, a pair of bored men with truncheons on their belt were huddled under the awning arguing the merits of employment with a merchant house. I wished them both success. They looked fat and slow, my favorite would-be watchman.

If Clar was having Isaac's watched, they were being professional about it. Hospur stomped past and the two bouncers hardly even paused as one of them explained the murky details of staying alert by drinking well, the full bladder being his secret. Hopefully neither would damage themselves trying that.

The theater was only a thrown rock from the docks. We headed straight downhill, we were far more likely to run into Gob's men wandering about in Uptown. If a patrol was staking out the border in between, we'd have to hope they weren't ambitious enough to try Lye's sword. His face had congealed into a jaw-clenched severity that didn't bode well for anything that slowed us down. In the end, the trip to Anias was slow - Hospur's pace was an unrelenting stomp-pause-stomp - and tense, but nobody tried to arrest us or kill us.

Lem's shop was dark; it was well after midnight. The nightly fogging devolved into an ambitious rain that soaked through leather and ran in rivers down the collar of my coat. With the walkways and streets deserted and our pace dictated by the steady and consistent pace of the priest, I entertained myself imagining what a desert would be like. Somewhere I'd read that a person could trick their body into warmth by envisioning coals. Instead, my teeth chattered and drops of water sprayed into my face as I slapped the door to get the leach to open for business.

It was hard to hear over the tearing sheet sound of the rain. There was no point in standing under the eve, gusts of wind drove the rain into any crevice and cranny making sure everything was miserably wet together. I slapped the door again, a sustained pounding to force Anias out of sleep. My hand throbbed, but I was going to wake him or the dead, whatever got me out of the storm.

A burly naked man holding a cleaver burst out of a door across the boardwalk featuring the severed head of a ram burned into the wood, "Tides and Deep take you I'll gut you like a..."

Lye had his sword out and leveled at the stall owner before he could finish his rant. He dropped the cleaver like it had grown teeth, backed into his half open door, corrected, and threw himself into his shop. I could hear someone inside followed by the poor man slamming the door shut. Lye's teeth flashed at me in the darkness.

"You are a bad person, poor fellow is going to have nightmares." I turned back to the door, hand raised but stopped when I saw a light from inside flare to life, "And there's our man. Let me do the talking."

Lye just shook his head, flinging rain like a wet dog only to be instantly drenched from all directions.

Anias Lem drew back the bar keeping us as well as the weather out of his shop and pulled the door in a crack which he immediately filled with the head of a broad bladed boar spear. The blade was vertical to keep the bar from fouling if he needed to jab through the gap, trust is one of the few items you can't find in Lower Myrport.

Lem didn't say anything, just grunted loud enough to be heard over the rain. As talkative as he ever was.

"Wounded man out here, Lem, let us in."

The only light was from inside so I couldn't see his face, just a head that was sized for his enormous bulk. Even seated his head was at eye level, I could see the shadow of it as he shifted - trying to see out of the crack he'd permitted.

"Which?" He said.

A hands span of tempered steel was still holding the gap, water torrenting down. Honestly, I was tempted to just shove my way in - getting stabbed would be drier at least.

"Let us in, he needs healing and we've got better things to do than try anything with you."

Besides, harming Anias would be like cutting my own throat. He was about as friendly as a spinefish, but there are some things even the docks won't put up with. Harming the man who cures the clap was probably one of them.

He said something I couldn't hear through the water running into my ears but the spear went away and there was a rumble as his chair slid away. I held the door while Lye led Hospur into the middle of the room. It dawned on me that this was Anias' bedroom as well as shop. Most businesses doubled as homes for their owners, cheaper than a second building and it paid to keep an eye on your stock. In the healer's case it seemed unlikely he'd be able to navigate stairs with his chair.

Once he finished poling himself back behind his counter, he set the weapon where he could reach it if we decided to try something. Nothing was said while he waited for us to shake out a bit of the rain. Although, when he saw Hospur walk, stiff as an oar, up to the counter his eyebrows shoved their way to the top of his forehead.

"Priestesses. Can't fix that."

"No, no, that's not the problem. He got stabbed, the wound might be going bad. Might be poison, we can't tell."

Talking to Anias made you start conserving words, like you had been wasting them frivolously.

"Hnnh. Where?"

Lye pulled up the priest's shirt and peeled back the bandages. They'd been red earlier where the blood soaked through from wounds that wouldn't clot. They'd turned a pinkish hue on the march. Without the covering, the slits of split flesh welled up angry red and started dribbling downward.

Anias reached around the side of the counter and produced a wad of linen. He scooted in close and pushed the edges apart with one hand, daubing away blood with the other. Lye moved to pull him back and I stepped in close and warned him off with a shake of my head. Hospur stood, face as slack as a tide, while

Anias poked and prodded, butcher-like, at the wounds. Even if he got better, he wasn't going to thank us.

The leach pushed back, flicked the hinged counter down with a bang, and folded his arms across his girth, "Up front, dirhams."

I dropped the last of my coin in front of him, "I pay my debts, Lem, you know that."

The dirhams smacked and clinked in the pouch like only money can. The sound of being broke. It was way better to have that sound going in my favor. Something I was going to have to rectify.

He hefted my money, eyed Hospur, and then set it back on the counter. That was bad.

"We're sort of pressed for time, if there's a problem say it."

Truth was, I was getting pretty raw. Too many people trying to kill me and not enough sleep.

Anias looked me up and down, rubbed his eyes and then massaged his forehead with both hands, pushing the flesh about. Finally he grunted again and shoved off toward the racks covering the back wall. The pouch was still on the counter and I knew he'd sensibly arranged his shop so that the really costly stuff was well out of reach, so on the back wall. Only a fool robs a healer but the Goddess nurtured the wise and the foolish. The sinking burbling coming from my mid-region was because my stomach was both empty and sober, and because healing Hospur was going to cost more than just the rest of my money.

While the leach was prowling through his inventory I sat down with my back to the counter. Lye raised an eyebrow at me and then traced his gaze back to the rattle clink of Anias at work.

"It's fine," I kept my voice low, a mutter really, "He would have turned us away if he couldn't fix it. I'm just resting my feet."

Sitting on the floor made him look even taller than he was. Just walking next to him I had a fine view up his nose. From this vantage it was like looking up at a parent. I cut that line off by burying my face in my arms and let myself doze off to the hiss of rain and putter of Anias.

Hospur's boot heel slamming down next to me broke my nap. In that middle state between sleep and not awake my mind screamed 'escape!' By the time I started thinking I was executing a perfect forward roll. Lye would have woken me if there was any danger. That thought was followed by an attempt to stop midway, leaving me sprawled out like a badly skinned rug.

At least he wouldn't tell anyone. Neither of the two laughed, Lye just shook his head as he helped maneuver Hospur into better position for Lem to apply whatever antidote he'd cooked up. I could smell scorched anise, something that was probably garlic, and an acrid scent that stuck to my tongue when I breathed.

Lye held the priest's arm up while the fat healer crunched in close, one hand spread the lips of each wound open while the other ladled in a paste, packing the stabs until the skin couldn't meet without being stretched.

That had to hurt worse than barnacles in your sheets.

Once the wounds were stuffed, the healer took a needle he'd held in his teeth and stitched the edges closed with tiny delicate movements. He made sure to go back over them a second time to close any gaps and then wrapped a bandage around Hospur's chest. For the first time that night the pale linen wasn't instantly soaked.

"He won't keep food till its absorbed. No sense talking about bed rest from the look of you."

"Thanks Anias, I owe you."

"You do."

There was nothing more to say, he'd call in that debt when he chose to. I had no idea why he wanted me to owe him, but he did.

Lye marched his friend back out into the night. The rain had moderated back to the more standard Myrport drizzle. What the locals referred to as a 'Heavy fog.' Without the noise of the rain, the pounding stomps Hospur made on the boardwalks sounded like a ram working its way into a castle.

After fifty feet or so of this I stopped and waited for the two of them. Once they caught up I stopped Lye with a hand. He couldn't see me in the dark and I didn't care to make even more noise, so I guided his hand to the sword on his back. He nodded, movement more felt than seen, and unfastened it. Anyone looking was going to find us, just head to the signal drum pounding away our location. Better to be ready when they got close. We moved on, this time with weapons out. Maybe that would discourage anyone from actually trying to kill me.

The walk back to the theater and Isaac's attic was almost as miserable as the trip out had been. Without the rain, the constant need to be ready for attack and the certainty that even the most callow spotter could find us frayed at me like a rat on a mooring rope. The farther we went without the expected happening, the worse it got. It was like waiting in line for your turn at the Orchid knowing you didn't have enough to pay and too embarrassed to just go home. When I poked my head around the last corner bordering upper and lower it was almost a relief to see a squad of the watch spread out in a half circle, behind them several men and one woman were huddled in the drier space offered by a nearby roof.

Looked like whatever was causing Clar and Gobineau's new alliance still held. Neither of them was in sight, the squad appeared to be answering to a solidly built corporal with scraggly sideburns and the crew from the docks would answer to whoever growled the loudest.

I stopped, feet nailed to the planks, trying to think of some way to even the odds or avoid the confrontation entirely. In a moment they were going to catch on to the steady metronome of Hospur's march and the jumble of bickering thugs tossing crude put downs at their natural enemies would turn into a mob of blades aimed at us.

The left side of my temple throbbed painfully and it felt like someone had turned my head into a solid block of jungle hardwood, the Tugali could probably make a canoe or at least a paddle out of it. Very slowly, I pulled back around the corner and turned to talk it over with Lye. Or talk it out while he listened.

They hadn't gotten close enough to alert the herd waiting for us, so I figured I'd be able to get back and pick a different route, one not overflowing with the local citizenry. I'd let myself get pretty far ahead, or the sound didn't travel as far as I'd been worried it did.

Two thoughts collided. If I was that far ahead, I wouldn't have heard if some especially ambitious part of Clar's gang coming up behind the two people I was supposed to be guiding, and I couldn't hear the sound of Lye's walk at all. Sprinting back down the walkway and looping around the blind alley I'd passed a little bit before nearly face planted me into Hospur's back. He was crouched next to Lye. The priest was slumped against the seaward wall of a stack of shanties. Hospur turned on one knee and steadied me with one long arm.

"What happened?"

It came out as a hiss, partly because I didn't want to alert our nearby friends and in part it was panic that something had gone wrong. Lem's cure didn't take. Of course, if they'd been attacked they would hardly have left the man with a seven foot sword standing there and there wasn't a chance Lye would have stood by or let them escape. I needed a nap.

"Spell wore off." Hospur's voice was thin, squeaky, like a boy as his voice hops around, "Feet are killing me, side feels like I've been stabbed again. I'm going to feed Isaac the rest of his books if he ever does that again."

Hospur shrugged, nearly clipping me with the crosspiece of his sword.

"Can you move? There's a sending off party down the way and I'd rather not be around to share in the celebration."

Hospur levered himself up using his free arm, grunted, and then slouched back.

"Not at the moment. If you hadn't already taken care of it, I think I'd like to kill that wretch. Maybe I'll bring him back so I can try."

"That's not possible, right?"

"Young man, I try not to tell Him what is and isn't." He

probed at the stitches, sucked in air and then let it out through clenched teeth, "Right now I can't decide to thank or hunt down the person who did this. I'll put him in line after Isaac."

"Well, it was that or let the wound go foul. I'll be sure to note your choice for next time though. If we keep chattering away here that next time could be sooner rather than later."

"Ah, well I've just had a spiritual epiphany, I forgive the stevedore who did this to me and you for arranging it. Despite the shin splints I've been granted as punishment for my many failures, I believe I can hobble, or perhaps crawl."

"Very kind of you. At the moment we need to figure out where to crawl to. There's a squad of the watch's finest, backed up by some rabble they wouldn't scrape up off the cobbles, waiting for us the way we came. The Triplets don't watch out for fools so it's a safe throw that there are more wandering the docks looking for us."

Spend any time up on the hill and it's easy to forget what dark is really like. Lamps, torches, and most people have a storm lantern fixed outside their door. Plenty of shadows, I would go hungry far more than I have if there weren't, but no real dark. On the docks, those sorts of luxuries buy food for the next day, or shelter from the rain, so they don't last long. When the moon wanes or the clouds are thick your eyes won't make out the fingers on your hand. Spend enough time and there are tricks to getting around when the space between walls is so black it's a solid thing. I couldn't see Lye move, but the moment he did, call it a combination of the air moving and the barely audible rasp of leather on wood, I knew. He was past me and headed for the welcoming party. Someone that big shouldn't move that fast.

"Tides! Wait!"

There hadn't been any crossbows visible when I peeked around the corner so that sword probably evened up the odds, quite a bit probably. Nothing in the time I spent learning the best ways to avoid getting killed had covered what to do when your opponent has a great sword. I could extrapolate though. Run. Of course they had swords and numbers. And I wouldn't want to be on the committee that reported the failure to Clar and Gob. All it would take is one of the dozen or so to get around behind Lye and end it.

"Here." I found Hospur's hand and pressed a knife into his palm, "If anyone comes this way, stab them." Then I sprinted after the warrior.

"Rearguard, perfect." Hospur called after me.

Lye was already around the corner by the time I caught up with him but the streets were quiet so I pulled up short. No reason to provoke anything more hasty than we already were. If they thought it was just one crazy near giant, maybe they would make mistakes they would avoid if he wasn't alone.

"Drop the sword. You're detained. Councilor's Writ. Put that thing down and that'll be the end of it."

That would be the corporal. He sounded about as eager as you'd expect facing down someone who could behead you half a block away.

Councilor's Writ was interesting, though. Myrport is governed by a council, drawn from the oldest and richest merchant houses. The selection process is part heredity, part election, and all corrupt back alley deal, betrayal, and counter-betrayal. Entire generations have been assassinated for a vacant seat.

Once elected, a Councilor could act, either as the voice of the council or by fiat - sometimes both in one day. In the case of my father it had been the former. Somehow he'd made an enemy of the council, the councilor who'd ordered the arrest had done the rest. Councilor's Writ meant that the watch was acting on the personal authority of a member. The unlucky men and women hanging from the gallows didn't care which was which, but for us it meant that whatever happened on this street corner probably wouldn't come before the council as a whole. Each member maintained a public facade of neutrality towards the others while behind the scenes their relationships ranged from pigs around a trough to outright hatred.

"Come now, I've got a squad. And these fine citizens," the

corporal sounded like he'd bitten into a crabapple, "have graciously volunteered to assist in your detainment. Drop the sword and tell us where the others are."

I dropped into a crouch and very slowly peeked one eye around the corner. If anyone was both sharp-eyed and looking for things at knee height, they might see me, but there are things sound doesn't tell you. Things like the two thugs with crossbows standing in the back of the pack.

The corporal and his men had tightened up when Lye sprinted around the corner. They had weapons out, stubby swords with both an edge and a point, and each of them had a dagger or a truncheon in their off hand. Effective for crowd clearing, start swinging when everything is going to hit something, but less so in a fight against a well trained and armored man. Given years of practice and study two weapons can be a formidable thing. In the hands of an amateur, you're better off with a shield or just using two hands; try eating with two forks some time. The rabble in the back had spread out around the sides. All armed with knives except for the two crossbows. The bows probably belonged to the squad up front and the corporal had maximized his options. Crossbows are easy to use, point and pull the lever really. It was the sort of thinking that his superiors had probably promoted him for.

Lye stood, legs a comfortable distance apart, body angled so his left side faced the squad leader. His right hand gripped the leather wrapped blade in front of the crosspiece, his left rested on the pommel. The tip of the sword held down and out to his right, almost as if he'd forgotten to point it at his targets.

The crew in back were getting twitchy, one of them was bouncing on his toes and yelled past the watchmen, "Hey, you! You deaf? The man said to drop the sword."

Most of the time that was how it worked, murdering other people isn't natural. It takes training, fear, or rage. Usually a little bit of both the fear and rage.

The corporal flushed red and his head twitched back before he got himself under control. Right then was the worst time to start a squabble with his allies.

"I got this Dell," his voice was strained but even, "Sir, if you don't surrender, you'll hang by morning. Drop it and we can avoid that."

Dell waggled his tongue at the corporal's back followed by slamming his hips forward a couple times. That provoked a couple giggles and was all the permission one of the ones holding the crossbows needed. He pointed the weapon at Lye's head and yanked up on the lever holding the string in place. Crossbows are easy to shoot, but small targets are hard to hit. With the armored watchmen blocking good shots at Lye's torso, the head was his best shot. Bad technique did the rest. The crack of string and bow releasing tension sounded like a broom handle snapping followed by a knee-wobbling drone. Lye didn't seem to notice but the soldiers all jerked toward the sound, led by the corporal. The man's face had taken a deeper shade of red and his mouth looked like a snake, with its jaw unhinged, as he turned to scream at the offending crossbowman.

"You piece of fi..."

Seven feet of steel flicked up as its wielder skipped forward, closing the distance to place the second six inches of the blade halfway up the neck before travelling through the intersection of jaw and up across the bridge of the corporal's nose and exiting in a spray of blood, bone, and the dead man's eye out through the opposite forehead. Somehow Lye curved the path of the blade, forcing it down and pulling the hilt to his chest to score the tip through the next man, standing flatfooted next to his dead commander, carving a line through the ribs and out the stomach before whipping the blade around in a spin. Lines of blood glittered in the air painting streaks and arcs on the walls and cobbles.

Each step whirled the sword high or low to pass through another body. Every blow calculated to land where it wouldn't lodge or bind. The third watchman was still turning towards the falling corporal when the edge of the sword caught his neck on the completed turn, the force built up on the spin launched his torso at Dell. The head tumbled lazily down. Lye arrested the blade, using the hand on top of the cross piece as an anchor and rotating the pommel like an oar to harpoon the fourth watchman through the gut before slashing free to slam into the last of the squad with the flat of the blade, pulping the man's arm and lifting him through the air before hurling him against an adjoining wall.

Lye froze, sword swept overhead with the blade angled down at a sharp angle. Three people dead and the other two convulsing on the cobble. The petty gang member who'd shot at Lye hadn't even lowered his weapon to reload. There hadn't even been time to be pants wettingly terrified. Just a pack of dock trash and me with our mouths open and anything that could contract squeezed into diamond hardness. Dell was on his ass staring at the headless body that had bowled him over. His feet kept moving in different directions under a stream of contradictory orders. The sound of rawhide scrapping over wet slick cobble from his shoes was strangely loud. Like the brain wanted to notice that or anything to avoid reviewing the moments before.

The one with the still loaded crossbow recovered first, "Dell? Dell. What do I do? Dell, what do I do?"

His weapon was surprisingly steady, the point aimed somewhere chest height with just a little wobble. If not for the acrid stink of chum in the air it could have just been the unfamiliar weight of the weapon lending a little tremble to his grip.

There are two ways fear can go, some people panic, some get angry. Dell went out mad.

His voice started as a squeak, "You squibs waiting for a drink? Get him!" He shoved the corpse off his legs and went for a knife strapped to his leg.

The first crossbowman stepped back, grabbed another bolt, and then tried to reload without using the foot stirrup while chanting, "shoot him, shoot him," at his partner.

The rest of the gang spread out even farther, this time with a healthy respect for Lye's reach. The ones to the flanks began circling to get behind. Lye appeared to be ignoring the lot of them, concentrating instead on the crossbow and the man aiming at his chest.

"Tides take you, Kirney! Don't be yellow, shoot him!" Dell had the knife in his hand and was crouched, waiting for Kirney to shoot.

With a bolt in his chest, Lye would be just another lion taken down by the numerous jackals.

It is possible to kill someone with a thrown knife. If you can get your target to stand very still, if you practice a great deal at throwing knives so that they land point first, and if your knife is heavy enough. The problem is, after you've thrown your knife, potential victims don't hand it back for another try or for use in the ensuing discussion about why you threw a knife at their face. Much like Dell, I carried a backup, which I'd left embedded in a window frame a few hours earlier. Since I'm the cautious type, I carried a second spare, which Hospur was using, probably carving his initials in the boardwalk with it. That left me with a single weapon, a nice heavy piece of master smithing I'd had forged after most of the nonsense had been beaten out of me by the sailors, dockworkers, and part-time brawlers turned pirates who made winning a fight their business.

"Renn, you are a fool."

Muttering to yourself is probably a sign, just like disarming yourself in the middle of a fight. In one smooth motion I stood, stepping past the corner, flipping my knife so that I held it by the blade, and over-armed it at the aiming crossbowman's stomach. The Mad Three were pants down playing cat's cradle in the privy. Do the gods use the privy?

The poor sod saw me, crossbow naturally following his gaze as he pulled the firing level and I had a split second to think, "Goddess, not again." Followed by the crack thrum of the bolt flying free to carve a line a hair's thickness to the side of Lye before whistling past me to end in a solid bang. Buried in the loose boards behind me.

My spine felt like seal fat. There was a soft moan that wasn't coming from me. My throw had been perfect, the man dropped the weapon, clutched at his stomach, and sat slowly down, contemplatively, staring where I'd hit him.

One of the two thugs who'd been trying to flank Lye waved his younger partner back. The order was acknowledged with a nod and the kid started tossing his knife from hand to hand as he approached me. It's the sort of thing that looks threatening but isn't very useful in a fight. Openings come and go so fast, making sure you catch your knife is a poor way to lose one.

"I know you." He said.

Bringing a knife to a sword fight is the sort of near fatal mistake my father would have disproved of. Failing to bring a knife to a knife fight? Assuming I wasn't carrying my guts in a bucket, I resolved to spend the next morning purchasing spares.

"Are we friends?"

If he thought he knew me, I was for talking about it over fighting. He was young. Still had all his teeth and none of the bulk men get as they age. It was possible we'd met in the course of a night's drinking and his name was buried under the ale I'd downed.

"Freelancer, word is you think too big. Dell says Clar doesn't want you dead."

My surprise was genuine, "Really?"

Dead is effective and efficient, traits that anyone thinking to become the lord of the docks would possess in spades or end up, well, dead.

"Don't much care. I'm betting he'll like your body just fine, after I gut you for Kirney."

He followed up with a pretend swipe of the knife.

Playing with your food is a bad habit. Especially when it's me. The kid and I were shifting, side stepping. Footwork is first. Hitting someone with a sword, knife, or fist is easy or impossible. It all depends on where you are...and you are where your feet are. Since I wanted to keep everything inside my skin, that meant keeping out of range of the guy with the knife.

Off to the side I could hear the rest of Dell's gang and Lye. Insults, instructions, and the axe-into-whale wooden sound of seven feet of tempered steel hitting a body. Intermixed with screams and groans. It was a creepy tingly sensation; not daring to take my eyes of the kid trying to kill me but not knowing if somehow another got past the tall fighter and was about to skewer me from behind.

A couple more passes, a couple close calls. He was quick, not as fast as he should be, but quick enough. Combined with the gusto of facing someone who can't really fight back. If he got careless, I could probably hurt him. If I saw it in time and cared to risk getting close enough. When he failed to get an easy cut he dropped the grin for tight lipped concentration. He lunged again, a full extension fencer's thrust forcing me to throw myself back. My foot slipped on something, warped board or slick of blood - impossible to say - I dropped into a roll and came up expecting him to be on top of me. Hands up to ward off the knife, better a hand or an arm than being opened up like a fish.

Instead I nearly bounced off Lye. Somehow he scooped me to the side with one plate-sized hand while the other brought the two-hander down with the other, guiding it against gravity really, as it dropped out of the darkness. The kid's instincts were good. He was hard on my heels, following up when his opponent was weak. The blade caught him in mid stride, crushing down through collarbone and rib before stopping in his midsection and torqueing out of Lye's grasp.

"Thanks."

Lye twisted his sword free before nodding in response. He pointed at the man I'd left my dagger in, slumped to the side in death.

"Yeah. Seemed like the thing to do."

I went to get it, trying not to think about how young that kid had looked. I'm only a few years older, but still. That's why the gangs are a dead end, they seem like the only way. That's what my ex-partner, Joh, had thought. He'd probably ended up just like these. Dead over something he'd been pointed at, by someone else who stood to profit. If a few of the rank and file die along the way, that's just the price you pay.

The copper tang of blood mixed with the pig sty offal scent of split intestines. I yanked my dagger free, stropped it clean on the corpse's jacket, and tried not to look at the kid's face as I stepped over his body to get back to Hospur.

The priest was where we'd left him, semi-conscious but he nearly cut me with my own knife before he realized who we were in the dark. We were finding our way by feel as much as anything and I nearly tripped over him.

His voice was weak, part delirium, "Gah! Easy marks, in and out, you said."

The cold prickle of a blade slashing an inch from my neck brought me up short. He was half aware and taking swipes at foes we wouldn't have seen in the daylight.

"Put that down!"

"Leave him, they catch us he won't live anyway, I said leave him!" Hospur said.

"Tides! Lye a little help here?"

I finally caught the knife arm. Even wounded he was still bigger, it took both hands to control the knife and he promptly clubbed me with his other fist. Lye stepped in and after fumbling a bit for a grip, pinned the priest until his fit passed. After that we were just two late night drinkers escorting a third up the hill. Lye did most of the carrying and I kept an eye out for patrols and worried.

# TWENTY

"Tell me again how you took Hospur to get help and came back with a catatonic priest, a marvelous black eye, and killed an entire patrol of the city watch?"

The question was probably rhetorical. Since she had my head in her lap while holding a damp cloth to the eye in question, I didn't think she could be too upset. Besides her fingers were light and cool. I would happily have murdered anyone who made her stop.

"To be fair, I didn't kill any watchmen."

"I'm sure they'll note that in your trial before they hang the two of you. I should have gone with you. Don't shrug at me, Isaac should have come, it was a mistake to split up, if they'd come in force at either of us? We can't take risks like that."

She had a point. The rabble in the alley could just as easily come for Isaac and the outcome would have been different. And then I remembered Isaac, with gouts of flame billowing out of his mouth, burning down a Deepspawn. Or it might have been horribly worse.

Isaac spoke up from the sick room, what used to be his study, "If it bears mentioning, there does seem to be improvement. The fever is gone and the smell as well. Although, as to that, I'm not entirely sure the new odor is an improvement. He didn't create a complete disaster."

Faint praise. Settle for what you can get, I guess.

"When can he walk? The longer we wait, the more trouble these two are probably going to find," she started running one hand through my hair, "and the more likely the temple catches on. As soon as word gets out about the other night, things are going to start piling up."

I felt like a shark that's just hit a school of herring. The school explodes in a flash of silver and the shark is left wondering what happened.

We'd come through the door to a wall of questions. Before long we'd run through the whole trip, gotten Hospur as comfortable as we could on the table, and Sylvie prescribed a wet compress for my eye - which was threatening to swell shut. Since Lye wasn't going to volunteer, I was trying to describe the fight with one hand. Describing combat with one hand is a lot like tying a knot with your lips. After the third contradiction from Lye, he didn't think much of my narrative style or my attempts to mimic his prowess with a wet rag as my weapon, Sylvie called a halt with an exasperated, "Give me that." And I wound up narrating from the floor while the swordsman illustrated and she applied the compress for me.

My eye hurt like hell but I don't remember being happier. We sat like that for hours, after the second rendition we started talking about the proper ways to combat superior numbers and then the best way to marinade the legs of a bird I'd never heard of. They'd talk about something for a few minutes, shifting between old arguments and new with the easy familiarity that old friends create over the course of countless hours. Somewhere in there I fell asleep.

Hospur woke with the false dawn, shaky, pale from blood loss and fever, but he could walk. By early afternoon we were all awake. My mouth felt like it was growing the ooze that covered underground cave walls and my spine was probably never going to be straight again. But I was awake and alert for the first time in what felt like weeks.

"Whoever wants the key, for the money or whatever, they aren't going to let us sit here for another night. I'm amazed they didn't try for it during the day. Besides if I don't get a chair soon, some of these books may become a permanent part of my skin." I said.

I dug a particularly offending title out of my kidney and tossed it to the side. Isaac had given up protesting our treatment of his books hours since.

"I wish we knew if they were doing it for the money or not." Sylvie said.

"That much money, to make Clar and Gob play nice, that I would like to see. If I hadn't seen them standing arm in arm I wouldn't have thought there was that much gold in Myrport. Still, it can't make much difference why, this sort of thing wouldn't bother either one with or without knowing the reason."

"It matters because if they are just tools, proxies, there will be a limit to what and how far, if not, there will be no limit to which they cannot be goaded." Isaac said.

"Well that's a cheery thought. Of course, they wouldn't be working together if either one could do it by themselves. Once we're in the temple we should be clear. Besides the flensing flesh-eating cannibals, I mean."

"They don't eat...Expert, I may ask them to make an exception for you."

"You have a plan for them, I mean besides offering me up for supper?"

The smile I got back was not reassuring.

"The Goddess has not always relied on the faith and goodwill of the kingdoms that line the Inner Sea," Isaac explained, "Her temples have often served as fortresses and redoubts. A common failure when building such a bastion is failing to prevent the defense from becoming a trap. An illustrative example would be the Last Stand of Verri..."

"We know the song, Isaac." Hospur's voice was weak, deep breaths were painful.

"Of course. The tunnels and their entrances are hidden and guarded," there was a small pause, the tombstone of a lost argument, "but we plan to pick one, progress to the Repository, and then make our escape by boat with the outgoing tide. The general opinion is that if we do so with sufficient alacrity we shall overcome any opposition with minimal harm inflicted and be away before sufficient force can be redirected to oppose us."

"Some of the people there were...are... people I should have been kinder too." Sylvie said.

"And most of the rest are just following their callings, however imperfectly." Hospur said.

Sylvie flashed him a smile, however the discussion before had gone they were swimming together now.

That left me still ignorant though, "What if it goes wrong?"

One night a group of us got into a half-cask we got for cost at the Net and Hook. We were well past feeling warm and toasty and someone, probably Joh or maybe Jak, came up with the idea of stealing a skiff and rowing it out past the jetty line. The jetty smothers the waves, go out past it by a couple feet and the chop turns a skiff into a ride worse than a spooked horse.

Somehow we not only stole a skiff, but a handful of us rowed it and the half-cask out and into the swells. The skiff rode up each wave and dropped out of the sky to meet the next. Not a minute into it I'd lost everything in my stomach leaving a burning in my nose and a twisting hollowness with every lurch.

Asking the question felt like that.

A childhood of training followed by years of experience said to plan for it to go wrong. That's not pessimism; it's how I didn't end up like a long tally of mostly disposable peers. There was no matching experience in working with a crew that had a bond and trust like this. The nearest I had was my ex-partner Joh and that had worked out about as well as an anchor without a chain. Last night I'd decided whatever Sylvie wanted sounded better than good, and so far they'd treated me the same as if I'd earned my place. The part of me I like to drown in bad gin kept asking when that was going to end.

A good con isn't so convincing that the mark never notices, the good con never has a pebble under the shell for the mark to find. As the afternoon wore on the waiting, waiting for them to spot the imposter, was like the top of the swell before the boat crashed into the next trough. They'd fit around me better than the wallow in my bed but sooner or later comes the guy in the back saying, "no that one." And I'd be the pebble.

Whatever he does, the good con doesn't get himself noticed by asking questions.

"How do you mean, wrong?" Sylvie said.

"What if we aren't fast enough or the Tugali are guarding

your secret entrances, or the key doesn't work, or anything really."

The pile of books to the left became the most interesting thing in the room; anything to avoid eye contact. This was the sort of planning I did as a matter of habit but it felt disloyal somehow to point it out. And what in storm and reef was that all about? It was a sensible question. It was just a question nobody else had asked.

"If there are Tugali, we do what we must. If the key fails…I don't know. Isaac?"

The skin on his face dawned a ruddy red, "My research is clear, the key will work - probably better than your trap finding. "

It was a fair point, I'd blundered through the crypt blind and stupid enough.

"In the chance that it doesn't, we'll try the front door, the Priestesses should love that. One way or another, we get the keystone. Lack of speed does not equal failure. It means we may not all be making it out."

Nobody said anything after that. She hadn't offered to let me out of going and that felt good. We all found some piece of leather that needed oil worked into it or a notched edge that couldn't be seen but still a few strokes with a stone was required. That voice tried to tell me I was a fool but I couldn't hear him over the urge to whistle.

People who whistle should be used for dredging.

# TWENTY-ONE

Four walls, one door (with a better lock than it deserved), no windows, and two beams strong enough to hold my weight. The roof was an accumulation of tile and flatboard that made it not leak. That's equity in Myrport, roof leaks are a fact of life. The shelving I'd put up held little mementos. A spoon, a hand-sized painting in a ridiculously over carved gilt frame, the doorknob I'd popped clean out of the door rather than play around with the poison Hurndek's private secretary had lacquered on. Too bad he had a habit of getting chattily drunk.

The ten-pound hammer cost too much and left me hitching my pants all night but the look I imagined on Hurndek's face when he saw his counting room wide open and bare as a newborn was worth it. It was the only really dangerous memento I had. The rest was just bits and pieces, tools in need of repair and spares.

Hurndek hadn't lasted the winter, face down in the mire, like his predecessor.

The doorknob I wrapped in a piece of burlap and tossed down to join its previous owner. The rest I left, whoever annexed my little square of dryness would get a little boost in income to go with it. Maybe they would build more out of it than I had. Probably not, but my head was still minnowing, thoughts bouncing off invisible walls to dart sideways into the next wall.

"Go'n somewhere?"

The painting hit the floor with a crack that dropped its value by at least half. My fingers were numb and my heart couldn't decide between crawling out of my mouth or the more direct punch through the ribs.

There really aren't any secrets Dockside, just information that someone hasn't offered the right price for…yet. Since I wasn't breathing through an opening in my neck, Clar's man wanted to talk. I knew it was him without looking. The way he talked was one, but nobody else was going to through the trouble of finding out where I lived. He'd found out and put someone to watching.

It was stupid, but sometimes that isn't enough. There's something about being the author of my own goodbyes. It was why I'd gone to see my father and now it was why I my sails were flapping in the wind.

"I'd invite you in but I didn't invite you. I don't have what you want. The deep knows I wouldn't give it to you after that nonsense yesterday." With one foot I nudged the pieces of frame and painting out of the way in case the talking ended badly. I shouldered off the ruck I'd just finished tying up and deliberately placed a hand on my dagger, "So why are you here?"

He was as blank and thin lipped as ever, not even a twitch on his face as I very clearly set myself up for a fight.

"Yesterday 'n last week are the why, but things are fluid." He cleared his throat, started to spit, stopped, and then leaned out before firing at the boardwalk.

Showing manners too. There wasn't a reason I could stack up why he'd start caring what I thought.

"Tell me about that." I said.

"The way'n I see it, you're pretty far out'n the wire'n there's no net. No safety line neither. That can change though."

"Do tell."

My mouth tasted sour, like waking up the afternoon following drinking in the dawn. Which was sort of the case, Clar's lieutenant was there to shake me awake.

"Simple facts, you work for me'n my people don't go native. Make sure the dice throw right'n you get the benefits of employment. Forget who's hand is on the coin'n you'll get The View."

The gibbet was oft known as The View. Supposedly it offered a spectacular view of the harbor. Once in a lifetime, as it were.

"I'm not really interested in long term employment, you may have heard."

"Fair enough. We'll go week to week. Any week you feel like, you can hang."

"I'm otherwise employed currently."

Windows or a back door was looking like the sort of home improvement I should have looked into. He'd have those covered even if I had one though. Going through him might work. But nobody becomes Clar's hatchet man by being a pushover. So... probably not.

"Figured, it's one of yer appealing qualities. Yer going to be insurance. Go with them'n when the moment is clear'n good, you jump'n I say jump."

"What makes you think I'll do this after what happened to Dugal?"

He looked at me for a while, long enough for sweat to make the grip of my dagger tacky and I had to fight the urge to shift my weight. Staying still is harder than you think, but I'd had entire nights of hiding a foot and a half behind a not quite sleepy enough watchman to practice. And I'd walk to the gibbet myself before showing weakness in front of that piece of creepy boot scraping. Finally he cleared his throat, spat at the walk outside my door and took a seat like the chair was his. Since it was the only chair, that left me standing in the corner of my own place with no place but the cot to sit.

"Clar likes you, so I'm explaining something you already know. Yer a tool, a piece of work to get things done. That's why this girl wants you along. Why Clar's willing to give you'n other chance. Soon as you don't, you get tossed back'n they find a tool that get things done. Now, you got a choice. You get things done for Clar, you breathe a while longer'n get paid. Otherwise, you play pretend'n get tossed aside, like Upper folk do, when they get done with you. Then I'll catch up to you'n there won't be more chances."

Never a good moment when your best rebuttal is, "No it isn't." Much as I wanted him to be wrong, he'd laid out how the world worked, or at least how Myrport worked. A week ago I would have been the first to point out Sylvie might feel bad about how she'd gotten me involved, but she'd still done it. Apology or not, there was no reason I had to think she wouldn't do it again.

Tides come to that she would and expect me to understand it was for her Goddess.

"Can see you thinking. You'n I both know how you move up the hill. It sure ain't doing the bidding of them that live up there. It's money, boy. You get yer head in line, do when I say do, you get a chance you don't have now. Sure, you earned some debts, Dugal'n so on, but she's gonna toss you away when she's done. You keep yer value, Dockside we don't throw away tools when we don't need 'em. You get a chance."

That could be true. Break them by the hundreds for a little profit, but not for boredom or fun. Mostly. The leash would be short, but if the profit looked good they might forgive. There weren't any better than me in the city that I knew of. That might be enough to keep Clar from deciding I looked better face down in the mire.

"I work for me."

"That's cute. You work for whoever pays, just like the rest of us. Here." He flipped a pouch out from behind his back and tossed it onto the cot, "Think whatever you like about yer job, when the time comes, you do what I say."

He stood in one smooth motion, oiled and quick, looked around the tight confines of the place I called home and then looked me in the eye and spat into the dead center of the room. So much for manners.

His way of saying he owned it now that I'd been paid, I think. Then he left, boots tapping softly down the walkway that passed my door. When I was sure he was gone, and whoever he had watching wasn't going to set fire to the roof or come through the door to add punctuation to his message, I finished packing. I left the door open, as much a signal as anyone needed that the place was vacant; the new owner could clean up the floor.

# TWENTY-TWO

"Down!"

My warning came as a startled squawk as much as a yell. Follow your own advice, right? The dive forward clipped my chin on the pavers and carried me under the path of the spear that scored a hole down the middle of the passage.

That's the problem with unguarded secret entrances. Eventually someone notices that an exit is an entrance and decides to discourage visitors.

The path in had been buried at the back of the temple stable. It was used for the mounts of the rich and powerful as they sought the favor of the goddess during temple hours and it was pleasantly unmanned after dark. The proprietor's house formed one wall with stalls extending out and ending in a massive bin-like structure that held the by-products of stabling horses. As far away from the house as possible…made sense to me. The whole affair was enclosed by a slat-boarded fence serving to keep the animals in, but did nothing to keep us out. After all, if someone was tempted to steal the owner's manure, he would probably lend them a shovel.

Which is exactly what we did. Hospur settled down on a bucket and conferred with Isaac while I kept watching the house for signs that the inhabitants realized there were people on their property, likely up to no good.

"Hsst, Renn, over here!" Isaac was in the back of the pile of horse droppings and urine-wet hay with a small lantern held high.

"Would you put that away, please?"

"I can't see without it."

"You can't see with it either, but anyone within miles can see you."

He looked blank, but he slid down the hoods so only the tiniest slice of light glowed through.

"Good enough. Now, why are you standing in a pile of filth?"

"The entrance is there. I think. I can't see now."

"That's too bad. So where's another one of these, one without a wagon's worth of manure on top of it?"

This was something like watching the sunrise and asking for a different one. Since this was Myrport, one that wasn't obscured by a layer of drizzle and fog. I'd spent a week cleaning out stables once, good view of the gardens - horrible job, once the pay was bouncing merrily in my hand I swore to never do it again.

"Funny, Expert. Do you prefer a shovel, or whatever this fork thing is called?" Sylvie joined us, arms full of borrowed tools.

"Spade fork. I can't wait to explain to the watch: Well sir, we're relocating this pile for, um, religious reasons...Or something."

The three of us began the process of shifting the waste back into the adjacent stall while Isaac and Hospur watched the road and the house. After Lye nearly beheaded me with a massive heave of straw and unnamable matter, we decided the lantern could be used after all.

The entrance was a slab of stone resting on a wooden platform. We levered it up, snapping a tine off the poor stable master's fork in the process, and from there it was a straight drop of about ten feet. The sides of the hole were lined with whitish powder and the stains of years of seepage ending in a rancid smelling puddle that was quickly splattered onto everything as we jumped down. Since Hospur was in no condition for acrobatics, I went last and helped lower him down to Lye who plucked him from the edge and set him down into the hall leading from the hole. He reached up to take his arbalest and ducked farther in as I splatted down on the churned scum.

"Now that is vile." Walking my feet back and forth in place a few times cleared most of the muck but not the smell. Solid footing restored but new boots went on the list.

"Isn't it?" Isaac had wrapped cloth around his mouth and nose making him look a bit like a clerk turned to banditry.

"Shame we can't replace all that." I said.

With the covering removed, and the slab propped up, someone was bound to notice come daylight and probably sooner. Would they summon the watch, or would The Mad Three decide enough was enough and send them straight to the temple? No reason the gods of luck should come to the aid of the priestesses, but divine motives were inscrutable for a reason.

Lye shrugged at me and then made himself small so I could slip up ahead of him. Time to be the Expert again.

The passage leading to the temple was man-sized and lined with stone bricks. Evenly spaced beams that turned out to be carved stone kept the ceiling in place every six paces or so. The walk from the stables to the temple courtyard might have taken a minute or two but the would-be temple defenders had to contend with the confluence of the mountain, the swamp below, and the growing city above. Escape routes that get dug up the next time the local burgher decides he wants a basement or flooded when the tide is right are equally pointless.

We slipped into a steady exchange, I would traverse each length of hall looking for defenses and hoping there were none to be found by my feet. When I reached the next turn, a quick signal to the others brought them forward and repeat.

Within minutes I found a tripwire, hidden in the join between pavers. It was the pattern that gave it away. Masonry is generally staggered, each stone or clay piece offset from the next. When it comes time to finish of a section, smaller pieces get cut to fill in each line so they all meet at the same place. That place is never in the middle of a hall. But there it was, a perfectly straight line bisecting one half of the passage from the other. I sank down on my heels, not daring to move either foot in case I'd already put my weight on the trigger for something. There hadn't been any give, none of the slight grind of stone sliding on stone that usually gives a pressure trigger away.

Finally I waved Lye closer. He had the arbalest in one hand and a ship's lantern in the other and I needed a better view. Sure enough, maybe a quarter inch of space lay under a strand of mottled grey wire. Tripwire wasn't really correct. The strand was too low to catch the shoe, the designer probably viewed that in the same way a master smith views a stone club. Most people don't so much step, as swing the foot forward. That's what makes a tripwire work, the foot swings forward, catches the line, pulling the catch, and releasing mayhem on the unwary.

What made this one so ingenious, and so frightening, was that someone had looked at that setup and thought to herself, "The problem here, the reason bodies aren't piling up in my hallway, is that the wire is too visible, I should do something about that." The something was to notice how people walk, drop the tripwire almost to floor height, and then use a wire strung tighter than a miser on tithing day. If not for the extra bit of trickiness in trying to hide the nearly invisible line in the brickwork, one of us would have brushed the wire. A kitten would have set it off.

A quick warning to Lye, he nodded, and I stepped over the trigger line using high knee bend steps. A little extra caution to avoid trouble. The tall swordsman moved to mimic my actions and I scooted back out of his way. As my heel came down the paving stone rocked under my heel with a teeth itching grind.

"Down!" I was screaming the warning and hurling myself further down the passage before I realized why I was doing it. My chin bounced off rock flooring sending a wave of white across my vision, teeth cracking into teeth with force that left my jaw aching. The sound of raw meat hitting hot iron chased a glint of metal followed by stretched out wooden shaft. Ending in the crack of rock shattering.

"Expert?"

"Yesh?" The muscles in the back of my jaw spasmed and ached.

"Hospur says he doesn't mean to be critical but getting yourself killed is a poor way to meet his god."

"He really needs to tell me more about that."

A quick check on Lye got me a shrug. He was examining the crossbow for damage. Since nobody was wearing the spear, best to move on. This time with a certain amount of reverence for someone willing to design an entire floor and a fake, probably fake - no chance I was going to test it, tripwire around a simple pressure plate to kill me.

Sylvie popped her head around the corner, "He says, 'No.'"

What sort of priest doesn't talk about their god?

"I'm pretty convert-able currently. Near death'll do that to you."

"So they tell me. Ready to go on?"

Not really, no. More like a stiff drink followed by the bottle it came from. Mistakes like the one I'd just made ended lives and suddenly that included more lives I cared about than just mine. Being independent meant nobody at your back if things went keel up. Someone else helping was probably nice, being on the wrong end of luck was a lonely thing. But it also meant somebody else's hangover, bad night at the Orchid, or need to sing opera while picking a lock didn't become my problem. So I'd wrong footed the trap after being gulled by its long dead designer. A week ago that would have been a close call and a story to tell at the Pike. Not so simple now. If Lye had been a little wider or a breath slower? If Sylvie had followed a little closer?

Once upon a time, Josie got me a deal, some unsmelted silver of the purity he liked (not very) that involved crawling through an abandoned sewer shaft. I had to push myself along with my toes and hope that nothing blocked the tunnel since I couldn't bend my knees or arms for leverage. The whole time I had to breath in small gasps like taking a fist to the stomach. Took most of an afternoon and smelled like burning tar. That wasn't the bad part. The bad part was when I got stuck. I'd no idea how long it took me to get free, but the memory of it still made my heart race and my mind numb. It's the sort of memory that goes well under a thick layer of denial mixed with whatever is handy and can peel paint off the wall.

Thinking of someone else sprouting a spear because I glad-handed a trap made me feel like that. Vomiting seemed like a good idea. I knew better, it was time to suck it up. Get the job done, something my father used to say, "Whatever the job takes, you get it done." Not really helpful advice, I could feel my breath coming in pants.

Lye stepped up and quirked a shoulder and set the arbalest down, checking to be sure it wouldn't slide or fall. From tip to tip the thing nearly spanned the hallway. The arms and stock were polished to reflection out of a thick-grained wood and then lacquered to keep moisture from warping or rotting the weapon. It could easily stave in a skull just by dropping it on the unwary but damage like that might skew off the aim. A skilled shooter could put down a man in armor at a hundred yards; the care Lye put in to the weapon said much about his ability to make that kind of shot.

When he was satisfied it wasn't going to roll off like a loose barrel, he turned and looked down at me. The passage was portioned for a normal adult, a good six inches clearance for me. Someone Lye's version of tall was crooked over and still bouncing the top of his skull off the stone beams.

Once my attention was focused it was hard to look away without feeling like I was plugging my ears and babbling nonsense to avoid hearing something. He made a show of breathing in and out, big pantomimed breaths. Breathe, idiot. Useful advice that made me feel like a child for following…until it worked. The fat man on my chest stepped off. The babble in my head agreed to take it up with me later. Lye reached out, gave my shoulder a squeeze that threatened to shatter a collarbone, and reclaimed his weapon.

"Thanks."

He shrugged.

"It's just, you know. That was close. Sorry."

Another shrug, this time accompanied by a small crook of the lips. He scrunched around to create a gap between his chest plate and the bands of steel that covered the hips. A streak of angry red scar traced from his stomach around to his back. Whatever caused it would normally have killed its victim. The tissue bore the tracks of stitching, little whitish lines crisscrossing the red. Somehow he'd lived through it without healing.

"Ok, granted, that was closer."

Lye nodded, seeming satisfied that he'd made his point.

"I don't know why he shows people that," Sylvie walked up during the viewing, "don't give him any sympathy; he treats every little scratch like he should get a medal."

That earned her a dignified sniff and he set to re-layering the plates to do the job of preventing the sort of injury he'd shown.

"Well, it's no crossbow bolt through the body, I guess. Sadly, the scar from that isn't as excessive, but there's still time tonight, maybe I'll get lucky."

Lye grinned at me. He rolled his shoulders and twisted in place to verify everything was set properly before retrieving his arbalest…and promptly tapped his head on the ceiling like a carpenter checking for a stud. The grin fled in favor of a sour scowl as he made shooing motions toward the next turn.

The passage wound through the underside of Myrport; drunk and with no idea where home was. After several twists and double backs it widened out into something like an underground hall. The far end featured an archway just large enough to allow passage in single file. To either side of the archway lay horizontal slits, likely for use by defenders to fire down the passage without taking return fire by attackers. There was maybe fifty paces from the tunnel mouth where Lye and I crouched and the firing slits. About twenty feet in, matching pairs of polished brass lanterns burned. The oil carried the rancid bite of seal fat. Polish and the smell of burnt oil meant that someone at least checked down here now and then. Guards or servants, possibly both.

Running full out, a man might make the distance in eighteen seconds. Depending on how alert the guards were that probably meant he'd only be shot once. Of course that assumed there were guards. Maybe there weren't. Being shot by a "maybe" crossbow bolt didn't seem like it would hurt less.

If there were guards, they were patient and quiet. My ears picked up the scraping sound of metal knee on stone and our breathing. But none of the drone a pair of guards will create as they try and hand off the boredom between themselves. Of course, we were well into Tugali territory now. They might not pass time on watch like standard watchmen.

Motioning back down the tunnel, I led Lye back to where Sylvie waited with Hospur and Isaac. She raised an eyebrow but waited for what I had to say.

"I think we're here. Area up ahead looks like a guard post. No sign of the Tugali, but it's lit and anyone waiting at the far end could hold off an attack pretty easily."

"They won't attack without provocation." Sylvie said.

"I bet showing up in a secret escape route counts as provocation for most people."

"No, they'll give you a chance to go back. They're sticklers; the Temple doesn't start until we pass that point so they won't do anything until we cross the boundary. They'll show themselves to warn you, nothing more."

Every instinct my father beat into me and, every one I have learned since, blazed like a midsummer bonfire. That room was designed to hold off an invasion as surely as if it was a castle wall. No fortress stands by letting invaders walk up to the wall before challenging them.

"We'll approach, I'll talk to them. Hopefully I can convince them to let us through."

So that's what we did. Sylvie went first, palms forward, arms out from her body. Lye and I followed her and Hospur tried not to look to much like he was relying on Isaac to stand up straight.

The walk itself was like watching a wet shirt dry, with chance of an unseen arrow flying at you. It was the longest fifty paces I've ever walked, looking for the glint of glass tipped death the whole time. Fifty paces. Did they use the blue glass for their arrows or steel like everyone else? Forty. Come to think of it, did they even use bows? Thirty. Those slits didn't seem like they'd work for thrown weapons. Twenty. How far could a person throw something like a javelin? Ten.

There were two of them, one to each side. They'd been standing, backs to the wall, waiting. Without a sound, each stepped into view. The one to the right filled the opening, arm raised to throw. His fellow stood behind, weapon in hand.

The tips were translucent stone, blue glass, whatever. Question answered. Each held a short, maybe three feet, shaft tipped in the distinctive Tugali material. The base was socketed into a stick with a ladle end cupping the wood. The long end of the ladle was grasped with the last three fingers of the hand and then the thumb and forefinger pinched the haft of the javelin in place. A couple shafts poked up behind their head and a second javelin was ready in the off hand to launch after the first.

Sylvie stood, hands still out, breathing calmly.

The tribal protectors of the priestesses were partly myth in Lower Myrport. We knew they were real, but it's one thing to talk about them, another to see one. Temple services were for people who could wear silk and woven fibers, who had nice clothes they wore on holy days. People who tithed. Even then you weren't likely to see them, the guardians kept out of sight unless they thought one of their charges was in danger. Some sailors claimed to have seen their boats approach, but usually the teller was angling for a free drink.

Up close they were just men. Their skin was the white of a salmon's stomach; the lamps turned their faces yellow. Each had straw blond hair, pulled back from their faces and held in place by a strap of leather just behind the ear. Neither wore more than simple pants drawn up at the knee, fastened at the waist with a belt, and buckle of plain metal.

Put either one of them in clothes and maybe a hood and they could have gone anywhere in Myrport without a word. That thought bothered me more than if they'd been gnawing on a leg bone.

There's almost as many languages in the Inner Sea as there are kingdoms and Myrport hosts most of them. Spend any time in the docks and you'll start to pick up the version the locals use, for sheer survival if nothing else. But encountering a conversation in a tongue you don't speak is part of any given day. If that means pantomiming for your wine, that works too. I developed a taste for racki after I tried to order a bottle of gin one summer and the proprietor was from one of the desert kingdoms on the eastern coast. Ordering in a place you don't know is a gamble anyway. If you don't want to eat fish brains or something, pay attention for to more than the words.

Sylvie stood, still as a dead calm breeze. The Tugali guards matched her statue for statue. They stared at her, we stared right back. She'd been clear on the plan, when we met them, she'd do the talking. we weren't to appear threatening or hostile. Of course, standing there in front of the very threatening and hostile tribesman, all sorts of questions occurred to me. Things it might have been good to cover back when that was possible. They weren't likely to treat this like a child's game of tag, call a halt while we conferred off to the side and then resumed play once we'd hashed it out.

All I had were the parts you can tell without words.

So instead, I stared at the one in front. And worked over in my head the thought about how normal he looked. Normal in a distinctly hostile way, but that wasn't uncommon. Folks get pretty personal about money, threaten what they think is theirs and hostile is just the start of what you can expect. Happened often enough over a game of Sevens. Get a family man on a losing streak, maybe rolling on money he couldn't afford to lose. Something happens to make him think the game isn't fair, it never is, so call it less fair than usual. He'll start looking at you exactly like that Tugali was looking at Sylvie while he works up his nerve. If it isn't handled someone ends up face down in the mire.

Exactly like that.

My body was in motion before my brain could say I was overthinking. Did the tribesman see me start and react? Did I see muscles in his arm flex, ripping the handle forward and down in a chopping motion, and act? Maybe we both reached the same thought at the same time. My first step brought me even with Sylvie, I threw my weight into her from the side. She'd felt me coming, half turned to stop me. The look on her face would have terrified me if I'd had time to think about it. Right or wrong she was going to kill me if the Tugali didn't.

Which they nearly did. The shove knocked her off balance. She dropped into a roll instinctively to buy space to recover, using the momentum of the push to get away from her attacker. Leaving me standing nearly where she'd been as the javelin bored a hole in the air close enough to feel the wind of its passing in my hair before threading the space between Isaac and Hospur.

Sylvie bounced to her feet, both hands out to the Tugali guards, shouting something in what had to be their language. The one who'd thrown never missed a step. He brought the ladle device up, socketed the next javelin, pinching it in place with thumb and forefinger. Each motion was precise and practiced as a seamstress finishing a seam. No doubt he'd been drilling that exact sequence since before he'd come to the temple.

Isaac had stepped in front of the priest, shielding his friend. Hospur looked like his pants were bunching up but he also seemed likely to pass out. Instead he settled for a two hand grip on his mace since he wasn't up to holding a shield.

Sylvie and the Tugali were snapping at each other, both speaking rapid fire, both on the verge of yelling.

At first it seemed like he must be mad at me. Sylvie sure was. The glances I got could have cleared barnacles off a ship hull. Somewhere between, "I'll deal with you later' and 'I'll hand them your liver for a snack." The javelin never wavered from Sylvie though and neither of the tribesmen paid me any attention at all.

Maybe that was normal for them. All sorts of people under the sun, or the fog, this was Myrport after all. I'd stolen a matching set of rings and neck bands from a trade delegation where all the men had their eyes sewn shut at birth. Something about the sight of evil preventing their entrance to heaven. Practical solution to a spiritual problem, but strange.

The more Sylvie tried to calm them, the more agitated the two seemed to get. The one in back was mostly hidden behind the other, but he had started hopping and shifting from foot to foot.

Sometimes he would shout something over the top of his friend, interrupting Sylvie. Each time she flinched, soon her hands were clenched into fists and she had stopped talking altogether. Instead the first Tugali was off on a rant, getting louder and louder, flecks of spittle sparkling as he showered her with abuse.

"Sylvie?"

She didn't look away from the one streaming the Tugali version of hate and bile, "Yes, Renn?" Using my name probably wasn't a good sign for me. She was talking without moving her lips, staying eye to eye with the tribesman. He'd got the smell of chum in the water in his nostrils, soon he'd be the shark hitting the meat again and again long after it was dead. It sounded more like 'Yetth, Wenn.'

"What now?"

"Not sure."

"He doesn't seem like he wants to let us pass"

"Not really, no." Isaac said. "He's upset."

"That part translates pretty well. You speak Tugali?"

"Read really, but enough. He's calling her, well, I'm not sure that translates. Heretic, deceiver, something about 'slattern of the devourer,' if you take his word for it our fearless leader has been a busy spreader of lies and defiler of virtue. That part is probably exaggeration."

"Thanks Isaac." Her voice could have made a drowning man thirsty.

More than a couple times I've worked offloading cargo. It's an easy day job to get and it provided something even more valuable, access to the interior of warehouses. With the coastline moving farther and farther away from the city, the docks chase the harbor out to sea. Warehouses that are in prime location one year require laborious transport through new construction a few years after. Merchant captains hire the cheapest labor they can to make that trip and Myrport invented the principle of you get what you pay for. Watching a harried skipper rain insults, kicks, and generationally hoarded curses on a half drunk day hire for dragging a bale of batiqued silks across the boardwalk instead of a proper shoulder carry is worth a few hours of low pay by itself. These were masters of their craft, abusers of both character and virtue on a grand scale.

Judging from the virulent shade of pink the Tugali was turning, he'd missed his calling. He was on the edge of heart failure or stroke. That would have been fine, he'd already attacked us once. The room stank of it, a sourness in the mouth, the remembered odor of blood. The finger loop on my knife chafed as I filed away at the edges.

Lye slid behind me, sword held vertical in front of his body, one hand caressing the pommel and the other at the base of the blade. The last twelve inches of blade were unsharpened and wrapped in leather for that purpose. After the fight the night before I'd discarded any assumptions about how fast he could maneuver that thing. Having him in front of me would have been comforting, nothing about my jacket was going to help if one of those glass tipped darts came my way. Of course the way Sylvie told it in the bar, steel wasn't much protection anyway.

That put things right back where I was used to in a fight. Don't get hit. Good advice if you can follow it. Avoid getting distracted is an excellent place to start. Don't start paying attention to the guy with the mast sized sword who isn't going to hit you instead of the violently irrational man with a javelin or six aimed at you or your friends.

Instead of keeping my eyes front, I was watching Lye when the tip of his sword flicked out. Like watching a fly that tempts the frog just a hair too close. One second the frog's staring at you, not a care in the world, the next there's a memory of motion interrupted by a snap and the sound of pieces of javelin hitting the far wall.

Sylvie's sword glittered in the yellow light, ever angle precise and every step perfect. Bringing the blade up in front of her in classic blocking technique against an overhand blow, using the edge to create a slanted surface to glance the incoming weapon down and away from the defender's head. Her attacker was running through the exact same sequence to reload his ladle assisted throwing hand. That's the problem with drill, it's reliable but predictable. As he was socketing the next javelin he stepped toward us and to the side to clear a throwing lane for his partner.

Sylvie met him there, sword sweeping up to catch the javelin behind the head, flipping it out of his grip. Instantly she reversed direction. Wrist torqueing, blade held lightly but firmly, she drew a line down his torso. His mouth gaped wide and then gritted down in pain as the blade flayed open a inch deep cut from collarbone to waist. It wasn't fatal, merely painful. Before he could recover, she reversed again, using the same slashing motion across the chest muscles and into the neck, severing something that sprayed blood out as he dropped his ladle and clutched at the gaping cut that was decorating the area with his blood.

The other tribesman stepped into the gap created by the first. Reddish eyes locked onto mine, he chopped his hand down. The blue glass head flashed as it spun, again Lye flicked seven feet of steel, snapping the wood and sending the pieces to bounce off in the distance like someone dropping a rake. While I was busy not thanking The Mad Three, Sylvie spun and punched the tip of her sword down through the man's torso. Just as quickly she gave the hilt a wrench to the side as she pulled it back, severing as much of the dying tribesman's internal organs as she could.

After that it was just quiet and the smell of blood spreading. Hot saliva soaked my mouth and there was a vague feeling I should have do something useful. The realization that my big contribution to what had just happened was provoking the deaths of two people squirmed in my gut like a mud slug. That wasn't fair, the fight would have happened anyway, worse case I just moved the timing up by a few seconds, a minute, something. And then stood there like a gawp-jawed ship's boy walking into the Orchid for the first time. The look had been there though. The slug squirming in my gut might be asking what if, what if I'd read him wrong? But I'd have gone for the pot if I'd been around a Sevens circle with the Tugali. He'd been about to jump and the when didn't change anything.

Sure, and that changed anything, being right gets you

nothing on the docks.

Hospur pushed past Isaac to join Sylvie. She stood looking down at the corpse of the second man. The first one was still twitching, blood wasn't spraying anymore, but the flood seeped into a spreading pool causing little ripples as his wounds overcame the rest of him. The tip of her sword dripped the dead man's blood into the forming pool. The priest found a scrap in his satchel and handed it to her, finally grabbing her free hand and folding her hand around it.

"Did you know them?" Hospur said.

If she heard, she ignored the question, instead applying the cloth to blade, working the steel clean before addressing the smears and splatters on the basket hilt.

"We knew it might, probably would, come to this." Hospur kept his voice calm, reasonable.

The rag was worked into the nooks, blood gets everywhere, with a viciousness that made me want to be someplace else. Go look down the hallway for the reinforcements that had to be coming. Definitely not a subtle entrance, get into a loud screaming fight then kill people messily. Spitting seemed disrespectful but the thought of swallowing made me queasy.

Hospur tried again, "Speed, Sylvie, remember? If you can't do this we need to get out now."

Finally she rolled her shoulders, mimicking Lye adjusting the set of his armor, slammed the mostly clean sword home, and pinned me to the floor with a glance, "We'll talk later. Let's go, you first, me next, the rest follow."

Given a choice right then I would have taken the option for getting caught and hung rather than have that promised later. It had been the right call, doing the right thing, for the right people, wasn't that supposed to swing in my favor?

And why have me lead after that? To keep me where should could see me like some toddler that gets into it the moment you take your eye off them? Nobody booby-traps areas they traverse regularly, that's a good way to start misplacing family members. Uncle gets a little too far in the sauce and loses the toes off his left foot sort of stuff.

My stomach was doing flops and my thoughts were moving faster than a cart full of smuggled rye on cash out. It kept circling back on itself. It had been impulsive and unplanned, but running through it didn't change it anymore than diving to the bottom makes the bay shallower. He'd meant to kill her, execute her by attacking without warning. Whatever she'd done was a death sentence, she'd said as much. Those two had meant to carry it out.

That would be just the thing to console myself when she dropped me back in the tavern she'd fetched me from. Wrap my arms around all the gin they had and wait for Clar to clean up his loose ends. There's no fairness - my father taught me that and Myrport was always there to remind me if I started to forget.

So fine. Back to the docks, back to what I knew. I was good at that. Besides, nobody lasts forever at the top, or even at the top of the bottom. Make myself scarce for a while and Clar would be someone else as sure as fog replaces fog. Finish the job - rule one. Then maybe take a boat somewhere I could take care of myself. So that's what I did, gave myself a good shake, faced towards the center of the temple and stopped the runaway cart that had replaced my brain.

Mostly.

Sylvie was just behind me to the right and I could feel her, like the heat of a boiling kettle just before you grab it.

Just past the archway sat a couple chairs around a small brazier of unlit coal. After them was a series of narrow passageways lined with brass doors the size of family portraits you can get in the cheaper parts of Upper. People buy them when times are good to show off even though all the babies look like old men and the eyes are dead. When we came to a turn, Sylvie would point and I would head down the turn she chose. We didn't talk and I didn't look; the sensation was there as clearly as if she was pushing.

It was the not being yelled at that was worse by far, than if she'd just chewed on me for a bit and then stormed off in a huff. I think that would have been better anyways. Instead it gnawed at me, ate away, flaked off my composure like paint on the windward side until I was ready to stab someone just to have something to say.

The Lady of the Tides provides, or something.

Passages tighter than a beggar's last coin turned into larger halls, these with correspondingly bigger doors. Horizontal like a bread oven, made of brass and stacked three high. Long rows of the wealthier dead. Each buried with whatever worldly goods survived the tithe. Paid so their remains were safe in the protection of the temple.

A week ago I, or anyone I knew, would have gleefully strangled his mother to be where I was. A week ago if someone suggested I'd be jogging past them without the least urge to check inside I'd have taken his drink away.

Instead we moved on with hardly a glance. Names were cast into the cover plates but by that time we'd accelerated beyond hustle to just short of a run and only the need to avoid wrong turns kept us at that speed. It must have been agonizing for Hospur and I could hear the choked wheeze of Isaac's breathing when the halls morphed again into a series of intricately decorated rooms.

Each was fronted by a carved stone effigy. The carvings were two-faced, a reference to the goddess of the tides in her aspect forms of low and high tides, in the styles popular when endowments were settled. Usually one would be the husband and the other the wife. A couple were parent/child and even one that appeared to be a young/old version of a particularly narcissistic corpse.

I dropped the pace when we hit the first one. Sylvie wanted to push on, the warmth roiling off her spoke her intent clearly, pushing and prodding behind me.

"Take these carefully, way too easy to run into a pack of your...the guards."

"They don't just hang out in here."

"They didn't, but they know we're here, so they're going to be looking for us."

"We don't know that, you saw the crypt tunnels, probably nobody heard. I used to get lost down here, it's good for that."

"Maybe. If we do it my way we don't have to be wrong. Something I was taught, it's served me well enough."

Taught by my father, as it happens. There were things I'd learned since; how to use a knife, how to get gulled a little less by people like Josie the Fence, but it was his foundation that trapped me. The weight of that anchor felt heavier right then than it ever had. People hide their valuables, it's a hazard of the profession but I endure. Finding them isn't usually too hard; it's the picture frame that sits out from the wall a little far, the area rug where nobody sits, or the sneak thief trying to be something he's not.

"Just trust me." I said and then instantly regretted it. If she'd trusted me she wouldn't be seething behind me where she could keep me from dumping the bait again. I moved into the room to shut myself up.

The slower pace also meant we could hear. The Tugali may have been incorruptible foreigners with supernatural weapons but they were also guards and guards don't sneak. Soon the sounds of groups calling back and forth like pods of sailorfish floated through the chambers. Dive underwater with a pod, it's a spooky sound. It probably didn't help that I could reach out and touch a dead body if I wanted.

In the end we surprised each other. One of the Tugali hunting patrols jogged around the corner ahead at the same time that I moved into the next room. The slower pace let my natural impulses back out. A lifetime of thieving begged to look inside just one of the tombs. Well that, and I'm pretty sure I wouldn't be seeing any free drinks the moment I revealed my total failure to loot anything.

Somehow it seemed unlikely that Sylvie would see it that way.

I looked up and they looked over and we each stood rooted while we worked out our individual differences with the gods of luck.

The mausoleum had a distinctly new smell - fresh corpse

and fresh mortar. The passage we'd come through still hadn't been completely finished, bare stone instead of tile for the walls and ceiling, and the statuary in the room itself was freshly painted adding a sharp tang to the air. Each of the walls had spaces carved out for the future dead, but only one of them had the ubiquitous brass door sealing an occupant inside. Dominating the center was a circular block of stepped marble…probably the future home of a statue.

The thrumming snap of Lye's bow broke the startled standoff.

A heartbeat after, the bolt hit. Echoing a meaty slap that launched the lead tribesman back into the arms of his companions. His weapons clattered as they fell from nerveless hands amid a babble of command and counter order. One grabbed his friend and tried to support the corpse as he pulled it back out of the fight but there isn't much that cures a man of being pinned through the chest. The floor under them was instantly blood slick.

The other three snapped into the same drill as the ones we met earlier, wooden ladles up, javelin socketed, and I dove forward, rolled and came up with my back to the pedestal centering the room, as blue tipped missiles whipped past. Sylvie and the others vacated the middle at the same time letting the darts fly past to echo back to us where they landed.

The arbalest was tossed aside, value is relative when someone is trying to kill you, and Lye had the sword out again, stance wide as he covered the rest. Even he wasn't going to slap three or four of those out of the air if they launched at once.

I was up, legs pumping to close the gap before they could finish their reload drill.

Normally having a knife out when you collide with someone is the sort of danger I avoid. It's pretty easy to stab yourself like an amateur in the middle of a dog pile. This time I played the odds. One of me, three of them. Dagger out in front; a spear extended with my arm as the pole. By the third step they had reloaded, but by then I was too close to stop. Feet churning, I threw myself at the nearest as they chopped down driving the javelins into the air.

None hit. Somehow all three went under or over. Something coming straight at you is tough to counter and maybe I got more luck than I deserved.

Then it was my turn. A brief glimpse of wide pink eyes as the unfortunate target realized he'd lost the chance to do anything more than absorb the impact. My fist driving the knife through the upper ribs as his eyes got even wider and then a crumpling windmill ball as we spun into the Tugali next to him, collapsing under our combined weight. Something slammed into the side of my head, the grip of the dagger torqued away - nearly taking my finger with it.

The Tugali cushioned my fall, entangling and trapping as we went down. The sound of individual cries mixed in with the grunts and shouts of pain - like throwing a blanket on a mob of squabbling cats. Deadly intent became something happening somewhere else, even my finger - probably broken according to some far off spectator in my head - failed to hurt through the motes of sparkle floating around my vision. The watcher started screaming at me, get up…get up…get up, and something buffeted my head again. But it was a long way off; a knocking on a door floors away in one of those multi-story merchant prince's compounds. I tried to fend off the blows to my head, tried to rub my eyes clear to see.

Stabbing people is a messy business. Blood covered everything, my chest was wet with the blood of the man I'd speared and then used to break my fall. It was all over my hands and promptly all over my face as I pawed at the source of the blows and then in my nose, mouth and eyes.

With a twisting lurch I threw up all over myself and the Tugali.

It seemed like the thing to do at the time…or my stomach thought so anyways. There's lots of ways to win a fight, lots to lose one too, spewing all over my enemy was new. The Tugali was trying to club me to death, with the haft of one of his javelins, while trapped under the bulk of his dead friend and me. He recoiled as I lost the contents of my stomach over all three of us. He went from trying to murder me to scrabbling for escape in a blink.

Without the pounding rearrangement of my brain, I started to focus. Cold sweat covered me and I nearly followed his example. Getting away…anywhere away…sounded really good. The far off voice in my head rejoined me and I clamped down on that impulse - killed it as sure as I'd killed the man who had my dagger buried just above his heart.

"You come at me with a knife and we're gonna be friends, real close, you get me boy? Distance is the other guy's buddy, that's for the girl with a sword; a knife fight is the next closest thing to being born." The drunk who taught me that was shaped like a monkey and had more scar than skin up his forearms.

If I let that Tugali get out of arm's reach, he'd come to his senses and those javelins would finish the job. The other two would take their shot once they could be sure of not hitting their friend.

Stomach muscles still spasming, I grabbed a handful of pant. The leather slipped and twisted as he struggled to break away. Something caught for a second and then ripped free of my hand. The pain it caused was a blessing, clearing away the last of the fog. I found the finger ring on my knife, wrenched it loose with a popping crunch and another spray of blood, and then overhanded it like an ice hammer spike into the guard's free leg.

His agony howled down the hallways, and I lurched forward using the dagger to pull myself toward him before tearing the blade free and burying it again in his abdomen. The screaming choked off into a gurgle from the blow and I let him go. Between the spraying blood from his thigh and the fist-sized wound in his stomach he wasn't going to be getting tricky with those blue tipped darts anytime soon…or ever.

The floor lurched to the right. The voice trying to keep me alive was screeching at me to get up and get moving. Stationary is for the dead and the about to be dead. My stomach was a hard ball of knotted and salt lacquered rope, forcing its way up past my lungs. I gave in, closed my eyes, and everything went quiet.

Opening one eye made it worse, but not as bad as having both competing for focus.

Lye was checking the arbalest for damage; his sword was propped behind the stone base that I'd used for cover. The other three were out of sight. Rolling into a sitting position made the room wallow like a skiff at the bottom of a trough. By that point there was nothing to come up but stomach itself though. Sylvie and Hospur bracketed me a moment later. She had a scrap of something that she'd gotten wet. With one hand she started wiping my face clear, the other she held the back of my neck. It was cool and light; I could feel it in the tips of my fingers.

"Expert, is any of this blood yours?" Her voice was cool and light as her touch.

"Nuh." My mouth wasn't any more cooperative than my eyes.

"The way that last one was using his head for a drum, I doubt he knows. I'm well enough to help him but I doubt we have time. There's more on the way." Hospur said.

"Probably. We can't stop. You and Isaac will have to take him. Maybe you can do something while Isaac gets through the seals."

Then her hand was gone, replaced by Isaac and Hospur lifting me to my feet. A poor trade under any circumstance. Made worse by the waves of sea-sickness that went in and out whenever I tried to see where we were going. The twisted lurching in my stomach kept pace with the ebb and flow tide of nausea, until I just closed my eyes and allowed myself to be led at a stumbling half run.

There's a kids game they play on the docks. Two kids tie a leg together and then race another pair along a stretch of straight boardwalk. Running - loping really - being held up and guided by a pull or a shove was like that. Early on they pulled up short, dropping my arms amid a flurry of shouts. Opening my eyes just swam images and after images, so I squeezed shut and huddled where I was...too sick to care. After a moment they were back, hauling up, forcing me to stand and run some more. The running helped though. Soon I had an eye open that revealed only one of Sylvie and Lye ahead.

Sometime in the run we'd come up out of the crypts into a small underground village. The hallways were carved from the rock of the mountain and then sanded smooth giving them a glossy sheen pocked with thousands of little holes. Every so often there was a rectangular shaft leading away where the ceiling met the wall. They were eye-level for Lye, he pointed one of them out to Sylvie.

"Ventilation, keeps smoke and bad air from collecting."

Otherwise it had all the trappings of people living in the same ways everywhere. Doors with signs hung outside to advertise the selling of fish or ale. Every so often a larger open space with benches and tables, all deserted but with the debris that people leave behind in a hurry. Sylvie didn't try any doors, she just led down arbitrarily chosen passages that ended in stairs or another identical hall.

My stomach felt well enough to start complaining and my vision was mostly average. Every step felt like the dead man with the javelin was taking another whack, but I was recovered enough to care about living.

When we did stop, the door Sylvie chose was the same solid panel of polished wood as the others. No hinges on the outside, but that could be because it opened inward or someone had gone through the effort to hang the door with butt hinges recessed into the frame. It's not unusual for bedrooms and such where the occupant fears murder as well as theft. Since people like that keep their valuables close at hand it's something the aspirant to ill-gotten wealth learns to overcome. Personally, my favorite method is to use the window. Since I hadn't seen a window in hours that felt like days, keeping track of time is tricky while being chased by cannibals through underground warrens, I had to hope Sylvie had a solution.

"Isaac?" She stepped aside to clear space in front of the

door.

"This is it? It's beautifully done then. No warning, no chance of falsely triggering it. Much like the street performer, the charlatan who hides the..." Isaac started, looking at me obliquely.

"Isaac. We're a little pressed for time, if you don't mind."

"Fair enough. Would you like the door to be usable or not?"

"It doesn't matter, there are other routes, ones not available to us. Unlikely they'll follow us up this one." Sylvie said.

"In that case, Lye, right about here." He pointed at the spot he meant and then stepped aside to stand with Sylvie.

The tall warrior braced his back against the opposite wall, steadied himself with both hands out to the sides, and then launched both heels into the spot he'd been shown. The impact sounded echoes out like the breaker on a ship's hull. The door split from floor to ceiling about six inches from the wall. The larger part swung inward without a sound. Somewhere the craftsman who'd fashioned the concealed hinge felt his soul get a little smaller as his work was crushed beneath Lye's heel.

"That was subtle." I said.

"I think they know we're here already." Hospur appeared to be feeling better. His shield was on his arm now and some of the color was back in his face.

"Still."

"Talk about it later, Expert. We have to keep moving."

Beyond the door sat a squat iron staircase wrapping around itself into the ceiling. The metal shined with scouring from years, generations probably, of wire brush strokes to keep it free of rust.

Sylvie's lips were a line and the tendons in her neck tightened as she approached the circular staircase. I had a pretty good idea how she'd known about this way in. Iron wasn't useful for much of anything in Myrport. Salt air and water ate out nails faster than they could be built on top of. Whatever reasons the temple sisters had, it would have been just the thing to keep unruly and homesick young girls in line.

"Probably best if I go first." No slur in my voice either, if not for the angry brawl happening in my skull I would have felt fine.

Well, that and the smell. My shirt and pants stuck and began to rub as I walked. Nothing a good dunking wouldn't fix but I didn't envy anyone down wind.

Sylvie gave a small negative shake and followed it up with an even smaller smile, "No, there's nothing on these," the smile grew to include perfect teeth, "besides, your approach is a bit...enthusiastic."

"Seemed like the thing at the time. In retrospect, I think I'll invest in a helmet."

"I can't really see you with one. Maybe don't lead with your head next time."

"Thanks, I'll try that." I shot back.

This time the smile reached her eyes before she turned, inhaled, and took the stairs two at a time. The entire structure rung with each step like a tone-deaf bell. Anything up there definitely knew we were coming.

# TWENTY-THREE

A whole lot of things could have been at the top of those stairs. My bet would have been a room full of wiry white skinned, pale red eyed guards with a taste for my flesh.

Instead we found an old woman in priestess robes sitting in the center of a circular room. Next to her was the Goddess of the Tides, Mother of the Inner Sea, Queen of Mists, and so forth, carved out of green veined marble, polished to a mirror sheen. The dome above the statue bathed its subjects in pre-dawn light, creating a dappling blue haze through the glass.

The statue was even more impressive than I'd imagined listening to Sylvie describe it. Hidden away in the nave of the temple through massive double doors only the initiated ever passed was a masterwork, the culmination of the sculptor's art that even the wealthiest patron would never see.

If it were possible to extricate it from the temple, the thief who'd done it could establish their own seat on the council for the selling price...After being ritually drowned for profaning the most holiest thousand square feet of Myrport, of course.

The Goddess' feet were supported by a slightly raised representation of rocky coastline complete with a wave cresting behind her ankles. The priestess sat with her back supported by the stony wave and one translucent calf.

She was in that in-between state of being old without being decrepit. If she'd been walking about town she would have been someone's sprightly grandmother complete with walking stick she didn't need, but used anyway.

"Tides wash you through life and back to the mother." She said the words with an easy cadence, said a thousand times with the expectation of thousands more.

"Mother, sister, daughter, her waters return." As she said it, Sylvie did something with her hands we couldn't see from behind. Something in her voice would have set a cat's fur straight on end.

"No, some waters never return, I think. Or perhaps they do and should not in your case."

"That isn't yours to decide, priestess."

"No? You were never a willing acolyte but I suspect Sister Ellery managed to impart temple governance on even you."

"She did. But you are neither the goddess nor the priestess who speaks with her voice, Sister Fann."

So, not all warts then, but definitely something personal between them still. From what Sylvie had said before, Sister Fann was probably responsible for the long hours of familiarity with the iron stairs.

"The proper form of address is in the third aspect, my child." The woman sounded like the gull that's just snatched the herring. Something ugly and gloating made its way into her pronouncement.

"I should be more surprised than I am. How did you manage that?"

"Her hand on my shoulder, of course. Opposing your blasphemy helped. I would thank you properly, but when we tried that you let others suffer in your place."

"Felity." The name escaped Sylvie's composure in a choked spasm.

"Yes, that was her name. You have much to answer for." the priestess took in the rest of us, "More now. There isn't even a precedent to cover what you've done today. Water wears. To think even the armies of Hebrinda selected only female soldiers to loot the Goddess and yet you have the gall to stand before Her with not just men, but a speaker of heresy."

Hospur mimicked Lye's shrug and paired it with a complacent smile.

"I've stood in the presence of the Goddess in this very spot; your actions since that day make me doubt that you can say the same." Sylvie said.

The priestess straightened, her expression hardened, no longer someone's favored grandmother, "Witless child, you know nothing, the delicate walls of spun glass that keep the Temples safe, generations of work playing kingdom against kingdom, you claim to be something we gave up before this temple was built. We did it to avoid turning the combined might of the kings of the inner sea against us for our meddling. This desecration would undermine the cause of the Goddess throughout the Inner Sea."

"She doesn't agree."

"She? What, this old girl?" With one spotted hand she smacked the carved leg over her head, "Honey, take a young woman just getting comfortable with herself, prime her with a wash of ideas about how special she can be, how important, then starve her a bit, deprive her of sleep, and miracles are the least of what can happen."

"That's not how it was."

"Of course it was. I've watched it for fifty years after it happened to me. We provide them with the vision, they do the rest. It's a statue, girl. I prayed for twenty years after my initiation without a word, without so much as a whisper. When I was elevated to turn wasted daughters into my fellow priestesses, I prayed for another decade. I've spent more time in prayer than you've been alive and you think to tell me what she says? The traditions have lasted for millennia and through me they'll last another millennia and no trumped up sprite with fever dreams is going to change that."

"Why?" Something about Sylvie's voice reminded me of the sound of ropes snapping under black clouds and rain you had to hold your breath to walk through.

"Because it works, dear."

"What about the ice? Every year the mire grows and the Ring weakens. I've been there; entire fortresses are gone, covered in ice too thick to break through. You know what that means."

"It means nothing. It means a few sailors drink too much and talk too much."

"I've been there!"

"So what if you have? You had to go somewhere when you fled judgment. Why show any more sense than you showed when we offered you the chance to recant your heresy." she paused, tapping the carved head of her stick against the floor.

"Those fortresses have stood the ice at bay since before the Tugali fled, you know that, why are they failing now?"

"No concern of ours! Age, the will of the Goddess, the work of gnats, it is all the same. Enough child. You have tested enough of my patience. It is time for this to end. You will submit to the will of the temple as is just and your friends will be turned over to be hung as thieves."

"Does that ever work?" It seemed like the thing to ask. Every part of me itched from drying blood and worse and something about her voice drove spikes into the throbbing over my right eye.

"You will keep your silence. Pray I don't ask for more than a simple execution. You dare speak where you stand unwanted, the cast off birth of a street beggar. "

"That was fairly personal. You and my mother must have been close, sisters, or just coworkers?"

The grandma was gone, replaced by snarling hatred wrapped in spotted skin and painful looking wrinkles. She shoved the foot of the walking stick into the floor and leveraged herself upright. Her lips glowed purple in the light radiating from above the divine representation, glistening as she licked away the dryness.

"You debased spend of a man! How dare you? When they hang you, it will be a gracious end to your gutter bred mewling!" Flecks of foam speckled her lips as she chopped off each word.

"Expert…" Sylvie started.

"Running out of time…she can't stop us and she's really sort of annoying. Let's get what you came for and get out before the Tugali decide to come in here after us."

The doors on the opposite wall were barred shut, the light streaming in from the dome rippling the wood. The whiter light of dawn had begun smothering the darker blues currently cloaking the room. My chest felt like I'd taken a bite of a beehive, empty and full of things flitting every direction at once.

"She's stalling Sylvie, I don't know why or for what, but she is."

Days spent out on the edge of the moorings watching traffic from all over the Inner Sea taught me something. Overbuilt galleons from the North Kingdoms with their red tinted hulls, sleek sail driven trade sloops from the Eastern Edge, multi tiered galleys with bank on bank of oars, and all outnumbered by the flat wallowers build locally from whatever imported lumber was cheapest. All follow the same rule. The ship under way has the right of speed; everyone else gets out of the line of traffic or gets driven under in the inevitable collision. The priestess had a plan and all her sails were already run up and if Sylvie waited much longer, that plan was going to plow us under.

Every single intuition and carefully honed awareness I'd been taught and discovered screamed like a stuck seal to get out, get moving, and don't stop until we were somewhere that worshiped turnips and temples was what they called their version of The Orchid.

Except that hadn't worked out very well before. Blame it on being in the presence of a god if that helps. It wasn't that though. It was less divine inspiration and more about being tired, run down, beat up, and cresting a wave of decisions that hadn't worked out quite like I'd planned. For all that, things weren't as bad as they could have been. Besides being trapped in the heart of a fortress where my presence was both illegal and a form of sacrilege punished by slow painful death I was actually approaching a state beyond fear, perhaps. Instincts and experience could take a long walk off any pier. Long walks in Lower were dangerous regardless of the pier length. It was her call and I wasn't going to make it for her.

Instead I wondered if she would like to kiss me. Possibly I was not quite underway with all sails.

"Enough girl. Do not further your crimes. Surrender and face the judgment that should have been yours. Set aside your weapons and be done with this."

"We both know that isn't going to happen. I will get what I

came for. Give me the keystone."

The priestess looked like she'd reached for cheese and had a mouthful of butter instead, "Keystone? What keystone? Is that what you are after? Something else to do with the Ring? Should it make me feel better you aren't here for gold or worse that you desecrate this sanctuary for foolishness?"

"If it's foolishness, then give it to us and we will go."

"Almost I could, child. If I didn't have dead guardians and that overblown prat, Poulsen demanding I turn you over. Of course by law and custom I'd then suffer the fate that awaits you. Just a little ironic given the last time you left."

"Fitting though." Hospur said. That left the priestess with her mouth wide as a door and turning snapper red.

Sylvie unfolded her arms and waggled a finger at Hospur behind her back, "I regret the deaths. It was not the way I was hoping for. Please, give us the stone. The ice is spreading, ask the Tugali!"

"Ask them yourself!" With that, the priestess raised her walking stick up and then swung the carved head down with both arms. The wood splintered into the floor, shards of splinters spraying out causing her to recoil from the impact. She collapsed back into the statue, bounced off its marble shin, and fell into a tangled heap of robe and frail old woman.

Sylvie lunged forward and pulled up short.

The far wall and doors danced and then shattered like the reflection in a stomped puddle, reveling double rows of chalk pale men arrayed to either side of the doorway. Each held a toasted cream shield in full guard position. The front rank carried swords the length of a forearm that scattered the dappled blue light against the armor and shield of the Tugali next to him. The back rank held spears; shafts made of the same toasted cream and headed by deep blue flat leaf blades.

"That is not an improvement." I said.

A deep thrum, bees under assault by a stick, spread through the room. The last scraps of the spell of hiding fell away; panes of distortion, warping parts of the ranked Tugali, as they fluttered to the ground and pooled toward the Goddess' feet. With it, the statue base of waves and sculpted stone, started to flow and melt. Tendrils of marble formed a latticework over the fallen form of the priestess.

On top of the angry buzz the front row of guards stomped forward a pace, naked feet slapping the stone in perfect unison.

"HUAH!"

The cry ripped into us from the front rank. Followed by a perfectly simultaneous grounding of the shields, the flat bottom edge striking the floor. It felt like someone had hit my soles with a stick.

"I think I preferred the javelins. Sylvie?"

She was staring at the crumpled priestess, ignoring the ruckus across the room. "Hmm?"

Lye walked slowly to the right, undoing his sword as he fanned out.

"Turns out the sneaky minx was hiding twenty armed men up her sleeve. They seem unhappy with us." I glanced behind me to see Isaac shifting furiously through bits of paper and script

Behind the shield wall, each of the spears was flipped end over end, shafts cutting the air, ten crazed hornets joining the maddened bee noise, and then stopping dead.

"HUAH!"

Feet slapped down into a single ear cringing smack. Now that the back row was uncovered by the grounding of the front line, I could see the shields the back rank held were smaller and round. Over their shoulders each sported a quiver of the smaller javelins.

"Tides...My big mouth." I said.

"Well, once we close with them, they probably won't throw."

"That's great news, Hospur."

"Keep the toughs between you and them. If they don't kill us all, I'll do what I can." He still wasn't moving naturally, favoring the side Dugal had stabbed, but he slid out to the right with his shield up. The flanged mace he favored dangled from the other hand, partly hidden by his body.

Sylvie caught my eye as she slipped her sword sheath from its hanger before tossing it behind Isaac, "Ignore the drill, it's meant to scare and rattle."

"Effective. Definitely rattled."

On the other side of the room the front rank started tapping their shields against the floor. Slowly, each impact sending little shocks to be felt through my shoes as well as heard. Each tap was followed by a low chant, "Cha Meyte!"

"What are…oh no." Sylvie said.

Her attention fixed on the Tugali like a drunk on the last bottle. Whatever they'd said was bad, but I didn't have time to ask. We were playing house odds and that never ends well for anyone but the house. Isaac was up to something back by the stair, pieces of parchment mixed with paper shed away from him as he searched for something that would even our odds. Or at least I hoped that was what he was doing. Maybe he was looking for a blank sheet to write last words on. It was probing to be a good time for that.

The Tugali shields smashed down in a steady rhythm, still chanting but accelerating. The words had changed, "Cha Oya," accompanied by a percussive roar. The entire temple had to be hearing this. I had a pretty good idea what happened when it was too fast to keep up and the five of us against twenty trained warriors would make a smear that would take a lot of mops.

"HUAH!"

Somehow they all stopped at the exact moment, ending with a guttural explosion.

There were little differences, this one pulled back his hair with a tie, that one had a leather vest reinforced with plates of the same material as his shield, but tides take me, I couldn't tell if one was their version of an officer. If there was a signal I didn't see it. The silence was sudden and oppressive, the way the air seems wet and solid right before a lightning strike.

…and then I was busy.

The ten in the back hurled their weapons forward, arms

straining. The bigger spears arced upward even in the smaller room; not like the flat throw of the javelin. One of those fat, broad heads would hit like an axe head though. Hospur was down behind the wall of his shield in an instant. To the right, Lye hardly moved, the sword torqued through the air while he watched it, seeming amused by the antics of his hands and blade. It sounded like he was pulling sawclaw legs off for dinner, a couple pops and a crack that send pieces of spear pin wheeling off to the sides of the room and then a susurrated meatier thunk, as the ones he hadn't hit landed in shield and stone.

Hospur lunged forward, closing the distance between himself and the advancing wall of shields. The priest treated the raised shields as targets, pelting them with his mace. His own shield turned into a pincushion, dangling several shafts from where javelin heads had embedded themselves. Rather than tossing it to the side he slapped it again and again against the wall to his left, forcing the shafts into the faces arrayed against him. Somehow he had a half dozen trained soldiers recoiling and blocking blows from both, rather than attacking.

Lye struck the other side a second before his friend; his blade was as long as he was plus three feet of reach. His approach was direct - an overhand crushing blow at one of the shield men. The pale soldier flipped his shield nearly horizontal, trained response easily interposing the block. Against a normal blow it would have easily parried. Against Lye it was a life saving but flawed maneuver. The force of the strike drove the shield back, crumpling him with it, driving the hapless soldier into the man behind him and throwing them both out of the line into the hall behind. His fellow lost the javelin he'd been preparing as he was thrown onto his back hard enough to shatter teeth and sever his own tongue. They were both out of the fight.

Sure as rot follows rain, the little javelins…big darts, the distinction wasn't clear while I was trying to make myself fit behind a marble thigh, came for us a second later.

Sylvie appeared to be in a daze, like someone had slipped her something, spice root in her drink. Somehow she batted away the couple that would have hit her. She was talking but not to anyone in the room. Her sword was in constant motion, conducting to something only she could hear. I could see the key in her other hand.

My father would have laughed, "This is why you don't do heroics, boy. Thieves are like servants, better unseen and unheard. Both skimming from wealthy, come to that. Now get me another drink." I told the voice in my head to get his own drink.

Hospur was in trouble, he couldn't get through the guard and the ones on the end were flanking his shield side despite his attempts to keep them honest. As one of those general rules, a shield trumps a dagger no matter how well used. Daggers are close in weapons and a shield works as well as a wall for keeping a little personal space.

At that point I'd committed at least half a dozen crimes that would get me sentenced to death in any kingdom bordering the inner sea, one more wasn't going to make it any worse.

"Sorry about this," if there wasn't a decree against using idols of the Goddess as a climbing aid I was sure there would be if I survived the fight. The marble folds were excellent hand and foot aids. Using the netting of stone covering the robed woman as a step stool, I scrambled up like there was money to be had. Once I was standing on the massive shoulder I discovered I was exactly where I planned to be and a spectacular target.

Several of the javelin tribesmen were down, the rest were reacting to Lye's rampage on their right flank, backing away from Hospur, but they stopped when they saw me and started hurling as fast as they could pull missiles from their quivers. The air was suddenly full of sparkling blue tips driven by wooden shafts. The head of the Goddess deflected a few and I kept moving, watching for my moment and hoping Hospur would last long enough for my plan.

He nearly didn't. Later we discovered the stitching on the stab wounds ripped. How he managed to keep the staccato blows going while simultaneously deflecting the stabs aimed at him is probably an actual miracle. It is possible the Three hated the

Tugali more than they dislike me.

Just before I jumped, he slapped aside a sword blow, driving a splintered spear shaft sticking out from his shield across the cheek and into the eye socket of a particularly offensive tribesman. Whatever the hapless man had done to so offend the gods, he paid a second later as he dropped shield discipline and his sword to cover the ruined eye, now a mass of scarlet and raw bone. Without a pause in the pattern, Hospur flicked the mace, light as a kiss, the sound was like dropping a gourd, and the corpse collapsed underfoot. Skull caved in from the blow, another hazard on a floor that was slick with blood and discarded weapons.

Some fights are over faster than you can muscle down a shot of bad booze. Some have a life of their own. Move, counter, and repeat. Continue until something gives way and one side assesses victory and the other defeat. Size and numbers usually predicts one from the other. Blind stupid risks, almost never.

Hospur backpedaled from the man he'd just dropped to avoid being gutted like a fish and the Tugali pressed in, they had the advantage and knew it despite their luckless friend.

So I stepped off the outstretched marble arm, heels locked together, arms tucked, like jumping off a board into the water. The man I was aiming for had some instinct, maybe he sensed movement overhead, I had a glimpse of open mouth and wide red irises before my boots crushed down into the middle of the remaining line. I kept my knees locked until I felt the initial impact and then rolled with it, just like I'd been taught.

Of course the practice floor hadn't been littered with men, shields, and naked blades. The hapless target under me crumpled under my feet, I twisted and folded at the same time and the two of us flowed into a third who pushed back, trying to steady his friend, forgetting his hands were full of sword and shield. We split the difference. The shield punched into my side and something slid and popped, driving the air out of my lungs. His sword slid into the man breaking my fall with a gristly tearing sound before the combined weight drove us to the floor.

Somehow I rolled past and back onto my feet. My throat was locked closed. Chest spasming to get air, but nothing would flow. A kitten could have finished me off. My dagger was still in my hand but the need for air became my only focus. My mouth worked like a trout, ribs grinding as I tried to force air where my throat was determined nothing should pass like some doomed hero holding a nameless bridge.

Panic fought with panic, I'd lost track of the fight. The next thing I was going to feel was the shattering burn of a blade.

Instead there was nothing and finally air. The muscles in my throat gave in to the need to breathe and then caught again as my lungs filled with air and promptly reconsidered the wisdom of that as bone rubbed on bone. I settled for little gasps, short pants that were absorbed in the stomach rather than moving the ribs.

"That was closer than I'd like." Hospur's breath was coming in gasps.

The best I could manage in reply was a nod and a hand waving him off.

The one who'd stabbed his friend was down, his face a scarlet mix of blood and crushed bone. Another one lay where he'd fallen, skull caved in from behind. Several of the back rank were down as well. Lye was smearing blood off himself and his sword, wiping at the steel with a rag that was redistributing more than cleaning. Streaks of blood tracked out of the chamber where the remaining Tugali had broken and ran while I was choking.

Early morning sun streamed and spotted the walls, mixing with fluids pooled on the floor. Desecration and worse. Piety wasn't part of my training but what we'd turned that place into was hard to look at. Sylvie stood where I'd left her, lips twisted, eyes locked on the senseless priestess. The impromptu lattice dome had flowered open from the top, blossoming into petals of stone that left the priestess asleep at the center of her magical flower.

Wet streaks tracked down Sylvie's face. She'd done what she knew she had to, bringing us to that spot, but anyone who survives the docks can tell you there's a difference between the thing you have to do and liking it.

"Sylvie?" I wiped my glove off and reached for her shoulder.

"Mmm?" She didn't move away.

"We have to move, where's the keystone?" My hand felt like it was glowing, maybe with a large sign announcing its presence or a trumpeter. I wanted the connection but didn't have a clue how or when to remove it. Should I let it drop now? Or now?

"She has it." Isaac joined us, book tucked under one arm, while he tried to put his recovered pages into an order that made sense, "That's what she used to set the trap and create this," He waved a hand at the melted and fused stone. "She must be a formidable woman, it should have killed her."

"What? Hiding a small army? Why we didn't do that."

"It would take a while to explain to someone like you."

"The short version is fine."

Lye gave up on his cleaning and moved over to watch the door. Hospur finished checking the fallen and bent over the priestess, he was holding his side like it might come apart if he let go.

"Ever seen a horse race? The riders use a bridle to control the horse, right?" Isaac said.

"I may have seen a race, yes. And yes."

"The keystone is like a horse without a bridle and a trained rider."

"The keystone being the bridle?"

"Yes, exactly. You are quicker than you look. I would have theorized that much unmanaged power would have killed her if I hadn't seen it. I suspect the only reason it worked at all was her familiarity with this specific place and perhaps the place itself."

"That's why we didn't do something like it then?"

"Yes, that is why we didn't attempt to channel sufficient unnatural power to shorten our lives by half."

"That's too bad, because in minute or two, the ones who ran away are going to meet up with the other hundred or so, and come invite us for breakfast."

Isaac swallowed and redoubled his organizing.

Sylvie reached up, squeezed my hand, and crouched down, rummaging through the fallen priestess' robes. A second later she lifted an arm and pulled back the barrel sleeve to reveal a thin gold chain looped around and around from elbow to hand until it formed a metal sleeve of its own.

Embedded in the fleshy palm was a piece of opaque white crystal. It would have fit right in at a market square, another unfinished bit that the locals used to fashion into cheap jewelry or as a focus for an icon. The stone was half covered by the woman's skin, a raw reddish border against the milk of the keystone. Removing it would take a knife and a willingness to draw blood, no shortage in the room at the time, in retrospect.

"That's the other reason, it's the keystone in a very literal sense, it's part of the building it powers, or in this case, the person. If it is threatened, it seals itself away. Sylvie broke the seal, that's what the keystone was for, but there's no telling what that did to the priestess. Removing it may kill her, but the damage done by shattering the seal may render that a kindness." Isaac shrugged, "Renn is correct though, we have a tide to keep."

"Let me do it, if I can save the hand I will." Hospur took the woman's forearm from Sylvie and started the task of separating skin from stone.

I found a sudden urge to join in the watch at the door.

Getting out of the temple proved much simpler than getting in. The ritual path to the sanctum passed directly through the audience hall that sees supplicants who come to the temple for healing, worship, and the burial of the dead. It was large enough to build a ship in and completely vacant when we got there. The patrons and priests who had been there, fled when the Tugali had. Tendrils of smoke from still burning incense swayed through the morning light. We kept to the side columns and made our exit. The outer gate guards were city watch who were tasked with keeping the poor and disreputable at bay. We definitely fit the description of the latter, but since we weren't trying to come in, they took no official notice.

Normally, I existed in a one sided truce with the Watch, I wished them no ill, and they felt the same. Mostly because it's tough to wish bad luck upon someone you don't know exists. In this case I felt a little bad for those two. About five minutes after we left, give or take, their world was going to come down around their helmets.

# TWENTY-FOUR

The line between Upper and Lower Myrport differs depending on where you view it from. Walk up the hill a stretch and the houses start growing legs, thick beams to keep the floors level over terraced gardens and the view stretches out over Lower and docks proper. Lower Myrport, including all of dockside, stretches out from there. A mottled scab covering the mire, bounded on one end by the rocky foot of mountains. At the other, shipping from the inner sea snuggles up to be weighed down once again before dropping sail and making way past the break and into open water.

Down at street level where the smell of rotting mud is beaten down by the rain, the lines are harder to see but easy to hear. People, navigating up and down the winding streets, can tell where they are simply by the sound of their steps. Boot heel on paver and you're in Upper; when it becomes the hollow knock of board, you're back in Lower. For a few yards the buildings look the same, their owners struggling to keep up a façade, but it fools nobody.

Relief at the sound of the boards beneath my feet, didn't make it past the twisting in my stomach. I was prepared. Sickly sure that at some opportune point Sylvie would stop. She'd be poised and assured. Gracious in thanking me. She'd offer some reward, for services rendered, which I would take.

There was gin to buy and Clar and his man would be looking for me…possibly Gobineau, as well. If there was enough, maybe I could lay low long enough for them to lose interest. Or long enough that Josie wouldn't see more profit in selling me than paying me.

"Expert," Sylvie kept her voice low but I'd been waiting for this. If I'd thought my stomach had wound itself as far as it would go, it gave a lurch flop to prove me wrong. Somehow she still smelled of spice and trees.

"That's it then, world saved or whatever it was we were doing?" Sometimes the choice between an inch at a time and the whole tail is better if you do it yourself.

"Yes. Now we…" she started.

"I understand. Look, she really was stalling. I know should have…you know I'm not sure what I should have. I had a friend once, Joh, he'd do the same thing…act on impulse.

I just thought…if you need anything when you come back. This thing with Clar'll blow over. Just ask around, leave word at the Pike, the Net-n'-Hook…or even that place with the boat on the sign. You remember, the one from the other night? Just make it worth a few dirhams to the staff and they'll pass on…what?"

Sylvie looked like she'd eaten the bait, mistaking it for lunch, and couldn't decide between spitting it up or swallowing. Since I'd been staring at anything to avoid eye contact, it was Hospur who'd caught my eye and shut me down, practically making fleet signals to get my attention. A small family could have wintered over in the heat coming off my face.

Mouth big enough for my foot and a fat little coastal trader.

"What I was about to ask, before…whatever that was…was how do we get to The Dawnlight, our ship, ideally without running into any of your former associates. We," she circled me into the word with one gloved hand, "have an escape to make."

Somehow my skin got even hotter. Could I cook from my own embarrassment?

"Go easy on the poor boy, Sylvie, he looks like he might have sweating sickness. Bed rest might be the thing." Hospur was the sort of man who offers a mug of ale to the drowning.

"I'm sure they have a spare hammock aboard."

"I'm fine." More mumble than declaration. Ancient wisdom noted that it isn't possible to choke and die on your own appendage. This time it proved correct.

Isaac put on his lecturers voice, "It might be brain fever. Onset is sudden and without apparent symptoms."

"Thanks, Isaac, don't you have a book to eat, I mean read?"

"Now, now, Renn. Isaac has a point, any frothing or urge to spit?" Hospur's face was guileless.

Sylvie's question still hung unanswered and served as a distraction, "Not in an actual sense, no." I directed at her. "We should get moving or it won't matter which route we take."

With the newfound friendship between Clar and Gobineau, it probably didn't matter anyway, but it takes time to make decisions and then more time to round up forces. The watch doesn't travel any but the major routes during the day and not at all at night. Any attempt to stop us would come from Clar and those wouldn't be soldiers, standing around armed and ready.

The riches of the Inner Sea pass through Myrport, but mostly they don't head into the city. Instead they spend some time in the warehouses and then back onto a different ship heading to their port of sale. That fact help keeps folks like me from starving; we do what we can to see that some of them stick around a while. No thanks necessary. Even so, there are some things that need to make the trip to dry land. For that there are a couple accepted paths that navigate the boardwalk, depending on who the owner feels like paying protection for safe travel.

The prior few months had changed even that. Clar held most of the juicy bits. Some holdouts did exist in places, like the Runs. Which weren't worth the trouble or returned a bleeding stump when someone tried to grab them. Going through those would avoid or slow down interference from whoever was yanking Clar's strings. It would also probably get us killed. They don't like strangers, especially armed wealthy strangers. Those they hate.

"Do you trust them?" I said.

"Trust who? You lost me" She was bouncing on her toes. The space between ready and numb is fingerling small and just as easy to let slip.

"The captain of the ship, The Dawnlight. These are direct people. If they know about what happened in the Temple, they'll want to keep you where they can control the environment. While we're in the city they can try again, as many times as it takes. If they can cut off the exit. So can they?"

To her credit, she took the time to consider the question. Most folks don't take the time to review their assumptions. 'Of course Terr is trustworthy, we've been friends since playing pilgrim stones in the cobbles', then it turns out Terr sold them out for some silver coins and a free night at the Orchid. We moved at a half jog while she thought.

Faster would have been nice, but Hospur's wounds were blushing his shirt as the blood mixed with sweat in pink streaks he kept covered with a clamped elbow. He was tough as a one eared street dog, but his face was developing lines and a pallor that aged him by a few decades. Sylvie watched him like the dog's mother, but the ship and rest was the best we could do for him.

"Haas owes me and doesn't know Myrport. He'll be there for us." She said.

"In that case, they'll be on the docks. They'll have connected you and the ship by now, they can combine forces - and not spread them across Lower Myrport."

Just to keep things honest, I picked out a route just off the standard channel. The decay and demolition cycle that maintains the docks doesn't allow for things like streets, so residents navigate by being lost creatively. The mountains are one way and the ocean is the other so as long as you head for one and away from the other, you can never be really lost. Like most things, it's the details in the middle that matter. By the second or third week the clues that tell a blind alley from a dogleg become second nature.

Pickling my insides on a regular basis may not be great for health and longevity, but it does mean I know most of the drinking spots within earshot of the docks. Windows aren't a big feature of building in Lower Myrport. They let in rain and cost money. Luxuries like that are reserved for people who aren't focused on eating and staying warm, in that order. Knowing what was waiting for us before we stepped into the open might mean the difference between a glorious escape and a messy bleed out. Fortunately I knew of a place, it started out as a business office for a merchant house that doesn't exist anymore. Eventually it changed hands and the new owner gravitated to the never-ending demand sailors have for drinking and spending their pay. A place called Savki's. It was cold enough to preserve meat and the windows got boarded over instead of replaced; mornings should see it deserted which made it perfect.

We wound our way past most of the dead ends and before mid-morning we were standing outside the back of Savki's.

"Tide and Reef, I don't remember it being this bad." Hospur said.

I think something died." Isaac had a hand over his mouth pinching his nose.

There's a smell - part rotten grain, part sour urine - that's unmistakable, fronting the quays.

"On reflection, perhaps we should take up the option of surrendering to the local thugs. If nothing else so I don't have to inhale ever again." Isaac moved up to the first step leading to what passed for a kitchen.

"That's not a good place to hang out. Soldiers and criminals are lazy, they won't look for us here. Besides, if I'm right, we should be able to go in the back and out the front. From there it's a straight shot to where the Dawnlight is…or as straight as things get." I said.

"Have you looked at what you are standing on?"

Isaac was referring to the slatted construction of the walk just next to the steps. Since the standard waste disposal involves tossing whatever is in the bucket off the steps, he had a point. If the curious had a lantern, they could see the mire through the gaps, set about the width of a hand between the boards. The wood had long since acquired a patina of grease and filth. The back of a drinking establishment is not a good place to stand if you value your footwear. Footprints smucked the goo here and there; leading to a desire to burn your shoes and get up on something that didn't slide under you like chewed gristle.

"Just don't light anything on fire and we'll be fine."

"Keep it simple then," Sylvie said, "Lye goes first, Expert, you and I to the sides, Isaac help Hospur. I can see the blood, you dolt, stay out of the way and try not to get killed by some amateur with a knife."

Lye shrugged, unfastened the sword from over his shoulder, and slipped by me to get to the steps where Isaac made himself skinny to make room.

"There's nobody back here. I told your boss that the last seventeen...tides!"

The flat board that served as a door slapped open to bounce off Isaac. His arms whipped around a couple times before he teetered over onto the boardwalk he'd been escaping. Sludge fanned out from the impact, liberally coating his pants with dark globules that deformed into ooze.

The shove came from a bale sized man with a face that was more pock than skin. The steps gave him the height to get a brief glimpse eye to eye with Lye before the door whipped back and was caught by his forearm. He stared at us staring at him, hand steadying the offending door.

"What the..." If he'd been a smarter man his nose might still be straight.

++Instead he was cut off by the pommel of Lye's sword, jabbing out by two hands gripping the leather wrapped section at the base of the blade. It hit the bouncer on the nasal bone, just below eye level, with a wooden sound and a spray of blood, spittle, and mucous. Both eyes tried to focus on a point an inch out and he sat back, remained upright for a heartbeat, and then his head hit the wood floor behind him. One foot kicked out and then he was still, chest rising and falling in a burbling snore.

"Well, there goes simple." I said.

"I'm going to be sick." Isaac sat where he'd landed, hands thick with muck like a wet hawk trying to dry its feathers after a miss.

"Be sick later," Sylvie hauled him upright by the armpits, "he did warn you."

"That is of great comfort right this moment."

Any snappy retort was cut short by a female voice calling

from deeper inside, "Durk, you get distracted by the kitchen? Check it's clear already."

Temptation burbled up like the soup Durk was supposed to be skimming. I covered my mouth with both hands and plugged my nose to approximate the comatose bouncer's nasal whine, "Said it's clear, tides take you!"

"That never works!" Sylvie was smiling, it wasn't going to make things worse, "Get ready, this is about to get messy."

"Suck bilge, didn't have to be difficult. Back in an hour."

"I don't want to know what that cost your soul, Expert. Lye, haul that out so we can get past. I hope you have a change on the ship Isaac, you're going to have to burn those."

The kitchen was just barely worthy of the name. I had to wonder how Durk maintained his size off of it without dying from the spoilage. Lamb and poultry corpses were stacked to one side of the back door, next to a bucket - half full of yesterday's fish. The juices from both formed a small trickle out the back door, adding to the ambiance. There was no oven for the bread, just a shelf to store what they brought in, next to a pit of coal peat, keeping a pot the size of a small child going. No amount of lucre could pay me to taste the contents. The odor of rotting permeated the room, somehow worse than the mire and sludge from outside.

"Remind me not to come back here."

Hospur chuckled, "Son, I see a long sea voyage in your future."

"Suddenly fish and dried pork sound delicious."

Sylvie shoved the swinging door to the common room hard, banging it back on its hinges and letting it recoil back to be stopped by her boot. A sensible precaution if there was anyone lying in wait with a crossbow. There wasn't, just a surprised looking drunk and the man tending bar…probably owned the place. Or, judging from the exchange with the sleeping Durk, part owner with a majority share held by Clar.

Sylvie let the door rest against her foot for a breath and then pushed through to confront the hapless man frozen in mid polish, damp rag in one hand, clay mug in the other. He looked ready to bolt but stuck in a cycle of terror. The gods of luck hate everyone but they were making a special point for him. When things sorted out, whatever happened to us, his odds were bad.

Sylvie cut short any plans for running off to warn his unwanted business partners, plucking the mug from his hand with the tip of her sword. He immediately switched to polishing a forehead that went all the way back to his ears.

"Sorry about this, we're just passing through." I said.

I felt a little bad for the man. He'd lost the small amount of color he had, bottom lip trembling. Running a business with the likes of Clar was a tense affair when times were good. If they figured out he'd let us use his place to access the docks, not that he had any choice, they'd take their time making an example. Mostly that's what they did, collect money they hadn't earned and kept their business going by fear. It made my line of work look positively noble.

"Cut him up a bit, make it bloody." It might not work, but it might save his life.

"What?"

"Maybe make it look like we forced our way through. Who knows, maybe some pretty young thing will take a liking to rakish bar owners with scars."

I moved past her to check outside. Only a couple windows remained, perfect for our purposes.

Slate grey washed everything outside of the window making seeing anything for certain hopeless. The difference between raining and not, is always a little arbitrary in Myrport. The fog swamps in when it isn't beaten back by a steady drizzle. Call it the difference between wet and damp. The tide was on the verge of changing, cargo laden outbound ships called to each other, bells ringing. The sails were just solid blocks of fog at any distance leaving wooden spires, painted or left raw depending on their home ports, gliding in and out of view.

Ships wouldn't be arriving anytime soon. They came in with the tide just as they left, using the Mother's natural cycle. That was good and bad for us. Inbound vessels needed unloading which meant the piers would be swarming with day laborers, crew, and the parasites in charge of taxes and duties along with the muscle to get their cut. Crowds like that are easy to get lost in, something that would have aided our escape. On the bright side, no inbound vessels meant spotting Clar or Gob's men would be easy; it's hard to blend in sitting wet on an empty dock.

"And there they are." I resisted the urge to duck back, motion draws the eye. "Sure we can't wait twelve hours or so? A little misery is good for character, according to my father."

Lye was peeling a turnip that had seen better days while giving the barman significant looks to discourage adventurism. He gave a snort at my suggestion.

"Tempting, but I suspect that woman won't fall for the voice trick in person. You'd need to be two of you." Sylvie leaned over my shoulder to check the view.

My skin tingled at the proximity and I stopped thinking about the clump of irritably wet thugs enjoying weather and time of day wholly unfamiliar to their way of life...and mine for that matter. My brain buzzed and bounced around like a fly caught in a ship's lantern around her.

"Ouch. I need to cut back then. 'getting fat with all this sedentary living."

"I suspect you'll get some exercise soon." Her tone was unreadable but the feel of her breath on the back of my ear slathered whitewash on my thoughts.

I ducked back away from the window and tried to force my mouth to say something practical and focused. It came out as, "So, um, right?" Not witty, not focused. The skin on my cheeks started to heat up again and I swear she could read my mind. Lifting a full cask of nails was easier than breaking eye contact.

"If the Dawnlight is still here, we're going to have to find it. Let's go see if anyone objects."

Spitting out a chunk of un-chewable turnip, Lye shoved through the door to the piers.

# TWENTY-FIVE

The transition from shoulder squeezing boardwalk alleys and buildings constructed out of whatever lumber could be found, including the wall of your neighbor, is hard for some folks. A line of warehouses, offices, and watering holes hold back the nothing. Most days the view was a shade of grey meeting the black green of the ocean, but every so often the rain failed to trade with the fog and it was just undulating ocean touching sky. Off to the left a single dark line marked the breakwater. It wasn't so bad on the incoming tide; stacks of crates, piles of goods baled for shipment, and barrels containing goods that couldn't be shipped any other way, marred the sight lines. Once everything was stored or shipped, the lack of cover made my spine feel loose and wobbly.

The moorings resemble steps laid on their side, long straight stretches ending in a right angle leading to another stretch. Something to do with how the current works to keep the depth constant by letting sand build up on the stops. The Dawnlight was somewhere on the end I'd guided us to, North Dockside, but the mist hid anything more than a hundred feet away, coating skin in a layer of wet as soon as we ventured out.

A small huddle stood around an oilcloth draped figure watching the madness out in the bay as ships jockeyed to hit the gap between the breakwater and the rock foot of the mountain. With low visibility there was always the chance someone wouldn't back down and there'd be the timber-snapping echo of a collision. If the gods of luck were especially spiteful the matchup would be uneven and it would be the endless splintering roar as the smaller one was driven under. Sound suffered as badly as sight in fog, mixing direction and distance into ethereal soup. Anything to break up the boredom of staking out a stretch of cold wet dock. One of the group, a shivering under-fed boy maybe sixteen, glanced over at the stretching creak mad from the cheap leather strap hinging on the door.

Sudden realization made the slow trip through boredom. When it hit, it fired off in a spasm, comically, as he tried to alert the person taking shelter, seated next to him on the pylon, and nearly toppled over the edge. He was a sad loss to the acting profession that specialized in overplayed royal jesters.

The woman under the oilcloth snatched the boy's wrist off her arm where he'd grabbed for balance and gave it a sharp twist, sending the offender to his knees - forced to follow the torque or suffer a broken wrist.

One of the others, a burly hairless man glistening from the wet, snapped at the kid, ""Mucking idiot! Keep yer hands off!"

"Aigh! Sorry! It's them!"

"What? Tides take you for a fool, whyncha says so?"

The woman lurched upright and spun to face us, her rain protection dropped over the edge, forgotten. Since she'd likely stolen it...that was someone else's loss, more garbage floating in the sludge under the walk. The four of them spread out a few steps and then stopped. Hands on their knives but without drawing them.

"Hey, you! Hold up!" The hairless man was in full bluster trying to recover from being surprised.

Since we'd already stopped, Lye just gave him one of the shrugs that filled in most of his parts of a conversation. He took a bite of his turnip and chewed it slow while he waited. He still had his sword out, blade balanced on his shoulder with the other hand. Sylvie and I flanked him a step or so back. Sylvie's sword dangled, point not quite brushing the wood at her feet. Isaac and I were the only ones without a weapon out, but I suspected Isaac had something up his sleeve and I could ship in a weapon from across the horde infested steppes before they could cover the twenty paces between us.

The woman's lips had a faint lilac tinge; sinew and bone pushed out the angles that made up her face and hands. Stretching out skin like she'd starved away any hint of fat until all that was left was feral instinct. Her hair was pulled into a tight orange-red tail behind her. Making your way up in the gangs took some amount of ferocity, strength, and intelligence - she looked like she was making it on pure, hungry mean. A handful of gang trash wouldn't even slow us down but something about her reminded me of rat sickness where they have to cut the animal's head off and then dig out the teeth after it bites.

The other one said, "Someone wants a word. Yer either gonna be with me like little ducks or I' gonna have her," He waved a hand at the hungry-looking redhead, "tack yer guts up to dry while you hold open the hole." He glared up at the sky as if he expected it to clear up and provide the sun for his plan instead of just making everything wetter.

"No." Sylvie opted for the no negotiation plan.

"You're outnumbered and that...," I pointed at Lye's sword, "says you're going to apologize for bothering us and go the opposite direction."

"Naw, that won't work." He said, "Tell Clar we found them." Then he stepped back leaving the woman in front.

She flicked the back of her hand out, catching the kid on the ear, startling him into a trot in the opposite direction.

The spokesman parodied a bow, "Nowhere you can go, we can't follow."

The kid staggered off, holding the side of his head where she'd caught him. I made a note to get Lye another crossbow. Chasing after him was out, the tide was working against us - if we didn't get on board soon we'd be trapped in the city - not that the other three would just let us go. Oldest mugging trick in the books, older than the bump, have a weak looking but quick decoy grab something, anything will do, when the owner gives chase he gets led into a pack of your friends, who club him and strip him. Sylvie looked like she was about to order exactly that, but I reached out and gave a little shake to warn her.

What followed was about as awkward as anything I've done. We didn't know where the Dawnlight was, so we headed north toward the breakwater, figuring the captain would be where he had the most room to maneuver and figuring it would take whatever help the kid scared up longer to get to us. The grinding teeth and rage coming off the crew boss as we edged away instead of chasing after the bait roiled in the space between us. After a short huddle, she sent the other lackey after the first and then she and the bald speaker tailed in our wake. They managed the distance professionally, never close enough to get caught if we turned on them, never far enough that we could risk taking our eyes off of them. We walked like sawclaws, sideways with pincers out threatening everyone.

"They couldn't be more irritating if they started singing. We should throw them in with whatever that is floating down there." Hospur waved at the brown foam coating the water as it roiled in and out, stirred up by the collision with the structure underfoot.

"Probably don't want to know. If we tried, they'd run, like a pack tiring out the moose." I didn't like it anymore than he did. "They might have lovely voices though."

"Nothing about her was lovey. Her inside is reflected on the out."

"You prefer them with more rounded corners?"

"Much as I hate to interrupt setting Hospur up with a dock rat, that's the Dawnlight." Sylvie pointed north to where the hulk of a ship could be seen as a slightly darker patch of fog.

The stem was toward us, we'd guessed correctly. The lurch of relief was physical. A cluster of darker spots in the mist flowed along the dock beside the hull. That meant the captain, Haas, was ready for a speedy departure. Cutting lines sounds good in theory but there's enough work aboard a ship without splicing extra rope. Having crew down and ready to cast off made sense.

"Anyone feel like a jog, I hear it's bracing and comes without reinforcements from behind." Hospur said.

The sooner we got aboard, the less likely any response the kid gathered would catch up. We moved into something between a really fast walk and a run, still keeping a couple eyes on our escort.

I looked back, "Um, Sylvie?"

Running with a sword is the sort of thing people don't do

much, "Yes, expert?" She was mostly trying not to cut one of us.

"She's not following."

"What?"

There was a shout from the sailors milling about alongside the Dawnlight. Two of them, a large blob and a smaller, probably normal sized, one held back, the rest fanned out across the dock. All of them held poles, boat hooks maybe, for pushing small craft away or drawing them closer. They'd be pretty useless for a ship the size of the Dawnlight.

"That's not right." Sylvie stopped.

Not by a long shot. Leaving port is a complicated business. Anyone with the wherewithal to stand-up, can handle a boat heading in a straight line. Captains earn their keep entering, leaving, and when something goes wrong. That's when you can find them out on deck, orders flowing, watching and correcting. The deck of the Dawnlight looked like the middle of the night; not a soul moving and certainly no mates echoing instructions from the deck. The men I'd thought were crew preparing for departure looked to be something else.

Sylvie's face was grim enough for a full tribunal, "I don't care who it is, we break through and get on that ship, Haas won't have let them take it without burning it to the waterline."

"Assuming..." I have a suspicious mind, sometimes it controls my mouth.

Money and blackmail work on most everyone, my little chat with Clar's spokesman proved that. Sylvie's jaw clenched and I didn't say anything else. If she thought he was loyal, I was hardly in a position to push the issue.

The next fifty paces we did in silence. The ship grew sharper in the mist, low and long, hardly wide enough for a cabin below decks, two full masts and a long spar thrusting out towards us. The hull was a dark green, nearing black in the fog and everything above the deck was washed a contrasting white. Lumps the size of a cart, fore and aft, were the only mar on her sleek lines. Just the sort of thing to lose, the moment it was out of reach, with a heavily taxed cargo. It was a good thing Haas wasn't a local.

Gobineau had his fingers in all the local smuggling pots. Smugglers tend to gravitate to each other like thieves and fences.

The poles resolved themselves into spears. Spears held by watchmen dressed up to look like docksiders. Hopefully whoever they'd taken the patched trousers and shirts made of sacking and bale cloth from had gotten a few dirhams and not a fist. The men and women wearing the new old clothes had a bit too much stomach filling out at the waist. And they'd had to use the leather belts from their previous outfits since cord and twine do a bad job of holding up swords. That and nobody who had a choice would give up their shoes for going barefoot in Myrport.

"That's about far enough," The smaller of the pair in the back stepped up between two of the spearmen and spat a glob at a particularly offensive plank in front of him.

It really was an nasty habit, I couldn't be the only one bothered by the gooey black spittle. Maybe they were used to it, none of his pretend gang members seemed to notice.

"Your'n getting any farther. Yer cut off. Now, give me the Key'n the stone'n maybe some of you get on the boat'n leave."

"No." Sylvie was feeling chatty.

There are fights that can't be won, your only option is to curl up and hope they stop kicking you. The trap was around me and it was the sort that keeps squeezing the rat until its skin splits and it suffocates from the pressure. Clar wasn't going to leave his cards unplayed. I wondered if they would stop kicking before I died.

"Look girl…yer outnumbered, trapped'n if you push me, I'll hand you over to the council or the temple. Either way your friends die'n I still get what I want."

"A lot of trouble for a share of nothing. Step aside and let us on our way."

"What you hold is worth any trouble'n we both know that."

Sylvie stiffened, like a cat that's suddenly aware there's another cat after the same fish. If she'd suddenly puffed up to look bigger and started spitting, I wouldn't have blinked.

"Why don't you go tell…what was his name? Clar? To take

a swim with a barrel full of ballast. It's not going to happen."

If any god or goddess loved me the mountain wall behind the city would erupt into lava, the moon would collide with the ocean, anything to interrupt this conversation. The gods of luck are insane. They hate everyone, but they had a special ire for me. This was what the condemned man feels, head encased in black, air choked off by a mouthful of burlap, waiting for the half second kiss of cold steel before death.

"She's closing the gap again, Sylvie." Hospur said. He had an eye on the pair following us, "…and she has friends."

The kid and the second thug had rejoined their boss along with a double handful of typically scrawny gang members holding an assortment of knives, with the odd gaff hook or table leg club. The mob was moving forward slowly, fanning out as they walked, urged on and chivvied into formation by the woman who'd sent for help. She had a pair of matched daggers held pommel first, blades trailing. She either thought it looked intimidating or knew how to use them and I wouldn't know until she was in arms reach, not a good range for surprises.

"What Clar wants is no longer'n issue. Last chance before I get what I want by washing yer blood off'n it."

"We're not going to change our minds. Get on with it. You might want to start running; you'll need the head start." Sylvie said.

"Is that so? Renn, do you have anything to add?" He smiled, lips tight together but looking like a shark in a pool of chum regardless.

Sylvie's head jerked, more of a twitch, and I could feel the space between us thicken, vibrate. My hands and feet felt like cork, to light for anything but floating, in that tingly you've-sat-on-them-for-too-long way. Wait long enough for something and when it comes, it's still surprise, panic and nausea. Nothing but the sound of the Dawnlight's hull rubbing, shifting, up and down for a moment as it shifted from "us and them" to "them, them, and me."

Alone. It felt like being overboard in high seas. No boat, no land.

Slowly, eyes locked on Clar's man, she stepped forward and shifted, putting her back very carefully to me. Nothing else. She didn't say anything…just planted herself where she was most vulnerable. After a second, the others followed suit, each putting their backs to me facing out, a defensive circle with me at the center.

"No. I'm good. I work for her." Sylvie and Isaac shifted without a word to make room for me.

"I bought'n paid for you!" Black spittle flecked the Man in Brown's lips and he clenched his hands like he had them around my throat.

"Next time try without the drugs and the threats. Catch more fish with bait than clubs." The light feeling was gone from my hands, migrating to my head. I squished the urge to smile, people were about to try to kill me and all I could focus on was the couple feet between me and Sylvie.

He drew a forearm across his face, streaking the brown leather of his sleeve, "Kill them! Make sure'n he lives, I want to gut'm like one o' his fish." He waved the thugs behind us forward and stepped back behind the line.

"Here they come!" Hospur faced the way we'd come, shield up, mace trailing behind again.

Sylvie motioned Isaac to the inside of the circle, "Even the odds." Something buzzed past a foot or so high to hit anything. Isaac ducked and started talking to himself while sorting through strips of parchment tacked onto his robe.

The watchmen closed up into a tight line, left leg leading, with spears out in front, one hand back to drive the points forward. One of them, probably a corporal in uniform - a little grayer and lined than the others - started calling out cadence, "Left, huh! Left, huh!"

"That's nice." I did start smiling. We were outnumbered, trapped, and probably about to die, and I couldn't have been happier. It probably showed.

Hospur took in my happy smile, "Did something hit you in

the head again? Now may be a bad time to bring it up, but there's a lot of people with sharp objects about to try and kill us." Hospur's tone was conversational.

One of the rabble hurled a bottle, better aimed this time, forcing him to flick the edge of his shield up. The glass hit the shield, spraying splinters of glass around us in a rain.

"You can take the soldier out of the city…" It's possible I was letting the emotional high run away with my mouth. All those feet slapping down in time was a temptation I couldn't resist. I snapped the button off the pocket holding the carefully wrapped package of caltrops and turned to use my body to shield my hands from view. It felt a little odd, keeping my back toward a bunch of people with spears, but I had to wait until they were closer, the little foot spikes didn't weigh enough to throw very far.

Something heavy hit Hospur's shield with a dull crack before falling to the dock. He was intercepting anything that looked like it would hit inside our little circle, leaving a dribble of bottles, stones, and what might have been manure to trail over or by. If we hadn't been in the middle, it could have been a miniature riot, the mob on one side, soldiers to put it down and enforce order on the other. Yelling coming from the direction of the Dawnlight joined in, but they would have to take care of their own problems, for now.

"Lye, let them come to us!" They were nearly in range of my throw but that was also close enough for his reach.

He glanced over, saw what I was about and took a small step back, enough to tell me, 'after you' without using words. Sylvie moved to stand next to Hospur and I snapped the square patch of leather holding the caltrops forward, flicking a hundred or so half inch missiles to land in an arc before the advancing spear line.

They made a noise like scattering pebbles, hail on board, tick – tick - tick. Hardly heard over the steady, "Left, huh!" unless you were listening for it. A couple looked for instruction, changed orders, at their corporal but she kept the steady rhythm, maybe an extra firm, "Left" paired with a slight flourish added to the forward thrust of her spear to refocus her troops on the business at hand. The uncertain snapped their heads back straight. If they hadn't been as corrupt as a four month old peach I'd have felt a little bad.

Something smacked into my back, bounced off, reminding me that was only half of our problem. I checked Lye, he pointed back and gave me a nod that I decided meant he could handle the spearmen. Isaac was crouched behind the bulk offered by a man in full armor and a shield. He'd selected a scrap of parchment and was mouthing the words, speed reading through the spell before actually doing it.

"Take your time. I'm sure the mob of knife wielding scum throwing their garbage at us will wait." Hospur punched another missile, an unfired brick from the way it burst into a cloud of red and pebbles flying back toward the pack, out of the air with his shield.

"Both at once is going to be bad. On three, charge." Sylvie said. Something had clipped her in the cheek leaving a streak of blood and a slight puffiness.

The front of her armor was smeared brown from another missile. I nearly took a rock to the head staring at her.

"One. Three!" She and Hospur surged forward followed by me a half second later as my brain caught on and I jumped to catch up.

They had maybe three steps lead on me but both were in armor and running is something I get lots of practice in. The dock thugs weren't more than thirty paces away and we halfway across before the redhead could react. She'd been arguing a wager with the man next to her, set to throw another clod of manure.

Behind us I heard the corporal shout as we sprinted, "At 'em!" It was probably the right thing to do, catch us from behind as we hit the far line instead of letting us split them, if they hadn't ignored the other information, probably….and if Lye had let them.

A couple of the disguised soldiers stepped on the spikes. Razor sharp steel plunged through leather soles and skin. They were trained and disciplined, if they screamed from a half inch hole, I didn't hear it, but no amount of training could make them keep running. Then they ran into Lye in a mass of splintered spear shafts and unstoppable blade. The hobbled ones were the lucky ones.

"Hey! You lot! Here they come!"

The redhead hurled a rock in my direction but I didn't see where it went and then we were on top of them. Hospur hit first, ramming the flat of his shield into his target, the bottle thrower who'd made the mistake of taking his eyes off us while he fished for a weapon. He still had a bottle in his left hand and looked up as he pulled at his knife, it was caught by the hilt on the braided rope he used for a belt, his eyes went wide and then he disappeared behind a wall of wood and iron banding with a beefy smack and a spray of glass shards and blood. The force of the impact brought Hospur up short and launched the thug backwards through the air - landing with the grace of a dead flounder ten feet beyond the others.

Sylvie and I were next. She led with sword extended, lance style, running flat out at her man. He had a makeshift club he was tossing from hand to hand. Probably more concentration than he had to spare. The point bored into his cheek and burst out the back of his skull, a bloody nail sticking too far out the board. She whipped her wrist to the side to keep it from binding in the wound and kept going, letting her sword trail behind as she shot through the gap she'd created.

The corpse slid off her blade and she spun to pin a second through the side as he turned to follow. She lunged twice, arm extended, like practicing with a target, catching him in the exposed ribs. The blade slipped off the bone, slicing into the gaps above and below and through to lungs. Blood foamed out of his mouth and he fell on top of her first victim.

Charging a group of armed men is the sort of thing swords, or spears, are for. This occurred to me when I was about two steps away from the gap-toothed grin facing me. Armor...a sword, I needed to make a shopping list. Not really the time or place. I pulled up short and threw myself backward. The smell of rum and sweat swamped my nose as he over extended above me. I dropped one hand back to catch myself and punched upward with my dagger. It was more wild swing to keep him honest than anything else. The tip caught him in the armpit and ripped up into the socket, spraying blood as the blade lodged and then wrenched free, as I rolled to the right.

Gap Tooth, if he lived he'd be Lefty - creative nicknames are part of the profession, staggered backwards howling. Even drunk his interest in the fight was gone. No telling if he survived. The sinewy redhead darted in to disembowel me before I could regain my balance, and yes, she knew exactly what she was doing. All I could do was keep my weapon between us and evade. She kept her steps small…perfectly centered. One blade or the other was constantly stabbing, slicing in, or flicking towards my face. Within a few passes, I stopped even pretending to counter, backpedalling to keep far enough that she couldn't follow anything close enough to disembowel or blind me. Her face was frozen; her lips carved into a snarl. Her breath came in little snorts through flared nostrils.

She had me backed against the dock edge and I was about to jump, swimming definitely a better option than being stitched open. She'd gotten close a couple times in a matter of seconds, leaving burning lines on my neck and chest. Just as I was setting my feet to throw myself backwards there was a crack like a mast splitting, followed by a blurred rush in the corner of my eye and something hurtled into the planking. The ground shuddered with impact and the redhead pulled a thrust that would have opened a valley in my stomach. She called out something, half looking over her shoulder.

Lower Myrport is a big place. Even so, word gets around about certain things. Who to go to if you've got a satchel full of someone else's jewelry, who waters down their wine - everyone, which parts of town to avoid with a full pocket of coin - all of it, and who to avoid offending or else they'll feed your fingers. The redhead was definitely on the last list and it was a miracle of the worst sort that I hadn't heard of her. Make a mistake in fist fight and you'll get a light show or end up puking your guts out on the floor. Make a mistake in a knife fight and you'll be picking your guts up with bloody fingers instead.

The redhead was faster than anyone I'd ever faced and she was nearly fast enough. She started to correct almost instantly, backpedaling, both knives out, too late. I took one knife on the palm, hand going numb as I swatted it aside; the other went over my shoulder as I dropped it, driving in and under the other blade. All my weight went into my right arm, slamming it forward as I caught her just under the rib, driving in, slicing upwards as my hand slickened.

Her face never changed; a rictus of nostrils and teeth an inch from mine. Half of me expected her to start biting, piranha like. Her breath smelled like peat, a heavy earthy loam. With my left arm and the dagger I shoved her back, slicing the wound open as she fell.

To my left, Sylvie and Hospur had decimated the remaining thugs; several were down, bleeding and cradling smashed bones. At least two made the correct choice and were sprinting into the mist. They'd need good lies if they expected to live through reporting their failure, but that was probably a better bet than facing us. Most of the watchmen were down as well, pieces of spear and men were strewn across the dock. The corporal in disguise and two others were forming a line protecting Clar's man across the space I'd spread my spikes on. Spears out, but not even remotely steady, badly spooked and a single loud noise away from panic. The bodyguard was down, stuck fast to the dock by a twelve foot pole thrust through his abdomen like a collectors prize beetle. Somehow he wasn't dead, arms and legs scrabbling at the wood trying to free himself.

The mouthpiece had both hands spread wide, showing empty palms. After what happened to his bodyguard that made a fair amount of sense, except the logical source for something like that, Isaac, was muttering so fast I couldn't make out words and shoveling scraps of paper into his cheek like a squirrel waking up in the last week of fall.

Blame the wash of relief, the surge of life, cold and fresh as a rinse bucket after a soak. Or maybe I'm just slow. The lot of them weren't paying any attention to us, they were locked onto the Dawnlight like someone was about to light a fire out of debt markers. The canvas sheeting on the bow was gone, revealing the lump I'd seen earlier as a siege bow, a ballistae.

Visibility was too poor to make out the second lump on the back end, but it was an easy guess they came in a matched pair. Sailors swarmed around the weapon. I couldn't make it out what they were saying but the cadence of orders and response drifted down from her decks. Ballistae are meant for ship to ship combat, not the sort of weapon to pick off a single man, at sea the goal was to punch a hole around the waterline on the hull. Tied up and without waves and wind to compensate, the crew had waited until the armed men on land were well and fully distracted by a maniac with a greatsword, before taking a shot. I found out later they missed, they'd been aiming for the line of spearmen. Gave me the shakes when I thought about what could have happened if they'd cheated left instead of right. But the end result was worthy of a round of drinks anyways. What our foes didn't know, we could make work.

We'd won, but winning a fight meant people were dead and that still left a sour taste. I needed to get clean and we needed to get aboard and away from Myrport. There was a lump in my emotions when I rolled that over in my head. It wasn't clear what was under the lump, something, maybe big, maybe not. The box you shake to find out what's inside and nothing rattles. My father would have flicked out the stick, "loot first, escape second, think whenever." Yeah, I still hated him.

The kick caught me completely blind.

There are some basic rules in a fight. Don't make mistakes. Don't uncover for anything but the kill. You'd think that spending time with someone who gobbles books and spews flame out of his mouth I would have added, "Don't assume stabbing someone in the lung and mincing her internal organs means she's dead."

You'd think.

Her foot slammed into my leg just above the ankle with the force of a two inch iron pry bar. I went down hard. The dock reached up and body slammed me, I barely got my mud covered hands up in time to keep from leading with my face into the wood. My own elbows shoved the air out of me and I head butted the dock with only the back of my hands for cushion, washing my vision with sparkling white. My mind went from desert sober to three-day binge in a second. Why were my hands muddy?

A gasping choke for breath later she was on me, one hand crushing my throat the other tangled up in my hair. Her arm was solid rock. Sinew, bone, and muscle crushing and twisting. Somewhere I could hear Isaac's voice; garbling off all the hard consonants on words I couldn't repeat. The redhead sitting on my chest decided I wasn't dying quick enough and slapped the planks with the back of my head. Each time it felt like something stabbed my temple where the javelin butt from last night had hit me, only with the blade this time.

I lost track of everything except the steady pounding and the roar of incoming waves pulsing in my ears. My hands were still clawing at the fingers crushing out my breath but without air I might as well have tried to pry iron bands.

A long fingered hand, encased in plate reinforced leather, grasped the redheads face, digging into one eye socket, another finger snagging her open mouth, yanking her head sideways. She twisted to avoid losing an eye and let go of my hair to fight off her new attacker. Her other hand still clenched at my throat but just having the pounding stop was a relief. Blessed silence is relative, the roaring in my ears continued but without the world sized drums, choking to death seemed tolerable.

Then she was off of me entirely, huge gasping breaths brought the world back into focus. Lye was standing over me, straddling me in place of the redhead. He had her by the head in one hand and the other strained to retain hold of one thigh as she bucked and twisted to get free. Someone grabbed my arm and then another pair of hands on the other arm. When I started to wrench free, the first person slapped my shoulder.

"You've done enough, Expert, time to let Isaac earn his keep."

"Howwuh?" Eloquent, I was not. My throat felt scraped and salted, like I'd skidded downhill on it.

"Golem, nasty creation, someone is really upset at us." Hospur answered my question as they half trotted, putting as much space as they could between the fight and me.

Lye still had the creature but it was clear he was tiring. She was getting more and more movement as she turned and arced, throwing herself around to break his grip. Her free foot lashed out, snake quick, catching him across the nose. Blood dribbled out and he staggered for a moment but didn't let go. The two of them were completely silent, Isaac's chanting reached a shout and he crumpled the last bit of writing up and swallowed it - muscled it down - and then gave a sharp nod. Lye whipped around in a circle, once, twice and then let go, first of the things head, then as her weight whipped out, her leg.

Arm wrestling the fighter went right off my list. The redhead hadn't been big, but she'd been heavier than she should. Lye's throw flung her out off the pier, arcing up and over the water at least twenty feet. Right at the peak of the throw, Isaac screamed one final word. A spout, more solid pillar of blackish green water surged up, crashed into the woman, enveloped her, and then hurtled down to the ocean below. The impact sent a second spout geyser-ing towards the sky, nearly as high before dissolving into sea spray and foam.

"Suddenly I don't feel like sailing." I said. Croaked really.

For once Lye looked as tired as I felt. He had his hands on his hips, panting mouth open and nostrils wide. He gave me a shrug and walked to where he'd dropped his sword to rescue me. Clar's man was gone, along with his three surviving watchmen. Between the gang members who'd escaped and them, they'd have to explain to Clar and whoever was steering Clar's rudder. If they lived through that, we'd be long gone.

Hospur and I leaned on each other and made our way to the

Dawnlight. We passed the bodyguard along the way. It turned out to be my old gambling buddy, Gev. Bled out, nailed to the dock by a stray shot. He wouldn't lose any more Sevens games. Maybe the insane gods of luck hated one person more than me. Gev never could roll a winning set.

# EPILOGUE

The Dawnlight's bow chopped down through another swell, sending slices of water leaping out away from the hull in glimmering sheets before splashing down over the top of the wake. Rather than pounding down like the fishing boats I was familiar with, a jerking vibration your legs automatically adjusted for amidst chaos where each man shuts out as much as he could to do a job, the Dawnlight was the wave on top of the wave. A sabre cut compared with the chopping axe of other ships.

A squad of sailors armed with short bladed chopping swords and backed up by another scattering posted in the rigging met us at the side when we approached to board. Each of them wore broad pants cut from undyed canvass and sleeveless shirts that buttoned in the front. A step back, another sailor stood with his sword thrust through a rope looped around his waist fiddling with an unlit pipe.

"Good ending to those lot, wouldn't even let me step off for a smoke. The only pleasure of land and I miss it for a brawl you could have down the way."

"Didn't stop you from firing on them, did it Haas?" Sylvie said.

"Oh, well, the crew needed practice and they were tiff'ed about shore leave. They get unruly if I don't let them stretch their legs." Haas grinned around the pipe stem and the matching smiles from the men and women around him explained why the soldiers hadn't boarded the ship to wait for us.

"Sorry, maybe next time. I'm grateful you are ready to make way. I don't think we're welcome here anymore...and get Hospur stitched up before he bleeds to death."

"Not even aboard yet and she maligns us lads; makes a man long for an honest life. Run out a platform for them, I'll go wake the surgeon."

Haas turned away yelling the endless chain of orders needed to cast off and maneuver a ship out of harbor and into the open sea. We were escorted below, most of which was taken up by a space sectioned off by barrels tied and netted securely to the sides with hammocks strung up in the gaps for crew off shift. A pair of cabins, each with an iron banded door, capped off either end of the below decks.

The crewman leading the way, a short woman with the reddish tan a life at sea gives you, found me a spot and a spare change of clothes. The moment I'd scraped off enough of the dried and undried filth coating me, I fell into a hammock and let the fatigue take over.

The next day bells pried me out of my coma and hunger drove me up top. A purple bruise swelled over my ankle and up into my calf making walking trickier than shipboard usually is. After waylaying a sailor to find a chunk of bread and matching cut of cheese, I found a place near the bow that was far enough out of the way to avoid being asked to move and settled into the easy rocking motion.

Sylvie found me there, letting the sun cook my skin. Food forgotten in the sleepy murmur as the ship went about its business. She joined me leaning against the rail, turning her face up to catch more warmth. One eye was virulently purple, the look of badly applied makeup over a small dark line of split skin.

She caught me looking and grinned, "You look terrible. Hospur said nothing was broken though."

"I'll have him tell my ankle then. Glad to hear he's alright." My voice rasped, giving me a whispery tone.

"Lost nearly all the blood he had but one of the hands sewed him back up and he was up this morning acting like nothing happened."

"I suppose I should thank Lye, I thought she…it…was dead. If he hadn't pulled it off me I wouldn't be getting too much sun."

"If we started keeping score, nothing would ever get done."

"What are you doing now, what's next?

She stared at me until I finally met her gaze, "We…"She

paused for me to get the hint. "…are going to restore the Citadel Ring. It'll be dangerous, as someone once told me, insane. But I have people I trust with me."

We stood there for a bit, letting the sun scour away the week before…maybe a life before for me.

Finally I took a deep breath, "Thanks."

"You're welcome." She shifted next to me, hip kissing mine lightly, "Now we're even."

I lost track of the sunlight I hadn't seen in months, the hum of sails being adjusted, or where we were going. For the moment all that could sort itself out, I was busy thinking about perfect lips and a tingle that spread from where her leg touched mine.

# ABOUT THE AUTHOR

Thad lives in the Willamette valley of western Oregon where he studies anthropology and writes. Find out more at www.thadwind.com.

www.ingramcontent.com/pod-product-compliance
Lightning Source LLC
Chambersburg PA
CBHW071445170626
46811CB00007B/2488